'I shall not altogether die,
A mighty part of me will escape the goddess of death.
Again and again shall I rise,
Continually renewed by the glory of after time.'

Horace, Ode 3. 30

Tom Johnson is a classicist and musician with a career in technology. He lives in London with his wife and three children.

For those we fear to lose.

Tom Johnson

SILVER PLANET

AUSTIN MACAULEY PUBLISHERS™

LONDON • CAMBRIDGE • NEW YORK • SHARJAH

A CIP catalogue record for this title is available from the British Library.

ISBN 9781528934428 (Paperback)
ISBN 9781528934435 (Hardback)
ISBN 9781528967860 (ePub e-book)

www.austinmacauley.com

First Published (2020)
Austin Macauley Publishers Ltd
25 Canada Square
Canary Wharf
London
E14 5LQ

1. A Solar System Hosting Human Life, Light Years from Earth

Sound Hunter

Jonathan Powers blasted out of Elephant's Trunk. 'I nailed it, Filia! Recording's in the bag.' He had captured the sound of his solar system's most spectacular wormhole.

Filia Wrens punched the air from the safety of an orbiting shuttle. 'Yessss!' she cried, flooding his helmet visor with shooting stars.

Jonathan twisted his single-seat levitator in doughnut circles and scribble-sloppy lines, carving his JP initials into the golden dust rings of a nearby planet. 'I am, and always will be, a sound hunter,' he roared. There was no argument from the quiet, pondering cosmos.

'Jonathan, hurry, the worm will breathe you back in,' yelled Filia. Elephant's Trunk was a tidal wormhole. Tidals sucked you in and spat you out. The sound hunters joked that they were allergic to space-borne particles. They sneezed.

Elephant's Trunk was plagued by the sun-kissed dust of the Tilmenian corona, an arc of seven splendid planets, each with its own dazzling rings. The Trunk was the tentacle end of a vast dark hollow that lay gasping at the centre of the crown.

Jonathan had positioned himself near the tip of the Trunk before the Elephant had inhaled. He'd been sucked inside and catapulted out with the amber-hail exactly as planned, but not everyone emerged in one piece.

Jonathan accelerated and docked his levitator in the shuttle bay. He removed his dust-encrusted space suit and sprinted to the observation deck where Filia was waiting.

Jonathan grinned from ear to ear as he ran, knowing he was moments away from being showered with praise like a big shot who's brought home the galactic bacon.

'Yuk, you stink of Elephant odour,' blurted Filia, pinching her nostrils after embracing him. Jonathan raised his sweaty hands in mock surrender. 'That's worse, you lunatic,' laughed Filia, waving conditioned shuttle-air into his face.

'More please!' he howled with delight as the public space bus began its return journey to their home planet, Centurian, the only habitable planet in their solar system and as far as the people of Centurian were aware the only planet capable of hosting human life, anywhere.

Jonathan and Filia had just turned sixteen and been allowed to spend weekend nights at the nexus of sound hunting, Rockmore Space Junction.

Rockmore was the busiest space hub on Centurian. It was situated at the heart of the planet's capital city, Geocentrian, and it served a constant stream of mining freighters travelling to and from thousands of desolate moons as well as public shuttles visiting places of natural fascination such as Elephant's Trunk.

Filia had recently joined Jonathan's school, Tempo Chorium. They'd met briefly a long while ago in nursery classes, then spotted each other several years later going in and out of a local piano teacher's house, but hadn't crossed paths since.

The connection had helped break the ice and Filia had quickly come to share Jonathan's passion for space rock, a genre of magic-music in which sounds were recorded in the wild using spells of capture, then brought back and distributed in music halls for bands to sample and develop with spells of shaping.

Magic-music aficionados would cram the platforms of Rockmore Space Junction whenever the sound hunters arrived, itching to get their hands on the latest recordings.

Filia and Jonathan had become part of the scene, carefully inspecting shuttle origins and flight paths to predict which new samples would best suit their taste or pique their interest.

The Tilmenian run, in and out of Elephant's Trunk, was the sound hunter's rite of passage. It was an unwritten rule that until you conquered the tidal ride, you could not be called a sound hunter. This baptism in dust embodied the basics of sound hunting: timing, the opportunity to capture incredible sound and a moment or two of danger.

Filia had thought Jonathan was mad to attempt the Tilmenian run with so little experience of sound capture and next to no training in bust-outs, the label given to these pressurised tidal rides. But Jonathan had insisted, confident as ever in his flying skills.

The boy racer had succeeded and was almost ready to assume the sound hunter accolade he coveted so dearly. There was one more box to tick: the recording had to be stellar. An original blend of magnificence.

Jonathan and Filia leapt off the shuttle as it pulled into Rockmore, locked the levitator they'd hired back into its slot and opened the sound container. The recording was perfect.

The foghorn of Elephant's Trunk blew once at the start and then at the end like a ship that owns the ocean. In between was the sneeze, the crash-landing sound of a seashore wave as it smashes the sand and rushes to a gentle conclusion.

Jonathan and Filia stared at each other in triumph as they replayed the recording again and again. 'Oh my gosh, that's going in our next track,' cried Filia, grabbing and shaking Jonathan's arm with joy.

They took the uptown dronibus home. Jonathan walked Filia to her door. 'Hey, thanks for watching me,' he said.

'Oh, not at all, you really did nail it,' smiled Filia. 'See you Monday morning, seven-thirty dronibus; none of your usual time-lapsing, Mr Sound Hunter.'

'I'll be right on time,' grinned Jonathan, turning to walk away. Filia reached out but he was already halfway down the path. He looked back as he opened the gate and paused, noticing she was about to say something.

'I, er,' hesitated Filia, 'I just wanted to say, thanks for being such a good friend since I joined school, and make sure you wash that filth off.'

'I will,' beamed Jonathan, saluting her before bounding up the road.

2. Earth, Southwest London, England
The Ghosts of Friendship

'You're quite shy, aren't you?' asked the registrar in charge of admissions. Fifteen-year-old Jonathan Prior was mortified; that was the one thing he didn't want anyone to think. Porchester was a school for confident, curious boys who looked people in the eye and fitted into their vision. Jonathan searched for the correct answer: a few words, one word, a sound. He had no reply, not even an excuse for silence. He wasn't going to get in.

His parents, Stephen and Florence Prior, shuffled uncomfortably. Jonathan could tell he'd let them down. 'I will contact you in two weeks, once we've finished the other interviews,' concluded the registrar ominously as he showed them the door.

Stephen Prior drove like a bat out of hell. On the face of it, this was to make sure that Jonathan was only a little late for class at the school they all hated, Grovecourt. All three of them knew the extra twenty miles per hour were the revolutions of a man who wanted more than he had and blamed everyone else for his lack of achievement.

Even at the best of times, Stephen Prior was a thoroughly dislikeable person. He worked as an accountant in a bookbinding shop but secretly fancied himself as a writer rather than a mender or bean counter.

He had once attended a writing class. The teacher had told him that writing a book was like dressing shaggily to offload garden waste at the dump before returning home, jumping in the shower, combing your hair and getting ready to go out.

It was messy at the start, but the home stretch would come and finally the process of polishing it off before celebrating.

Stephen never managed to get his brain beyond the dump; his thoughts tangled like weeds and stank like compost.

The intensity of under-achievement drove Stephen to spend little time with Jonathan and Florence, preferring the company of his delusions of grandeur instead.

He was convinced Jonathan should follow in his footsteps, despite the lie of his own happiness. The best school, top marks in all subjects and a career in an established profession.

Jonathan's grades consistently failed to meet his father's expectations and his father made sure he knew it. Jonathan looked to his mother for support. She seemed too frightened to interfere. He hoped she cared enough to one day take his side and confront his father.

The Priors' clapped-out banger screeched to a halt, exhaust pipe just about clinging to the rattled chassis. Jonathan ran to his classroom. 'There you are, Jonathan, you're in time to read out your "Where I Live" assignment,' announced his English teacher, Mrs Flowers, as he sat down.

'This'll be good,' sniggered Jasper Manley. Everyone duly laughed, except Mrs Flowers, who froze, powerless to intervene.

Despite her inability to punish even flagrant abuse, Jonathan considered her an ally. She was blissfully inconsequential, not a judgmental bone in her body. He often worried whether she too cried herself to sleep at night on the days that Jasper and Carter Manley, brothers grim and cruel, ran riot.

Jonathan pressed the sharp end of his compass deep into his desk. The puncture was barely visible in the splintered wooden surface, attacked countless times by anxious hands.

He reluctantly stood up and glanced out of the window, delaying public performance and certain embarrassment for as long as possible.

A little robin was bobbing and pecking frantically on the grass. It stared right at him, eyes like warm yellow suns, not the usual darkness of a robin's pitch black pupils.

Sensing the encouragement of other birds too, he looked Jasper and Carter Manley in the eye, imagining himself piercing these two Cyclopean monsters with deadly pencils, and stuttered precisely how he felt.

'I–I live in a crossword, where every word is work. My sentences are–are corridors that lead to bookends, stuffed upright. The walls of my house are so h–high that the only thing that climbs over them is sound and those sounds are strange. I–I don't know where they come from or why they treat me so well. They whisper comforting words that I do not understand, messages from the ghosts of friendship.'

'Jonathan, brilliant, you must keep it up,' gushed Mrs Flowers proudly. 'One day, we will enjoy reading his books, won't we, everybody?'

'Nerd,' heckled Carter Manley.

The bell went and Jonathan wandered alone in the schoolyard. He plucked up courage to talk to Joe and Patrick. They hadn't seemed as instantly repulsed by his stuttering weirdness as others in the class.

'I–I really liked the sound of your house, Patrick,' Jonathan offered.

'Well, you're not going to see it,' Joe shot back. Patrick looked confused but fled towards the dining hall, preferring Joe's claws to joining Jonathan as isolated prey.

'Scrape,' snarled Jasper Manley, taunting Jonathan's failure to infiltrate another circle.

Jonathan made it through to the end of the day and headed towards Battersea Park. It was where he went for solace and to drown himself in the sound of birds. 'The fairy's off with the tweeting fairies again,' Carter Manley yelled after him.

The same robin fluttered past and Jonathan picked up his pace. The birds appeared to care, but they couldn't speak to him or speak up for him. True friendships came with conversations, words that ignited laughter or plumbed the depths of failure, worry and despair.

Jonathan sat below the hollow of his favourite oak. He talked and sang, repeating sounds that got a reaction from the attentive robin. The birds chirped constantly. They seemed as frustrated as him, as if hoping for a breakthrough so that he could join the park life chatter.

His mother phoned and Jonathan ambled home. That evening, his parents' yelling was horrendous. Jonathan frequently wondered how they made it through the night alive and how much of their fighting was because of him, or something else. He ate alone in silence, ran upstairs to his room and buried his head in his pillow.

Next day he woke at the crack of dawn and went straight to the piano, which he'd loved playing from an early age. He closed the door so he wouldn't disturb his parents.

Jonathan had a crystal-clear memory of the sounds he'd heard at the oak in Battersea Park the day before and transposed them into notes and chords. He'd followed this routine every morning for a long while.

Jonathan recorded everything he played, naming each piece of music with a date and the word "conversations". No two conversations were the same, which added to the intrigue and excitement of what would come next.

He closed the lid gently, tiptoed into the kitchen and made himself breakfast. He noticed that his vision was more blurred than usual. He'd hit his head a few weeks before, slipping off one of the oak's branches. His eyesight had troubled him ever since.

Jonathan's mother burst in, knotting her dressing gown as she marched. 'Mum, I think my eyes are getting worse,' he said.

She gazed at him closely. His mother looked terrible. Her watery ten-gallon eyebags were hideously swollen. Jonathan found himself staring at them. They were smothered in oil and wrinkled with pain. She sensed his concern and turned away. 'The doctor said your condition would correct itself soon,' she yawned. 'Try not to let it worry you in the meantime.'

Jonathan's father breezed into the kitchen. 'Ch–cheer up, Jonathan, y–you'll be okay,' he said with typically dismissive stuttering bluster. His mother busied herself with the nearest pointless task, parallelising knives and forks on either side of plates, right-angling spoons. His father shoved her out of the way and stuffed the knob-end of a croissant into his mouth as far as it would go.

Jonathan couldn't bear it; not just their blatant lack of interest in him, but the tension and how he was caught unfairly in the middle of two pathetically juvenile adults. *Sod it, I've had enough,* he thought, *I'm going to start a normal conversation.*

'I saw that friendly robin again yesterday. She helped me ace my creative writing assignment,' he smiled, delivering his news without one unnecessary syllable.

Jonathan's father slammed the front door without saying goodbye. His mother breathed a sigh of relief. 'That's wonderful,' she remarked, clearing up the breakfast.

Why doesn't she ask me to recite it? fumed Jonathan.

Fed up with waiting, he changed tack. 'The robin is the state bird of Michigan, Wisconsin and Connecticut, you know,' linking his passion for songbirds to the more traditional topic of geography in the hope that it would make a difference.

His mother looked at her watch. 'We'll talk more in the car. Get yourself ready, dear.'

Stephen thought Jonathan's preoccupation with birds was the cause of his suboptimal performance at school. Florence tried to discourage Jonathan's obsession by brushing the subject aside whenever he brought it up. She would do anything to avoid Stephen's wrath.

Jonathan stopped himself from erupting in anger and focused on his immediate worry: his blurred vision. 'Mum, my eyesight. I'm scared; the headaches are getting worse too. Help me,' he pleaded.

'I have an appointment with the doctor to go through the latest scan today. I'm sure it's healing itself as expected. Be extra careful crossing the road on your way home,' she warned.

'I'd rather you met me after school,' insisted Jonathan.

'I will do my best,' she replied. 'I'll phone the school if I can't make it. The appointment is right before you're due out. Hurry up now.'

Jonathan struggled all day; the migraines were missiles, not bullets. He asked Mr Boulder, the games teacher they nicknamed Achilles due to his bulging fuselage, shoulder span and superhuman speed, if he could skip football. 'I'm having trouble with my eyesight, sir. I–I don't think I'll be any good in goal.'

He could tell Achilles was annoyed. Jonathan knew none of the other boys wanted to go in goal so his weakness was handing this strongman a headache of his own. The boy who did get the goalkeeper's job would be sure to let Achilles know how he felt, Jonathan too.

'Okay Prior, but maybe you shouldn't be here in the first place. I'll write a note to your parents to that effect,' boomed Mr Boulder.

'Oh, thank you, s–sir,' hesitated Jonathan, almost changing his mind, knowing he'd get it in the neck for making his parents look irresponsible.

Everyone left for games and Jonathan went to Mrs Flowers' classroom. She was his form teacher and that was where he would wait until his mother arrived to collect him.

3.   Southwest London, England
The First and Last Conversation

'I'm sorry, Mrs Prior, the results of the scan are not good,' began Doctor Sharp. 'Jonathan has a rare form of glaucoma. I'm not surprised he complains of headaches and poor eyesight.'

The doctor paused to allow Florence time to contemplate his assessment, which contained nothing other than overtones of potential disaster.

'Go on, please, doctor,' she requested nervously.

'The degenerate blood cells created by his fall are not clearing themselves out in the way one normally expects.'

'What do we do then?' asked Florence.

'I will refer you to another specialist, Professor Edon at the university hospital. Jonathan will need surgery. Rest assured, this can be cured and he is not in immediate danger, Mrs Prior; although the operation should be carried out soon to avoid any risk of permanent damage to his eyes.'

Florence left and broke down in tears as soon as she closed the car door. She was worried for Jonathan, but that wasn't all that frightened her. She'd promised Stephen she would renew Jonathan's medical insurance but hadn't done it yet. She was terrified that the cost of carrying out Jonathan's surgery in time would be enormous. Stephen would be unforgiving and punish her for the financial consequences.

Florence needed time on her own, a moment of peace before another fight, so she drove to the Raging Red Lioness, as she liked to call it.

She ordered a large glass of red wine and snuck around the back for a cigarette, finding a corner seat just in case anyone she knew happened to wander past and peer over the fence.

Florence ripped open the packet and sparked the flame. She then phoned the school and left a message. 'The rush-hour queues are awful, I'm so sorry. I'll be there to collect Jonathan in thirty minutes,' she groaned.

*****

Mrs Flowers strode into her classroom. 'Your mother called, she's stuck in traffic and will be another half hour.'

Jonathan knew Mrs Flowers would have to stay until he left. 'I'll walk home,' he said.

'Are you sure?' asked Mrs Flowers.

'Yes, I feel much better,' nodded Jonathan.

Mrs Flowers said goodbye and Jonathan texted his mum not to worry, saying that he'd make his own way home. He didn't tell her that he would be going to Battersea Park first.

But as he set off down the road Jonathan suddenly found his eyesight worsening and he slumped on a wall not far from the school gates.

He hauled himself up, eager not to lose time in the park and looked carefully left, then right, before getting ready to cross the road.

As he stepped off the pavement he saw the friendly robin pecking furiously at the concrete in front of him. 'I'll be okay,' he smiled.

Jonathan was certain he heard the robin reply, 'Hurry, Jonathan, hurry,' but as he opened his mouth to answer, he was blindsided by a bus and immediately lost consciousness.

The emergency services arrived in minutes and contacted Stephen and Florence, who made their separate ways to the hospital as swiftly as they could.

Stephen got there first. Jonathan was on life support and the prognosis wasn't good: he had next to no chance of recovering.

Stephen yelled truncated stammering accusations down the phone at Florence as she swerved past outraged cyclists, her face as wet and miserable as the depressing city streets, pelted by an unexpected downpour of hail and thunderous rain.

'You–you–you should have made him wait at school,' Stephen bawled.

'I know, I knooowww,' screamed Florence, trying to comprehend what she had done.

She rushed into the hospital and threw her arms around Jonathan, then fell to the floor beside his bed, clutching her dying son's hand as she wept. She couldn't speak. There were no words to describe her grief and guilt.

Florence prayed in silence as she cried and cried. She'd never really thought about God. She didn't know what to believe—God was a subject she'd planned to return to later.

But now, out of nowhere, she needed a miracle. Florence needed God to exist and poured her heart and soul into prayer. 'Please, God, forgive me, I beg you, and look after my amazing boy, help him get better—please allow him to live.'

4. Centurian

The Boy and the Bus

'Stop messing around in front of the mirror, you tart!' messaged Filia.

'I'm not,' replied Jonathan.

'You are,' typed Filia, laughing. 'I can see your six-foot silhouette grooming itself. I'm admiring it from across the street.'

'Seriously, Filia, something's not right. Wait for me at the dronibus stop and I'll tell you more when I get there.'

Jonathan stared at the bathroom mirror. He could see a boy, roughly his age, being hit by a mode of transport that he didn't recognise. It was the second morning in a row that these images of carnage had darkened the glass.

They vanished, replaced by the baffled glare of his grey-blue eyes and the ungovernable mess of his riotous walnut hair.

His parents and teachers viewed this crowning glory as a rebellious mushroom cloud. He dutifully leaned over and flattened the offending explosion in the basin, showering himself in the process.

Jonathan cursed and unbuttoned his soaking shirt. 'Come on, you're late,' shrieked his mother, Presette. He buttoned it back up, ran downstairs and decided not to bother with his usual mountainous four-cereal breakfast, spooning up the paltry remains of his parents' scrambled eggs instead.

Still ravenous, he stretched his arm into a top cupboard and grabbed his father Lucius' badly concealed stash of choccoli, a fast-acting nutritious snack—"boosts parts of the brain other snacks cannot reach" plastered all over the packaging.

The stairs creaked, warning Jonathan of the arrival of a prying parent. He stuffed one handful of choccoli into his mouth and another into his trouser pocket and veered awkwardly past his suspicious father.

'This is ridiculous. Get a grip, you bloody idiot, you make no effort to be on time. Last chance or no more late-night excursions to Rockmore.'

Lack of sleep during the weekends was not the only reason his parents disliked Rockmore. They hated the fact that he'd all but ditched piano for the sound hunting scene. Music was not supposed to be dangerous. They had no idea he'd risked the Tilmenian run and would have grounded him indefinitely if they'd smelt the faintest whiff of space dust on his clothes or hair. Fortunately for Jonathan, he'd mastered the art of creeping past his parents' bedroom without a sound.

'I do make an effort, I'm making sure I look smart for school,' objected Jonathan.

'Try harder, and don't talk back,' yelled his father.

Jonathan closed his door and glanced at the mirror one more time; there was nothing, only him. He rushed back down but couldn't find his shoes. He cast a spell of convenience so that they'd lift themselves out of hiding and make their own way towards his feet.

Centurians had enjoyed the use of magic for just over a thousand years although spell casting was tightly controlled by a government who dictated how many times anyone could do anything. Sixteen- to eighteen-year-olds were allowed ten convenience spells per day.

The shoes did not appear so Jonathan cast the spell again. Still nothing. Jonathan hadn't exceeded his spell count—far from it—this was his first convenience spell of the morning. He cast the spell repeatedly until they finally floated out from behind the coat stand and motioned towards his feet.

Jonathan examined his shoes. He couldn't see anything out of the ordinary; they were the same old unpolished clobber. He looked behind the coat stand. There was nothing that could have stopped them from moving. Something was wrong with his magic. Jonathan swallowed hard, he was scared. He had never experienced any problems with his magic.

5. Southwest London, England

Storm Pandora

Stephen and Florence had not left Jonathan's bedside for several days but were suddenly interrupted by a nurse telling them to go home, collect any precious belongings and drive to the storm shelter closest to their house. Severe tornadoes were powering towards London from the south coast.

'Storm Pandora will cross the M25 in three hours,' warned a policeman outside the hospital, swaying with the trees as he looked up at the turmoil in the sky. 'The fellow on the news said something about geostrophic winds, whatever the hell they are; hell itself, probably. He said they normally only ever invade the harshest parts of Earth. Hurry up!'

Pandora's line of unstoppable screwdrivers marched through defenceless England, mutilating hedgerows, cars and carriageways, and against all odds, the maelstrom gathered strength and speed as it progressed inland.

As soon as they arrived home, Florence began filling a suitcase with items that reminded her of Jonathan, including a heavy hardback book she'd given him for his seventh birthday, Mythical Strongbirds. She hadn't touched it for years and a thin layer of dust had started to form on the front cover.

It had been Jonathan's favourite read at the time. Its stories and illustrations had spoken to him in a way that she and Stephen were never able to. She cradled it in her arms before placing it carefully in her suitcase, hating herself and her husband for not loving and understanding their son.

Stephen and Florence joined hundreds of people sheltering in the Grovecourt sports hall, their nearest refuge. There was no indoor football, only fear and emergency food.

The television, set up on a stack of chairs in the corner, beamed pictures of Pandora's tornadoes twisting steel as effortlessly as earth and spewing their tangled destruction into the sky.

Mrs Flowers was amongst those who came up to Stephen and Florence, offering condolences. Her eyes, like theirs, were craters of sorrow. 'I can't imagine what you're going through, I'm so sorry,' she choked. 'Jonathan was so talented, so polite, such a joy to teach, I'm so sorry.'

A local government official arrived, promising that the damage would be repaired as soon as the storms had passed but his words fell on disbelieving ears as they always did.

'I'm bored, there's nothing to do,' moaned Jasper Manley, kicking one of the exercise mats that were pushed up against the wall. His brother, Carter, addressed the issue by lamping him one for fun and a brawl ensued.

The government official stepped in and fell over without receiving or landing a blow. The force of his own lunging arm had brought him to the floor. Echoes of laughter bounced around the sports hall and for a moment, everyone's minds were diverted from the howling gales outside.

6. Southwest London, England

The Learning Bush

As the worst of the storms approached London, a robin called Rose was giving a philosophy lesson to a group of younglings and their families deep inside one of her favourite bushes in Battersea Park.

The space was packed. Birds with superior hearing had volunteered to hang off the perches farthest from the makeshift lectern at the centre. Lighter, more agile birds had situated themselves on the most frangible stick-seats and the elderly occupied the bird-equivalent of the front row and the royal box.

The birds called this bush craft, the art of optimally arranging yourselves in a green and brown space. There was no need for magic. This was something that came to birds quite naturally.

Rose was well-known and highly respected by woodland and garden birds of all species. Everyone worked themselves into a frenzy of anticipation when the location and timing of her philosophy lessons were announced.

It was first-come, first-served, and queues formed early. They were never straight lines because birds disguised what was really going on as territorial ground-grabbing. No one wanted to delay the start of a lesson by inviting humans to wonder why so many birds were cramming themselves into a single small space.

This particular Battersea Park gathering was one of the most eagerly awaited talks of all. It was Rose's traditional end-of-year London lecture and it always took place during the period many humans called Christmas.

Rose was in full swing. 'Humans enjoy eternal consciousness. When humans die, their conscious souls travel across an invisible corridor to a second human planet where they join the mind of another person, losing all memory of their past life the moment their new life begins. The whole process happens very quickly. It's like waking up as someone else.

'When the person on the second planet dies, the cycle repeats. Their soul passes back to the first planet to yet another new life.

'This planet, which humans call Earth and birds call Opus, is linked to the planet Centurian. Centurians used to call their planet Earth, but their government changed the name a thousand years ago when they discovered magic and we birds have also adopted their name.'

Rose paused, giving the younglings a chance to take it all in. She smiled as she gazed at their gaping beaks. She then winked at a few of the parents and grandparents she recognised. The older birds were all familiar with what she'd said. They also knew what was coming next.

'And, my dear younglings, it is us, the birds, who brought eternal consciousness to humankind,' Rose declared. 'It is our greatest labour, our most precious magic.

'Long ago, powerful birds saw the souls of the dead being tortured and destroyed by an ancient evil that we call the Arc of Darkness, a force which has not shown itself for many an age.

'Sickened by the injustice of what they witnessed these birds created this cycle of eternal consciousness to keep human souls away from Arcan punishment.

'Spheres of woven magic called lumenests were placed at the heart of this planet, Opus-Earth, and at the heart of Centurian. These eternal cores are the beginning and end points of a soul's journey between the two planets.

'Our purpose is to protect the workings of eternal consciousness so that humanity never again experiences such suffering after death.'

A strong gust caused the bush to sway violently and a covering from a nearby skip narrowly missed enveloping them. One of the younglings leapt off her perch, thinking that jumping was necessary to avoid being trapped. Rose shot across and caught the bird to chirping applause.

Rose spoke to two fellow robins, Jaden and Enchoir, 'These storms might be more than freak weather; I must investigate. Can you do the watching-without-being-found and homing-without-getting-hurt slots now? I'll be back shortly to finish off philosophy.'

Basic education was compulsory within weeks of birth to prevent birds from being harmed and there was always a winter safety lesson at the end of Rose's Christmas lecture.

Jaden flew over to the teaching platform. 'Quiet please, I'll run through the safety briefing quickly while we wait for Rose. Point one: humans moving fir trees into the warmth of their homes in winter does not mean indoors is a safe place to hang out and chat. Point two: attention please, quiet please.'

The younglings weren't listening. They wanted more philosophy. Jaden and Enchoir knew a lot about the lifecycle of a human being but Rose was far more proficient in human teaching.

'What are the current threats to human eternal consciousness? Rose mentioned protecting it,' asked an inquisitive starling named Gardencrates. 'I understand you can't speak for Rose but please tell us what you know.' The younglings fell silent, hoping the robins would answer.

'In my opinion, there are two dangers to eternal consciousness,' Jaden replied, relieved to have got her audience back. 'First, the vile race of Skulls. They are servants of the Arc of Darkness but unlike their ancient masters, they are very much present in our world today.'

'Oooowww,' oohed the younglings, some of whom had heard their parents whispering about these rapacious creatures.

'Skulls travel secretly in wind-form. They invade humans during sleep and stay inside their minds until a person dies. Humans do not know they are there.

'A Skull-invaded human has no prospect of eternal consciousness. At death, the Skull assumes wind-form again and carries the invaded human's soul to the dungeons of Terminus, the Skull planet.

'The soul is then tormented and destroyed. The Skull survives this final ruin of human life and waits for the Skull lord to order it out into the world once more so it can steal again.

'Humans look the same after invasion but their character is often tarnished. Even placid and contented people can become short-tempered, sometimes hurting those around them as well as themselves.

'It is difficult to identify a Skull in wind-form or detect invasion while a Skull is breaking into someone's mind.

'We do our best to save humans with spells of waking if we suspect invasion and we try to intercept the malevolent breezes if we spot them before they attack.'

Gardencrates' eyes bulged, as did everyone else's saucers. It wasn't Rose, but by holly, this stuff was good.

'Our second concern is keeping eternal consciousness secret from humans,' continued Jaden. 'The purpose of eternity is to protect human souls from punishment after death, nothing else.

'At the inception of eternity the elder birds agreed that human behaviour would change for the worse if people discovered the truth.

'Humans would be consumed by a desire to control which new life they joined. And just think how they would treat us if they thought we might possess the magical power to help them choose. Not everyone can join the life they wish for. We would become objects of disappointment, enemies perhaps. We would no longer be humanity's secret friends.

'Anything else, Enchoir?' asked Jaden, when she'd finished.

'Oh, hum, yes I think there's a third concern,' said Enchoir, puffing herself out; appropriate, she thought, for the high-minded cogitations of philosophy.

'We must look after ourselves. We can't tell humans how important we are so we need to watch out for number one—us. If we take our eye off the proverbial ball, or start dying out, who will protect humans from Skulls?

'Please, therefore, everyone, listen to the winter safety lesson. It is directly relevant to our purpose; the preservation of eternal consciousness.'

'That was excellent,' smiled Jaden.

'Thank you,' beamed Enchoir, her feathered cheeks displaying a tinge of crimson.

The two robins decided it was time to return to the safety briefing. Gardencrates, however, had not yet had his fill. 'Is there ever an occasion when a human experiences past consciousness?' he asked.

'No, absolutely not,' replied Enchoir. 'That would confuse the heck out of the poor creatures.'

'Although,' Jaden interjected, 'there is a rare condition, conscious transference, where the new consciousness may see images of the previous life for a brief period.

'This can happen when death is assured but a living element remains; someone in a state of deep coma, for example, a sort of confused animation if you like.'

Rose sent Jaden and Enchoir a private message. 'You are both doing a fabulous job but I'm worried these storms might flatten our bush. Please evacuate the audience without causing alarm. I'm going to see Charlie and find out whether there's any hope for our friend, Jonathan Prior.'

Rose flew to the hospital grounds and landed next to Charlie, a young robin who had adored Jonathan and spent countless hours with him at the oak tree in Battersea Park.

She was also the robin who had tried to warn him about the bus and she'd not left the hospital for fear of missing one of the doctors' updates.

'There's no hope for him,' Charlie wept. 'His musical ear and his understanding of sound were beyond anything you or I imagined possible in a human, Rose. I can't even begin to comprehend what we've lost.'

'It is a total catastrophe,' groaned a pigeon called Albert who was wandering in circles around them. 'We've known the lad for years and will miss him so. Not trying to be greedy an' all, but life will be a bloomin' sight harsher, starved of his company and his yummy crusty bread.'

'That is selfish and inappropriate, Albert, you're always thinking of your stomach,' sobbed another pigeon, Lorna, Albert's wife.

18

Rose bowed her head. 'There is much to ponder, and not only the loss of Jonathan Prior; the Skulls are more active than they've been for many a long year. We must monitor the breezes closely, but I'm also keen to discover who Jonathan Prior joins, or has joined. His soul may have already entered its new consciousness.

'This is what we will do,' said Rose firmly. 'We, his friends, shall fly through the corridors to Centurian and we'll learn the destination of his soul on the way.'

Lorna looked nervous but Albert perked up. He was one of the best long-distance flyers in the neighbourhood. He loved an adventure and always dreamt of seeing the bird corridors between the stars and planets. 'No need to get your tail in a twist, dear,' he grinned. 'You have a falcon in pigeon's feathers to accompany you on the crossing.'

Lorna ignored him and stared at Rose who gave her a reassuring flaps-up. 'You've nothing to worry about,' chuckled the robin. 'Charlie and I have journeyed to and from Centurian many times, and it won't take nearly as long as you imagine.'

'Will six months of supplies do it, Rose?' asked Albert.

Rose smiled. 'It will take about a day of Opus-Earth or Centurian time. The bird corridors transcend all the rules of life and light. They are woven with the same spells that hasten human souls to new consciousness. Speed is one of the most important properties of corridor magic. We cannot risk a soul being stolen in transit.'

Albert and Lorna stopped in their tracks and glared at Rose in disbelief, but the robin wasn't looking at their wide golden eyes, she was studying the swirling shadows in the London sky. 'We meet here in one hour,' she sighed. 'I must first make sure that everything is as it should be in the park.'

7. Centurian

Spellology Exam

Jonathan raced out of his house before slowing down to a fast walk very quickly. Rushing was considered extremely bad form by the Centurian government. According to their own broadcasts, it polluted the atmosphere with disorder.

Convenience spell counts were docked as punishment for so-called "rushing yards". A rushing yard was motion outside registered sports facilities and running routes where both feet were off the ground at the same time and excessive distance was travelled. The government never published what "excessive" meant so the system couldn't be gamed.

Forfeiting convenience spells often led to greater tardiness, incentivising further illegal rushing yards; a vicious cycle that Jonathan had experienced on a number of occasions.

Each time he'd been penalised, Jonathan had begged his parents for spell donations to help him out of trouble but the government didn't allow spell transfers and he'd been forced to plan his journeys carefully to earn his way back to a full spell count.

'Goodly morning,' called Mr Occidoriens, Jonathan's neighbour, doffing his hat without his hands. Politeness, alongside timeliness, was a founding principle of Numberalism, the word used by Centurian's leaders to describe their counting style of government; every spell was valuable, no matter what it did. Jonathan nodded politely.

Two parrots darted synchronously from either side of Mr Occidoriens' hat rim. 'Goodly morning,' they sang.

'Well done, Polyglot, and you too, Talkalot,' exclaimed Mr Occidoriens, casting spells of repetition that sent the goodly morning message into the skies with sprinkles of silver.

Jonathan's mother, Presette, looked on disapprovingly through the front room window. 'That man is wasting energy again. Even the low-power wide-area spells of display drain something of significance from the grid.'

'You're an energy zealot, Presette,' scoffed Lucius. 'Should we stockpile spell count in case the evening greeting creates an occidental power outage?' he laughed.

'It's a very important topic, Lucius, and not one to belittle with your stupid caustic humour,' Presette retorted.

'Don't you think you were too harsh on Jonathan this morning?' Presette asked pointedly, turning to the subject she cared about most—her son.

'No, he's fine, he knows we're simply looking out for his spell count,' Lucius responded, dismissing Presette's question that wasn't a question.

'Calling him a bloody idiot was totally unnecessary though, don't you think?' countered Presette.

'Okay, okay, I'll sit down with him when he gets home and apologise,' replied Lucius.

Jonathan reached the top of the road. Filia was waiting for him, holding on to a prime position near the front of the dronibus queue. 'Nice work, sorry I'm late,' he sighed.

The seven forty-five landed half a foot from the ground. They boarded and took the last two remaining seats.

'I still can't get over Saturday night,' beamed Filia. 'I must be on my hundredth replay of that recording. You ready to mix the sneeze into some mega-tracks this weekend?'

'I'm ready,' smiled Jonathan as the crowded dronibus took off.

'So, what was up with you this morning? Still got space dust stuck in your hair?' laughed Filia.

'Er, yes,' chuckled Jonathan hesitantly.

There was a boy from their school standing right over them. Jonathan could tell he was listening. He didn't want anyone to know he'd had a problem with his magic. Sound hunting would be out of the question if word got around that he might be magically handicapped, the name given to the few Centurians who couldn't use magic in the normal way. Spell failures in the middle of a bust-out or any other sound hunting manoeuvre could be fatal.

'I meant to ask, who was that dude you were talking to in the shuttle bay before you began your run?' said Filia, sensing Jonathan wanted to say more but wasn't comfortable doing so with the boy hanging over them.

'Oh, Glitch Hopper, a real pro,' Jonathan replied. 'He was telling me how hunting is better than ever with the latest shuttle-technology cranking out deep space round-trips in less than a day, samples hardly losing definition in storage, even with low-power spells of containment.'

'No way. Isn't he the headbanger who brought back the magnesiim-to-magnesiim collision sample?' gasped Filia, bolting upright and realising she'd missed an opportunity to meet one of Rockmore's most renowned heavy metal hunters.

'That's him,' nodded Jonathan. 'He watched the chart futures for months, spotting the asteroid's collision course and predicting when impact would happen.

'He hitched a ride on the one mining freighter that had any chance of getting him close, and guess what, I got a message from him last night offering to take me on as an intern in the summer break.'

'Wow,' said Filia, flatly.

'I asked if there was space for a friend and he answered just as I was leaving the house. You're in,' smiled Jonathan.

'Yes!' grinned Filia.

The dronibus stopped and some of the passengers disembarked. The boy who'd been standing over them saw a seat and grabbed it.

'What's wrong?' whispered Filia.

Jonathan didn't reply; he was wondering if he should even tell Filia about his magic not working. He had his eye on a new sound capture opportunity and she might object to him taking it on if she feared for his safety.

'Hey, that was a question, sound-buff,' said Filia as the dronibus took off.

Jonathan leaned over. 'When I woke up, I saw a bizarre image in the bathroom mirror—a boy being hit by some sort of vehicle.

'It's fine; it disappeared pretty much instantly. Probably some random magical interference. Maybe a neighbour watching a diabolical movie without focusing their spell-zone accurately.'

'You're not behaving like it's fine. Not sure I'd be alright either. Who watches horror movies in the morning?' frowned Filia.

'There was something else, something really freaky; my convenience spells didn't work, straightaway at least.'

'You're sure you pronounced the magic paths correctly?' asked Filia.

'Well, I suppose I might have been distracted by the weirdness in the mirror. Perhaps I did get the phrasing wrong. I'll tell you if it happens again,' Jonathan smiled.

Filia was about to ask more questions but Jonathan interrupted. 'Let's forget about it, please,' he said. 'On a more important note, just because the Trunk recording's dynamite that doesn't mean we should ignore our other new tracks, like the one you started last week. It's got massive potential but needs a load of work, don't you agree?'

'Why? I was thinking it was almost done,' objected Filia.

'You're joking? It's over-complicated, too clever by half; sounds like a boffin girl like you,' cried Jonathan, looking confused by her response.

'You're jealous, aren't you?' Filia snapped back, skewering him with her hazel-brown eyes. 'Jealous because Mr Archaneus said I was the most creative Spellologist in his class.'

Jonathan laughed and Filia elbowed him in the ribs. He loved the way she'd get so serious then kick herself for rising to his bait.

'I wish there was a magic-music section in today's Spellology exam,' remarked Filia, fidgeting with her books. Jonathan's face dropped.

'You forgot the exam was today, didn't you?' said Filia.

'No, not exactly, I just haven't been thinking about it,' Jonathan replied.

'You'll be fine. Remember what Mr Archaneus said, use the big three: spells of recall, understanding and indexing during the with-magic sections, and don't worry, everyone hates the without-magic sections. They're lonely, bring some chocolate.'

Jonathan closed his eyes and shook his head. 'I forgot the chocolate as well.'

'Here you go, emergency rations,' winked Filia, plonking a bar of Centurian Chunkie in his hand. 'You'll feel like him when you're done—a hero,' she laughed, pointing to the wrapper. It depicted a Numberalist soldier dragging a broken-down dronibus full of screaming people away from a cliff edge.

'You really are properly prepared, thank you,' Jonathan smiled, putting the bar in his bag.

Filia and Jonathan arrived at the school gates and stepped onto the gravel track. The hedgerows were perfection and birdsong filled the gardens and quadrangles of the Temporium, the name most people used for the Tempo Chorium School of Magic and Music.

The bell tolled and Jonathan and Filia went to their form rooms to register before making their way to the theatre hall.

Jonathan sat down at his allotted desk and opened the exam paper. Question one: "In which year did Agrippina II ban the use of spell transfers?" He cast the spell of recall; nothing came back. He cast it again; nothing.

He moved on to question two, comprehension: "Read this passage and choose which spell, or spells, would best resolve the situation."

It was a story about two people misunderstanding each other through no fault of their own and ending up in a raging argument.

Jonathan was certain this was what Mr Archaneus called an antibiotic situation; a solution could be found using magic, but the magic had to be administered correctly.

Jonathan cast a spell of indexing to leaf through examples of antibiotic spell sequences. Nothing came back. He cast his spell again and again. There was no response. Jonathan was completely distraught and simply wrote, "Spells of Calming".

By the time he'd reached question fifty, halfway through, Jonathan was sure he'd only got five right at most.

He drilled his pen into his desk in frustration and decided to cast a spell of understanding on himself, asking the spell to explain why even the most common school-spells were failing. It returned "unknown source of interference".

Jonathan immediately went into an even greater state of panic. The spell's response was uncharacteristically vague. It was useless. The spell of understanding always spoke the truth and it was invariably crystal clear. That was a government promise. You ask, we tell you, you take responsibility.

'I'm in trouble,' he mouthed across the room to Filia who had noticed something was seriously wrong.

Jonathan fought back tears. There was so much at stake. The Spellology exam determined which classes each pupil would join the following year. He was desperate to be with Filia, who he knew would score spectacularly well. Everyone wished they had Filia's memory and mind-speed when it came to magic. Mr Archaneus was right; she was a stunning Spellologist.

Not only that, Jonathan loved school, he loved Spellology. He had revised hard and deserved to do well. He would be brandished incapable through no fault of his own. Worst of all, he'd be kicked out of the Temporium if he scored a low D, the dungeon score.

When the exam was over, Jonathan whispered what had happened to Filia but made sure they didn't talk about it until they'd left school.

On the way home, Jonathan gave her a blow by blow account of his dismal performance. 'It's clearly something that's not you; it'll pass. I bet they'll let you retake next week,' she said, holding his hand tightly and not letting go until they arrived at his dronibus stop.

'I hope so, Filia, I hope so,' he choked.

Jonathan wandered into Bushley Park, the heath and parkland at the top of his road. He was not ready to go home; he was dreading telling his parents.

As soon as he set foot in the woods, the familiar tweeting of afternoon park life was drowned out by what sounded like the world cup final of crickets versus locusts.

He glared at the trees and began to pick out words inside the wall of noise, then the buzz of conversation. It was coming from birds. That was impossible. No one could hear birds talking. He stood transfixed, listening.

'Here comes the one with silly flattened hair, Uncle Glorious. I knew his grandfather, that's where he gets it from.'

'Ah, but my father knew his great grandmother over in the Meadowlands,' replied another voice.

'Stop showing off, Sister Victorious.'

'Be quiet, Auntie Laborious, concentrate on the count.'

'Boy with silly flattened hair?' Jonathan mumbled to himself.

'How, how? He heard us, Uncle Glorious, he heard Brother Imperious' rudeness.'

Jonathan glanced up and caught sight of a group of flustered treecreepers losing control of their trunks and careering off.

He looked down and noticed two robins and a pair of pigeons. One of the robins stared right at him and spoke.

'Don't worry about the always-arguing-descriptornyms, I mean, treecreepers, that's what you humans call them. They only want to outdo the crows and be first to reach a full count of locals before sundown.'

Jonathan froze, flabbergasted.

'I know,' continued the robin. 'It's difficult to fathom their obsession, isn't it? The Notorious and Parsimonious families are always battling it out, long-time tribal rivalry. Cross-clan breeding hasn't helped; internecine warfare to us, a terrific racket to you, for which I apologise. I'm Charlie, by the way.'

'I–I'm Jonathan,' he spluttered. 'And you don't need to apologise, please. I love the sound of birds.'

'You're being Numberalist polite surely, Jonathan, it's a terrible noise, don't you think? And it's not just treecreepers feuding with each other or fighting it out with the crows, the other woodland jousters are part of the hullabaloo as well.

'Maybe you're saying it's alright because you're new to hearing it. Tune in every day and you'll turn deaf or mad, or both. Only saving grace is HE is not here anymore.'

'Er, who, who is HE?' Jonathan gasped.

'HE is, or rather was, Spitz Atme, the ugly possum. Oh my, he was butt-ugly, excuse my birdish. Hiss, click, hiss, growl, hiss, sneeze, splatter, and then all over again hiss, click…you get the picture.

'He spoiled the woodland with his slobbering sounds. If you got too close or tried to tell him to be quiet, you'd be showered with pond-filtered saliva.'

Jonathan instinctively wiped his face. He was shell-shocked. Centurians believed they could send messages to birds and other animals using spells of one-way creature communication. There was never much of a response, and certainly not any meaningful form of spoken reply.

Jonathan, however, was experiencing full-blown two-way creature communication. He was conversing with a frantic little robin who was embarrassed by the noise in the park.

'How–how is this conversation happening?' gawped Jonathan.

'I don't know, Jonathan, but I'm overjoyed you can hear me and I'm very excited to meet you, so forgive my babbling away. I just don't like the way treecreepers talk about people, and the noise *is* horrendous. I don't want you to feel unwelcome or to shut your ears to more conversation,' said Charlie.

'Th–this is incredible, wonderful, Charlie. I'd better go home now, but can we talk more tomorrow?'

'Absolutely,' Charlie replied. 'I'll be here; same time, same spot, same racket.'

Jonathan smiled and watched, dumbfounded, as the robins and pigeons flew off into the silver-blue skies above Bushley Park.

8.   A Castle in a Faraway Corner of Space

Flickering Silver

Grandmaster Mizmiq scanned the ceiling of his observatory inside Castle Spinneret, a rustic haven in a pocket of space far from Centurian or Opus-Earth.

The grandmasters were powerful spell weavers who took human form and humans would have described them as wizards if they'd ever come across one, which they hadn't.

The grandmasters were the birds' friends and allies in safeguarding eternal consciousness and the number of living grandmasters was a matter of debate amongst both the birds and the grandmasters themselves.

Some had been missing for decades, others centuries, a few for millennia. It was generally agreed around thirty were still in circulation, somewhere.

Castle Spinneret was their collective home and it was where these adventurous wizards would meet if they wanted to talk about the universe or simply observe it from afar.

Every grandmaster had their own observatory in the castle grounds and their magical ceilings represented the real state of planets and stars.

Grandmaster Mizmiq's attention was drawn to Centurian. The silver luminescence surrounding the planet flickered. It stabilised, then flickered again, like a lightbulb losing and regaining its source of power.

Billions of people casting spells round-the-clock had created a silver sheen roughly one kilometre above Centurian's surface. This shallow silver enchantment was harmless. It added beauty and wonder to the planet, a sort of benign magical exhaust.

The silver sheen could be admired from the ground or from space and as a result, the birds and grandmasters had named Centurian the silver planet. Its own human population used the term as well.

Mizmiq had never seen the silver planet flicker in the thousand years since its people had discovered magic and he was considered one of the most watchful grandmasters. The kaleidoscope of shapes and coloured dots that glittered inside his deep blue eyes were the markings of his intense examination of everything from supernovas to shadows in the canvas of space and his gaze seemed to glow with a radiance that no other grandmaster could match.

Mizmiq's eyes shot across the ceiling to Opus-Earth, Centurian's sibling planet, so-called because the two worlds were joined by the magic of eternal consciousness. Everything there seemed exactly as it should be. Opus-Earth shone with its usual sapphire-blue purity as it sat between its fellow planets of Mars and Venus.

The grandmaster summoned the Centurian globe from the ceiling. The silver circle hovered above his cupped hands and he closed his eyes and searched for anomalies in the magic used by the people of Centurian.

There were two parts to a human Centurian spell: the words, which were simply a verbal expression of what someone wanted, and the pitch.

Each spell had to be spoken at the correct magical pitch, otherwise it was nothing more than a wish.

The problem for humans, unlike birds or grandmasters, was that they could not speak or hear sounds in the frequency band of magic.

Centurians, believing that a magical spectrum existed, had decided to experiment with sound modulation and they eventually found a way to turn words into spells. Spell instructions still had to be pronounced, however, using particular notes that were thought to contain distant harmonics of magical frequencies.

These human pronunciations were known as "magic paths". They bridged the gap between human and magical sound and modulation towers monitored every inch of Centurian air space, elevating spoken paths into the frequency band of magic while Centurian shuttle craft bristled with technology that enabled spells in airless space.

The people of Opus-Earth had not found the frequency band of magic. The birds and grandmasters believed that one day they might, but there was no indication that they were close or even had an inkling of where to look.

Grandmaster Mizmiq spotted an anomaly in the log files of the Centurian grid, the Numberalist government's mechanism for distributing and controlling magic.

A sixteen-year-old boy, Jonathan Powers, was generating numerous spells that failed even though he was pronouncing their magic paths correctly.

Mizmiq cast a spell of understanding, which returned "mind magic". The grandmaster immediately leapt up and marched around his observatory, holding the silver sphere of Centurian tightly with both hands.

Mind magic was a form of spellcraft where outcomes were willed into being using thoughts alone, and although speech was not used to cast such spells, they became sound after they were conjured. They existed as magical notes.

This explained why most of Jonathan Powers' spells were failing. He was casting two spells at the same time and the sounds generated by each spell were cancelling each other out.

One was a spoken magic path, the other a spell initiated by the mind, and because the two spells were giving the same instruction, they created identical wave frequencies and those frequencies were not always in sync. Thoughts could occur slightly before speech. That was when they were cancelling each other out.

The boy was experiencing what any scientist or sound engineer, familiar with magic or not, would call Destructive Interference.

How mind magic had come to be present in a sixteen-year-old boy was beyond the grandmaster. Only birds and grandmasters could conjure such spells.

Mizmiq sent the Centurian globe back to its position in the ceiling. It flickered again. He'd found no explanation for Centurian's flickering luminescence.

Mizmiq decided that there was nothing more the observatory could tell him. He would have to do something he'd not done for many years—take avian form and fly through the transcendent bird corridors to Centurian.

Mizmiq hurried across a garden colonnade to his study. He locked the door and scrambled up a near-vertical ladder to one of the higher shelves and surveyed a row of dusty ink jars, mumbling to himself as he read the labels; 'vitreous fluid, don't need that, amputated gas, definitely don't need that, where's the blasted metamorphic rock? Aha.'

He paused and inspected a lapis lazuli-studded ampulla with the words "mastic fantastic" scrawled down the side. 'Got it!' he exclaimed.

Mizmiq grasped the precious vessel and gingerly, for a many-thousand-year-old, negotiated his way down the ladder, keeping his body weight forward and his thick silver-threaded cloak as far as possible from the open clasps of his going-away boots.

There was a knock at the door and the key fell and clanged like a badly rung bell. 'Hang on!' he shouted, irritated at being disturbed.

Mizmiq peered through the keyhole and saw the inquisitive eyeball of his assistant, Skrieg.

'What is it, Skrieg? I'm busy.'

'I have your mid-morning tea, sir,' the grandmaster's assistant replied calmly.

'I told you I don't need it today; in fact, I'm cancelling it going forwards. I'll see you later this afternoon in the dining hall.'

Mizmiq waited a few minutes and then checked again. Skrieg had wandered a short distance but was still hovering.

'You're like an Opus-Earth helicopter consuming fuel and occupying space. Go and ask grandmaster Sporadiq if he needs a buzzard to help him test his potions,' he yelled, stuffing a thick piece of papyrus into the keyhole.

Mizmiq opened a drawer in his desk and rifled behind some parchments. He grabbed a feather quill, dipped the feathered end inside the ampulla and spread a clear viscous liquid in a circle in front of him.

The gummy gel floated in mid-air exactly where it had been drawn. He reversed the quill and used the sharp tip to carve a line through the magically adhesive paste.

The grandmaster felt a breeze across his face. He had created a lapisphere, the traveller's jewel, a circular opening that acted as a gateway into the bird corridors between the stars and planets.

Mizmiq placed the quill and the ampulla of gelatinous travel-gum in his cloak pocket and cast the avian spell of flight. He assumed the shape of a great hawk and darted through the circle into the Alpha 1 corridor.

The birds and grandmasters had named each sector of the corridor network with one of twenty-four letters. Numbers were used to designate regions within a letter sector.

Twenty-four sectors seemed to work well as a proportional topography for the part of the universe they'd so far managed to cover with their transcendent corridors.

The birds and grandmasters had originally created their own symbols for each sector, but later adopted the human Alpha to Omega lettering scheme as it had the right number of characters and they liked the symbols more than their own.

It was possible to enter either Alpha or Omega from one focal point, Castle Spinneret.

A lapisphere opened on the north side of the castle would take the traveller to Alpha, then on to Beta.

A lapisphere drawn on the southern side of the castle would open a gateway to Omega and from there one could fly on to Psi.

Mizmiq shrilled with joy as he rocketed through the corridors, firing on all his mighty air-guzzling hawk-cylinders. Corridor travel was fast, extremely fast, and Mizmiq had missed the exhilaration of transcendent flight.

9.   Centurian

Destructive Interference

Lucius and Presette sat opposite Jonathan in silence, wondering what could possibly have caused his magic to fail so catastrophically during his Spellology exam.

Jonathan had told them that his spell of understanding had returned "unknown source of interference" as the reason for his disastrous performance and his parents had asked their family doctor to make an urgent home visit.

'You are sure this isn't a simple case of mispronouncing magic paths?' suggested the doctor as soon as he stepped through the door.

'I know them perfectly,' answered Jonathan, offended by the question. He proceeded to cast a convenience spell to lift his shoes towards his feet but nothing happened.

Jonathan scribbled the written form of the magic path on a piece of paper. 'Look, here it is. Like I said, I know the correct paths inside out.'

The doctor nodded and asked Jonathan to repeat the spell again and again, recording every element of sound. Nothing happened each time he cast it.

'Your intonation is indeed spot on,' announced the doctor. 'I believe you have a very rare condition, Destructive Interference. You are casting two spells at once and they're cancelling each other out. There is a sort of echo when you speak.

'Put your shoes on, Jonathan, and this time cast a spell of convenience to remove them,' asked the doctor.

Jonathan did as he was instructed and much to his relief, the shoes untied their own grubby laces, slipped themselves off and landed neatly next to the hallway wall.

'How extraordinary, there were two spells again, but also numerous derivative harmonics,' gasped the doctor, examining his Spelloscope.

'The second spell and all its associated sounds were close to running counter to the first, but not close enough to interfere.

'It is a type of polyphony for sure, but it is not a classical polyphonic DI condition, for two reasons.

'Firstly, the sound-signatures have too many dimensions, there are decaying echoes as well. I have never seen such a pattern or heard of one like it.

'Secondly, your physical voice—your vocal chords, mouth and throat—are producing only one magic path, a single spell instruction. The duplicate spell and the strange harmonics around it are not being generated by any part of your body. Physical anomalies are always present in Destructive Interference. They are the source of the problem in all the cases that we know of, but not in this instance.'

Jonathan, Presette and Lucius stared agog at the doctor, terrified and glued to his every word.

'The question we must answer next is how global it is. Is your Destructive Interference linked to particular spells or spell categories, or is it a broader issue?

'I want you to make a record of every spell you cast over the next week and note down whether each one is successful or not. Let's hope the vast majority of spells work first time,' concluded the doctor with a faintly optimistic smile.

Jonathan was devastated. He had been diagnosed with the worst disability imaginable, one that prevented him from using magic.

He'd studied so hard to get to where he was at school and had finally made his mark on the sound hunting scene. Everything was being ripped away. He was faced with a world without magic.

'What is the cause, doctor?' asked Presette, fighting back tears.

'I'm afraid I do not know. It's as if he's speaking with two tongues, or more, but we can only see one, and given there are no visible physical anomalies, I also don't know how to treat it.

'I will send an emergency message to the Numberalist counting controllers so he doesn't get punished for exceeding his spell count while we gather more data. I'll request a thousand per day. That should easily be enough.'

Jonathan went to his room, locked the door and screamed. He told his parents to leave him alone, despite their pleas.

He spent the night looking for anything that mentioned Destructive Interference. One article particularly resonated because it was about a well-known musician, *Tanglehill Piper Disappears, Presumed Dead*.

Everyone had heard of the Piper. He was famous for jumping up on stage uninvited at concerts and playing along with the musicians. Jonathan had seen him once at Rockmore's Central Hall in his coloured cloak.

The Piper's life had been blighted by Destructive Interference and the article talked about how he'd only ever been able to cast spells successfully by using his flute.

He had tragically disappeared during the weekend. His flute had been found at his home, but his body was nowhere to be seen.

Jonathan woke up early, eager to ask Mr Mercer about the Piper. Mr Mercer was his form master and the school's woodwind and percussion teacher.

Asking him about the Piper would be a perfect way of finding out more about Destructive Interference without letting on that there was anything wrong with him.

Getting ready for school was miserable. None of his convenience spells worked, even the simplest ones: clean-clothes-finding, sink-rinsing, face-moisturising, pimple-pulverising, brushing, flossing, mouth-washing. His room was a complete tip and he was an even bigger mess.

Jonathan wept as he tied his shoes and butchered his tie. He hurried out of the house and sent Filia a message asking her what dronibus she was on. He cursed—messaging magic still wasn't working. He'd been trying to get through to her all night.

Jonathan gazed up at the trees when he reached Bushley Park. The birds seemed to be tweeting away normally, and given he was already late, he decided to wait until the end of the school day before heading into the park to look for his friendly robin.

Jonathan was one of the last pupils to get to school. On his way into class, he saw Charlie landing on top of a wall that bordered a fountain at the centre of one of the Temporium quadrangles. Jonathan was delighted and went over to the robin.

'Hello, Jonathan. I noticed how upset you were at the dronibus stop. I thought I'd come and cheer you up,' she chirped.

To his amazement, Jonathan was able to conjure a reply that he himself could hear even though his lips stayed firmly shut.

'Thank you, Charlie, my magic's falling apart; I'd love to ask some questions. I'll come and find you in the break after my form lesson.'

'I'll be right here,' answered Charlie and Jonathan was sure he saw her smile before she darted off.

Mr Mercer had a drawn face and it was impossible to tell how old he was, or what he was thinking.

Sometimes his skin looked flat and leather-tanned, particularly his bald patch; at other times, it was pale and undulating like ripples on a pond and it was unclear whether these were lines of thoughtful wisdom or restless worry, or both.

His pupils' inability to read or second-guess him kept everyone on their toes and when he spoke his appearance was frightening which unsettled his students even more; he could look almost as contorted as Mrs Struth, the deputy headmistress, and nobody wanted to get on the wrong side of her.

'How are we all today?' said Mr Mercer, once his class was all accounted for.

Jonathan stuck his hand up. 'Sir, I have a topical woodwind question please, about the Tanglehill Piper. He had something called Destructive Interference. My mum was telling me about a friend who has it too. I wondered if you knew what caused his illness and how his flute was able to help him with his magic? I couldn't find anything that explained it.'

'It is an awfully sad story, Powers. He was a friend of music, always welcome on every stage, and a friend of mine, I might add.

'I don't know how his disability came about. He didn't know himself; I asked him once. Nor do I understand his end. I think he had a special magic about him. Some say his flute whistled magic paths that couldn't be counted by the grid.'

'That's illegal, and impossible,' cried a voice at the back.

'Indeed,' sighed Mr Mercer.

'Maybe he was disappeared by the government,' whispered another voice.

'I heard that—utter rubbish,' growled Mr Mercer, his face presenting an especially tortuous warp.

Filia wrote Jonathan a note and handed it to Julius Fog, Jonathan's long-time friend, so that he could pass it on to him.

The folded paper, with the letters "JP" on the front, fell to the floor as she gave it to Julius.

Julius reached down but another boy grabbed it first and read it out: 'You think you have DI?'

The whole class stared at Jonathan. Filia was beside herself; she'd crushed the person she cared for most, in public.

Jonathan couldn't believe what she'd done. He looked straight at her and raged at her in silence.

'Is Jonathan contagious?' yelled a boy with an enormous boil on the side of his nostril. It was Larry Dyers; he was paranoid about health.

'No, Dyers, relax,' said Mr Mercer. 'Powers doesn't have anything wrong with him. Even if he did, you know full well the Numberalist Healing Service has conquered contagion.'

'Wait a minute,' shrieked Larry Dyers. 'If Jonathan's casting spells outside the grid like the Piper, his disease can't be stopped with the usual antidotes. He is contagious.'

The whole class erupted with laughter. 'Be quiet!' ordered Mr Mercer. 'In the last six and a half minutes of our form lesson, I want you all to use the manuscript paper on your desks to write the correct notes for the magic paths of these spells,' he declared, clattering his drumstick against the screen behind him.

'Anyone with a score greater than ninety-five per cent, and that includes drawing them perfectly, will receive a prize from Professor Harvester. If anybody gets all of them right, I'll eat my soup with my drumsticks.'

The class began writing furiously, looking up from their desks and glaring at Jonathan as they scrawled. Jonathan felt sick with anger and wanted to explode. He was an outcast.

Mr Mercer's magic drumsticks rolled across his desk, indicating that they were permitted to leave the classroom.

Jonathan marched outside. Filia and Julius followed.

Filia put her hand on Jonathan's shoulder but he pulled away. 'What were you thinking?' he cried.

'I'm so sorry, Jonathan. I'm such an idiot,' said Filia, burying her head in her hands.

'You think I'm done for, don't you?'

'No, I don't,' answered Filia, exasperated. 'I made a stupid mistake; I don't think you have Destructive Interference at all.'

'That's what you said though, Filia! You wrote it, and you and this moron published it so that everyone could know. And what's more, you're right, it's what the doctor said last night when he came to my house. I have Destructive Interference.'

'Why didn't you tell me?' wept Filia angrily.

'I did tell you. My messaging doesn't work, does it? I'm disabled, crippled. You think that I didn't want to tell you? How could you think that, Filia?'

'Stop it!' demanded Julius. 'I'm the idiot here for dropping the note, not Filia, and I'm sorry, Jonathan, but there's no way you've caught something like that out of the blue.'

'Just leave me alone,' Jonathan seethed, walking off. They let him go.

Jonathan approached the fountain. He made out the shape of a small bird basking in the sunlight on the wall while the water glistened and gurgled happily, cascading down the fountain's marble shelves into the mosaic basin below.

Jonathan's spirits lifted. He recognised the bird. It was Charlie. Maybe his mysterious new friend could help him understand what was happening.

'Charlie,' he called, again without the slightest movement of his lips. He glanced back. No one seemed to have heard him. 'Charlie,' he shouted.

There was no reply. As he drew closer, he felt a knife in his heart. Charlie was completely still.

He ran to the wall. The beautiful, delicate robin lay dead. She'd been mauled. It looked like an attack by a wild animal or a savage and powerful bird.

Jonathan knelt on the grass and sobbed. He then inched his fingers towards her feathers, shaking. 'You must have suffered so terribly,' he wept, touching her. 'I wish I could have helped you. I'm so sorry I didn't come sooner.'

Jonathan cried and cried for the little robin and for what he too had lost. He would have given anything for one more conversation.

10. Centurian

The Sound of Broken Shards

Grandmaster Mizmiq hovered and glanced up at a line of silver lettering woven into the corridor ceiling. It marked the beginning of the Gamma 12 sector of the bird corridors. "γ δυώδεκα," he whistled with delight, careering off along the final stretch of his journey to Centurian, which lay at the heart of Gamma 12.

After a few more hours of flight, Mizmiq came to a full stop and opened a lapisphere into the silver-blue skies above Bushley Park. This was where he'd detected many of Jonathan Powers' spell-casting anomalies.

Mizmiq had sent a message to Rose, asking her to meet him. He and the robin had been the closest of friends for many, many years.

But Mizmiq had sent his message to Battersea Park on Opus, where Rose was most often found, and had assumed that he would reach Centurian well before her. He was surprised to discover a reply waiting for him inside a tiny parcel of air as he glided high above the trees.

The robin's reply directed him to a holly bush deep within a woodland area of the park. Mizmiq knew the spot. He'd met Rose there before, although not for quite some time.

'Grandmaster hawk, you haven't aged a jot. I'm so glad you managed to find your travel paraphernalia,' she winked.

Mizmiq chuckled. 'It is marvellous to see you, Rose. It took me hardly a moment to locate the ampulla, and not only that, there was enough fast paste to conjure private lanes all the way; the traffic was an inconsequential blur,' he declared proudly.

Rose's expression quickly changed to one of sadness. 'What is it?' Mizmiq enquired.

'A young robin has been murdered, Charlie was her name. It happened earlier today; all the hallmarks of a screech owl. The Skulls were bold enough to have it attack in broad daylight.'

The horror of Charlie's death welled in Rose's eyes. She shook in rapid vibrations, as if freezing cold in an icy wind, but this wasn't the motion of a robin fighting the bitterness of winter, it was the shuddering of an angry, grieving bird.

'Your message was intercepted and brought to me just in time, Mizmiq. I was about to take Charlie's body back to her family on Opus.'

'Where was she attacked?' asked the grandmaster.

'At the Tempo Chorium School of Magic and Music. Charlie was striking up a friendship with the new consciousness of a very special Opus boy called Jonathan Prior. He was close to conversing with birds, Mizmiq, but was tragically killed in an accident outside his school.

'Jonathan Prior's new consciousness is a Bushley Park local, Jonathan Powers, and he *is* able to speak with us.

'Not only that, his ability to converse with birds isn't some miracle of Centurian human magic, he is using avian magic, mind magic.

'At one point, he could hear the whole park. I've cast a spell to ensure that he only hears birds who address him directly. I wanted Charlie to continue her friendship.'

Rose looked straight at the grandmaster and smiled. 'This is why you are here, is it not? You have observed mind magic in your ceiling, in a sixteen-year-old boy named Jonathan Powers?'

Mizmiq grinned. 'Right you are, my insightful little friend. However, I had imagined his mind magic would be limited to duplicates of human spoken spells, an extraordinary thing in itself, but he is conversing with birds you say, incredible.

'I will test him, Rose, and unearth the full extent of his abilities while you travel to Opus.'

'Agreed, and I will join you after Charlie's birdsong lament. Jonathan Powers' address is 34 Tildesline Avenue.'

Rose placed an image of Jonathan in the grandmaster's mind and raised her wings in readiness to leave but Mizmiq stopped her.

'I saw something else, Rose. The silver planet flickers in the observatory ceiling. I do not understand why.'

Rose bobbed about in frantic circles, pecking the ground as she went and saying nothing for a long while.

'I do not know either, my friend,' she replied eventually. 'Perhaps Jonathan Powers' mind magic and Centurian's flickering are linked. Two such mysterious events occurring at the same time are unlikely to be a coincidence.

'Let us see where your assessment of Jonathan Powers takes us. I will return in a matter of days. You are as observant as ever, grandmaster,' she smiled. 'Thank you.'

Mizmiq circled Tildesline Avenue. Jonathan had told Mr Mercer he wasn't feeling well and he'd been allowed to leave school early. Mizmiq spotted him as he got off his dronibus at the Bushley Park stop and followed him down the road.

'Jonathan Powers?' he said, swooping past.

Jonathan ducked and almost lost his balance in fright. 'Wh…what?' he blurted, speaking in plain Centurian.

The grandmaster landed on the wall outside his house. 'My name is Mizmiq. It is wonderful to meet you.'

'Don't sit there,' gasped Jonathan. 'Can we talk while you fly? People will think I'm mad. You're not the type of bird that's supposed to be on a garden wall.' Mizmiq didn't move.

Jonathan rushed into the kitchen and grabbed a packet of thick cut ham. 'Go, take it all,' he insisted, tossing it as far as he could beyond the hawk.

The grandmaster didn't flinch. 'Jonathan, I know why you're able to understand me and other birds.'

Jonathan hesitated before turning to close the door.

'Don't shut me out,' begged Mizmiq, 'we must talk inside.'

'No, tell me while you're flying so no one sees us,' Jonathan demanded.

'Have you had trouble casting spells?' asked Mizmiq, ignoring his pleas.

Jonathan looked down. 'Yes, I've been diagnosed with something called Destructive Interference,' he whispered.

'The magic that lets you understand me is the same magic that causes your Destructive Interference,' said Mizmiq.

Jonathan stared at the hawk, stunned, then ushered the bird along the hallway and into the music room. His parents were both at work.

Mizmiq perched carefully on the head of Jonathan's bass guitar, trying not to scratch the lacquered wood with his claws. Jonathan watched nervously. It was his prize possession.

Mizmiq noticed Jonathan's discomfort and lifted himself into the air above the guitar but clobbered his head on the ceiling.

He tried to crash-land on the piano but slid off, knocking over Presette's harp as he beat his wings to break his fall.

The harp struck the wood floor and Jonathan cried in despair as he set it upright. It had been severely dented, but as he inspected the damage he glared at the harp in amazement—it was repairing itself.

The towering bird perched on Jonathan's guitar again, a hooked claw on a hooked head.

'No, you are not going to use my bass as a branch,' ordered Jonathan.

Mizmiq launched himself into the middle of the room once more but this time he shattered the glass chandelier in the process.

'Nooooooo,' shrieked Jonathan. Not even Julius, who was notoriously clumsy, could have achieved such consummate destruction in one manoeuvre.

But rather than witnessing priceless shards splinter a gleaming waxed floor, everything drifted in ultra-slow motion without touching the ground.

Jonathan marvelled at the particles of glass floating inside the room. He understood where each scintilla fitted, and without calculation, he willed the scattered blades back together and they began to re-join one another.

Their movement was accompanied by instruments in the room celebrating the moment each piece slotted into place. It was the most uplifting music Jonathan had ever heard.

'How can I capture this sound, this moment?' cried Jonathan.

'Ah, you are a sound hunter,' mused the grandmaster.

'I am,' nodded Jonathan proudly.

Mizmiq sighed and Jonathan sensed the answer would disappoint. 'I'm sorry, Jonathan, you can't, no one can. We cannot capture any of this and take it outside.'

'Outside? I don't need to record it and take it outside, we can play the music live through the instruments in this room using spells of performance,' Jonathan explained.

'Jonathan, no, what I mean is we cannot take this experience anywhere other than where it is. And where it is, is not here.' Jonathan looked completely confused.

'You are in a place we wiz…ahem, birds, call Twilight. Inside Twilight, time is compressed but everything else expands. Senses, objects, thoughts—they are all sharpened.

'You are surrounded by what we call Candela Lumen power—an energy that makes light, sound, everything take on characteristics that do not exist in our living world.'

'How does it work? How is it doing this? The music, the chandelier,' gawped Jonathan.

'*It* is not doing this, Jonathan, *you* are doing this. You have created an Opening into Twilight,' smiled the grandmaster, astonished by Jonathan's ability to conjure not only avian spells, but ones that summoned Candela Lumen power.

Jonathan's mind spun wildly in stark contrast to the visual and musical harmony of the room. He'd never known or imagined anything like what he was experiencing, and he felt safe, exhilarated.

Mizmiq paused, watching Jonathan take it all in, then continued, 'Objects can be drawn into Twilight and exposed to Candela Lumen power before being put back into the world.

'That is how you are repairing my clumsiness. Okay, I did fall off my perch and bash the chandelier on purpose to test you, but this is your magic, Jonathan, not mine.'

'But I didn't cast a single spell?' protested Jonathan.

'Ah, but you did, Jonathan, you did,' grinned Mizmiq. 'Your spell was a form of magic we birds call mind magic, spells conjured by thoughts alone. In this case, an instinctive reaction: your desire to reverse a catastrophe.

'Spells of the mind exist, like all magic, as sound, but spoken human paths are not needed to elevate them into the spectrum of magic.'

'How do we bring others in, into where we are, my friends, so that they can hear this music?' asked Jonathan.

'We cannot invite anyone in unless they too are able to cast avian spells that draw on Candela Lumen power. I would wager your friends do not possess such magical ability. To be here, you must be capable of existing here.'

Jonathan's face fell. He thought of Filia and Julius. He wanted more than anything to share these sounds with them.

The final shard slipped into place and an invisible finger plucked one last angelic note on the harp, and as the sound faded Jonathan was certain he saw the strings bending ever so slightly in a satisfied smile. He then felt the Twilight Opening shutting and sat on the floor in shock.

'What about my sickness, Destructive Interference? Can I use mind magic to cast everyday spells in my own world?'

'That is something you have already been doing without knowing it, Jonathan. Your spoken paths failed because you were casting spells of the mind at almost exactly the same time to will the same outcomes into being,' replied Mizmiq.

'How do I get better at it and make sure one spell doesn't interfere with the other?' asked Jonathan excitedly.

'The only way for you to initiate one spell instruction at a time would be to no longer speak magic paths and cast spells with your mind alone. Thoughts cannot be silenced when you are wishing for something, so you would need to silence your speech instead,' answered the grandmaster.

'But what would people think of me, wandering around casting spells without speaking? I'd be a freak show, and what would the government say?' objected Jonathan.

'I'm afraid there is a greater consideration. I do not know how the Numberalist grid will react to a human conjuring Openings into Twilight.

'Unlike some of your mind spells, which are being counted it seems—hence your own people's diagnosis of Destructive Interference—those that reach into Twilight might not be countable at all because they draw on a power that exists outside this world.

'It is also possible that the initial notes of your Twilight spells might generate incredibly high spell counts as the magic forges a path into the Twilight realm.

'Either way, the government is likely to forbid you from using magic altogether,' warned Mizmiq.

Every Centurian knew that if magic could not be counted and controlled, it was not allowed. Another founding principle of Numberalism was the equal availability of magic for all.

'Then I will not use Openings when I conjure spells with my mind,' said Jonathan.

'I'm sorry, Jonathan. Without training, you will not be able to choose whether your mind creates Openings or not, and even minor spells might use momentary Openings simply because the magic has decided that that is the most efficient way to achieve an outcome. You must learn how to control your Openings, Jonathan.'

'Will you teach me?' pleaded Jonathan.

Mizmiq flew beside him. He lifted a wing and placed it gently on Jonathan's shoulder. 'The thing is, Jonathan, I don't think I can teach you and I'm not sure other birds will be able to train you either.

'I felt your Opening, but I could not hear the magic that began it so I do not know how to prevent you from reaching into Twilight.'

'Why couldn't you hear my magic?' cried Jonathan.

'Perhaps it is because you are human. I have not met a human able to wield Candela Lumen power.'

'Why then has this magic come to me?' exclaimed Jonathan.

'I do not understand how or why it has found its way to you, but I promise you this, Jonathan, I will be your friend for as long as it takes to answer that question and cure your Destructive Interference.'

Jonathan wept, and held his head in his hands.

'I will return soon,' sighed Mizmiq. 'I must tell a dear friend of this. She will help us determine what to do next. Avoid drawing attention to yourself. Use as little magic as you can. In fact, try not to think or speak the paths of any spells at all. I'm sorry. I know that sounds impossible, but if you can restrain yourself things will be much better.'

Jonathan looked up. The front window in the music room was open and the hawk had flown.

11.   Terminus, Planet of the Skulls

The Dispossessed Lord

Duggerrid, lord of the Skull race, rose from his throne in the dungeons of Terminus. His fleshless skeleton stood nearly five metres tall, almost as high as the damp rock-walled cavity that was his home.

A teardrop climbed over the precipice of his eye socket, solidified into a brilliant diamond, then plunged, striking the cold stone floor.

Duggerrid's hand shook as he stretched down, and he dropped the diamond several times before finally pinching and swallowing the precious jewel.

An intense rush of sadness instantly shot through his vulcanised shell.

Skulls longed to be human. They toiled endlessly in the dungeons of Terminus, hoping to manufacture human feelings out of the remains of the souls they'd carried there and destroyed, but sadness was the only emotion their artistry had been able to conjure.

Nevertheless, it was a piece of humanity and so it brought joy.

Duggerrid cracked his neck backwards and screamed his pleasure into Pleonec Tower, the megalith needle that stabbed the thundering skies above the Skull planet.

The cherished diamond's effects quickly wore off and the Skull lord's heartless shell tensed with pain.

He raged at the agony, which always stung as the pleasure of humanity lost its strength. It was a Skull's punishment for seeking a human life.

Duggerrid directed his anger at a Skull cowering in an unlit corner of his audience chamber. 'I have heard reports of incompetence in the latest Opus insurgency, Senestophar. Was I wrong to put you in charge of such a large invasion force?' he scowled.

The astrostrategist, Senestophar, stared out of the shadows at the empty space where the diamond had lain, envious of his master's human moment.

'All our ships came out of transit at the same location, my lord, not far from London, England. I have eliminated the commanders of the errant vessels for not spacing their entry correctly.

'The violence of their combined arrival made concealment in a natural Opus weather system impossible,' explained Senestophar.

'Their ships took the form of a mild tornado, but only for a short time. The anomaly soon passed after the crews changed from shell to wind-form and dispersed. The ships were scuttled without incident and they dissipated unseen.'

'You should have checked the accuracy of the matterline before initiating transition in the wayward ships. Attention to detail is how we will maintain secrecy and successfully invade humans at higher rates,' fumed Duggerrid.

'I will examine the matterline for each ship myself next time,' answered Senestophar defensively, but Duggerrid did not like his tone; he demanded perfection and if that could not be attained, he considered those at the top of the command structure accountable for failure.

'How can I trust you with invading a human in sleep if you can't get the transit right?' yelled Duggerrid.

'I have skilfully aided many invasions, my lord,' retorted Senestophar. 'I helped my predecessor, the Opus astrostrategist Dormidion, who mistakenly came out of matterline at the nearby red planet causing—'

'I'm not interested in you putting your former commander down,' interrupted Duggerrid.

'My lord, if I may…without me, Dormidion's own invasion would not have been successful. Let me at least explain what happened,' begged Senestophar.

Duggerrid was seething, but he was short of experienced astrostrategists, having let too many invade humans who were living longer than he had predicted. He was prepared to hear Senestophar out.

'Dormidion and I assumed wind-form and entered the target's home without any hint of wake, not even a breath of agitated breeze to warn the watching birds of the possibility of invasion,' said Senestophar.

'Our air vibrations beat the skin protecting the victim's eardrums and as expected, the foolish human brain was talked into allowing us in and we scarred its visual cortex with terror.

'I watched as Dormidion wrestled for control of the dream, my lord, respectful of his higher rank. But he was too slow and I could tell that the human was going to wake before the dream portrayed his death so I introduced a new mortal horror, a drowning.

'I did not leave until the human saw himself die in the dream, giving Dormidion a way into his consciousness. He still lives inside that human today, as you know.

'I remained on Opus and observed Dormidion's new existence, and yes, I was jealous of his victory, but I also felt much pride, pride at my craftsmanship inside the dream, for Dormidion's invasion had left not a scratch.

'The human's family and friends did not notice any changes in character. There was no new petulant behaviour.

'Death had clearly occurred long enough before the target woke for Dormidion to occupy the human's consciousness without disturbing his mind in any way.

'No bird will be able to detect the truth: that a Skull lies within that man,' Senestophar declared, growing in confidence.

Duggerrid was suddenly distracted. Minium, his chief intelligence officer, hobbled into the chamber smiling and holding up a glass phial.

Minium's stunted, mangled shell could not be changed into wind-form. He was therefore incapable of invading a human and had resigned himself to serving Duggerrid on Terminus.

Minium's greatest satisfaction was receiving the Skull lord's praise and what Duggerrid wanted from Minium was information that exposed mistakes and lies.

Skulls feared Duggerrid but they hated Minium. He was their enemy, not merely the fawning servant of their ruthless master.

Duggerrid thrust his arm downwards, almost to his knees, grabbed the phial and placed it inside one of his eye sockets.

'You lie, Senestophar,' he howled. 'You introduced the most out-of-the-ordinary weather event ever seen in that part of Opus.'

Senestophar's worst fears were confirmed when Duggerrid turned to his roll-master, Skor, who kept the record of which Skulls were next to leave the dungeons and attempt invasion.

'Do not condemn me, my lord,' pleaded Senestophar.

'You lied to me,' roared Duggerrid. 'Mark him down to the bottom of the invasion line.'

'Very well, my lord,' replied Skor, whose own disfigured skeletal structure belied an uncanny ability to memorise every Skull's position in the invasion line. Duggerrid had tested him on many occasions and he'd always responded with the correct ordering.

Skor led the defeated Senestophar away. Duggerrid slumped back on his throne and bemoaned his own fate.

He was forbidden from seeking completeness, the word Skulls used to describe their own state after invasion when they were able to experience the emotions of the person whose eternity they'd stolen.

The Arc of Darkness, the power that had created the Skull race, considered Duggerrid indispensable as a ruling presence on Terminus. Skulls obeyed him without question. Only under Duggerrid's tyranny would Skulls remain slavishly and efficiently focused on invading humans and carrying their souls to destruction in the abyss of Terminus when they died.

The Arc of Darkness had promised the Skull lord that he would be released from service when human eternity was finally annihilated and it had assured him that such a day would come.

The Arc's own demons would destroy the lumenests once they'd gained sufficient strength by feasting on the ashes of human souls in the hellfires below Terminus. Only then would the Skull lord be free to enter a human mind.

Duggerrid craved the end, the demons' triumph and his own completeness in a mortal life.

He had also been promised a further reward. Duggerrid had been told that when his human victim died he himself would rise up and take his place alongside his creators as an eternal elemental being, one who judged humans after death.

But Duggerrid did not know how many lives had to be captured and burned before the demons could bring about the end of the eternal world.

And with Senestophar's failure, the demons' coming felt almost out of reach but for the Skull lord's own faith in the words of the ancient power that had created him. And even those words, he now found himself questioning.

Duggerrid twisted his dagger into one of the hundreds of painless incisions that littered his cheeks, pondering how to accelerate the end of eternity.

He paused, removed the blade, brushed the white dust from his face and grinned. 'Guard, get me Kazeg,' he ordered.

Moments later, General Kazeg entered the chamber. He was Duggerrid's second-in-command.

'We are going to pursue a new course of action,' announced Duggerrid. 'Invasions in sleep are not progressing quickly enough. We will invade Opus openly, dig down and butcher the eternal core.'

Kazeg smiled with warmongering pleasure. He hated stealth and was itching for an opportunity to raise hell in open battle. He had never thought that this day would come, given Duggerrid's reluctance to fight the most powerful birds.

'It will be a great victory, my lord. The birds and grandmasters will not expect such boldness. They will not be ready for us. Do we know if killing the Opus core means the end of the Centurian lumenest as well?'

'We do,' proclaimed Duggerrid. 'I sent a Skull agent to Castle Spinneret. He entered unseen in wind-form and successfully invaded the assistant of the one they call Mizmiq.

'He found evidence in the evil wizard's study that the death of one core signals the doom of both. Prepare the ships for invasion.'

General Kazeg strode out of Duggerrid's audience chamber and within minutes, the clamour of war was echoing through the dungeons.

The Skull planet, Terminus, orbited a dying sun in the Delta 13 sector of space. Opus-Earth's solar system lay in Epsilon 45. The crossing would be swift.

Skulls had mastered matterline travel, a way of transporting objects at incredible velocity between pre-determined points.

Matterline travel was not always as accurate as they wished, but it had the same transcendent magical properties as the bird corridors; a magic that made the speed of light look like walk in the park.

12.   Southwest London, England
Winds of Mass Destruction

Storm Pandora had eventually petered out and Stephen and Florence Prior had returned to the hospital. Jonathan's injuries meant a miracle would be needed if there was to be any hope of him waking from coma.

Stephen held Florence's hand. She pushed him away and broke down, 'I could have prevented this. I will never come to terms with what I've done. The doctor said that while there was no immediate danger, he'd be needing surgery soon. I should have collected him. There was something seriously wrong with his eyesight.'

'Wh–why didn't you make him wait?' stuttered Stephen.

'I wasn't thinking clearly. I wasn't only worried about him. I was terrified of you,' Florence snapped angrily. 'I wasn't ready to come home. I couldn't face telling you what the doctor had said.'

'Why?' demanded Stephen.

'I had forgotten to renew Jonathan's medical insurance. We may not have been able to afford the operation in time and I couldn't bear to confront your hate and blame so I phoned the school and told them I'd be late. I didn't think he'd leave before I got there. I needed time alone. I was afraid, afraid of what you would say; that is what killed Jonathan, my fear of you. You,' she sobbed.

Florence felt a renewed sense of hurt as she cried out the truth while Stephen's disbelief gave way to spitting fury. 'Y–you are saying this is my fault?'

'Yes,' she screamed. 'You never allow me to speak. You never sit down and listen and work through problems with me, you never forgive me for my mistakes. You are so cruel. I hate you.'

Stephen went apoplectic with rage. 'I–I gave him and you everything and you accuse me of not doing enough?' he yelled. 'And all the while, you could have prevented this by telling him to wait until you got to school.'

A doctor rushed into the room, ignoring their fighting. 'There are reports of another storm, only this time more dangerous. You will both be staying here until it passes,' he said.

Stephen marched out of Jonathan's room. Florence left shortly afterwards.

They followed a stream of people to a crowded reception area and stood on opposite sides. Everyone's eyes were on the television.

'We are taking you live to the Prime Minister who is holding an emergency briefing,' stated the newsreader abruptly.

'People of our great country,' began the Prime Minister. 'We have been struck by tornadoes, we are about to be beaten again, only this time it is every nation on Earth that will suffer.

'More than one thousand violent weather systems will reach ground level over the next twenty-four hours, pitching their destruction at all corners of our beloved planet. This is an invasion but with no known enemy.'

The audience at the briefing panicked, as did everyone in the hospital reception area.

Having given the facts and caused alarm, the Prime Minister attempted to offer hope.

'Although our enemy is of a kind we do not understand and we cannot therefore plan a defence with confidence, we are mounting one nevertheless.

'A front line is being constructed that will surprise our foe as much as it does us.

'Our co-habitants, the birds, are forming some sort of circle, creating wave upon wave of upward pressure that our meteorologists say will counter the impending attack. It seems the birds are powerful friends we have never really understood.'

The Prime Minister stepped back from his lectern, visibly shaken. Regaining his composure, he ended with the words, 'We pray to the birds for their help and salvation. May they watch and protect us now, and for evermore.'

Stephen and Florence fought their way through the petrified crowd to Jonathan's room and glared at the billowing skies from separate windows, fearful of what lay inside the storms.

*****

Rose shot out of a lapisphere into Battersea Park and laid Charlie gently on the ground. When her family and friends saw the robin's mutilated body, they were inconsolable.

Rose bowed her head and excused herself as quickly as she could, darting off to join the largest conglomeration of birds ever seen on Earth.

The bird population had swelled to twice its usual count. Birds had arrived from across the corridor network. Many were species that had never flown the planet's normally fair blue skies, desperate to support their distant cousins.

Every foreign bird hid its shape, colour and size with spells of concealment to avoid changing the scope of human knowledge. Even the giant five-foot red cardinals who'd never left the bird corridors managed to downsize successfully.

The Skulls had caught the birds by surprise and they were scrambling to coordinate a defence.

Birds did not operate with a leader making a speech; they all talked at once, twisting and turning in unison without one apparently telling another which way to swerve.

They settled on a plan of action quickly. Rose was to help direct the creation of a windshield covering the globe and she and the other leaders marshalled the birds into sixteen flight paths along evenly spaced lines of latitude.

These protective moving waves would strike the Skull storm ships as they descended to earth, preventing them from reaching the ground.

The waves took shape, coloured with the regalia of thousands upon thousands of sparkling bird species. They were like rainbows that appear suddenly in a tempestuous sky—lines of order and beauty amidst darkness and chaos.

At the head of the first wave was Elgarian, the lord of all eagles, hiding his hundred-foot wingspan as he flew.

'More golden brown on his head, don't you think, troops?' suggested Rose to the locals, trying to relax the throng by teasing Elgarian like a mother making fun of her Herculean son.

'Agreed, he's taken the bald thing too far, and feathers more out than in, please, Lord Elgarian,' added Fovea, one of the North American eagles. The birds laughed and after a few adjustments, Elgarian got the flaps-up.

Just below Elgarian were a flock of beat box birds from Gazong, an earth-like planet far from Earth and Centurian. It had no human inhabitants but boasted a bird population louder and larger than anywhere else in the birds' universe.

Their thumping lows and melodic highs magically transcended the noise of imminent battle, dictating individual flapping frequencies so that every wingspan contributed to the unified motion of the waves.

The Skulls had never seen or imagined anything like the defence that curled in front of them. 'Ram the smaller ones as they take their turn on the flanks,' bellowed Duggerrid to his captains.

'Aye my lord, the birds will pay a high price for their invention,' raged Kazeg at the helm of his battleship, the Turpitude.

Elgarian steadied everyone's nerves, bracing the birds for contact with the enemy line. 'No matter what happens, my friends, keep flying and stay inside your wave,' he demanded.

'Do not even think about chasing the Skull filth or their ships. It is not the victory of any one bird that will deliver triumph; it is the continuous momentum and coherence of each line.

'Billy, you and your cohorts of pneumatic metalpeckers are the exception. You may depart the lines and pound the enemy vessels. Drill them to crater dust even if that means going cross-eyed. You hear me, lads and lasses? Who needs eyeballs when your entire body and soul is on the line?'

'Not us!' they cried, attaching their metallic sheaths.

'Finally, twitches and switches, do your best to stay inside the waves,' declared Elgarian.

The twitches were quirks of bird nature, a variant of the chicken family. They shook every time they spoke and had a habit of stopping in mid-air, plummeting to the ground.

They lived mainly in the bird corridors, but could also be found on Centurian where they were valuable to humans because they produced twice the number of eggs of every other chicken.

Their kin, the switches, lived only in the corridors. They sported one wing that would oscillate faster than the other, causing them to fly in a curve, and they would turn upside down to plot their course back to the straight-line point—a constant S. Everything about them was lopsided.

The Skulls took their ships out of wind-form and the battle was joined twenty thousand feet above ground.

Duggerrid's flagship, the Marrowbone, broke through the flank of the equator wave but it could not force its way past the birds and it was carried along inside the wave.

The Skull crew launched defensive platforms and slaughtered anything that came near them with ribbons of lightning that poured from diamond-tipped rods, the Skulls' close-combat weapon of choice.

Duggerrid's dark magic had found a way to cage lightning in diamonds. He had also discovered that some shafts of light behaved like thinking beings when trapped, discharging powerful explosive energy in the hope of ejection. The Skulls called these weapons diaminds, living diamonds.

Billy and his metalpeckers drilled into the Marrowbone's underbelly and splinters singed their feathers and stabbed their eyes, making them bleed.

Any shards that reached a Skull's eyes simply disappeared through their sockets without the slightest discomfort. Their eyes were like black holes in the brain.

Skull destroyers and battleships followed the Marrowbone into the wave. Their crews slashed at the birds and the metalpeckers redoubled their efforts, risking all in their desire to sink the enemy.

'Downburst, get back,' warned Billy as a colossus class battleship disintegrated, evaporating into a new life as a collection of tropospheric air parcels, leaving behind only metallic dust as evidence of Skull craftsmanship for the humans below.

'Three cheers for the metalheads,' cried the Gazongians.

'Aaaaallllrrrrrrr,' came the resounding cross-species victory cry that the birds called the Shrill. On this occasion, they let it rip in a double-octave V major scale, signifying a major victory. It was heard all the way along each line of latitude. No one missed out on the news and everyone joined the chorus of celebration.

Duggerrid stood raging on the uppermost platform of the Marrowbone, willing the invasion on.

The battle looked and sounded like devastating thunder and lightning to the people of Earth. They did not see what was inside the storms and could not have imagined what was really at stake—their souls' onward journeys after death, not merely their lives.

Kazeg saw Duggerrid's squadron caught inside the equator wave and divided several hundred ships into convoys of ten and hid them inside a conflagration of menacing cyclones in Earth's atmospheric flow.

The crafty General had noticed how the stronger birds were moving up and down the wave, converging on focal points of attack, so he ordered his ships to strike at multiple locations around the circumference.

Kazeg would have broken through if it wasn't for the arrival of grandmaster Mizmiq. Rose had messaged the hawk as soon as she'd known of the Skull invasion.

The grandmaster shot out of a lapisphere at thirty thousand feet and descended on the battle. He cast spells of weaving that strengthened the wave wherever General Kazeg attacked and filled his threads with whispers of reassurance to comfort those who were in danger of losing heart.

Duggerrid and Kazeg saw that they would struggle to overcome the birds' defence and announced the retreat so they could preserve their ships with an eye to vengeance.

Nearly a quarter of Earth's birdlife was dead. Rose opened a lapisphere, dived into one of the local estuary corridors and emerged in Battersea Park. There were hundreds of bodies strewn across the ground.

Rose searched for Jaden and Enchoir, having last seen the robins a few miles behind her in one of the waves.

Mizmiq landed next to Rose and touched the worried robin with his wing.

'The scale of sacrifice is unfathomable,' wept Rose.

Mizmiq was silent with grief.

'Did you test the boy?' choked Rose.

'I did. He has extraordinary magical potential. He created Openings into Twilight and handled Candela Lumen energy with ease,' replied Mizmiq.

Rose stared at the grandmaster, flabbergasted. 'I never even thought to look and see if he might be conjuring Openings.'

'I fear the Numberalist government will take him away in an effort to understand his magic. We must help him, for his own sake, while we find out how and why this power has come to him,' urged Mizmiq.

'Yes, and we must move quickly,' answered Rose. 'We will fly without delay to Centurian and show him how to control his Candela Lumen power.'

'No, Rose, it is not that simple. A human reaching into Twilight was not the most astonishing thing I found. He did not begin his Openings with the spells you and I conjure,' said Mizmiq.

'What magical notes did he use then?' gasped Rose.

'That's the thing. I couldn't hear his magic. I do not believe we can train him,' sighed the grandmaster.

The little robin glanced up at the hawk, then at the death that surrounded them.

'It is not only the Numberalist government I fear. The Skulls must not learn of his power. He represents a threat whether he knows it or not, and the Skulls won't just steal his soul, they will kill him right where he stands.

'We must train him, Mizmiq, and if you or I cannot, we must find a way to carry him through the bird corridors to Eskatar, to the priestesses. They will teach him.'

Rose suddenly felt a circle of air trying to get her attention. It was a message, but it contained no words.

Rose shot off to its source. It was Jaden; the robin lay dying. She had lost most of her feathers and there were deep cuts across her chest.

'No, it cannot be,' Rose wailed. 'Come back, Jaden, come back.'

Jaden summoned the strength to speak, 'Enchoir is d…dead. She was struck by a diamind blast and fell outside the wave. I turned to help, others did too, but we were marshalled into line to keep the wave intact. Sh…she was too weak to get back inside. She is gone.'

Rose cradled the little robin in her wings but Jaden's heart gave way and Rose slumped to the ground, overcome with grief. The two robins had been as sisters for so many years. Like Rose, they had been blessed with long lives by the power of the birds' own magic.

Birds did not know what happened to them after death. Eternal consciousness for humans across sibling worlds gave them hope that a similar process of renewal might exist for them.

Most believed in a place they called Nihilimb, and that they would travel there after death, live a new life, then return to their corridored world, empty of memory and with a new identity but with the same continuing purpose: to keep humans within the cycle of eternal consciousness so that their souls would never again experience Arcan torture and punishment after death.

Mizmiq tried to comfort her, as did other birds who wept and remembered how Jaden and Enchoir had guided them and cared for them. The two robins were loved and known across so many of London's parks and gardens.

'Today, our hope for the truth of Nihilimb is greater than ever,' wept Rose, holding Jaden and staring through her tears at the devastating loss of life around her. 'Go now, my dear sisters, to Nihilimb, to the renewal of life,' she cried.

Rose turned to the grandmaster. 'Fly, Mizmiq, persuade the boy to begin his journey to Eskatar. Don't wait for me to finish the birdsong lament for Jaden, Enchoir and the other valiant birds of this park.'

Mizmiq bowed before the bird-throng and he too wept, acknowledging their sacrifice before opening a lapisphere and plunging into London's estuary corridors.

13. Centurian

Rockmore Space Junction

Jonathan sat at home in his music room, waiting. It had been several days since the mysterious hawk had left and he was worried.

The hawk had said that he was going to talk to a friend then return. Surely he'd not met the same fate as Charlie. Jonathan quickly put the thought out of his mind. The hawk was a powerful bird, not a tiny robin vulnerable to attack.

Jonathan had not been to school. He'd told his parents he couldn't face the idea of everyone pitying him as they watched his magic fail again and again.

Lucius and Presette had supported him without question and informed Mr Mercer that he was sick with an illness that had not yet been fully diagnosed.

Jonathan had said nothing to his parents about the hawk. The harp and chandelier were spotless and he'd checked every inch of the music room for feathers, including inside the piano. There was not even the slightest scent of bird.

Jonathan had decided he would tell his parents his outrageous tale of magic after the hawk's next visit. He wanted to finish the unlikely story with a solution to his Destructive Interference. Without that, they might feel obliged to call the doctor and he'd run the risk of being banned from using magic altogether by the government.

Filia and Julius had bombarded Jonathan with messages, apologising for making the class think he might be magically handicapped. He had replied with remorse for his anger and they'd responded with even greater remorse and longer apologies.

Filia and Julius had come around every day after school to see how he was and he'd told them about the hawk while his parents were at work.

Each time they came, Jonathan had walked wide-eyed across the music room playing the harp, piano and bass guitar, describing the notes that had accompanied the chandelier's floating shards.

Filia and Julius had listened intently, believing everything he said and looking out of the window as often as he did, hoping to see the hawk.

Jonathan had avoided using magic whenever possible, heeding the hawk's warning that it was unclear how the Numberalist grid would react to Twilight Openings, even momentary ones that he himself wouldn't notice.

The possibility of the government detaining him for not being able to control his magic was the one thing he hadn't told Filia and Julius. He wanted to go to Rockmore with Filia to see if they could try and enjoy their magic-music as if it was any other weekend night. If she knew his magic could put him in danger she might stop him from going.

Jonathan stood up and began marching to and fro across the music room. It was Friday evening and he and Filia had agreed to catch an early dronibus to Rockmore but he was agonising over whether to tell her the truth, or whether to say nothing and risk being found out by the government.

A message pinged on his awful, archaic phone. In an effort to use magic sparingly, he'd rummaged through his room, unearthed a battered old device and connected it to the network that operated without magic.

The phone and the network were both woefully unreliable. The message was from Filia and it had been sent an hour ago, telling him which dronibus she'd be on and what time it would arrive at his stop.

Jonathan hesitated before replying. He went to the window, hoping to spot the hawk's majestic shadow in the evening sky. His heart leapt, not because the hawk had miraculously appeared, but because Filia was outside his house and she looked stunning in her magic-music fan's uniform of boots, jeans and black leather jacket.

She was sitting on the garden wall, one leg hanging down, tapping the bricks with her heel. The other leg was propped up with her foot placed squarely on top of the wall. Her head was resting on her knee and she was staring at the ground.

Jonathan hurried into the hallway and opened the front door, and as soon as she saw him, she brushed her long auburn curls away from her cheeks, jumped off the wall and rushed to embrace him.

Jonathan felt the same surge of euphoria that had gripped him when he'd bounded up the road after they'd celebrated Elephant's Trunk. 'Ready?' she grinned.

'Yes,' he smiled, hugging her tight, his stomach spinning as if a thousand butterflies were trying to take off inside him.

Julius was there too. 'Five more minutes and we would have broken the door down,' he winked.

'I'm glad you didn't, not sure I could have fixed your damage,' laughed Jonathan. 'How long have you been out here? You should have knocked and come in.'

'Julius persuaded me to give you more time in case you were having second thoughts and worrying about people glaring at you if the magic didn't work,' answered Filia, bottling up tears. 'I was starting to lose it.'

Jonathan pulled her closer to him. 'Hey, I'm late because of my stupid phone. I only just got your message.'

'We're going to see you right, buddy, no matter what,' said Julius. 'If anyone gets even a glimpse of your spells failing, we'll dispel the myth, there and then.'

'Which one?' Jonathan chuckled. 'I'm demented as well as disabled remember, I can do crazy things with my brain.'

'Only the Destructive Interference myth, we want to promote the properly mad stuff—it's genius,' laughed Julius.

Jonathan allowed himself a half-smile, then looked down, wondering again how the Numberalist surveillance apparatus would handle his spells. 'I'm afraid there won't be any mad magic on display this evening,' he sighed. 'Not even a few bars of Jonathan Powers unplugged. This headcase wants nothing other than a regular Friday night out at the Junction.'

Filia gripped his hand and Julius put his arm across his shoulder and they made their way up the road.

They boarded the downtown dronibus. It was Julius' first visit to Rockmore, a fact that the other passengers were all made aware of shortly after lift-off.

Julius talked to people in the street on a whim. When he was this excited, he was unstoppable. Jonathan and Filia laughed as he strode up and down the aisle of the dronibus demanding to know which magic-music samples everyone thought he should listen to first.

His parents had refused to let him join Jonathan and Filia at Rockmore until after the Spellology exam. They knew how carried away he'd get. He was a passionate musician and he'd been itching to get involved in their magic-music making.

Julius and Jonathan had been writing songs for years. Julius wrote farcical lyrics, which Jonathan adored. Jonathan's songs were always serious, which made Julius' ability to get comedy spot on all the more precious.

Jonathan would start with incredible soundscapes using the magic-keys on the piano or the spell-extended harmonics of his bass.

Melodies and chords would follow. Julius would listen and think, listen more, then think again until his conveyor belt of one-liners was ready.

Jonathan would invariably collapse in hysterics during each song and struggle to recover.

Filia had begun to sing with them. Her voice was second to none. It could be elegant and powerful or gentle and intimate, whatever the music required, and she just about managed to keep a straight face when confronted with Julius' lyrics.

'I'm only semi-quavers away from the ultimate experience,' Julius bellowed, plonking himself back in his seat.

Jonathan half-smiled again, acknowledging Julius' playful exuberance but troubled by another bout of worry.

Filia tightened her fingers around his hand. Julius noticed his friend's anxiety and brought himself back down to earth.

'There will be a cure, Jonathan. The hawk's definitely got options up his sleeve,' he whispered. 'Besides, doctors all say different things. That diagnosis doesn't mean diddly-squat until you get a second opinion. There are lots of mystery diseases that come on suddenly and go away on their own.'

Jonathan feigned a smile but didn't reply. Filia was quiet too. Jonathan's ability to develop magic-music was as important to her as it was to him. What they did together simply worked and not only that, they'd discovered it on their own.

Composing magic-music with anyone else was inconceivable, it would feel like a betrayal.

The dronibus arrived. They jostled their way through the crowded underpass below the shuttle platforms and up the steps to Rockmore's Central Hall, the largest sound hub in the Junction.

Jonathan and Filia had a pre-booked booth which doubled as a soundproof mini-planetarium. You could sit in an open circle and listen to other people sharing their magic-music or shut yourself off and concentrate on your own creations.

Filia triggered the planetarium setting. Hundreds of glasslike spheres hovered in the ceiling and the rest of Central Hall disappeared and fell silent. Each sphere represented a planet or moon in the Centurian solar system and they all hung in their actual cosmic locations relative to the other blazing orbs.

Filia expanded the horizon to reveal nearby stars. 'Seat-belt on, Julius,' announced Jonathan, 'sound containers are in play,' and they laughed as Julius fumbled for a non-existent belt while keeping his eyes fixed on the galaxy of lights.

Julius' jaw dropped as he stared at one sparkling jewel after another, knowing that inside each sphere was the sound of that celestial body's geological character created from spells of structure to sound conversion.

He focused on one particular container that had specks of colour crawling around it like tiny trails on a map. He gasped, recognising the markings from pictures and from Jonathan's descriptions; they were the locations of event recordings made by sound hunters and voted by them to be of high enough fidelity and originality to deserve a place in the planetarium ceiling.

'Can I go first? Please!' cried Filia. Jonathan waved her on.

Filia pointed at the Seresind moon, also known as Thunder One due to the hostile weather system that hammered its surface.

The booming thump of Thunder One's kick-drum proceeded to pound their insides and Filia pointed at it repeatedly to set the tempo.

'I like the tough beginning,' smiled Jonathan, delighted that she'd chosen some solid rock to blast things off. 'Not the usual passive scene-setting of a Filia Wrens epic,' he grinned. Filia kicked him lightly under the table, being careful not to bruise his shin with her boot.

Filia added Larintine's golden dust rings and a crescendo of cymbals rushed through the booth. Then she chose the snare drum of Thunder Two while lining up the bright white stars of the Angels of Cryona, telling them to be patient before bringing the purity of their chorus to the fore.

Jonathan took a deep breath and spoke the magic paths that instructed Elephant's Trunk to join the music. He shook his fist in delight as perfect electro-static seashore waves washed over the wormhole's bottomless infrasound. His Centurian magic paths had worked first time.

Jonathan cast spell after spell, summoning magical notes and moods that lifted the music. He had no idea whether he was using mind magic alongside his spoken paths, nor did he care as worries became lost in the music.

'Lyrics?' howled Filia, overjoyed.

'Yes!' whooped Jonathan. 'One line each, I'll start.'

"Beyond the door is another world, below the floor a million miles..."

47

'Oh, can I, please?' demanded Julius, holding his arms aloft and knocking the Rhombidian moon out of position.

'Got to watch that one, big man, oval orbiting pattern, cuts right across the others, very impolite,' laughed Jonathan.

Julius waited until he was certain the moon was orbiting correctly again and he was sure that the cosmos hadn't experienced any unplanned collisions. 'You gone all shy?' teased Jonathan.

'I'll have two lines for that comment,' Julius retorted. 'Here goes, you guys are so darn serious,' he scoffed, 'what about…

Sixty games of solitaire later, Jonathan's orbiting his hundredth crater
Why does Julius get all the action while Jonathan's stuck in a tin contraption?

Filia and Jonathan burst into laughter. 'Love it. I've got some more lines,' cried Jonathan.

'There goes Rocket Man, here comes Superman, you'll see them twice every twenty years
Jonathan's still waiting for, er, Tincan Repairman to fix the fault in his forty gears.

Okay, that was terrible,' winced Jonathan, looking at Filia and Julius, who were bent over double.

'My turn,' yelled Julius. 'I can make something of it.

Turn the spanner, strike nail with hammer, systems choke back into life
What's this, a drone? A bird alone? It's Jonathan Powers; he's comin' home!

'There you go. I turned a story of galactic intraspection into a divine comedy,' shouted Julius before exploding into song.

'He's comin' home, he's comin' home; Jonathan Powers is comin' home. He's comin' ho…'

'Enough. Ridiculous. I've no idea why I'm laughing so hard,' bawled Filia.

'Insane,' cried Jonathan.

Filia looked at Jonathan and they nodded. She drew a line in the stars and Jonathan followed it with a parallel line. The piece was complete.

The ceiling went dark except for the stars, planets and moons they'd used in their composition.

'That, Julius Fog, is our sound constellation,' Jonathan beamed, admiring the pattern.

'It looks like an FJ!' gawped Julius.

'With an exclamation mark to the side!' added Filia, flinging her arms around Jonathan before running her finger down his forehead and tapping the end of his nose. 'I want lots more exclamation marks, Mr Sound Hunter,' she smiled, delighting in the fact that he'd lost none of his creative magic.

'We need to give it a name,' said Julius. 'Something describing a bunch of superheroes and a broken-down shuttle—Space Fiction—that's it, and it's more than a song name, it's a new genre!'

'Things starting to go downhill?' grinned Filia, looking at Jonathan.

'Yep, crash-landing,' Jonathan laughed. 'Julius Fog is undermining the reputation of magic-music as a high art.'

'No, we're not going downhill, far from it; we're levitating ourselves to new heights. If you don't like Space Fiction for our new genre, what about…what about…got it! Fogspawn,' yelled Julius triumphantly.

'Oh my, wow, he's lost it. Let's take him to the sound-stalls and try and calm him down before the next session,' Jonathan exclaimed.

They left the booth and walked to one of the junction platforms in fits of hysterics. T-shirts, jackets and every other type of apparel imaginable were on display, laced with the signatures of famous sound hunters and images of their mastery.

Jonathan saw Glitch Hopper. He was wearing his own colliding mining moons t-shirt. 'Hey, Glitch, what did you bring in tonight?' he called.

'Something unbelievable. You got a booth?' Glitch answered.

'Yes, Central Hall, come on,' replied Jonathan, introducing Filia and Julius.

'I found eleven of the Edgeland moons arrayed in a crown and their sound kicks ass. They've got more cosmic energy than any other sonic astral chain,' explained Glitch as they darted through the crowd.

They took their seats, activated the planetarium and Glitch spoke the magic path that played his sound constellation.

A confident swinging rhythm bounced across the booth and eleven points of light formed a tiny arc in the otherwise pitch-black ceiling.

'They only curve like this once a decade. Listen to the deep boom of one, the groove of three, four and five, the crash of six ricocheting off two and the hard frickin' rock of seven to eleven—ten totally tears it up at the end.

'I couldn't believe the interplay as the shuttle passed each one. Ten was the hardest to place. For a while I thought it might spoil the constellation's shape and the arc would become a broken bow, but—wait, here it comes, what an ending, eh? The whole thing's still raw and I've got one of the engineering dudes working on a ton of enhancements.'

'Can we have a copy and sample it?' cried Filia, getting up and twisting with the rhythm as he replayed it.

'Keep this one; publish it too if you like, you'll be one of the first to put it out there,' said Glitch.

He suddenly noticed the time. 'My next shuttle leaves in minutes. Gas explosion waiting to happen.'

'Where?' exclaimed Julius. Glitch hesitated.

'Julius is new to the scene,' smiled Jonathan. 'Not your fault, Julius, sound hunter etiquette, can't run the risk of others creating the magic first,' he winked.

Glitch ducked out of the booth. They listened to his invention over and over again. It was every sound hunter's dream; a constellation that was shaped like it was meant to be with incredible sound that had never previously been captured.

'The guy's a genius, and he's nuts,' grinned Julius, shaking his head.

'I thought you were about to volunteer to go with him?' quipped Jonathan.

'Back to work, you two. Let's write the next verse of FJ,' ordered Filia, laughing.

They sat up straight like children in a classroom and Filia spoke the path that opened her and Jonathan's magic-music library.

'I'm going to add Anvilian cow-bells,' announced Jonathan as their first session's work echoed throughout the booth.

'Arggh, you know I hate those, the clanging nonsense drummers love,' objected Filia.

She looked at Jonathan after a few seconds. 'You changed your mind?'

'No, they're there, can't you hear them?' he replied.

'No,' said Filia. 'Julius?'

'No, nothing,' Julius answered.

Jonathan cast a spell to increase the volume. 'I can't hear the song anymore, just the Anvil, it's doing my head in,' he shouted.

'Turn it off then,' yelled Filia.

Jonathan cast spell after spell but they had no effect. 'I can't stop it, help me, I can't control the volume either.'

Filia shut down the planetarium; the ceiling receded and the noise of Rockmore's Central Hall surrounded them.

Jonathan rushed out of the booth. Filia and Julius shot after him. 'Wait, Jonathan, wait!' Filia screamed, afraid she might lose him in the crowd.

Jonathan stood outside and raged. Filia grabbed him and wrapped her arms around him.

'I expected Destructive Interference at some point, Filia, but not torture,' he cried. 'I'm not going back in, that was hell.' Filia and Julius said nothing. They were as shocked and distraught as him.

It began to rain, hard. They moved to the shelter of the Central Hall doorway. 'Okay, I'll give it one more shot,' said Jonathan after several minutes, 'but you watch me and switch the whole thing off if I signal.'

'I will, I will,' Filia sobbed.

They went back inside and Filia restarted the FJ song but Jonathan's experience was even worse. The Anvil clanged inside the music without him even asking it to be there and only he could hear it. The volume grew, destroying the song and subjecting him to unbearable pain. Jonathan signalled and Filia immediately shut the planetarium down.

'One more try; play the song at the lowest volume,' wept Jonathan, but the same thing happened—the Anvil was there without being summoned.

Filia cut the music. 'I can still hear it. Stop it!' yelled Jonathan.

'I've shut everything down, Jonathan,' answered Filia in despair.

Jonathan ran outside. 'It's killing me,' he cried. 'I can't do this, Filia, I can't,' he howled as the Anvil pounded inside his head.

Filia held him tightly. 'I won't let go until it's gone,' she whispered and the sound eventually faded.

They made their way home. Julius hugged his friend after they got off the dronibus. 'We will never give up. Never. We will find a cure.'

'Thank you, Julius, thank you,' bawled Jonathan.

'All three of us will go to Rockmore tomorrow night,' choked Filia. 'We will try again together, Jonathan. This is still your calling.'

Julius left and Jonathan walked Filia home. 'I'll come to your house early and make you breakfast,' said Filia as they reached her door. 'Well, not too early, nine o'clock, it's a Saturday,' she smiled.

Jonathan's eyes flooded with tears. 'I'm not the boy I used to be, am I?' he wept.

'Yes, you are,' Filia replied firmly. 'You're the boy who conquered the Tilmenian run and you're going to beat this too.'

She kissed him and Jonathan's heart leapt like it had been catapulted out of Elephant's Trunk. He didn't let go of her lips and nor did she let go of his. Filia was everything and if she loved him, his life could fall apart all it wanted.

They saw a light come on inside the house and Filia quietly opened the front door. 'Remember, breakfast, Mr Sound Hunter. Get some sleep; I'll be booting you out of bed at nine.'

Jonathan crept down the path. He was so miserable and so happy at the same time. He wanted to scream his delirium to the stars; the butterflies were out of control and he felt like he was flying, properly flying—no shuttle, no wings, just Filia.

14. Centurian

Crime and Punishment

Filia knocked on Jonathan's front door. 'It's me! Open up.' There was no response. 'Come on, Jonathan, time to get up and admire yourself in the mirror, it's nine o'clock,' she shouted.

Filia's voice woke Jonathan up and he sent her a message, 'I can hardly move, I've been zapped, badly.'

Zapping was the colloquial term Centurians used for the punishment meted out to people who committed gross spell-count violations.

Zapping could be anything from a short sharp pain to frequent shocks over time depending on the number of excess counts logged by the grid.

Spells were added up daily and zapping would begin during the culprit's first period of sleep after midnight, or at midnight if they were already asleep.

The Numberalist government openly stated that the agony of being woken continuously was an important part of the penalty.

Spell-count abuse had to be dealt with aggressively not only to ensure equal use of magic for all but because the planet's natural resources had been stretched to the limit in order to power Centurian's spell-casting infrastructure.

If one zap was like touching boiling water, Jonathan felt as though he'd been drowned in fire. He'd clearly conjured a monstrous cocktail of magic at Rockmore and the doctor's allowance adjustment had not been remotely sufficient to cover the spell-count.

Filia read Jonathan's message in horror and immediately arched her thumbs and forefingers to create an emergency communication circle. The Numberalist Healing Service answered straightaway. 'Address and name?'

'Jonathan Powers, 34 Tildesline Avenue,' Filia replied. There was silence. 'Hello? Hello?' she said.

'I would stay well clear of him if I were you,' warned a robot-voice moments later. To the Numberalists, this was no accident. It was purposeful teenage rebellion.

'He's hurt, for goodness' sake, you heartless machine. Are you going to help him or what?' snapped Filia.

'He's been added to the queue,' answered the monotone voice. 'Estimated time of arrival seventeen minutes and twenty-nine seconds.'

Filia slammed the communication channel shut and messaged Julius. He lived on the other side of Bushley Park and it wasn't long before he came hurrying down the road.

They forced open the door and found Jonathan splayed out across the hallway floor. He'd crawled out of bed and managed to slide down the stairs but was too weak to haul himself up.

They sat him against the wall but he flopped to one side. 'I want eggs and bacon, and lots of it,' he groaned.

They moved him to a chair in the kitchen and rustled up a substantial breakfast which Jonathan began wolfing down as soon as it was placed in front of him.

'Last night felt like a firework display. I think I broke every rule in the Numberalist book,' he smiled. Filia and Julius were relieved he seemed to be perking up.

'Don't contact my parents, I'm feeling better already,' he said, between mouthfuls.

'You're hurt, they should know,' insisted Filia. 'I'm amazed they didn't hear you.'

'I didn't yell once during the zapping. They don't know. I feel okay, don't tell them, please.'

'Where are they anyway?' said Filia.

'At work, of course, married to their screens,' replied Jonathan.

'At least your parents do something interesting,' said Julius.

'I guess I shouldn't be too harsh,' smiled Jonathan. 'Dad just got promoted too. The Space Academy have made him a Flight Science Professor.'

'Wooo, how about that for a bloke who started out fixing levitators and other groundless vehicles in his garage,' grinned Julius.

'When's your mother back?' asked Filia, deadly serious and worried about Jonathan.

'No idea, lunchtime probably. She doesn't usually work all day on a Saturday, says the new engineering head is a tyrant though, so who knows.'

'Well, I've already called the Healing Service. We'll let them be the judge of your health,' said Filia sternly.

Two robots swerved to a halt and trooped out of an emergency surfer, a type of levitator which sacrificed accuracy in the corners for straight-line speed. They were surprised to find Jonathan eating and complaining only of a headache.

While Jonathan answered questions, Julius eyed his last portion of eggs. He hadn't expected him to finish the lot and attempted to snaffle half of what was left with a spoon. Jonathan blocked his arm and a dollop dropped to the floor.

'Stay still while we scan your pulse,' ordered the healers.

'Yes sirs,' muttered Jonathan, impersonating the healing-bots with a softly spoken squeak.

'Your pulse is a quarter-speed of a healthy human,' announced one of the healers, swivelling its head in a full circle of confusion.

'I feel totally fine,' objected Jonathan. 'There must be something wrong with your gadget, why not test it on your own pulse?' he suggested, winking at Filia and Julius.

'Your jokes are as bad as ever so you must be alright,' laughed Julius.

'It's not funny,' said Filia, holding Jonathan's hand.

After more swivelling, the bots pronounced their verdict. 'We will be back in thirty-three minutes with more equipment to carry out further tests.'

Jonathan and Julius fought over the last quadrant of eggs while the robots shot off up the road.

'Don't lie, Jonathan, do you really feel okay?' said Filia.

'Yes,' he answered, getting up and moving into the music room. 'I just wish the hawk would show up,' he sighed, more desperate than ever for the bird to appear and tell him what on earth was going on.

*****

Jonathan's mother, Presette, sat in front of her four monitor screens in the Numberalist Research and Development centre and bashed out another software build.

Centurians used computer programming to tie spell intructions together so they could create magical outcomes that were not possible with single spoken paths.

Presette had gone to work early and was nearly ready to quit for the day. She and her friend Stella had all but completed their month-long project to reduce the number of spells that were needed to construct a new type of modulation tower.

Sintax, the chief engineer, interrupted her and Stella. He was sporting his usual creased lab coat, and as he leaned over they got a close-up view of his disgusting brown teeth and the ugly thorn-like spikes of stubble that protruded from his chin. They called him the MVP, the most vile person.

'We had an outage last night in the grid,' he explained in his whining nasal voice. 'Traffic peaked just after one in the morning. We've never seen anything like it and the load balancers were completely decimated. Luckily, we came back online a few minutes later.

'I need you to stop what you're doing and join the others. I've been trying to keep as few people on the investigation as possible; an outage in the grid is obviously a sensitive topic.'

Presette and Stella had no choice, they'd have to stay. 'What was the cause?' asked Stella, inching backwards to avoid his honking breath.

'We don't know; that's the most troubling thing. There's a hole in the memory. We can't see who or what triggered the downtime.'

Sintax wafted off to crack the whip somewhere else on the vast open-plan engineering floor and they set to work.

'Stella, look, the last piece of code to be used in the calculation before the outage is old,' exclaimed Presette.

'No, that's not old, it's ancient. Oh my, it's an original part of the grid, C flat; caveman code,' gasped Stella, an expert in dead programming languages. 'It's an early cut of revert code from when magic began a thousand years ago.'

Reverts were the official government term for zaps; literally, "things that turned your behaviour back to what it should be".

'Do you remember those ancient picture books telling people about the dangers of unlimited magic? The vomiting baby always made me laugh, filling his milk bottle twice an hour while his parents slept—hilarious,' chuckled Stella.

'Yes, I do,' laughed Presette.

'I kid you not, this is that,' said Stella. 'One of the first Numberalist code dumps from the time when counting, limits and incentives began. We should bring it up to date.'

'While we fix it, could we allocate the Powers household some extra counts in the Convenience category? Finding spells would be good,' joked Presette.

'You really do specialise in chaos, don't you,' grinned Stella. 'Your earrings, Jonathan's clothes and Lucius, well, he's a lost cause, isn't he? Should we change your Replenishment count at the same time so that your taps dispense wine as well as water? That might help calm things a little.'

Presette laughed and nodded agreement.

'Look,' gawped Stella, pointing to one of her monitors. 'The code only kicks in when an individual's spell violations exceed four, five, oh my word, that's impossible, six zeros, over a million illegal spells in one day. Someone got zapped big time. The network hit a level it's never reached, or not for hundreds of years perhaps. Who on earth could have been mad enough to zap themselves like that, or even be capable of doing it?'

Stella moved her hand across the screen. 'The surge took power from all over the grid. Energy was drawn to one point...' Stella hesitated then grabbed Presette's wrist, '34 Tildesline Avenue. Presette, what's going on? Someone's trying to frame you.'

'Change the location in the log files, now, Stella,' whispered Presette.

'Wh...what's going on?' said Stella.

'Just do it, it's Jonathan. He's not able to control his spell-count. The doctor said he's got Destructive Interference, but duplicate spells to this level—no, something's really wrong with his magic. I'm terrified they'll take him away. Do it, please, Stella.'

'Where should I have the logs point to though?'

'Anywhere, outer space, I don't care, quickly Stella, please. If they've harmed my boy I'll...'

Sintax strode up to their desks and demanded an update. 'Er, we haven't found anything yet. Has anyone else?' asked Presette.

'You two are useless, particularly you, Stella, I would have thought it was obvious to someone with your background. There's very old code that needs to be rewritten. But before we do that, Stella, tell me what the log files say, you have the most experience of this code type.'

'Ah yes, we did find the old code. I thought you were after an update on the cause. We still don't know what brought on the surge but I'm making my way through the logs and it looks like a massive stream of reverts was sent to...here, oh, that's Numberalist government headquarters.'

Sintax was not happy. His next logical step had to be plucking up the courage to accuse his superiors of sabotage. He scratched his head vigorously before traipsing back down the aisle towards his office.

'Thank you, Stella,' choked Presette, clutching her arm.

'Don't thank me yet, I'm doing it now, wait, done, they'll never know.'

Presette called Jonathan, fearing the worst. 'Jonathan, are you okay?'

'Why, yes, what's up, Mum?' he was taken aback. His mother never called him from work.

Presette muted the connection. 'He's okay, Stella, he's okay!'

'Mum? Are you there?' asked Jonathan.

'Oh, yes,' mumbled Presette. 'I was worried the doctor hadn't upped your allowance enough and you'd be punished unfairly.'

'Well, I was actually zapped last night, Mum. I feel fine though.'

'Are you sure you're all right? You really feel okay?' said Presette.

'Yes, I have a headache, nothing else,' Jonathan replied.

'I'll ask the doctor to increase the limit,' said Presette. 'Try not to use any magic until I've spoken to him. I'll be home shortly.'

Presette turned to Stella. 'One more thing, keep a copy of the original logs, please. I need to work out what to say to the doctor. We have to analyse his peak rates, understand which spells made the count so high and make sure he doesn't use them again. I'm scared, Stella.'

'Presette, don't worry, no one will find out and I'll look at the log files at home. I've taken a copy. I'll let you know what we should do. Go and check on Jonathan. I'll tell the MVP there was nothing more you could help me with.'

Presette took the dronibus home and was relieved to find Jonathan, Filia and Julius composing a new song in the music room.

'What's it called?' Presette asked, examining Jonathan for signs of distress. Other than looking extremely tired, he did seem fine.

'Fright night,' grinned Julius. 'Always best to write when it's raw.'

'Yes, I do remember saying that to you two boys once,' smiled Presette.

Three healing-bots knocked on the door and Presette answered. 'We've been instructed to bring Jonathan Powers with us,' they said. 'He must undergo extensive testing.'

Presette went pale; further investigation might lead to her and Stella's cover-up. Jonathan appeared to be okay and she did not want him to go.

Jonathan came to the door and his eyes suddenly lit up in delight. The hawk was clinging anxiously to a branch inside a tree across the street.

It opened its beak and Jonathan heard a message. 'Don't go with them, they will not understand, you will become a medical experiment. Please, I will tell you more when they're gone.'

'I...I...feel quite faint,' moaned Jonathan, resting his hand on his mother's shoulder. 'Can you do the tests here?'

The bots swivelled. 'We will return in nine minutes,' they answered.

Jonathan hurried into the music room and flung open a small rectangular top window. 'Mum, I will explain,' he blurted as the hawk squeezed through.

'Close the curtains, Jonathan,' asked Mizmiq abruptly, swooping down and gripping Jonathan's guitar head with one talon whilst adjusting his ruffled feathers with the other.

Presette, Filia and Julius fell backwards onto the sofa and sat shell-shocked, watching; they could tell the hawk and Jonathan were communicating.

'Jonathan, listen carefully,' said Mizmiq.

'I'm not going to listen to anything unless my mother and friends can hear it too,' Jonathan responded. 'How do we let them into the conversation?'

'I'm sorry, Jonathan, I cannot do that,' Mizmiq replied. There were lines that he, other grandmasters and the most powerful birds would not cross. Helping humans understand birds was one such red line. A single whisper from a careless bird might reveal the secret of eternal consciousness.

The grandmaster braced himself, expecting Jonathan to pressure him. This was the most exceptional of circumstances and he might just give in, if pushed.

But Jonathan didn't press him. Instead, Mizmiq watched, amazed, as Jonathan closed his eyes and willed the magic of bird-communication onto his mother, Filia and Julius.

Mizmiq was astounded by the spells flowing from Jonathan's mind. Most of the magic was audible to the hawk and he understood it, but there were also gaps, moments of silence that the grandmaster knew were filled with sounds he simply couldn't hear.

Once Jonathan had finished, Mizmiq stared at Presette, Filia and Julius. 'Mother and friends of Jonathan Powers, can you hear me?'

They nodded, almost ripping the sofa's soft velvet covering in astonishment. Jonathan was ecstatic.

'Can you hear other birds? Words instead of tweets coming from birds outside?' asked Mizmiq, afraid that Jonathan had opened up the world of birds to his mother and friends.

Presette, Filia and Julius could only hear the familiar twittering of urban birdlife and shook their heads.

'Jonathan, what about you? Can you hear the birds outside?' enquired the grandmaster, wondering if Jonathan had inadvertently found a way past Rose's spell.

'No, I can't hear them,' Jonathan replied.

Mizmiq breathed a sigh of relief. 'I'm glad. The racket of some of the folk out there would drive you crazy,' he smiled, 'and don't worry, this magic is not counted by the grid. You will not get zapped.'

'I don't believe that, we will get zapped,' muttered Julius to Filia. Mizmiq eyeballed Julius with affectionate disapproval. 'I can hear you, young man, even when you're convinced my ears couldn't possibly pluck your sound waves out of the air,' he smiled.

'I–I'm sorry, I didn't mean to offend you, Mr Hawk, sir, I believe you, no zaps,' gulped Julius.

'Please, the name's Mizmiq,' chuckled the grandmaster.

'I'm, I'm Julius.'

'And I'm Filia.'

'And I'm Presette, M–Mr Mizmiq,' stuttered Jonathan's mother.

Mizmiq smiled at them and turned to Jonathan, 'You have an incredible gift, Jonathan, and I'm here to ask that we develop your skills. I created the circumstances that initiated your Twilight Openings during my last visit when you repaired the harp and the chandelier.

'But what you did just now, when you gave your mother and friends the ability to hear my words was to enter Twilight entirely on your own. You decided what you wanted and did it.'

Presette glared at the harp and chandelier, then at Jonathan. 'I was about to tell you everything, Mum, about the bird's visit, and there's not a scratch on your harp or the chandelier, I promise.' Presette was so utterly confused she didn't know what to say.

Mizmiq continued at a pace, 'We birds believe your magic signals the possibility of great spellcraft. There is a power in you, Jonathan, yes, you, even though you think of yourself as someone with a debilitating sickness.'

Jonathan opened his mouth, he had so many questions, but he stopped himself, noticing the hawk lower his eyes in sadness.

'The Numberalists will punish and confine you for this gift, but a graver danger exists.

'There is an evil at work in the world, you are not aware of it; invisible creatures we call Skulls who wish to harm humanity for reasons I am not at liberty to divulge.

'I worry that they will view you as a threat. Your magical skills might one day allow you to see them and stop them.

'They must not know of your power, Jonathan. Unless you learn to control your magic, they will find you. Training is imperative, not just for your own quality of life, but because your survival depends on it.'

Jonathan, Presette, Filia and Julius began scanning the music room in terror. 'Please, dear friends, you are not in immediate peril from these creatures,' the grandmaster reassured them. 'I believe one of my roles in these mysterious events was to find you, Jonathan, and to find you first.

'I can see and hear many forms of magic and I am able to identify extraordinary magical potential, and I see so much promise in you, Jonathan Powers.

'We must protect and nurture that promise. I will keep you safe. That is why I am here.'

'Then how do I learn to control my spells?' Jonathan choked.

'Alas, I do not have the ability to teach you as I said in my last visit, but there are others who can, and that is the good news I'm bringing with me this time,' smiled the grandmaster.

'Those who are able to develop your power are—how should I describe them— angels, yes, there is no other word so fitting. They are the priestesses of Eskatar and although their home is far from here, I will take you there and we will fly back to Centurian as soon as we can.'

'Fly?' gawped Jonathan.

'Did I say fly?' flustered Mizmiq.

'Yes,' exclaimed Presette, petrified.

'You definitely said fly,' added Filia, equally concerned.

Mizmiq swallowed. In his haste, he'd let slip the thing he'd planned to say last. He looked at them and smiled. 'There are secret corridors that can only be flown and I will cast a spell that allows me to carry you, Jonathan.

'The corridors are the quickest way to the land of Eskatar, and back. I expect us to be gone for a matter of weeks, maybe months at most. Please accept what I'm saying. You must come with me.'

Jonathan was distraught. He had expected the hawk to present a solution to his Destructive Interference on his return, not to ask him to fly to a place he'd never heard of. His mother, Filia and Julius were inconsolable.

'I will not leave my parents and friends. They come with me or I stay,' he demanded, fighting tears.

Mizmiq twitched frantically. 'Jonathan, I can only take you. There will be moments when I must conjure Openings and we will have to exist briefly in Twilight together. Please, the path to Eskatar must be travelled, and by us alone.'

'No,' Jonathan repeated. 'I will not go.'

'I beg you, Jonathan, please allow me to take you. The healers are coming,' warned Mizmiq.

They heard the robots pulling up outside the house. 'I can't go,' Jonathan cried. 'I cannot leave my parents and friends. Besides, what will the government do when my spell-casting footprint disappears? They'll order my mother to let them see me, and then what will happen? They'll interrogate her. There must be another way.'

Mizmiq suddenly turned his head almost a hundred and eighty degrees, the top window opened and he shot through.

Jonathan, Presette, Filia and Julius ignored the robots as they prodded the front door and wrapped their arms around each other. 'I will not let them in,' said Presette angrily.

Mizmiq circled the house, at a loss as to what to do. If he stopped the healers in an attempt to buy more time, an army of more aggressive robots would arrive in minutes. Should he take Jonathan against his will? How would Jonathan react? He might find a way to free himself once they were inside the bird corridors but that would put his life at risk—he might not survive in a bird corridor and he certainly wouldn't survive if he escaped into space.

'They're unlocking the door,' cried Julius. 'I'll—' But before he could finish, six healers marched into the music room carrying a stretcher.

'Get out,' shouted Presette, 'this is my home and you're not going to steal my son.'

They took no notice of her and grabbed Jonathan, forcing him down onto the stretcher.

'Get off,' he demanded, 'you have no right.'

Three of the healers held Presette, Filia and Julius while the others bound Jonathan. 'Untie me now,' he yelled.

'No, you must comply,' ordered one of the robots.

Jonathan was helpless; he couldn't even wipe the tears from his face. He moved his head just enough to catch his mother's eye. 'I love you, Mum, love you so much, Dad too, so proud of you both.'

'Jonathan, I love you more than you can know. I won't leave you there. Everything will be okay,' wept Presette.

Jonathan bent his head towards Filia and Julius as the robots tightened the clasps around his wrists and ankles.

'When I return, we will go straight to Rockmore. I love you, Filia, I love you so so much, I love you too, Julius,' he cried.

Filia tore at the healer restraining her. 'Noooo,' she screamed as they lifted the stretcher.

Jonathan tugged at the bindings and howled in agony; the more he fought, the more they zapped him with pain.

He resigned himself to doing what Mizmiq had asked, but as he conjured a message to the hawk, the healers stabbed him with a sedative.

The grandmaster saw them do it and sent a spell to bring him round but Jonathan did not respond.

The robots examined their instruments and when they were satisfied that Jonathan had been put to sleep, they prepared to set off.

Jonathan, however, was not asleep. While he was unable to see or hear anything, he was awake and fully aware of his situation. It was as if some magical force had placed a barrier between him and the rest of the world.

Jonathan told his hands and feet to try and slip free even though he couldn't feel them.

He sensed an Opening and willed the magic on. It engulfed him and a moving image began to form in his mind.

It was a bird. He recognised it, an osprey, a bird he loved. He'd watched them soar over the Meadowlands lakes in the Centurian countryside when he was a boy on family holidays.

A new memory consumed him, this time of a book about real and mythical birds of prey that he'd cherished when he was young.

The details in the photographs had captivated him and he'd adored the descriptions. Some of the words started coming back to him: 'osprey, ossifragus, the bone-breaker.'

Jonathan then saw himself, aged seven or eight, he wasn't sure exactly, turning the book's pages.

His tiny fingers settled on a picture, a photograph of an osprey grasping its catch and lifting it from the lake. The bird's magnificent pearl-white wings arched gracefully above the water and Jonathan's gaze was drawn to its talons.

He felt contact with the outside world once more; the stretcher, the fastenings. But he could now move his ankles. His feet had changed and the rest of his body was changing and freeing itself too.

'I–I'm the bird in my book,' he gasped, completely baffled by what his magic was doing.

He became more and more aware of his surroundings and felt the pinprick of the sedative again and realised that time had hardly passed.

Mizmiq, Presette, Filia and Julius watched dumbfounded as a great osprey rose from the stretcher. The robots lunged at the bird, but a circle of breeze opened inside the music room and the osprey disappeared.

Mizmiq swerved and darted in elation as the robots sped off in search of new instructions. Jonathan was free and he'd topped all his astonishing magical feats by becoming a bird, a spectacular osprey with dazzling silver plumes no less.

This was powerful mind magic at its brilliant best: creating whatever the imagination conceived.

Mizmiq had not even detected any echoes of the spell that he and the other grandmasters conjured when they took bird form. He was as gobsmacked as Presette, Filia and Julius.

The grandmaster cast a spell of finding as he twisted in celebration but there was no response. Mizmiq cast the spell again and again but couldn't locate the osprey and began to panic. Jonathan was not where he expected him to be.

Any bird leaving Centurian would open a lapisphere into a nearby estuary corridor, one of the narrow tubeways that led to the wider transcendent corridors between the stars and planets. There was no trace of Jonathan, anywhere.

Mizmiq sent Presette, Filia and Julius a message as he hurriedly conjured his own lapisphere and dived into the local Centurian estuaries. 'I will look after him, I promise,' he cried.

Presette, Filia and Julius heard him. They were speechless, terrified, wondering if they would ever see their dear Jonathan again.

15. Centurian

Communion with the Birds

'I must leave you and find Lucius,' sobbed Presette. Filia and Julius wiped their eyes and nodded.

Presette locked the front door and they walked up the road together. She then said goodbye and boarded a dronibus that would take her to the Space Academy in the centre of town.

Filia and Julius wandered aimlessly before stopping at a bench in Bushley Park. Two pigeons landed nearby but Filia and Julius took no notice of them. They were a common sight wherever people lingered.

The two pigeons were Albert and Lorna, the birds who had known Jonathan Prior and accompanied Rose and Charlie when they flew from Battersea Park to Centurian to discover whose consciousness Jonathan Prior's soul had joined.

After Charlie's death, Rose had suggested that they remain on Centurian rather than fly to Opus-Earth with her and the poor robin's body, explaining that she would be travelling extremely quickly and they wouldn't be able to keep up.

Albert had wanted to dive into the corridors anyway, confident he could remember the route home, but Lorna had persuaded him to explore Bushley Park instead and get to know the local woodland birds while Rose was away.

Albert and Lorna knew how fortunate they were to have stayed; word had reached Centurian of the Skull invasion of Opus-Earth and they awaited Rose's arrival with trepidation, afraid to learn the fate of their Battersea Park friends.

'Those two look as worried as us,' remarked Lorna. 'Aren't they the ones who are close to Jonathan Powers?'

'Right you are,' replied Albert. 'Maybe his sickness has taken a turn for the worse. I feel so sorry for him, holed up at home, but like everyone says, we mustn't worry because the powerful hawk will be back soon to help him.'

Albert and Lorna craned their necks, hoping to spot the magnificent hawk returning after his heroics on Opus-Earth.

'I actually spoke to him once, Lorna, a while ago, before you and I met. He was a special guest at a lecture on natural and unnatural breezes.'

'Good for you, dear, mixing with the stars. I always thought there was more to you than ambushing humans for grub and scavenging in the bushes,' chuckled Lorna.

Albert smiled at her fondly and for a moment lost his balance as he bobbed and bumped up against his wife.

Filia and Julius stared at each other, flabbergasted. They could hear Albert and Lorna's conversation.

Julius took a flattened sandwich out of his pocket, undid the transparent wrapping and let several large pieces drop to the ground.

'Look!' cried Albert, flying into action.

'Make sure you get the corner crust before the hungry one picks it up,' shouted Lorna.

Albert grabbed the chunk of bread and sprinted back to his wife.

'What a lovely wad of dough, Albert, you did so well,' Lorna declared as they gobbled it up.

'We're not supposed to hear other birds speaking, isn't that what the hawk said?' whispered Julius, putting his hand over his mouth and leaning close to Filia. She mumbled agreement.

They glanced about but found that they were only able to hear the two pigeons. 'Let's find out what's so special about our Albert and Lorna,' Filia smiled.

She looked at the pigeons. 'Don't be frightened, but can I ask, are your names Albert and Lorna?'

Albert and Lorna froze. How on earth did the girl know their names? They began waddling in circles in order to appear as unperturbed and pigeon-like as possible.

They were following bird protocol which required all species to behave in their usual manner when humans spoke to them. Any form of unnaturally close relationship might lead humans to suspect that birds were much more than they seemed.

'Don't worry, this is far stranger for us than it is for you,' smiled Filia. 'We're friendly locals, so don't be scared.'

Albert and Lorna gazed at the ground, then at each other in disbelief, then at Filia and Julius. They didn't dare say anything. They'd be breaking the rules of engagement simply by speaking.

'I wish I had some proper seeded loaf to offer you,' said Julius, holding out a sizeable chunk of his sandwich. He cut it in two. 'Here, half for you, half for me,' he grinned. Albert and Lorna didn't move.

'Ah, I'm sorry, so rude of me, there's two of you and one of me,' smiled Julius, trying to even out the portions, but the bread fell apart and crumbs scattered everywhere.

Albert and Lorna hesitated then helped themselves to the nearest pieces. 'Th...thank you,' said Albert, tentatively, deciding that if he was reprimanded for crossing the line, he'd plead necessity—the need to investigate how these humans were able to hear them. He whispered his plan to Lorna.

'It's p...perfectly served, thank you,' added Lorna.

Filia and Julius were delighted and Albert and Lorna gave them a faint smile before returning to their meal, heads down.

'I've created my own special sandwich,' announced Julius a few seconds later. Albert and Lorna looked up.

'I stuff the submarine with salami, scrape half the seeds off for you birds and the semi-smooth remains are called the Sheenside Salami Sandwich!'

'Only a few seeds for the birds?' scoffed Filia. 'What do you two think about that?'

There was silence as Albert and Lorna fretted once more about the rules. Lorna was the first to answer, putting her worry aside. They'd already gone too far she told herself, so they might as well get to know the two humans and see if they could indeed discover the mystery behind their magic.

'You wouldn't even part with the seeds, would you, dear?' Lorna chuckled, poking Albert in the flank.

Albert was caught off guard by his wife's directness. She winked at him and he relaxed. 'Alright, alright, generosity's not my strong suit,' he conceded, eyeing the delicious morsels.

Filia, Julius, Albert and Lorna began talking freely and quickly covered a wide range of topics, although some conversations flowed more than others.

Filia and Julius told Albert and Lorna about their meeting with the hawk and Jonathan's transformation. Albert and Lorna changed the subject whenever Filia and Julius probed on the secret bird corridors and the two pigeons looked genuinely bemused at the mention of a place called Eskatar.

There was no such awkwardness when it came to Jonathan's past. Albert and Lorna were eager to learn about his life and Filia and Julius were overjoyed to be asked so many questions about their incredible friend.

Recollections of Jonathan inevitably led Filia and Julius to share examples of his music. They sang the FJ song they'd composed at Rockmore and many of Jonathan's other favourites.

Filia and Julius were blown away by Albert and Lorna's singing prowess. The pigeons proudly declared that they were lauded as mastersingers by their own species, a baritone and soprano.

Filia and Julius were certain they heard notes outside their familiar audible range. Jonathan's spell appeared to have done more to their hearing than simply alter the norms of human and avian speech.

The two pigeons composed a new song in honour of Filia and Julius, "How lovely are thy crustings". They sang it, tweaked it, argued about it, then sang it again, each time with greater enthusiasm than before.

They explained how it took its form from a genre of music they themselves had invented, called an Allornia.

Filia and Julius had never heard a piece of music with so many trills. Lorna pointed out that trills were as common as crotchets in an Allornia.

Julius responded by revealing that he, Filia and Jonathan were also creators of a new genre of music, although the title was still work in progress—Space Fiction and Fogspawn being the two leading contenders.

Albert and Lorna loved both names and made them promise to write more music in the genre.

Filia told the two pigeons about the first song she'd sung with Jonathan on their way to school when they'd attended the same nursery classes,

'There are no wheels on the bus no more, this dronibus doesn't touch the floor. Levitation spells are better than before but we still get crushed in the passenger door.'

All four of them laughed and cried, delighting in the rhyme, but also mourning Jonathan's uncertain future.

Jonathan was, of course, in some sense Albert and Lorna's Jonathan too, in a way that Filia and Julius could never know, and the pigeons' tears were filled with memories of Jonathan Prior and the terrible tragedy of his death. They hoped the hawk would watch over Jonathan Powers so he could enjoy the full life that Jonathan Prior never had.

In between the tears, Albert and Lorna asked lots of questions about the nursery rhyme. They seemed disproportionately interested in dronibuses, and bits of old dronibuses such as landing gear.

Filia and Julius answered with as much detail as the pigeons wanted. They didn't think their obsession with dronibuses was odd at all. These were two Centurian pigeons enthralled by the ins and outs of human engineering.

The four friends finally parted. 'We will visit you in the park tomorrow,' smiled Filia.

'And I will spend the night assembling the largest Sheenside Salami Sandwich ever made,' added Julius.

'We will be waiting,' beamed Lorna. 'With extended stomachs,' declared Albert, sticking out his chest.

Filia and Julius ambled home, staring up at the stars and planets in Centurian's evening sky. They wondered which way was Eskatar and whether Jonathan was nearing his destination, hoping above all else that he was safe.

16. The World of Birds

Judgement

Jonathan fell through emptiness, unable to control his descent. He flapped wings that felt like arms and trampled darkness with talon-tipped stick legs.

The only sounds were those of his own panic; his rapid breathing and the thrashing of feet and feathers in the stillness of windless air.

As he pirouetted, his surroundings changed; he could make out stars in the distance, but they were blurred and impossible to identify.

He was also no longer alone. Other birds began to pass him, flying in all directions. Some glared disapprovingly, their faces faintly lit by faraway starlight while others nearly hit him, swerving violently at the last second.

Jonathan lost track of time and couldn't tell whether he was spinning down, up or along as one bird after another clipped his wings, doing their utmost to avoid him.

The rollercoaster finally came to an end when he was grabbed by a truly colossal bird.

He tried to swivel his neck to get a glimpse of his captor but couldn't; a pair of giant claws were arched over his shoulders either side of his head.

'Who in the world are you?' the bird demanded. 'Irresponsible acrobatics will cause a pile up in the busiest corridors. Most of us are in a hurry these days and lane inconsistency is unacceptable.'

'I, er, I'm from Centurian, Jonathan Powers, Bushley Park, sir.'

'Sir, hum, interesting choice of words. Don't you know who I am?'

'No, sir,' replied Jonathan, making another attempt to look at the bird but failing.

'I am Elgarian, the eagle. Very peculiar you are. Don't seem particularly birdy to me.'

'You're right, I'm not actually a bird, I'm a human,' answered Jonathan.

'Even more strange, never known a dead human to disguise himself as a living bird,' mused Elgarian.

'Dead? I'm not dead, or at least I don't think I am. I feel alive, although I've no idea where I am. I just fell through a hole in the air inside my house,' blurted Jonathan.

'Ah, more of a lost soul than a dead soul, he claims,' chuckled Elgarian.

'Please, Elgarian sir, I'm grateful to you for catching me, or capturing me, whichever it is, but where am I, please, sir?' begged Jonathan, terrified.

'Fascinating, you're getting less birdy with every question. You really have no clue where you are?' asked Elgarian.

Jonathan shook his osprey head as far as it would move in the eagle's vice-like grip.

'Don't worry, we'll get to the bottom of this soon,' mumbled Elgarian.

'No!' screamed Jonathan suddenly as they dived towards the tiniest of openings in what appeared to be an otherwise solid cliff face.

They emerged unscathed moments later above a vast expanse of water on the other side of the rock wall.

Jonathan stared ahead. There wasn't a single bird in sight. 'Nearly there,' Elgarian announced placidly.

'N…nearly where?' Jonathan spluttered.

'There, Savanna,' said Elgarian, propping his head up.

Jonathan gazed upwards and spotted a distant shoreline and far above it, to the right, a silver moon. 'Is that the Centurian moon?' he exclaimed, flogging the air excitedly.

'No, my funny friend, it is the Savanna moon. Now, look down, you'll see thousands of rafts crossing the lake. The moon reads the faces in the rafts and decides.'

'Decides what?' asked Jonathan.

'Who they should join, of course.'

'Wh–what…who?' babbled Jonathan.

'Unless you're a special case,' continued Elgarian. 'Then the agnostriches will want to have the final say. You are about to meet the agnostriches because you are without doubt a special case.'

'Agnostriches, I've never heard of an agnostrich,' said Jonathan.

'They are highly-revered and they oversee the lake,' explained Elgarian.

'Are they a type of ostrich? Flightless birds? Ratites?' asked Jonathan, picturing his bird books.

'Yes, and no,' replied Elgarian. 'Agnostriches are not flightless birds by birth. They experience the wonders of flight in their formative years before sacrificing this most precious gift when fully grown.

'Each raft has a keel that once lay below an agnostrich's breastbone. They willingly forfeit the part of the body that enables flight; the bone that allows wings to rise and fall with strength.

'It is an agnostrich's keel that guides a raft to the centre of the lake where the souls of humankind are lifted from their cradles by the moon.'

'Souls? Souls of humans? Humans have souls?' cried Jonathan.

'Yes,' smiled Elgarian. 'The souls of humankind fly onward while the rafts drift back to shore.

'Their keels rot over time and must be replaced by the bones of more birds. We have not found a way to fulfil our purpose without this sacrifice. Maybe it will always be so; perhaps it is right that a new beginning can only be given with great sacrifice.

'My advice to you, Jonathan Powers, is to be as respectful of their gift as I'm sure you will be of their power. They, alone, have the authority to prevent a dead soul from moving on to a new life.'

'There is life after death? There is another life?' Jonathan gasped.

'Of course, my friend, for humans at least. You really did miss out on school, didn't you, if indeed you are a bird, and if you're a dead human soul in disguise who's wandered into the bird corridors by mistake—the only other possibility—then best you enjoy the knowledge of eternity now. Once you reach the other side, you'll never remember this place, or this conversation.'

'What's on the other side?' gulped Jonathan.

Elgarian looked pensive. 'I think it best I don't say any more. You can find that out for yourself.'

They landed on the shoreline. The ground was mostly sand with the odd pebble or stick and it was warm and comfortable. Jonathan moved his new feet one at a time, trying to walk, but fell over.

He glanced up, hoping the eagle would help him, but his mysterious carrier had gone.

Jonathan itched his leg and found a tag. A large scruffy bird with an extremely long neck peered down and read the tag out loud to itself.

'I pulled this one out of a bird corridor, very strange, claims to be human and despite its appearance it might be true given he has no idea how to fly and no knowledge of many other things besides. Elgarian.'

The bird ushered Jonathan closer to the lake. Jonathan hesitated but the bird pushed him forwards and onto a raft.

Jonathan didn't get very far. The water started to ripple and the raft felt unsafe and he could hear tense conversations on the shoreline.

'Haul him out and have Thalamian check the raft,' cried one of the agnostriches.

Jonathan was brought back to shore and stood precariously on the soft ground in front of ten or so puzzled agnostriches.

'It's a human, otherwise the raft wouldn't have set off,' one of them suggested.

'Then it's alive, otherwise it would have progressed across the lake; we didn't ask it to come back and undergo onshore cross-examination,' added another.

'It can't be alive, Dusty, it's been inside the Centurian lumenest core, for Savanna's sake.'

'How do we know it entered the core? Read the tag, Struthion. It was found in a bird corridor.'

'Excuse me, if it's any use, I don't think I'm dead, although I can't be sure,' interrupted Jonathan. There was silence.

'It understands agnostrich, get the Chief Justice, now,' ordered one of the birds.

An especially shaggy, seen-it-all-before looking agnostrich joined them a few minutes later. 'All rise, Lord Agnostus presiding,' hailed another of the birds.

The agnostriches stood to attention, then sat down when the Chief Justice began his inquiry. 'What is your name?'

'Jonathan Powers, I'm a human from Centurian, I've no—'

'Okay, okay, I just asked your name for now. I must not to be influenced by your arguments. They might affect my judgement. Please be patient.'

Lord Agnostus stared straight into Jonathan's eyes. Jonathan felt an alien magical intensity examining every inch of his being. He sensed the other agnostriches inspecting him too.

'Doesn't seem like a bad egg in the slightest, no reason to deviate from a standard semi-contented consciousness,' remarked one of the agnostriches.

'But look how resilient he is. He could join hardship on the other side and make a difference,' objected another. 'Do you agree with that judgement, Dusty?'

'Yes. There's a wealth of creativity too. His mind is full of it, as plain as a moon without dead souls passing,' said the one named Dusty.

Lord Agnostus released his gaze and shuffled off, followed by the other agnostriches, leaving Jonathan to sweat and worry.

After quite some time, the Chief Justice returned and he sat with Jonathan a while.

'I have decided that someone needs to vouch for you, Jonathan Powers, if you are to be considered a bird.

'If nobody vouches for you, and there are strict criteria regarding who can vouch for you, then we shall revisit the human line of inquiry. Where that will end, I cannot say.

'Even if we find you to be a dead human, you will be a difficult case to judge. Your abilities suggest your soul would give great strength to someone struggling in a life of adversity.

'You would, of course, live that life as that person and there will be quite a number of agnostriches who will fight against such a judgement, deeming it unfair on you.

'We want the lives of all humans to improve, which means we do sometimes send people to lives they do not deserve. I cannot predict, in your case, where the competing arguments will lead us.

'We do not judge lightly and we always know whether the choice we made was right.

'The birds monitor the outcome, the new life, reporting events as they unfold so that future judgements can be perfected.'

'But I really don't think I'm dead,' insisted Jonathan.

'Dead or not, I believe you have an important life ahead of you, although I cannot foresee more than that,' sighed Lord Agnostus.

'Who then can vouch for me, as a bird?' wept Jonathan desperately.

'You must be recognised by a bird of your own species, and that bird needs to be someone who knows you. Only then may we be convinced.'

Jonathan dropped to the ground. 'I don't know any ospreys,' he cried.

'Elgarian, who brought you here, persuaded me to give him a little time to find one. He is quite some bird. You never know who might turn up,' smiled the Chief Justice.

'There's a hawk who knows me, is that close enough to my species?' begged Jonathan.

'No, I'm afraid not. The only creature that can vouch for you and accept you into their flock is another osprey,' said Lord Agnostus.

'What is the longest someone has waited here for judgement?' wept Jonathan.

'We've never taken more than a few years to decide,' answered the Chief Justice.

Jonathan was beside himself. 'Is there no way for me to go back?' he sobbed.

'No, Jonathan Powers, you cannot go back, forward, or anywhere else until judgement is complete. I'm sorry,' replied Lord Agnostus firmly.

Jonathan cried and cried. He wanted to hold Filia, his mother and father and Julius with his own human hands, and he certainly didn't care about Destructive Interference or threats to his life from invisible creatures.

'I do not want another life,' pleaded Jonathan, staring up at Lord Agnostus. 'Send me home. Please let me be myself again.'

Lord Agnostus lifted his wing, wanting to place it on Jonathan's shoulder, but it hardly moved. 'I and the other agnostriches will do all we can to help you, dear Jonathan,' he said, smiling but also wincing with pain.

Jonathan noticed and remembered what Elgarian had told him about the agnostriches' sacrifice. He tried to imagine what it would be like for a bird to forgo the freedom and pleasure of flight, but he could not fathom the cost of surrendering such a life—this was a bird who had no hope of ever being himself again.

'Thank you,' Jonathan choked, raising his osprey wing towards the frail, aging feathers that covered Agnostus' scars, 'Elgarian told me of your sacrifice.'

'He is a very good bird,' smiled Agnostus. 'An example to us all. Thank you, Jonathan. I'm glad I agreed to his request and I look forward to finding out who the lord of eagles brings to our shores to vouch for you.'

17. The World of Birds

A Voucher is a Ticket for Life

Mizmiq had not been able to locate Jonathan in any of Centurian's estuary corridors and rather than widening his search to the corridor network between the planets and stars, the grandmaster had decided to seek Rose's counsel.

Mizmiq messaged the robin as he approached Opus-Earth, fearing she would be disappointed at the news of Jonathan's disappearance.

The grandmaster received her reply well before he arrived and Rose wasn't disappointed at all.

She was as amazed as Mizmiq that Jonathan had turned himself into a bird but she was not in the least bit bothered about the task of finding him.

She was also relieved that Jonathan had managed to escape before the Numberalist government had taken him away.

'I was afraid you wouldn't have been able to coax him into leaving before it was too late, my friend. We will track him down, don't you worry,' said Rose's message. 'Hurry up and meet me at the great oak in Battersea Park.'

Mizmiq burst out of a lapisphere and made a sharp left turn, narrowly avoiding a collision with the southwest funnel of London's Battersea Power Station.

He dived down to the oak and found Rose pacing to and fro along one of the tree's solid upper limbs. 'Which bird did he become?' she asked right away.

'Guess,' winked the grandmaster.

'No, come on, tell me, how could I possibly know?' she complained impatiently.

'An osprey,' Mizmiq smiled.

Rose gasped. 'That is a good sign, a wonderful sign. A powerful bird, a good bird,' she declared.

Mizmiq began to recount the events that had led to Jonathan's transformation but stopped when he saw Rose was distracted.

The grandmaster looked in the same direction as the robin. She was watching a shadow on the London skyline that was moving purposefully and straight towards them.

'What is it?' Mizmiq cried. Rose did not seem concerned. Her expression was one of annoyance more than anything else.

'It is Elgarian. He's doing a poor job of concealing his true size,' she tutted. 'Thankfully, he remains reasonably well-hidden in the evening smog.'

Rose sent the lord of eagles a message, informing him that she at least could tell that he wasn't a natural accumulation of local weather and that he should adjust himself accordingly.

'I'm sorry, I didn't exit where I intended and thought I could get away with it for a short time,' he answered, almost out of breath. 'Thank you for spotting my error.'

The shadow vanished from the horizon and Elgarian arrived at the oak soon afterwards in the form of an Opus-Earth eagle.

'I bring news of a strange being called Jonathan Powers,' he announced, perching next to Mizmiq and Rose.

'He sits on the shores of Savanna without passage. He appears to be an osprey, although I have my doubts.

'I found him spiralling dangerously in one of the main thoroughfares. The agnostriches have decided that someone needs to vouch for him if they are to believe he is a bird.'

Rose and Mizmiq shrilled and beat their wings with joy. 'You two know him?' cried Elgarian, astonished.

'Yes. Thank you for plucking him out of the crowd and carrying him to safety,' laughed Mizmiq.

'Then I really have struck gold by choosing to come here,' grinned Elgarian.

'I will go and vouch for him, Rose,' smiled Mizmiq, all but taking off.

'Wait,' said Rose. 'He is an osprey. It is I who must vouch for him. The agnostriches will demand one of his own species, not merely someone who knows him.'

Mizmiq looked the little robin up and down, baffled, while Elgarian's grin broadened. 'I knew you would remember,' beamed the eagle. 'My concern was whether you'd think the magic could still work?'

Mizmiq's eyes lit up. 'The Gazong war,' he exclaimed, 'when the ancient atomhawks gifted the osprey's bone-breaking strength and form to you and a few other smaller birds to aid their fight against the Skulls?'

'Yes,' smiled Rose. 'I can recall the spell's notes perfectly, even though it was thousands of years ago and the atomhawks are no more. It was a miracle I will never forget.'

She bowed her head in thought. 'I have cast the spell on a number of occasions since, but with no effect. However, I've never spoken the notes on the shores of Savanna. I have never needed to.

'Given that eternity is the atomhawks' creation, perhaps the magic will find its voice beside the lake.'

Mizmiq nodded agreement. 'I do not see any alternative. There isn't a single osprey who knows him.'

'I will fly with you to Savanna, Elgarian,' declared Rose. She turned to Mizmiq. 'Grandmaster, we have a problem here that your wizardry is well-suited to solving.

'The Skulls are repairing their ships on the Epsilon 45.198 moon at the edge of Opus-Earth's solar system.

'Their fleet will be capable of matterline travel in a matter of days, perhaps hours.

'We need a powerful spell of entrapment to stop them escaping to Terminus while we muster a force large enough to attack them.'

Mizmiq thought about her request. He chuckled to himself. 'I know how we can keep them where they are.'

'We?' enquired Rose.

'Yes, we. Wizard-woven spells of caging work best with two or more grandmasters and I know just the man for the job,' he grinned.

18. Castle Spinneret

Grandmaster Sporadiq

It was mid-afternoon and Grandmaster Sporadiq was asleep in his study. His rooms lay high up in Spinneret's northern towers, the side of the castle where a lapisphere would open a gateway into the Alpha sector of the bird corridors.

Sporadiq spent most of his time either totally comatose or running around like a lunatic. Whatever his state, it was pretty much always a result of his obsession with concocting and testing new potions.

Unforeseen chemical reactions had produced some of his greatest discoveries; one of which was a sound frequency that enabled grandmasters to communicate with birds over long distances while still in human form.

That particular breakthrough had happened after Sporadiq had gulped down a knockout dose of deep-dreamer eight, a sweet-tasting syrupy fluid that helped the mind come up with answers to complex problems by putting the brain to work during sleep.

The sedative only wore off after the brain had spent at least eight uninterrupted hours subconsciously analysing the issue presented to it when the potion was consumed. It was monumentally powerful. You could end up dead to the world for days.

The grandmaster had dropped his ampulla of deep-dreamer eight as he passed out and the liquid had slopped over the edge of his bedside table and landed on his sound generator.

The generator was already wet with an experimental substance called audio-mould, a type of harmonic glue that was supposed to aid the discovery of euphonious tone clusters.

The combination of deep-dreamer eight and audio-mould caused the generator to emit a sound that was soothing to grandmasters in human form but loud and unbearable to birds.

Hundreds of birds stopped whatever they were doing in Castle Spinneret's normally peaceful gardens and gathered inside his bedroom.

They searched frantically for an off spell and screamed at the grandmaster, begging him to wake up and help.

More kept arriving, some having heard a faint yet irritating noise in bird corridors entire letter sectors away.

The infuriating sound was eventually silenced by a flock of exhausted and traumatised metalpeckers who erupted angrily from their lapispheres on the southern side of the castle. They had flown all the way across Omega from Psi.

The metalpeckers hammered the grandmaster's eyelids as gently as they could while making sure they were getting through to him.

Sporadiq woke, and even though he was in some pain, he was delighted that such a powerful sound had been discovered.

Mizmiq cast what the grandmasters called a beacon spell. The spell used the transcendent threads in the corridor walls to send a signal to Castle Spinneret.

Once it arrived the signal triggered an alarm in another grandmaster's study and a light in his observatory ceiling showing the wizard's location.

The beacon spell was a grandmaster's emergency calling card and the wizard receiving the signal would invariably drop everything they were doing and fly to the beacon's location.

Mizmiq hoped it would not be long before Sporadiq heard his request for help and fortunately for Mizmiq, his alarm sounded while Sporadiq was snoring face-down on his desk having swallowed a substance far milder than deep-dreamer eight.

Not only that, a second alarm happened to go off at the same time and Sporadiq was woken immediately.

The second alarm was the overflow foghorn of Sporadiq's version 10.2 liquidiflyer, a container for carrying liquids as air without compromising their original state.

He'd constructed the liquidiflyer so he could smuggle gallons of toxic potions through the bird corridors whilst avoiding the visibility and sharing rules.

Travellers were expected to offer up samples of whatever they ported. Sporadiq's intentions were not mean-spirited; he was genuinely worried about the toxicity and side-effects of his concoctions.

The grandmaster's deception was ultimately found out but the birds let him off with a warning, sympathising with his motives and admiring his invention.

Sporadiq rushed to his observatory and memorised the precise location of Mizmiq's beacon before casting the avian spell of flight.

He took the form of a long-eared owl and used his wings to ruffle up the annoyingly tidy matted tufts that poked above his head.

Satisfied that everything was to his liking, he scrawled an exceptionally messy lapisphere and dived into the Alpha 1 corridor.

Mizmiq sent him a message as soon as he picked up the long-range pings that signalled Sporadiq's entry into the Epsilon sector of the bird corridors.

'Thank you for coming so swiftly, my friend. We must trap the remnants of the Skull fleet that attacked Opus-Earth,' he messaged.

Sporadiq was completely taken aback. He'd slept through the entire battle.

The grandmaster eventually exited his lapisphere and cast the spell of breathing that enabled flight in airless space for a short period of time and it wasn't long before he found Mizmiq.

'A Skull fleet attacked Opus-Earth?' he cried when he saw the hawk.

'Yes, I should have guessed you were otherwise occupied,' chuckled Mizmiq. 'They delivered a near fatal blow.'

'A near fatal blow to an Earth planet? Are you employing a bit of warrior hyperbole, my friend?' exclaimed Sporadiq.

'No, if anything, it's a galactic understatement,' laughed Mizmiq.

'Then I am truly sorry, I feel awful not to have offered my services,' said Sporadiq.

'Don't let it worry you, my friend. The Skulls retreated before you were summoned,' answered Mizmiq. 'Now, I have much news to share,' he grinned, 'but first, we must hustle and stop the Skull ships from leaving the Epsilon 45.198 moon.'

'Hustle? Where did you learn that word, doesn't sound like grandmaster vocabulary at all,' smiled Sporadiq.

'Ha! Right you are. I heard the word on both Opus and Centurian. I'm trying to use more of the local lingo,' chortled Mizmiq.

The two grandmasters set off and when they arrived at their target they immediately began weaving a spell of entrapment.

Invisible threads spilled from the tips of their wings as they sped away from each other, creating a canopy that drifted silently towards their enemy.

Only when they lit the strings did Duggerrid see the danger and he wasted no time in ordering his battleships to find a way through.

The crews lining the platforms slashed at the meshing but they could not penetrate the weave.

The Skull lord was incensed. The ships' repairs were all but done and they'd been moments away from matterline travel.

Kazeg spoke to him, 'If we cannot get out, let us bore into the moon and use its broken structure to tear the enemy's cage.'

They loaded explosive diaminds into an empty ship and sent it plunging towards a deep crater while continuing to restore their other vessels so that they could be ready to accelerate to matterline velocity should any chance of escape present itself.

The Skulls detonated the diaminds inside the ship as soon as it struck the moon's surface and the devastation was far greater than even Kazeg had predicted.

They sent another ship down, then another, until the moon started to peel away from its centre and Mizmiq and Sporadiq were forced to watch in horror as spiralling landmasses severed their threads and disappeared into space.

The Skulls stared in awe at the power of their weaponry and the brilliance of General Kazeg's tactics and Duggerrid roared in triumph as he initiated the matterline sequence and fled with his remaining ships.

19. Terminus

The Shadow below the Throne

The Skull harbourmaster had his best troops lining the pier for the return of his overlord.

Duggerrid cursed the failure of his fleet in open warfare but as he stepped off the Marrowbone, he had already decided his next move.

The unexpected power of diaminds to tear open the Epsilon moon had given him an idea. A container filled with millions of these weapons might fracture Opus-Earth or Centurian and expose the eternal core.

The seas roared against the breaking wall. Terminus in Delta 13 was a storm planet constantly pounded by rain, thunder, lightning and ferocious winds.

Duggerrid gave orders for work on the container to begin and climbed to the upper platform of Pleonec Tower.

He raged against the cacophony and the skies seemed to respond by launching violence and fury back at him.

He cried out for more anger and the winds howled through the gaps between his joints, relieving the agony of his fleshless bones.

Duggerrid felt as though he controlled the world and its elements—that it was the power of his voice that was rousing the thunderous sky and directing its lightning to strike the planet so it could be drawn into the diamind factories below.

Content that his hatred had made its mark, the Skull lord clambered back down the precipitous steps that wound their way around the tower and pushed open a door at the base of the megalith. It slammed shut behind him, silencing the anger of the outside world.

The upper levels of the underground city were a sprawling mass of alleyways and caves, and every chamber was now a hive of activity dedicated to the creation of a bomb that could destroy a human planet.

Duggerrid marched for hours deep into the abyss, inspecting chamber after chamber.

The Skull arsenal of diaminds was well on its way to being replenished and work on the container was progressing in earnest, much to his delight.

Duggerrid stopped at the entrance to a narrow passageway and turned around to make sure no one could see him before stepping forward and disappearing into darkness.

After several hundred metres, he reached a wall and placed his skeletal hand on the wet rockface. A hidden door identified him and Duggerrid strode through.

On the other side was a small shuttle. He leapt onto it and sped down through an empty network of vaults and caves until he arrived at a vast cavern.

He jumped off the shuttle and hurried along a stone pathway that crossed the huge subterranean cavity. It ended at the wall of a circular cave that had no apparent opening.

Duggerrid pressed himself against the stone and walked through; the air inside the cave was still, rank and hot.

Duggerrid supplicated himself, stretching his hand upwards to where he knew the black ash-laden flames of his master were smouldering in the darkness.

A harrowing voice blasted the Skull lord. 'You failed. Now you are weak. You command a substantially depleted force and fewer souls than ever will be brought to Terminus to feed the demons. It will be an age before they have the strength to burn the world.'

'My lord, I have a new plan,' Duggerrid pleaded. 'One which will not take long to prepare. We have proven the ability of diaminds to break planetary structures.'

'I have seen the beginnings of your new scheme. It will not work on its own, but there is a way, yesss, deathssss,' hissed the voice. 'How long until the container is full?'

'Four nights,' answered Duggerrid.

'You have two, otherwise the opportunity is lossst and you will waste away on your throne, tortured by the stupidity of your reckless invasion,' warned the voice.

A glass phial fell to the floor. Duggerrid picked it up and placed it in one of his eye sockets. Its contents were clear.

'Centurian,' he grinned, removing the phial.

'Yesss, use the soulsss of the dead, the journey of the dead to the core, as well as the bomb,' howled the voice in the darkness.

20. The World of Birds

The Atomhawk's Spell

Rose and Elgarian entered the Epsilon Gamma superhighway, the widest Opus-Centurian bird corridor. It was mayhem.

Everyone from local corridor-dwelling birds to migrating survivors of the Opus war was struggling to make any sort of headway.

It wasn't just numbers holding everyone up; birds hovered and gabbled with strangers and friends, losing all sense of time and their surroundings as they recounted tales of gallantry and sacrifice.

'This place is a mess,' frowned Elgarian. 'I must leave you here, Rose, and embark on some serious traffic duty.'

'I will be glad of your help to speed me on my way,' smiled Rose.

The great eagle set about restoring order while Rose moved forward slowly, doing what she could to make her way through the chaos but coming to an awkward standstill on several occasions.

After a long period of little progress, she spotted a flock of fulmarine petrels doing a good job of ploughing through the traffic and tucked in behind them.

'Hello there, little robin, hard work, isn't it?' said the petrel bringing up the rear. 'We're trying to get to Savanna, you?'

'That is my destination too,' replied Rose. 'Mind if I tag along? I've rarely seen it this bad.'

'Are you sure you have the speed to navigate the Pelagic Gate? Have you completed the passage before?' asked the petrel.

'I have indeed,' said Rose. 'I've developed some unusual gliding skills for a robin and will be able to follow. Thank you for checking though, I'm Rose by the way.'

'Then it will be our pleasure, my name is Alesand. We can't wait to see the lake again, our home away from home.

'We've also heard there's a special case to be judged and I've brought my children all the way from the Atlantic shores of Opus to hear it. My youngest one, Naricorn, will in fact be visiting Savanna for the first time.'

Rose smiled, winking at the young petrel whose eyes were sparkling with excitement and anticipation. 'I'm sure this case will be one you'll remember forever, Naricorn.'

Rose noticed that Alesand's amber-webbed feet had been brutally torn and that threads of her tattered skin were flowing in the air.

'Your service in the Opus windshield will never be forgotten, Alesand. I hope the war didn't treat you too harshly,' sighed Rose.

'We are alive and Opus is free, for now. We were glad to serve our cause, despite the cost,' mourned Alesand. The fulmarines dropped their heads and Naricorn's eyes welled with tears as she spoke.

'You conceal great pain in your hearts, dear petrels,' said Rose.

Alesand wept. 'I lost two of my daughters. They were butchered inside the wave,' she replied bitterly.

Rose's stomach churned with grief. She thought of Jaden and Enchoir and as she drew alongside Alesand to comfort her she detected bloodspots behind her eyes. 'Your heart is not the only part of you that bleeds, you are fighting other wounds,' said Rose.

Alesand courageously dismissed her concern. 'I am doing well, thank you, Rose,' and turned to Naricorn, nervous for her child. 'We are close, little one. Remember, flat span. The passageway is narrow and you must pass through swiftly.'

They dived towards a tiny line of silver light in an otherwise dark rock wall. 'There, the moon is hard at work and the lake shines on the other side,' Alesand declared.

'Six across, one altitude,' ordered the petrel at the front. 'You will not be able to lift your wings.'

The petrels' hearts were racing. The Pelagic Gate was a shortcut to Savanna but it had to be navigated with precision.

Alesand spluttered as they entered the passageway. Rose and the fulmarines kept their eyes on her while pointing their heads towards the exit ahead of them.

Alesand slowed and Rose touched the edge of her wing to share her speed and Naricorn did the same on the other side.

A narrow shelf suddenly opened into the moonlit air above the Savanna Lake but when Rose and Naricorn flapped their wings Alesand began to fall.

Rose darted next to her, cradling the petrel in surprisingly powerful wings. 'I will carry her, we must get help quickly,' she warned. 'We fly straight to the Supreme Court beside the lake.'

*****

Eager watchers and commentators of many different species packed the galleries of the Supreme Court, a wooden rotunda not far from the Savanna shore.

Representatives from the twenty-four letter sectors of the birds' corridored world occupied two thousand assigned perches on the terraces. They were delighted not to be amongst the groundlings jostling for position in the pit below the stage.

In most Supreme Court cases, the agnostriches would decide and the audience would observe. Representatives could be consulted, but that was highly unusual and the agnostriches were always keen to avoid appointing a jury. The birds all agreed that how proceedings were run should be up to the Chief Justice and the other judges.

As Rose descended through the open thatched roof, she spoke the notes of the spell that one of the atomhawks had sung thousands of years ago to bless her with osprey form and strength.

To Rose and everyone else's astonishment, her shape changed and the tiny robin became a mighty osprey many times the size of the ospreys in the audience and of Jonathan who was being ushered out onto the stage.

The spell had worked, exactly as it had done during the Gazong war when the birds had fought the Skulls and their creators, the Arc of Darkness.

Everyone gasped as word went around that someone capable of atomhawk spellcraft had arrived to vouch for the osprey and the groundling crowd moved away as Rose landed in the pit between the galleries and the stage.

Rose lay Alesand on the warm dust and wasted no time announcing herself to the agnostriches who were watching from a balcony behind the stage.

'I am here to vouch for Jonathan Powers,' she declared.

Jonathan was overwhelmed. He stood, legs shaking, between the two great pillars that supported the roof above the stage and gawped in wonder at the splendour and authority of this incredible bird.

Lord Agnostus lifted his long neck over the balcony and gazed deep into Rose's gleaming golden eyes.

'We welcome a dear friend and a soldier of the Gazong war. Rose, the floor and the court are yours,' he smiled.

'Thank you, Lord Agnostus,' replied Rose, bowing before the Chief Justice.

While Rose recited the history of her own transformation and established her credentials as a true osprey, Jonathan was drawn to the wounded petrel.

He found himself looking beyond the bleeding cuts between her feathers and examining the full horror of her wounds.

All his concentration focused on healing the dying bird and he was no longer aware of Rose's words as he began to mend every damaged sinew in her broken body.

Alesand's strength returned and she flew up onto the stage, nestling beside Jonathan. 'Thank you,' she whispered.

Rose stopped, amazed, then spread her wings, smiling. 'There, my lord, is the evidence,' she proclaimed, 'the evidence that he belongs, like me, to a magical strain of the osprey family.

'Only an avian creature of magical descent, or great magical ability, could heal the wounds of a dying bird. I ask the court to allow him to fly free under my guidance.'

The Chief Justice silenced the crowd who had started to cheer and flap their wings so hard they were leaving their perches.

'Be still. I have come to a decision,' he cried. 'My understanding, of which I invite disproof, is this. Jonathan Powers is an osprey born of magic rather than bloodline, and as such and not least because there is precedent before our very eyes in the form of Rose, he should, in my judgement, be recognised as an osprey.'

There was no challenge. The other agnostriches nodded their heads in agreement while cheering and chirping erupted again in the audience.

21. The World of Birds

Becoming a Bird

After the galleries had emptied, Agnostus made his way down to the stage and sat next to Jonathan. Rose, Alesand and the other petrels waited patiently to one side.

'Jonathan, you are blessed with something called Candela Lumen power,' said the Chief Justice. 'It is a rare gift found to a small extent in hundreds, maybe thousands of birds at most, and to a greater degree in less than fifty who we call luminaries. You also have a generous healing heart.'

Lord Agnostus closed his eyes, deep in thought.

'When we talked earlier, I think I was right, Jonathan. You have a very important life ahead of you. Be strong, never give up, much depends on you, although exactly what I cannot tell.'

'Thank you, Lord Agnostus,' Jonathan replied. 'You have been kind to me from the moment I arrived. I am grateful.'

Jonathan hesitated before continuing, 'I wonder, my lord, now that my case is settled, may I know what's on the other side of the lake? Where I would perhaps have gone if the osprey had not vouched for me. I realise there is some form of eternity for human souls, but exactly what, I do not know; none of the agnostriches have wanted to tell me.'

Lord Agnostus contemplated his request, but not for long. He had to tell Jonathan the truth.

His own judgement was that Jonathan should be treated as a bird and all birds knew that the souls of the dead travelled to a second human planet after death.

Jonathan would also discover the answer to his question soon enough through conversation in the bird corridors.

The Chief Justice smiled at the young osprey. 'What lies beyond the lake is another human planet, Opus. It is Centurian's sibling planet.

'When the people of Centurian and Opus die, their souls make their way here, to Savanna. And after they pass the Savanna moon, they join the consciousness of humans on the other planet.

'Centurians experience an Opus life after death and the people of Opus begin new lives as Centurians, and all memory of past existence is lost in the moonlight.

'Humans never host more than one foreign soul. Some do not have a soul join them until far into later life, and others, not at all.

'You must never speak of this to humans, whether you become human again or not. It is our most precious magic and our greatest secret.'

Jonathan shot across to an open window, landing haphazardly. He stared at the shoreline, overcome by what he saw, what he now understood.

Grey human shapes were pouring onto the sand from two separate places roughly a mile apart. They were emerging as if out of thin air, jumping down onto the shoreline from invisible openings only a few metres above the ground and the agnostriches were guiding them towards the lake where they were boarding rafts.

'What you see are the exit openings of the eternal corridors,' explained Agnostus. 'One corridor runs all the way from Opus, the other from Centurian. There are no birds in those transcendent passageways, only human souls.'

Jonathan watched a line of rafts set off across the water. He followed them until they disappeared in the Savanna moonlight.

'There is no shore on the other side of the lake,' continued Agnostus. 'Only the pathways that complete a soul's onward journey to a new life. Quite a revelation, isn't it?' he beamed.

Jonathan simply nodded and wept, mesmerised by the magic of eternity, the revelation that Centurians were not alone in the universe and most of all, by the thought that one day he would wake up as another person on another world.

'Goodbye, for now, Jonathan Powers,' smiled the Chief Justice, shuffling off towards his balcony.

'Wait, please,' gulped Jonathan. 'Did someone join me? Do you know who that was?'

Lord Agnostus turned and sighed, 'That is a question only a human would ask, Jonathan. I will not answer it. I stand by my judgement, you are to be treated as an osprey, and I ask that you consider the implications of my decision carefully; what it means for us as well as for you. You have bird form yet you retain human memories and, dare I say it, consciousness.'

Jonathan nodded slowly. He understood, at least he thought he did. His mind was spinning.

Jonathan flew back to the stage and looked up at the great osprey that had vouched for him. The bird towered above his head, each one of its magnificent ivory feathers the size of a single bird's wing.

'How did I heal the dying petrel? I don't even remember casting a spell,' said Jonathan, gazing at Alesand and Naricorn who was clinging to his mother.

Rose grinned. 'I think you know the answer to your question; you've met a very dear friend of mine, a hawk who showed you that your mind is capable of reacting to things that are not as they should be.'

'Ah yes,' exclaimed Jonathan. 'It was my fear. I was afraid the petrel would die unless I did something, and I created an Opening into Twilight?'

'Correct, and as Lord Agnostus just pointed out, the ability to draw on Candela Lumen power is a rare gift indeed,' smiled Rose.

'Will I see Mizmiq the hawk, soon?' asked Jonathan.

'He is otherwise occupied for now, but yes you will. He and I are—how should I say it—thick as thieves,' she chuckled. 'You will be seeing quite a lot of both of us.'

Jonathan was delighted. He hoped the hawk might bring news of his parents, Filia and Julius when he appeared.

'I cannot thank you enough for vouching for me,' he said. 'I didn't want to cross the lake, even if there is another life waiting for me.'

'I am relieved too,' said Rose. 'We must explore your magical potential, develop it and embrace your journey wherever it takes us, and to do that, we need you very much alive and as you are,' she smiled.

Jonathan watched, astonished, as Rose changed back into her robin form. She looked up at him, her eyes glistening. 'We meet properly at last,' she grinned. 'My name is Rose, Jonathan, and I am first and foremost a red-chested robin,' she declared proudly.

Jonathan stared at her tiny orange-red feathers and black saucer pupils. There was something familiar about her. He thought of all the robins that he could remember; he pictured Charlie. 'Have we met before?' he asked, tentatively.

Rose bowed her head in sadness. 'I was with Charlie when she first spoke to you in Bushley Park. She was a dear friend.'

'How did she die?' Jonathan groaned.

Rose was about to answer when she saw Lord Agnostus peering over his balcony, beckoning her to come and join him.

'We will talk more of Charlie, and the cruelty of her death, after we leave,' Rose replied. 'Speaking of which, you have wings but you need to learn how to use them. Alesand, would you mind teaching Jonathan the basics and a trick or two while I talk with the Chief Justice?' said Rose.

Alesand was overjoyed and Jonathan and the fulmarines set off while Rose flew up to the Chief Justice's private room.

'There is something I need you to investigate, please, Rose,' began Agnostus.

'A raft that has been missing for days has turned up at the Opus souls' embarkation point.

'It was empty and should therefore have landed on the part of the shoreline where all rafts go for their usual checks before reuse.

'It will not be sent across the lake again. There might be something wrong with it. However, there is another possibility. Its strange behaviour may have something to do with the soul it carried.

'That soul was Jonathan Prior, Rose, the Opus boy you asked about when you visited recently and who, as you know, joined the consciousness of Jonathan Powers.'

Rose gasped and bobbed about in circles on the dusty wooden floor. 'Jonathan Powers is a magical phenomenon that I do not fully understand and Jonathan Prior had an exceptional mastery of sound that might have led to spell casting and magic. We will never know. I have no idea how to explain this,' she said.

'Nor do I,' sighed Agnostus.

'You don't think it indicates that Jonathan Prior might still be alive?' asked Rose. 'You said his raft is at the Opus souls' embarkation point.'

'Jonathan Prior cannot be alive,' replied Agnostus. 'His soul moved across the lake. Nevertheless, I would still like to conduct a thorough examination of his body. That is my request, Rose. Go to Opus, please, as quickly as you can, and let me know what you find.'

Alesand, Jonathan and the fulmarines landed back inside the Supreme Court.

'He is ready,' announced Alesand. 'And we've also taught him a few of our favourite high-speed gliding songs. He has a fabulous voice.'

'Excellent, we make for the Pelagic Gate,' said Rose, fluttering down from the balcony.

'I will lead the way,' insisted Alesand.

Jonathan didn't take his eyes off the water as they skimmed the surface of the moonlit lake. He was consumed with thoughts of home despite his freedom and the exhilaration of safe flight.

'Jonathan, you are staring without seeing, what are you thinking?' asked Alesand.

Tears filled his osprey eyes. 'I am glad to be free, but I'm not going home,' he replied.

Jonathan had told Alesand about his parents, Filia and Julius, but hadn't yet mentioned Eskatar, Destructive Interference and his quest to control his magic.

'I will make sure he gets home,' smiled Rose. 'We must first understand his extraordinary magical abilities.'

Alesand touched Jonathan's feathers and remained close to him as they flew. She glanced at Naricorn. They had suffered, but their path home was clear.

After a while, they saw the Pelagic Gate and Alesand spoke to Jonathan, 'We are going to stay and enjoy the lake,' she sighed. 'It is time to say goodbye. We are forever indebted to you.'

Jonathan looked at her, startled. She'd caught him off guard. He hadn't thought about saying goodbye.

'And I, you,' he choked, realising he would probably never see these birds again—birds who had become firm friends.

'Thank you for teaching me how to fly, Alesand, and you too, Naricorn. Goodbye, for now. I hope, very much, that we will see each other again,' he wept.

The petrels waved and disappeared in the undulations of the lake as he and Rose soared upwards.

Jonathan broke down and sobbed. 'I'm grateful for everything you're doing, Rose, but I'm frightened—terrified that I won't be able to retake human form,' he cried. 'Please, Rose, will I return home soon and be myself again?'

'I believe you will go back, Jonathan, and as the young man Jonathan Powers, but how and when I cannot see.

'The quicker we reach Eskatar, the quicker I think we will know. I would beg you therefore to see this journey as the best possible path home,' answered Rose.

Jonathan was silent, struggling to accept her words.

'Look, the Pelagic Gate is close, and that is where hope begins,' smiled Rose.

They glided through the narrow gap in the rock wall and into the Epsilon Gamma superhighway on the other side.

Elgarian had brought a degree of order to the corridor but it was still crowded and bustling with chattering birds. Rose led Jonathan through the traffic.

After what seemed a long period of flight, Rose stopped and hovered outside a fork in the corridor.

'Jonathan, you are flying superbly, I must say,' said Rose. 'Now, listen up. Many birds actually live inside the corridors, in bird planets, vast spheres that also serve as major junctions between the different sectors of our secret world.'

'Bird planets?' gawped Jonathan.

'Yes, just birds. No humans or other living creatures,' smiled Rose. 'Now, I have something I must attend to urgently and you will be making a short flight on your own to the gamma/delta bird planet.

'It is full of song and friendship and directly that way. The passage is safe. There are only birds in these corridors, as I said, and I will meet you there.'

'I'd rather we stuck together, can I not come with you?' gulped Jonathan.

Rose smiled. She thought about where she was going. She thought about Jonathan Prior and how he would have loved to have flown as a bird, and here she was, looking at the consciousness he'd joined, a boy who had become a magnificent osprey.

'I'm afraid not, Jonathan. You will be perfectly fine flying on your own. Go now, that way, please, the gamma/delta bird planet is not far,' she persisted.

Jonathan eventually gave up arguing and drifted into the corridor.

Rose waited and made sure Jonathan could see her whenever he looked back, but as soon as he was out of sight, Rose shot off, relieved that he'd begun the next part of his journey to Eskatar but at the same time deeply troubled by the mystery of Jonathan Prior's raft.

22. Opus-Earth

The Guilty That Justice Won't Sentence

Stephen and Florence had spent a short time at home following the near catastrophic storms that had hammered every part of Earth.

They were now back at the hospital but it wasn't Jonathan that had made them return, it was Florence's deteriorating health.

Guilt over her failure to stop Jonathan crossing the road when she knew his eyes were not right had crushed her and she was refusing to eat or drink.

Stephen tried to hold her hand as she lay in a bed beside Jonathan but she turned away and he fidgeted uncomfortably.

He glared at the television hanging on the wall. The only topic of discussion, as usual, was the Sky War, as it had become known. Stephen wanted to scream. The nonstop talk of birds had begun to prey on his conscience, reminding him of how callous and stupid he'd been to belittle Jonathan's passion and chastise him for pursuing it.

For Florence, every image or description of bird-heroics was another nail in her coffin. She hated herself for not standing up to Stephen and for ignoring Jonathan's love of these amazing creatures.

Rose landed on the windowsill. She was shocked by Florence's pale and weakening state and listened to her with grave concern.

'I want to die so that I can be with my son and beg his forgiveness,' Florence muttered to the doctor, who said nothing.

Stephen got up and paced the floor. 'It wasn't your fault, Florence. You were told he wasn't in any immediate danger.'

'You just want it all to go away, don't you?' Florence cried, knowing his platitudes were laced with rage.

'I'm not dismissing it, for goodness' sake,' he yelled, angry that she'd allowed her grief to take her to the point of self-destruction.

Florence wept and Stephen marched between the two beds, trying to stop himself from launching into her. He hated himself for thinking Florence's suicidal actions were selfish and clenched his fists, desperate to contain his disgusting abhorrent thoughts.

Florence sobbed and sobbed, hating him. She wiped her bloodshot eyes and looked at the doctor. 'I'm guilty, guilty of murder, but I'm a murderer justice refuses to sentence, and my sentence should be death.

'I knew there was something seriously wrong with his eyesight and I let him cross the road. My only excuse is my husband's cruelty and for that, there is no evidence other than my own.

'But my excuse should not forgive my actions; those alone mean I am guilty. I deserve to die.'

Florence pointed at Stephen. 'Look at him,' she wept. The doctor pretended to stare at her notes. 'He knows the truth but has no remorse. I beg him to understand why I was late to meet my son—fear of him—and I cry for the heartless man to admit it, to help me die a less tortured mother, but he doesn't pity me one bit, he blames me, he hates me.'

Stephen couldn't bear it. 'Florence, enough. You condemn yourself unfairly, you–y–you're wrongly convicting yourself of murder, dammit,' he barked.

'You are a sick man, Stephen Prior. You know the truth. If you had one ounce of human feeling in your cruel body, you would acknowledge your part in Jonathan's death and you wouldn't be angry with me for wanting to die,' Florence yelled. 'Go back to your miserable existence. I will deal with mine. Get out.'

'I'm sorry, Doctor, I don't know what to say, I–I...' Stephen stammered.

'You don't get it,' Florence wailed. 'Jonathan's death was easily preventable and you make me carry all the guilt, all the pain.'

Stephen grabbed hold of Florence, pleading with her. 'Get out,' she shouted.

Stephen looked around, worried that people would notice their screaming. He caught a glimpse of Jonathan, who was completely still, oblivious to the fighting and suffering he'd left behind.

Stephen slammed the door and strode out of the hospital, raging at the now quiet winter sky.

Rose wept, wishing she could tell Stephen and Florence the truth of human eternity or a version of it that might still hide the truth but give them comfort—that Jonathan was a ghost born into another dimension of existence.

And how she wished they could meet Jonathan Powers, the magnificent osprey, the consciousness that their boy had joined.

Rose conjured an Opening. She wove a single silver thread of healing. It was pure and bright, infused with Candela Lumen power and identical to the strands in the lumenest cores of Opus-Earth and Centurian that she herself had woven with other luminaries to give humankind eternal life.

She drew it out of the Twilight realm. It was invisible to anyone in the living world, including her, but she could still sense it and control it.

Rose placed the thread inside Florence's failing body. Florence felt its warmth as it curled and came to rest.

Rose wept again. She knew her gift of healing and life would last for perhaps days at most. She could not stay and maintain the Opening that gave her thread its Candela Lumen power. It was not like the lumenest threads that were so numerous and thickly bound that they were able to draw life-giving energy from Twilight on their own.

Rose hoped her thread would be enough to help Florence find a path back to strength. She also vowed to look for an opportunity to return and help her again.

She stared at Jonathan and cast a spell of understanding. There was no life other than the artificial animation of machines. The raft's strange behaviour was not the result of some lingering living strand hiding inside his body. The workings of eternity had judged his state correctly.

Rose flew off and looked for a concealed location to open a lapisphere. There were plenty of good spots deep inside the many shrubs and bushes that lay near the car parks and the one-way lanes that circled the perimeter of the hospital.

Rose disappeared into a thicket in a corner of the main car park, opened her lapisphere and began her journey back to Savanna where she would tell Lord Agnostus what she'd found before joining Jonathan at the gamma/delta bird planet.

23. The World of Birds

Warbler Finch, the Warbler Finch

Jonathan arched his wings for maximum control and mumbled his destination to calm his nerves: 'gamma/delta bird planet, gamma/delta bird planet.'

He ignored the passing traffic and focused on flying in a straight line, keeping to one side of the corridor.

'The faster I fly, the faster I get home,' he told himself, increasing his speed as his confidence grew.

Most of the stars beyond the transparent corridor walls were distant smudged dots. Occasionally, a closer star or other object would suddenly appear next to him like a huge swooshing brush stroke, causing him to swerve across the corridor into the flight paths of other birds.

After concentrating intensely for over an hour, Jonathan was exhausted and hovered to catch his breath. As long as he hardly moved, the vista of stars was clear and stunning.

Jonathan spied a constellation shape that resembled one of his and Filia's magic-music compositions and imagined himself telling her about it, at Rockmore, using stars and planets he knew to draw it in the planetarium ceiling.

Jonathan wept at the thought of such a perfect moment. It seemed far more like a dream than a possibility, and as his tears flooded the bright yellow disks that were now his eyes he instinctively raised a wing to wipe them as if it was still his arm.

He immediately let the wing fall and flap to keep himself suspended in mid-air. The corridor was shaped like a vertical oval and he was afraid he might not be able to take off again if he slid down the tubeway wall to what looked like a narrow channel at the bottom.

Jonathan took one final look at the group of stars before setting off, telling himself he would find a way to hold Filia again with human hands.

Jonathan whispered Rose's words as he flew: 'the quicker you get to Eskatar, the quicker you go home.' He sped on for several hours; his most sustained period of high-speed flight yet, but then he started to worry—had he flown too far?

He slowed down to ask for advice but none of the birds took any notice of him and he had no idea how to grab their attention.

Jonathan accelerated again and became distracted by a roar some distance behind him. He flew faster but the unsettling sound grew louder until it was right on his tail.

'Get out of the way. You're in the route master's lane,' yelled a dismayed, infuriated voice.

Before he could react, a line of birds in a wind-blown trance knocked him aside. They were swallowed up by the darkness ahead.

Jonathan quickened his pace and heard the same roaring turbulence in front of him and when he caught sight of the snake-like procession of birds he decided to follow, hoping they would eventually stop so he could ask where he was.

As both they and Jonathan swooped into a right-angled bend, a warning message erupted, 'Reduce speed, you are entering a planetary cruising zone.'

Jonathan slowed down straightaway but kept close to the now-twittering train of birds.

The corridor burst open, revealing a vast cavernous space and movement instantly felt like slow motion as the sheer scale of where he was became clear. 'W–wow, unbelievable,' Jonathan gasped, gazing across what looked like a giant bubble full of tens of thousands of birds.

'Gate twelve closing,' boomed a voice. 'Last remaining long-haul travellers to chi/psi, please board now.'

Jonathan hugged the tail of the bird-train while his eyes boggled at the distant glasslike horizon and the stars beyond.

The birds came to a standstill below a sign that read, *disembarkation point, gamma/delta nesting station, route-master express reserved.*

One of the birds glanced at Jonathan. 'Hey buddy, I'm Warbler Finch, a warbler finch, navigator and old-time corridor cruiser. Good to meet you.' Jonathan appeared puzzled.

'I know what you're thinking,' said the sleek but solid little bird, thrusting his chest-feathers out with pride. 'Not many earn the right to use the species name, but I'm one of 'em. We're hard-working birds and I'm a master-grafter.'

Jonathan smiled. 'I love warbler finches, Warbler, and I'm so pleased to meet a famous one. My name's Jonathan.'

'Your first trip down the gamma/delta black run?' said Warbler. 'It's quite a ride, eh? Be careful not to stray into the wrong lane next time. We almost took some of your feathers with us when we shot past,' he laughed.

'I, er, I will. I will be more careful next time. I'm not very experienced. I was lucky to get away with it, I guess,' Jonathan replied, his white cheeks turning a soft shade of pink.

'Don't be embarrassed,' smiled Warbler. 'Like I said, it's a black run; narrower than other corridors and tricky to stay in your lane. Even the first-time falcons veer off-course. They're too slick for their own good, if you ask me, not proper grafters like us finches,' said Warbler dismissively. 'You a one-world new-tuber then?'

Jonathan stared blankly at Warbler, deciphering his question. 'Yes, I suppose so. I'm from Centurian and I'm new to the corridors. In fact, this is my first bird planet.'

'Then you're in for a treat, welcome to the most magical part of the world of birds,' grinned Warbler.

'Huge air bubbles like this one lie at transfer points where the letter parts of our universe meet and change. In this case, gamma becomes delta and vice versa,' he explained.

'We call them bird planets because they're mega-spheres where no one can survive without wings. They're made of the same transcendent skin as the corridors and are just as invisible.' Warbler hesitated.

'Actually, that's not entirely true,' he smiled. 'These planets are big enough for humans to spot, unlike the corridors. They'd probably describe them as tiny cosmic voids; miniscule cousins of the supers, if they ever laid eyes on them.'

Jonathan's beak widened as he listened and recalled his Tempo Chorium astrophysics class on supervoids.

'But even if they did locate one of our planets,' continued Warbler, 'they wouldn't have a clue what they were looking at, of course. Hilarious, isn't it? We, the birds, watch over them while they stare into space and can't see us,' he laughed.

'Wh, what about an orbit? Does this planet orbit a sun?' asked Jonathan, scanning the stars that seemed closest to the bubble.

'No, bird planets are free-floating,' replied Warbler. 'They have no orbit and no relationship with any star, and what's more, their position in space is almost static,' he declared proudly.

'Look; down there, you see those burds? We call them burds, b-u-r-d-s. They're birds of burden; duckbill planetipushers.

'They work in shifts, hundreds at a time, keeping the thing suspended. Unlike the corridors, the bubbles need a bit of outside support.'

Jonathan became dizzy as he hovered, gawping in amazement at the grinding circle of work below.

'Now, look up,' enthused Warbler. 'You see that juicy great piece of turf hanging by a thread in the middle of the planet like an upside down mountain? That's the kernel. The largest bird feeders you'll ever see are found in these air planets. It's why we also call them nesting stations.'

Warbler delighted in Jonathan's discovery, pausing while the osprey's eyes followed the glistening streams of water plunging down the kernel's edges.

'I just never...knew, I mean...imagined...' mouthed Jonathan, gobsmacked.

'Follow me,' said Warbler, shooting off. Jonathan didn't let the warbler finch fly more than a few metres ahead of him.

Warbler led Jonathan to the far side of the kernel where a stage and hundreds of rows of semicircular terraced perches had been dug into the turf.

Two identical robin twins stood bowing to an adoring crowd. 'They're Bob and Nod, a comedy duo renowned for species satire,' chuckled Warbler. 'We're just in time for the encore.'

The two robins acted out a parody of the kingfisher, a species that was apparently supremely capable of finding things out, then editing and publishing the best bits for their own purposes. Warbler explained that they were the epitome of what some birds called information manipulation, others, storytelling.

In the sketch, Bloggin the kingfisher talked of his pride in portraying sifted truisms to the world but he was unaware that his own secrets were being exposed innocently by one of his children who thought he was doing his father a favour by raving about his sophisticated operation to a teacher.

'He can predict what will be on the news tomorrow, Miss!' exclaimed Bob who was playing the part of the youngling. Even the kingfishers couldn't help but laugh.

'They're fabulous, Warbler,' cried Jonathan.

'I thought you'd like them. Now let's find a place to eat and then somewhere to nestle down,' yawned Warbler.

They joined a group of birds helping themselves to the local feed. The light in the glasslike sphere began to dim and the chatter and birdsong that had filled the bubble faded to nothing more than whispers.

Jonathan kept his eyes on the horizon and noticed more stars sparkling in the cosmos, and he marvelled at the magic that was giving the bird planet its semblance of night and day.

'Get some sleep, laddie,' said Warbler as the bird bubble fell silent and the darkness of space glittered with brilliant twinkling gems. A few seconds later, the osprey's eyes had closed.

24. The World of Birds

Bridging the Chasm

When Jonathan woke, he glanced about hoping to see Rose. There was no sign of her.

'Where are you off to next?' asked Warbler, pecking a collection of tiny breakfast seeds.

'I'm waiting for a friend, then we're heading to a place called Eskatar. Do you know it?' said Jonathan.

'Know it? You bet.'

'How far is Eskatar? You sound like you've been there many times,' beamed Jonathan.

Warbler looked worried. 'It's not about how far it is, it's not possible to get there.'

'That can't be true,' protested Jonathan. 'I'm supposed to go there, on good authority from two friends, a hawk and a robin.'

'Well, making it possible to fly to Eskatar is why I'm here. At least we're on the same side, boyo, even though we're clearly from different planets,' he chuckled.

'Same side? What do you mean?' demanded Jonathan, exasperated.

'Same side because I'm one of the few birds who's courageous enough to try and cross the chasm,' answered Warbler.

Jonathan stared at the ground. He wasn't reassured at all.

'Here's the thing, Jonathan,' sighed Warbler. 'No way anyone's reaching Eskatar without crossing the Tau 6/7 chasm. It's the only way to get there. That's the bad news.

'The good news is that there's a debate starting shortly and I'm going to persuade this lot to send an expedition to bridge the gap. I've got an idea for how we do it that no one's ever thought of before.'

Jonathan was beside himself. 'Warbler, I don't understand a word of what you're saying. I was told I'd be travelling to Eskatar and that was that,' he cried desperately.

They were interrupted by the booming voice, 'Gather for the debate, we're starting on time.'

'That's the gamma/delta stationmaster, Scipio,' said Warbler; 'Elderly jacana, used to be up for an adventure. Now he's a tentative fella. Come on, we need to cajole him into rousing the troops. We'll talk more about Eskatar afterwards.'

The stationmaster stood on a rocky outcrop protruding from the kernel and set out his position.

'We cannot afford to lose more birds. The chasm is constantly watched and guarded by Skulls,' he declared.

'Repairing the air gap between Tau 6 and Tau 7 requires a spell of transition to be cast simultaneously from both sides and all those who've tried to fly to Tau 7 so we can attempt such magic have met their doom well before they've got there.'

Jonathan sat distraught as bird after bird got up to argue against trying to cross this seemingly impassable chasm.

Eventually, it was Warbler's turn. 'Finches are crackpots and this guy's an exemplum of his species,' chortled a goose sitting next to Jonathan. 'Get ready for the most ridiculous idea you've ever heard.' Jonathan smiled politely.

'What if we ask the duckbills to push the nearby air bubbles of sigma/tau and rho/sigma towards each other?' suggested Warbler. 'This would make the gap smaller.'

There was a deathly hush. Half the audience thought this the most outrageous plan they'd ever heard but they didn't want to offend the warbler finch by laughing out loud.

The other half were so captivated by its originality that they didn't know where to begin with questions about how it would work.

'Some of us could then cross the gap quickly and quietly with air-packs in a gliding migration formation,' continued Warbler, glaring directly at the geese. 'The spell of transition would be cast from both sides and the chasm would be bridged.'

'I like this guy, Gilda,' whispered one of the geese. 'We get to be a strategic part of the solution.'

'He's bonkers, Godfrey, and you're as mad as him,' muttered the goose sitting next to Jonathan.

Others spoke, none with as bold a suggestion as Warbler, and they all warned that any attempt to cross the void, let alone repair it, would result in a significant loss of life. The debate looked like running out of steam with no action.

Warbler was miserable and flew back to Jonathan. 'We all long to cross the chasm and heal it,' he groaned. 'I would die trying. My plan or an agreement to send a powerful expeditionary force is the only way you're going to get to Eskatar,' he sighed.

Jonathan suddenly perked up. 'Warbler, there she is, that's my friend,' he gasped. It was Rose and she'd arrived as the stationmaster was closing the debate.

Rose winked at Jonathan as she landed on the speaker's platform. The little robin commanded such authority yet again, and on this occasion without even taking osprey form. Jonathan poked Warbler proudly, 'I know her, I know her, and look, she's spotted me too.'

'Impressive,' smiled Warbler.

Rose began, her voice echoing throughout the bubble. 'I come to you from Opus in Epsilon 45 and the aftermath of the recent war.

'The Skull fleet is regrouping on Terminus. They will attack again and we may not be as fortunate.

'We must remake the Tau 6 corridor. We need the priestesses' power if the Skulls are to be defeated.

'This, my friends, is the challenge of our times. The only debate is how we achieve the necessity of Eskatar. Whether it should be attempted or not is no longer a matter of choice. It must be tried if we are to confront our peril with any hope of victory.'

Scipio, the jacana stationmaster, resplendent with his bright blue bill and rich brown plumes addressed the murmuring birds, 'Thank you, Rose. We must respect your wisdom, despite our fear.

'Reluctantly, therefore, and if the objections are in the minority, I will ask the jabirus to lead an expedition to the chasm.

'However, participation will be entirely voluntary. If the expedition fails or doesn't even take off we will consider Warbler Finch's plan.' Warbler was delighted.

The murmuring faded into silence and Rose flew over to Jonathan and Warbler. 'Jonathan, you have done so well,' she smiled.

'Why didn't you tell me about this chasm?' cried Jonathan angrily.

'I'm sorry, I should have told you, but I felt certain I could persuade the stationmaster and other birds to organise an expedition. There are many powerful birds here; birds who I know will volunteer and I will not be far behind,' Rose replied.

'What? You're not coming with us?' gulped Jonathan.

'I must first fly to meet our friend, Mizmiq. We will join you during your journey.'

'Why can't the hawk follow us, on his own?' demanded Jonathan.

'I must, er, do something, do something with him, which I'll tell you about when we catch up with you,' Rose replied.

'Then I will wait,' insisted Jonathan.

'There is no reason to wait,' smiled Rose. 'You will not be alone as you criss-cross the highways; you will be escorted by a strong company of birds. There is also every reason to hurry. Eskatar is your route home.'

Jonathan lowered his head. 'How long until I see you and the hawk?'

'Mizmiq and I are able to fly much faster than you. We will catch up in no time at all. We will be at your side well before you reach the Tau 6 chasm,' answered Rose.

The robin stared directly at Warbler and the warbler finch began nodding his head furiously.

Warbler gazed at Jonathan. 'You are quite something, Jonathan Powers, osprey. You're with me now; orders from the boss,' he said, giving Rose a winged salute.

'Do not be afraid, Jonathan. You will reach Eskatar, and see home again,' added Rose.

The robin darted off towards one of the bubble's exits. She was concerned. Mizmiq and Sporadiq were supposed to have met her and Jonathan at the gamma/delta bird planet.

She and Mizmiq had exchanged messages while she was flying to Opus to see Jonathan Prior and after the grandmasters had battled the Skull ships at the Epsilon moon.

They'd agreed to meet at the kernel and the grandmasters should have arrived before her. Rose had flown to Savanna on the way.

Rose careered through the corridors to the Epsilon Gamma superhighway at a speed any bird would have struggled to match and found a message from Mizmiq when she got there.

The tiny parcel of air hovered amongst thousands of others in one of the messaging clusters that were commonplace at intersections in the corridor network.

The message had detected Rose well before she'd even begun to inspect the cluster and sent its own signal to let the robin know it was there.

Rose anxiously opened the message and sighed with relief. The grandmasters were safe but they would not be joining her, and Jonathan, yet.

Mizmiq had received word from the birds on Centurian that Filia and Julius had been conversing with a pair of foreign pigeons, an Albert and Lorna from Opus.

The Centurian birds were in a state of consternation: Filia, Julius and the pigeons had been whispering together for days and were becoming dangerously friendly. Avian rules were being flaunted and bird secrets were at stake, quite apart from the issue of inexplicable magic.

Mizmiq and Sporadiq were on their way to calm the birds and throw some light on how something of Jonathan Powers' magic had been left behind. They would also be attempting to explain what was so special about these two Opus pigeons.

Mizmiq didn't know Albert and Lorna or their closeness to Jonathan Prior. Rose was certain he would discover that for himself, and quickly no doubt.

She smiled. Albert and Lorna wouldn't have willfully broken the rules but they would be relishing the opportunity to learn more about Jonathan Powers, the boy whose consciousness their dear Jonathan had joined.

Rose tried to put all the mysterious pieces of the two Jonathans' magic together; Jonathan Prior's mastery of sound, Jonathan Powers' transformation into a bird, the wayward behaviour of Jonathan Prior's raft and now two human friends of Jonathan Powers talking to two bird friends of Jonathan Prior. Centurian's unprecedented flickering in Mizmiq's observatory ceiling had also been weighing heavily on Rose's mind.

Rose could only conclude that a powerful magical force must have entered the world unseen, a force that was able to interfere with the workings of eternity but with intentions that were alarmingly unclear.

Staying close to Jonathan Powers was now of paramount importance. Jonathan was perhaps a conduit for this strange and powerful intruder, or maybe the intruder's aim was to exist as whatever Jonathan Powers would become.

Rose decided she would rejoin Jonathan after flying once again to Savanna and telling Agnostus about Mizmiq's message. She had to inform the Chief Justice of what she knew, whether it led him to answers or not. Jonathan was in good company, and with her superior speed, she would still catch up with the gamma/delta birds well before they reached the Tau 6 chasm.

25. Centurian

A Rare Breed of Magical Pigeon

Mizmiq and Sporadiq shot along Centurian's estuary corridors, the final leg of their journey to the silver planet in Gamma 12.

Sporadiq momentarily veered off in pursuit of a remarkably striking bearded grey owl. The bird's feathers, not just its beard, were exquisitely flecked with immaculate white markings.

Mizmiq reprimanded his fellow grandmaster. 'No diversions, Sporadiq.'

'I'm sorry, of course, we must not stray. I will be as focused as a missionary hawk,' he replied with an enormous owl-eye wink.

Mizmiq smiled, glad to have his old friend at his side. Grandmaster Sporadiq was unpredictable but that was a comfort in a crisis; anything was possible.

They exited their lapispheres in the dead of night directly above the silverzone, the sparkling sheen that glided approximately a thousand metres from Centurian's surface, far below the planet's wispy clouds.

The grandmasters swooped downwards and within seconds found themselves surrounded by a flock of chatterati, a species who were always on the lookout for corridor birds entering Centurian airspace.

The chatterati wanted to be first to know everything but their goal wasn't to hoard information, quite the opposite: it was to dominate the airwaves with their voices.

They were constantly flying, searching for valuable nuggets of news, and they certainly didn't sleep.

The chatterati exemplified a survival of the loudest definition of evolution. Every chatterer did his or her best to speak at a higher volume than everyone else in the hope of drowning out competitors and controlling a patch of air.

Once they'd secured their air space, they'd look to attract others to their proclamations, thereby experiencing the rewarding feeling of being listened to, the ultimate aim of every chatterer.

'My friends, please tell us exactly what's been happening,' said Mizmiq. 'We are here to help contain the situation.'

The birds answered at the same time and it was impossible to understand what anyone was saying.

Mizmiq spotted an old friend in the thick of the chatter—Chirp, one of the elders. He motioned to speak to him.

The other birds reluctantly let Mizmiq through, pointing out that Chirp was a bird of formidable wisdom who did indeed have a right to be listened to; he currently held the record for the highest lifetime word count and as a result had received the coveted title of orator.

The birds were also quick to add that he'd been world number one for twenty-six weeks and would have continued to bombard the grandmasters with statistics if Chirp himself hadn't interrupted them.

Chirp had decided that Mizmiq represented a major opportunity to up his word count on a whole variety of subjects. Mizmiq made sure he got his question in first. 'What on earth are they all saying?' cried the grandmaster.

'Well, you've heard about the girl and the boy, Filia Wrens and Julius Fog of Bushley Park,' answered Chirp. 'And you've heard about how they've been breaking bread and talking with two pigeons, an Albert and Lorna who are visiting from Opus, surname Trafalgar, which we've heard is a common surname amongst the Opus pigeons.

'Well, now, where was I, that's right…what's causing concern is not merely reckless disregard for our engagement protocols, it's the fact that a couple of foreign dough-ballers managed to open a line of communication before us,' complained Chirp, almost spitting his words out in disgust.

'There's a lot of us chatterati who feel put out, and rightly so. This is our turf, and our species' entire reason for existing is to fraternise, consume and broadcast information for the greater good of our beloved planet.'

Mizmiq and Sporadiq shook their heads disapprovingly, sympathising with Chirp and the outraged chatterati.

'It's got to the point where some of us are tempted to break the rules, Mizmiq. There's even a debate as to who's going to represent our species and strike up a conversation first, and if words don't work, there's talk of trying anything and everything from dancing to sign language.'

'Chirp, no, use your influence to get everyone to restrain themselves,' said Mizmiq firmly. 'I will speak to the pigeons. I will also stop the boy and the girl approaching them.'

'As you wish, Master Hawk,' sighed Chirp.

Mizmiq and Sporadiq thanked him and explained that on this occasion, they were unable to stay and share corridor news. It was imperative that they ascertain whether Filia and Julius' peculiar behaviour had been spotted by the Numberalist government.

Chirp resigned himself to having to wait and he and a large contingent of chatterati directed the grandmasters to a bench in Bushley Park where they said the two pigeons could be found feasting, day and night.

Albert and Lorna were there. They were working through a cornucopia of crusts. The chatterati shot back up to their preferred altitude and left the grandmasters to it.

'We are here to talk to you about some mutual friends, Filia Wrens and Julius Fog,' said Mizmiq, as he and Sporadiq landed beside them.

'Pl–please don't be angry with us, Mr Hawk, Mr Owl,' cried Albert and Lorna, frightened that the moment of reckoning was finally upon them. 'We wanted to get to the bottom of how they were able to hear us. We are truly sorry.'

Mizmiq smiled. 'I think I would have done exactly the same as you. Please don't worry.'

Albert and Lorna couldn't believe their ears. 'So–so we can carry on getting to know them?' they gulped.

'No, not in the same way. The Numberalists mustn't suspect any untoward behaviour, avian or human. I would ask that you do not engage at close quarters for a while. I will deliver the same instruction to Filia and Julius. Where do they live, please?'

'Filia lives on that road over there, number one, first house on the corner, and Julius is 12 Dovelake Avenue; it's on the other side of the park,' Albert replied.

'Thank you, dear pigeons,' smiled Mizmiq, preparing to leave.

'Oh, er, one more thing before you go,' grinned Albert. 'I believe we've met before, on Opus. It's Albert, the baritone mastersinger.'

Mizmiq was not so certain, but smiled courteously nonetheless.

'In Battersea Park, my local stomping ground, at the lecture on natural and unnatural breezes,' Albert continued.

'Battersea Park, you say,' mused Mizmiq. 'Ah, of course, it is lovely to see you again, Albert, and I imagine therefore that you were also friends with that extraordinary boy, Jonathan Prior?'

'Oh, yes, lifelong friends, Mr Hawk,' sighed Albert, gently touching Lorna whose eyes were welling with tears.

'I'm so sorry for your loss,' mourned Mizmiq. 'That was a terrible tragedy. Look after yourselves; you are clearly an extremely rare and important breed of magical pigeon. I will return soon.'

Albert and Lorna stared at each other in amazement. The famous hawk had called them magical, rare, important. They were overwhelmed and beamed with pride as they waved their wings at the hawk and owl who vanished in the moonlit sky.

26. Centurian

A New and Vile Sorcery

Mizmiq spoke to Sporadiq as they flew. 'I will visit Filia and Julius,' he said. 'You should look for Grandmaster Tortriq, please. He's been masquerading as a Centurian human for years and has worked his way up the government ladder. He has become a special adviser on magic no less and has rooms in the eastern tower at the heart of the government district in the city centre. Ask him what the Numberalists know about Jonathan—Filia and Julius too.'

'Will I recognise him?' asked Sporadiq.

'He hasn't changed one bit. He's even kept his permanent frown,' laughed Mizmiq.

Sporadiq smiled and shot off while Mizmiq glided down to Filia's house. When he was certain he wouldn't be seen, the grandmaster cast a spell of opening and squeezed through a window in her bedroom. Filia woke instantly. She was at first startled, then overjoyed. 'You're back! Where's Jonathan?' she cried.

'He is on his way to Eskatar. All is well,' grinned Mizmiq.

Filia gazed out of her window, disappointed by his answer.

'Have you been approached by government officials asking questions about him?' said Mizmiq abruptly.

'Yes, they don't believe he actually turned into a bird at all. They think the whole thing's a trick, a spell of illusion,' she replied. 'They're convinced he's been dabbling in illegal underground magic. They think he's gone into hiding.

'I told them I had no idea where he was. I mentioned Rockmore and suggested they search the junction platforms or any other place a sound hunter might want to go. I also said there was no way he'd get into illegal magic and that I was sure it wouldn't be long before he came home.'

'Very good, behave normally and keep pretending that you expect him to show up soon,' smiled Mizmiq.

'Pretending? He will show up soon, won't he? And not as a bird, I hope?' said Filia.

'Yes, he will, soon,' Mizmiq replied. 'I'm sorry I can't be more precise. Now, has anyone asked you why you've been spending so much time with the two pigeons?'

'No,' answered Filia.

'That's a relief but you must be more discreet. The government will notice eventually. It is best you keep your distance for the time being, please. I've told Albert and Lorna not to expect you at the park bench, so don't worry about letting them down.'

Mizmiq drew breath. 'I'll contact you later today, after I've visited Julius and attended to a few other matters.' He raised his wings then paused. 'In fact, let me teach you a long distance communication spell before I go; one the government won't pick up. Use it for messaging me, and the pigeons if you must, or Julius, and tell me straightaway if anyone probes you further on Jonathan's whereabouts.'

Filia nodded.

'We'll use Julius as the object of our communication in this example,' continued the grandmaster. 'Focus your mind on the last image you have of him. The spell works best, more quickly that is, with a recent picture. Close your eyes if it helps.'

'Okay, done,' confirmed Filia.

'Open your eyes and place the image directly in front of you,' instructed Mizmiq. Filia opened her eyes.

'Hold the image right there and when you're ready say a brief message using the highest note you've heard when listening to the pigeons. You'll know your message has reached Julius when he turns towards you.'

Filia did as Mizmiq said. 'He's not looking at me. I can hear someone screaming,' she cried.

Mizmiq darted out of Filia's bedroom, shedding feathers as he shot through the window.

When he arrived at Julius' house, Mizmiq heard fighting in the back garden. 'Tortriq!' he shrieked. The grandmaster, a powerful raven, was attacking someone.

Mizmiq was devastated and launched himself at Tortriq, tearing him away. 'Have you lost your mind?' Mizmiq yelled.

Tortriq recognised Mizmiq's voice and glared at the grandmaster. 'Mizmiq, he is possessed by a Skull and was trying to break into the boy's house.'

The man lashed out and Mizmiq saw the dark hollows of a Skull's eyes. The grandmasters sent shockwave spells of destruction into the man's eye sockets, shattering his poisoned bones.

Tortriq cast a spell of burial and the dead man's body melted into the ground while Mizmiq sent Filia a message to let her know that Julius was okay, and that the screaming had been something else.

'I'm sorry, Tortriq, but a Skull in human form is an abomination I thought impossible,' shuddered Mizmiq.

'It is a new and vile sorcery,' spat Tortriq. 'Only when I confronted him did I detect the truth in his eyes. Invasion cost this human his life, not merely new consciousness after death. It is the same dark art that has poisoned the screech owls; one that gives Skulls control over living beings, and now even humans, it seems.'

'We have much to talk about,' sighed Mizmiq.

'Yes, we do,' agreed Tortriq. 'I think it is likely that some in the Numberalist hierarchy have been ravished by this same sorcery, making them subject to Skull control as well. The creature we destroyed was sent here by the government, Mizmiq, as part of an investigation into the disappearance of a boy, Jonathan Powers.'

Mizmiq grinned. 'The boy is safe. He has left Centurian.'

Tortriq listened intently as Mizmiq told him about Jonathan's magic, the inaudible notes in his spell-sounds and how he and Rose were hoping to cross the chasm so the priestesses could unravel the mystery of his magic and help cure his Destructive Interference.

'You are a great observer, grandmaster,' smiled Tortriq, when Mizmiq had finished.

A light went on in a room at the top of the house and Julius appeared at the window, rubbing his eyes and scratching his head.

The grandmasters stood absolutely still and waited until he'd moved away before launching themselves into the early morning air and setting course for government headquarters.

27. Centurian

Calculus Augustus VIII

Grandmaster Sporadiq had reached the heart of Centurian's capital city, Geocentrian.

The government district was a maze of right-angled buildings, hexagonal courtyards and perfectly parallel colonnades. At the centre were three triangular towers.

Sporadiq circled the eastern tower where Tortriq had been given a spell experimentation suite by the head of the Numberalist government, Calculus Augustus VIII.

Spell experimentation suites were incredibly well-built to limit collateral damage from powerful spells and when Sporadiq sent Tortriq a message, it simply bounced back, blocked by the spell-proof walls.

Sporadiq pressed his eyes against a small circular window and spied a red light twenty or so metres inside. Next to it were the words, "Special Adviser absent or busy".

Sporadiq looked about and spotted a faint glow at the top of the middle tower and flew across to find out what it was.

As he approached, he made out the soft radiance of a lamp in a dimly lit room. The long-eared owl perched carefully on a window ledge, peered inside and recognised the black and white chequered robes of the Calculus; Augustus VIII was marching about, talking to someone in a lab coat and gesticulating wildly.

Sporadiq cast a spell of hearing and tuned into their conversation. 'No, Sintax, no. I need all the engineers working on the diaminds. They must be ready by tomorrow night,' demanded the Calculus. 'Only then do you have my permission to resume your investigation into the grid outage.' The man left in a hurry.

Augustus VIII opened what looked like a safe in the far corner of the room and Sporadiq pushed his face against the glass to get a clearer view.

The Calculus removed a bright object, examined it, then placed it back inside the safe, slamming the door shut and yelling in frustration.

The volume was unexpected, causing Sporadiq to lose his balance, but he managed to cling to the windowsill, fanning his wings to steady himself.

The Calculus swung around. There was silence. Sporadiq concentrated on regaining his foothold but moments later a grasping hand smashed through the glass, strangling Sporadiq and pulling him across the window's jagged panes.

Sporadiq spun his head in a full circle to loosen the attacker's grip and went pale with fear when saw the unmistakable pitch-black eyes of a Skull. 'Augustus VIII, possessed,' he muttered in disbelief.

The Calculus cast spell of fire and Sporadiq immediately responded with a spell of protection, and as fire met woven light the Calculus' study burned and its windows shattered, releasing flames and thick flakes of ash into the air.

Unsure he would survive another onslaught, Sporadiq sent a desperate message to Mizmiq. The grandmaster heard his friend's cry for help and accelerated. Tortriq could not keep up with him. 'Hold on, Sporadiq, hold on, I'm coming,' Mizmiq cried.

The hawk sped towards the middle tower and shot in and out of Augustus VIII's study like a bullet through a whirlwind, grabbing Sporadiq on the way.

Mizmiq kept flying until they were outside the city and finally landed in a quiet field. Tortriq joined them and the grandmasters wove spells of healing to close Sporadiq's wounds and ease the stinging pain of his burns.

'Thank you for saving me,' Sporadiq mumbled weakly.

'That was a close call,' smiled Mizmiq.

'The Skulls are forcing the Numberalist engineers to create diaminds,' choked Sporadiq.

'That makes no sense,' pondered Tortriq. 'Why not bring the weaponry to Centurian using the secrecy of their ships?'

Mizmiq and Sporadiq did not reply. They did not have an answer.

'I will be accompanying the Calculus and other government officials to the Spellenaria festival. I will find out what I can,' sighed Tortriq.

'The moment we unearth the truth, we destroy him,' cursed Mizmiq. 'The people of Centurian will have to elect a new Calculus.

'Come, Sporadiq, we fly to the engineering research and development dome. That is also where Jonathan's mother happens to work. She will be glad of news of her son,' said the grandmaster.

*****

Presette slumped back down at her desk in the engineering centre. 'How did it go? Same interrogation all over again?' asked Stella.

Presette nodded, her eyes filling with tears. 'I've told them a hundred times I've no idea where he is. It's killing me, Stella, I want the answers too,' she cried as Stella put her arm around her friend.

A message alert pinged on their consoles. 'They're here,' groaned Stella.

'What?' asked Presette.

'The most stupid specs you've ever seen,' Stella replied, opening her file. 'We were given the heads up while you were being questioned. We're tasked with creating circular, hollow diamonds about the size of a small child's fist and stuffing them with a volatile light source.'

Stella skimmed through Sintax's instructions. 'The requirements are even more ridiculous than I imagined,' she exclaimed.

'What are they for?' sighed Presette, opening her copy.

'The MVP said they'll be used as explosives for mining craterite-bearing ores.'

Craterite was a metallic substance of exceptional strength. It could also be moulded. The precious metal was forged from rare minerals that were found inside the inner strata of Mars Munera, a hostile planet that lay at the edge of Centurian's solar system.

The minerals were extracted by burrowing probes. These so-called magic moles would set off explosions and gather what craterite-bearing shards they could before crawling back to the surface.

'Using diamonds as dynamite is insane,' muttered Presette. 'Yep, it's nuts,' whispered Stella, reading out the requirements:

The objective is to create the largest possible explosion with the smallest possible device.

Early experiments indicate that a new type of light inside a flawless diamond casing will produce a proportionally greater force than any other incendiary.

The dimensions of the diamond are set out in the Appendix. The thickness of the casing must adhere to the specifications precisely. The diamond needs to hold as much volatile light as possible in its empty cavity whilst maintaining structural integrity until it is detonated.

We do not understand the light fully, but it must be treated as if it has significant mass, hence the diamond's hollow centre, and it needs to be able to "see out" as it were, which is why the clarity of the diamond is a critical part of the design.

'Surely this is joke,' laughed Stella. 'The light has feelings and needs to be able to gaze through the diamond so it can enjoy the view before obliterating itself? What the heck have they been drinking?'

'How are we supposed to test it? Blow up the engineering centre?' chuckled Presette. 'And look, they want thousands of these violent jewels. Good luck with that!' she cried.

Presette and Stella left a series of spell sequences running to make it look like they were taking the problem seriously and went for a walk in the grounds outside. Mizmiq and Sporadiq flew above them. They'd been listening to the conversations in the engineering dome and although they were convinced that craterite mining was a nonsense, they hadn't identified the real purpose of these variants of Skull diaminds. Whatever the truth, it was a bomb factory and engineering had to be stopped.

'Presette, psssst,' whispered Mizmiq.

Presette jumped and Stella noticed the bird too. 'That's your mysterious talking hawk?' she gasped.

'Yes,' Presette smiled.

They followed Mizmiq and Sporadiq to a nearby tree and the grandmasters concealed themselves in the leaves and branches above them.

'Where's my son?' Presette demanded.

'He is well,' Mizmiq replied.

Presette asked question after question and Mizmiq apologised for the lack of detail in each of his answers.

'The hawk doesn't know where Jonathan is, or won't tell me,' wept Presette to Stella, relaying what Mizmiq had said.

'What about the owl? Does he know anything?' asked Stella, glancing up at Sporadiq's friendly rounded features and scruffy ears.

Sporadiq peered back at her and smiled politely.

'I'm afraid the owl can't offer you any more information than I, Presette,' said Mizmiq. 'The important thing is that Jonathan is safe, and well on his way.'

Presette translated again for Stella who shook her head, dumbfounded. She couldn't decide which was more unbelievable; Jonathan becoming a bird and flying to another planet or the arrival of animated light on Centurian.

Mizmiq spoke to Presette. 'Those diamond explosives are not going to be used for mining minerals,' he warned. 'They're going to be deployed somewhere else. We need to sabotage the operation.'

'How on earth are we supposed to do that?' objected Presette.

'Can you add something to the build that will weaken the diamonds or let the light out gradually?' Mizmiq suggested.

'I can't simply plant some sort of virus unnoticed; I'm being watched. They think I'm hiding Jonathan. Even if I wasn't being monitored I'd be caught,' answered Presette.

'You must try,' pleaded Mizmiq. 'I can't openly intervene. The government would start locking up every bird they clapped eyes on.'

They were interrupted by a screeching voice. 'Get back in here right now.' It was Sintax, striding up the path towards them.

Mizmiq and Sporadiq gripped the tree and didn't dare move while Presette looked at Stella. They were thinking the same thing: Most Vile Person. Presette mumbled a message to Mizmiq, 'Okay, I'll do it, I hate this place.'

'You are so brave. Thank you, Presette, thank you,' whispered the grandmaster.

28. The World of Birds

Leaving the Nest

The bustling gamma/delta nesting station was more like a beehive than a bird bubble.

The birds who'd volunteered to fly to the Tau 6 chasm were darting to and fro across the kernel, placing food and fresh water in small transparent sacks.

The food and water instantly became air once it touched the skin inside their tiny bags. These miniscule portable pouches were minute versions of the liquidiflyer containers that grandmaster Sporadiq had invented to disguise potions as weightless air.

The birds would suck the air out of their sacks during long periods of flight and the magical vapour retained not only the nutrients from the original food and water but also much of the taste.

The bags bulged as the birds made sure they were stuffed full. An overflow valve meant it was impossible for the sacks to burst. This was a feature Sporadiq had chosen not to include in his earliest versions of the liquidiflyer. Leaks would have merely increased his chances of being caught.

The courageous travellers began to gather at one of the many opulent fountains that soaked the kernel.

The Jiggles family was the first to arrive with their sacks. They were jabirus; tall yet agile birds, and supremely proficient in aerial martial arts.

The dad, Jigsy Jiggles, led the way, followed by his three sons—Squigbox, Squigsy and Squijy—each of whom he'd trained to a high standard.

Warbler was next. He landed beside them and called Jonathan over. Warbler had woken early and decided to let Jonathan sleep while he made them both several sacks of nourishing food and mineral-rich water.

Jonathan was delighted that Warbler had chosen for him. He was daunted by the prospect of having to choose from the kernel's countless treasures.

'How and when was the Tau 6 corridor broken?' asked Jonathan, sniffing an enticing parcel of air but stopping himself from guzzling it down.

As Warbler opened his beak to answer, a booming gong echoed throughout the bird planet.

'This is not a drill,' cried Scipio, the stationmaster. 'Incoming Skull ships. Everybody to the kernel. Stay away from the planet's edges, and Duckbills, get inside now and let the pendulum support the bubble.'

'This is how the corridor was broken, Jonathan; Skulls, but a long time ago,' replied Warbler. 'Attacks on the corridors and bird planets are rare these days, and ineffective, thank goodness.

'Occasionally, they cut the outer weave of one of the corridors and we repair the damage once they've gone.'

The nervous birds looked on as a squadron of Skull battleships drifted silently towards the nesting station, diaminds glowing like lanterns in the darkness.

'Are those lights the same weapons they used in the Opus war?' gulped Squijy, the youngest of Jigsy's three sons.

'Yes. What you see is lightning drawn from the skies of Terminus and caged in diamonds, but don't worry, son, we are safe here,' said Jigsy.

The first salvo of diaminds struck the bird planet. They exploded on impact and the bubble's glasslike casing shuddered.

The bombardment continued for what felt like an age but the Skulls could not penetrate the planet's seemingly indestructible skin.

Jigsy spoke to Scipio. 'They are concentrating their fire on a single point to move the planet off balance. We will need to send the duckbills back outside to keep the bubble stable if the pounding doesn't stop.'

Scipio looked at the duckbills. They too had identified the danger and were terrified.

'The Skulls want us to think the planet will list, Jigsy,' said the stationmaster. 'They want us to open the hatch so they can torch the kernel by firing their bombs into the bubble.'

'Scipio, it is a real threat,' warned Jigsy. 'We must be prepared to act. I, too, would be heartbroken if I had to place such gentle, hard-working birds in the line of fire. I will go with them and do what I can to keep them safe, if it comes to it.'

'We will wait until it is absolutely necessary, my friend. The more bombs they waste in the meantime, the better,' answered Scipio.

'I will protect the duckbills too,' offered Warbler.

Jonathan and many of the other birds stared at the warbler finch in astonishment. His species were not thought of as front-line soldiers.

'We warblers aren't the strongest, but we can dodge missiles better than most. I will divert the bombs away from the duckbills,' said Warbler.

'If we are required to fight, you boys will come with us too,' added Jigsy, nodding to Squigbox, Squigsy and Squijy.

Jonathan gripped the soft kernel turf, listening to the conversation. The minutes passed. 'We are tilting badly, station master. It is time,' cried Jigsy.

'You go in twenty seconds,' ordered Scipio.

Ploris, the oldest of the duckbills, asked a dozen of her flock to make ready and moments later they left the kernel with Jigsy, his three sons and Warbler. They waited a safe distance from the hatch.

Jigsy sent a private message to Scipio, 'The Skulls must not be let in, even if that means leaving us outside. We have air tanks so will be okay for a while.'

The bubble was perilously close to tipping as the diaminds continued to find their mark. The birds had never experienced such a relentless assault.

Jigsy barked his instructions. 'As soon as the first hatch fastening buckles, Warbler will go through and draw their fire.

'He will fly a short distance up the bubble before returning. You duckbills will have approximately thirty to forty seconds to build the suspension's momentum. Lads, we defend the hatch. Any Skull that comes close will be snapped in two.'

Warbler had survived close scrapes before and showed no fear. The three jabiru boys hid their terror and clung to their father while Ploris hugged the petrified duckbills.

One of the hatch fastenings erupted as the angles became too acute, nearly slicing through one of Warbler's wings. Jigsy gave the signal and Warbler shot out, darting up the underbelly of the bird planet.

Jonathan and the birds sheltering around the kernel watched in horror as the Skulls diverted their fire towards the hatch. Several duckbills were killed as they made their way through the opening and others were wounded, but Ploris could not stay and help them. The clock was ticking.

With her troop depleted, it took Ploris longer than expected to force the pendulum back to anything close to suspension speed.

After fifteen seconds, they had stopped any further leaning and ten seconds after that, the pendulum was rotating fast enough to begin lifting the bird planet towards its correct position.

The Skulls ordered one of their ships to move alongside the bubble so that its crew had a better chance of striking Warbler.

Ribbon and fork lightning flared like snake tongues as the Skulls lunged at him with their diamind-tipped rods. But even at close quarters, their weapons could not touch the elusive warbler finch.

The duckbills let go of the pendulum when they too were attacked by Skulls lining the platform of another ship and the planet began to lose altitude and stability.

The Skulls saw that the bubble was vulnerable once more. They intensified their assault and a second hatch fastening was flung from its joints.

The duckbills responded by putting everything into what they knew would be their final push and managed to raise the bird planet once again.

After thirty-five seconds, Jigsy reopened the hatch and Ploris gave the signal that enough was enough for now.

The duckbills and Warbler hurtled back inside but Jigsy hesitated before closing the hatch. One of Squijy's bright red toes had been caught under a casing joint.

Squijy quickly freed himself but lost his balance and fell away from the opening. Jigsy went after him and the Skulls trained their bombs on the two jabirus, and fired.

'Close the hatch,' yelled Jigsy, seeing the danger. 'No,' screamed Warbler.

Squijy was struck in the face by a diamind blast as Jigsy grabbed him and as soon as they'd shot back through Warbler slammed the hatch shut.

They hovered barely metres away, worried that the remaining fastenings would not withstand another onslaught.

Thankfully, the Skull weapons fell silent and they wheeled their ships about. Their arsenal was empty and they did not want to risk a counterattack without the means to defend themselves.

29. The World of Birds

The Jabiru's Heart

Squijy lay in his father's wings, his flesh scorched and mauled by the diamind, and Jigsy whispered his name again and again, but the young jabiru did not reply.

Tears flowed from the jabiru throng's cheeks as Jigsy flew across the bubble and laid his son down on the kernel's healing soil.

Squigsy and Squigbox were inconsolable. 'I should not have taken him,' Jigsy sobbed.

The jabirus did what they could to heal Squijy's wounds and revive him, but it was no good. Squigsy and Squigbox held their brother and cried and cried while Jigsy wrapped his wings around all three of his boys.

Jonathan wept for the young jabiru and for his brothers and father. The look of grief and failure on Jigsy's face was heartbreaking and it was not long before Jonathan had to turn away in despair.

He thought of Alesand and Naricorn, and how their world too had been blighted by the cruelest misery of all; the suffering that comes with the loss a child.

Jonathan willed himself to cast the same spell of healing that he'd conjured in the Supreme Court of Savanna.

His pulse slowed to a near standstill, although he did not feel short of breath and his thoughts were clearer than ever.

Jonathan had come to understand this strange state and its two extremes: an almost lifeless heart coupled with a lucid active consciousness—his mind preparing to leave the living world and enter the Twilight realm.

Jonathan spoke to Jigsy, 'Sir, may I hold your son?'

The grieving jabiru moved away, allowing Jonathan to approach his boy.

The poor jabiru's face had been disfigured horribly by the diamind blast and Jonathan felt sick with anger at the murderous brutality of his death.

Jonathan cradled Squijy in his osprey wings and held the jabiru tight as they travelled together through his Opening and into Twilight.

Jonathan found himself able to see every part of Squijy's body, just as he had Alesand's, and bit by bit he healed his wounds with threads of Candela Lumen light. And when he was done, he placed one final thread in his heart, which he knew had somehow come from his brothers, and rejoiced as it began to beat.

Jonathan willed himself and Squijy back through his Opening and when he looked up at the speechless birds he wept with happiness.

'How–how is this possible? Who are you, osprey?' asked Jigsy, embracing Squijy with the young jabiru's brothers and sobbing with joy.

'I do not know,' Jonathan replied, barely believing the truth of his own miracle. 'I do not know who I am or why I'm able to do this,' he said, weeping and smiling at the cheering birds.

Jonathan stared at Squigbox and Squigsy. 'I do know, however, that my magic would not have worked without something from you. I hope I did not take too much?'

Squigbox and Squigsy did feel faint, but whether it was their elation or some mysterious transfer of strength to their brother, they could not tell.

That night, the gamma/delta birds filled their planet with song—songs of wonder and celebration, including verse after verse of the ancient epic that told the story of the creation of the air planets.

Squijy, Squigsy and Squigbox did not let go of each other. They thought of their mother who had tragically passed away through illness soon after Squijy's birth.

Jigsy, too, remembered his wife and his eyes welled with tears as he gazed up at the stars and hummed the lament that he always sang when he mourned her.

Squijy suddenly looked at his father. 'Dad, I think I heard Mum's voice when I was with the osprey. I wasn't sure earlier, but now I'm convinced,' he smiled.

Jigsy held his precious boy tightly.

'And it wasn't just her voice that I heard. She said something to me,' he beamed.

Jigsy sat up, startled. 'What? You are certain? Little one, what did she say?'

'She said that, in time, we would see her again. Do you think that's true?'

Jigsy's heart was pounding. He wanted so much for it to be true, and after what they'd witnessed, who was to say his son hadn't heard his mother's voice?

'Yes, I think we will see her again,' Jigsy smiled; Squijy was ecstatic.

When the birds gathered at the fountain the following day, the stationmaster was presented with a serious problem. Almost all the birds in the gamma/delta bubble wanted to fly with the osprey to the Tau 6 chasm.

Scipio set about persuading as many birds as he could to stay. Defending the bird planet wasn't the only issue. The kernel needed constant attention because visiting birds expected to find plentiful supplies of species-specific fare, not just any old grub. A stationmaster's reputation depended on the freshness and variety of his food and drink.

'You are embarking on one of the most dangerous quests ever conceived,' he shouted as the birds lined up. 'The chances of coming back alive are close to zero. Maybe they are zero, perhaps even less than zero.

'And if you're worried about surviving inside an air planet, well, there's nowhere for any corridor bird to return to if the nesting stations disappear. No bird planets, no corridors, no nothing as we know it,' he cried.

Ploris got up to speak next, 'I envy you all your adventure and I wish there were two ospreys like Jonathan, so one could remain here.

'I implore as many of you as possible to stay with us duckbills. We are your support, keeping the planet suspended in the gravest of times, but we also need your protection, and support.

'Every day, we, the burds, embark on our work gladly. We bear the burden with an immovable sense of rotating duty…'

Ploris hesitated, realising she'd confused herself as well as the other birds. '…immovable sense of duty in every rotation.' *That's better*, she told herself.

'There are no greater folk than the bird folk in the watching over and caring of others, notably our human friends,' she continued with renewed confidence. 'Please also care for your own.'

Ploris had left their beaks and hearts hanging. The birds felt awful and took pity on the duckbills and the stationmaster, berating themselves for being so shortsighted.

They proceeded to negotiate and agree who should remain and who should go in a matter of minutes.

Jigsy led his troop towards one of the bird planet's exits. Warbler, Jonathan and Jigsy's three sons were right behind him.

Warbler looked at Jonathan. 'This time, my boy, we will succeed. The Tau 6 chasm will be bridged.'

Jonathan smiled. 'And we will fly on to Eskatar together, won't we?' he said.

'That we will,' grinned Warbler. 'We will see you right, laddie. We will be at your side, until the robin says we're done.'

Jonathan rejoiced. He felt a new sense of hope. He was with friends who were going to stop at nothing to help him find a way home. He would, after all, see Filia, Julius and his mother and father again.

30. Centurian

Anger Lights the Way

Presette and Stella were battling to come up with a sensible way of sabotaging Sintax's diamond containers.

They'd been racking their brains for hours while at the same time crafting elaborate spell combinations that looked like they were tackling the requirements but were in fact doing nothing.

Presette had sought ideas on how to derail Sintax's secret operation from the hawk, twice leaving her desk and wandering into the gardens outside the research and development dome, but his suggestions were always ones that she and Stella had considered and dismissed.

The hawk had eventually flown off with his owl friend, explaining that he would return after consulting another bird who was apparently trying to discover the project's true purpose elsewhere.

Sintax summoned everyone to an unscheduled meeting. 'How nice of you to join us, Presette. Pleasant outside, is it?' he snarled as Presette walked past and stood to attention alongside the other engineers.

'Vile,' coughed Stella, making sure Sintax didn't hear the word. 'Person,' coughed Presette immediately after her, stopping herself from laughing.

Sintax didn't appear to notice and addressed the engineers, 'Proximus has managed to create the perfect diamond encasement, light filament and triggering mechanism, and what's more, his code does it by joining together only ninety-seven spells.'

The young and ambitious Proximus grinned uncontrollably as he lapped up his master's praise. He was the engineering chief's archetypal prototype; an early stage know-all who worshipped the MVP. Presette and Stella had nicknamed him the protobof.

'The spell sequence diagrams and code translations of the magic paths are being sent to you as we speak,' continued Sintax, 'and Proximus will be handing out examples of the finished product shortly.

'Our task now is to build as many as we can, and quickly. We need ten thousand in two hours—entirely possible if you all step up. Shut down any other programs that are running on your machines and don't leave your desks.

'Presette, stay where you are. The rest of you may go,' Sintax concluded, waving the engineers away.

Sintax's miserable slaves loafed back to their consoles while Presette stood alone, terrified.

'If you take another of your ridiculously long breaks before we're done, I'll lock you out for good,' spat Sintax angrily.

Presette gritted her teeth. She knew being defensive would backfire. 'I'm sorry' was all she said.

Presette returned to her desk, raging. She wanted more than anything to obliterate the MVP and Stella suggested they engage in one of their favourite activities to try and calm her down.

They'd developed a game where they would display sticky note messages to Sintax as he patrolled the floor. Success meant getting him to notice a message without understanding the joke.

Presette ripped off a giant orange rectangular sticky note and inked the words "DELETE THE MVP" using a permanent marker. She attached it to one of her monitor screens.

Sintax marched by, peering at it but ignoring the message. Stella and Presette punched the air under their desks as he disappeared down the aisle, planting one foot after the other in his customary robotic prance.

'Too many five hundred terabyte chips for breakfast?' chuckled Stella.

'Or he's about to give birth to an explosive,' warned Presette. They laughed hysterically.

Proximus arrived moments later with examples of his masterpiece. As soon as he'd moved on to the next pair of engineers, Presette gripped the diamond casing and pretended to crush it.

The light inside quivered as if agitated, and the more she aimed her fury at it, the more it flickered and shone.

Presette calmed herself and the light began to fade, but when she allowed her hatred to boil over again, it almost burst into flame.

'Stella, it's responding to me, to my anger,' she gasped.

'How, how?' said Stella, flabbergasted.

'I've no idea, but I think there's a way to stop these bombs exploding. We should cast spells of calming and set them running in an infinite loop inside the casing.'

'Genius,' whispered Stella and they went to work.

'What are you two doing?' demanded Proximus, suddenly appearing at their desks squelching on a banana. Presette and Stella cringed. The protobof was as physically repulsive as he was self-serving.

Presette blurted out the first thing that came into her head, 'We're testing the volatility of the light.'

'That is no longer a requirement. You would know that if you'd bothered to read the updates,' smirked Proximus. 'Follow the instructions properly.'

Proximus swaggered off and Presette was about to scream when Stella grabbed her. 'Ignore him, Presette, he's an ugly pompous brat,' she said.

Presette seethed. 'You build the bombs, Stella, I'll calm the light.'

Presette cast hundreds of spells of calming, filling the hollow of every one of Stella's diamonds.

'Coffee?' said Stella after a while.

Presette nodded. 'I feel totally spaced out. I'll have to take one of these calming diamonds home,' she smiled as they made their way into the food hall.

'Careful what you say,' mumbled Stella, pointing ahead. Proximus and Sintax were talking at a nearby table.

'The bots are taking a break?' tutted Presette.

'Looks like it; setting a bad example,' Stella laughed quietly.

Sintax got up and came towards them. Proximus followed. 'Come with me, both of you,' ordered the MVP, striding back to his office.

'Get inside,' shouted Sintax, slamming the door behind them. 'You are ambushing our work. Why?' he screeched.

Stella opened her mouth but Presette interrupted, 'Because you are the most disgusting, inhuman person I've ever known,' she cried. Stella couldn't believe what Presette had said.

'You will pay a heavy price for your insolence, Presette Powers,' growled Sintax.

Proximus smiled smugly in the corner and celebrated his victory by gnawing his revolting fingernails with ravenous glee; Sintax would reward him handsomely and Presette and Stella would receive the harshest of punishments, and rightly so.

Sintax and Proximus conferred briefly. Presette and Stella overheard Proximus explaining that it was too late to reverse Presette's spells of calming. The time had come to ship the diamonds and they would have to abandon the damaged explosives.

'You have caused irrevocable harm,' yelled Sintax. 'You will be dealt with in the severest possible way.'

Sintax left his office and came back minutes later with a Numberalist government enforcer who shouted and pointed aggressively at Presette, 'I hereby charge you with destroying government property. You will be detained for at least thirty days. We have all the proof we need.'

Sintax looked at Stella. 'As for you, although you are clearly complicit in this criminal activity, we are still examining your spell history to establish the scale of your crime. You will learn your fate within the hour.'

Presette broke down in tears, realising what she'd done. They would find out about Stella's log file tampering and she would suffer the same punishment, or worse.

Presette lashed out at the enforcer as he took her away, while Sintax restrained Stella who was screaming and weeping for her friend.

Presette was led through a door near Sintax's office and into a long corridor. At the end was a lift. The enforcer bundled Presette inside and she sat alone on the floor as it travelled down and down.

The lift finally opened and Presette hesitated before stepping into a damp rock-walled chamber. Someone seized her and dragged her along a metal-grated walkway before throwing her into a small room with only a bed and a basin.

Presette knelt on the ground in despair, listening to the cries of anguish coming from the adjoining cells.

The air was foul, polluted, unbreathable. Presette did not last long; she passed out and collapsed.

Her cell instantly filled with the swirling currents of wind-form Skulls lusting after her humanity.

The Skulls fought over their prey. They knew that only one of them could win; human souls could not be shared and the victor would be the first Skull to persuade her mind to portray her death in a dream.

One of the Skulls decided to crawl through the cracks between her lips, and it hacked into her consciousness well before the other evil breezes had even come close.

The torment of seeing her death in a dream woke Presette. She wailed and screamed in terror, but it was too late. Her soul, her life after death, had been taken.

The Skull now battled for control of her living conscious mind. This was the vile sorcery Mizmiq, Tortriq and Sporadiq had witnessed. If successful, the Skull would own her thoughts and actions before she died.

Speed was critical and the Skull inflicted as much pain as it could to force her mind to give up quickly. It knew her poisoned body would not last long, perhaps only days. Her flesh would wither and she, and it, would become one; a skeletal creature capable only of shell or wind-form.

It would then keep her soul captive and enjoy her memories until it was ordered to cast the final remnant of her human consciousness into the hellfires below Terminus.

It was not long before Stella was brought to the same dungeon and thrown into the cell opposite. She could see Presette writhing and begging for the torture to end, and she stared horrified at the black pits that were now her eyes.

Stella cried and cried for her closest friend, and for the brilliant generous mind she'd loved. She wept for Jonathan too. If he did ever, one day, return, it would be to a world without the beautiful mother he adored.

31.   The World of Birds

The Prescient Aquila

After many hours of high-speed flight, Jigsy made an announcement, 'We are going to bypass the eleven nesting stations between here and omicron/pi.'

'How?' cried his entourage in unison.

'By flying through one of the ancient expressways. It will save us an enormous amount of time. You all heard the robin, we need the Eskatar priestesses' power to fight the Skull filth, and given what we saw at gamma/delta, we need their help urgently,' said Jigsy.

There was silence. The birds knew of the corridor although none had flown it. The expressway led to an ancient junction, the Omicron interchange, a crossover point in the early corridor network and a precursor to the first bird planets.

Qybil, one of the Aquilae; graceful eagles renowned for accurately seeing into the future, interrupted the hum of passing air shortly after Jigsy's announcement.

'What if the expressway is torn?' she asked. 'We'd be forced to use our oxygen tanks. We might even run out of air.'

The birds began to whisper. 'Did Qybil just say the expressway is torn and we're likely to end up stranded in the middle of nowhere without any air? Did I hear that right?' gulped Machian, a logistics falcon.

'Quite probably,' replied Fovea, the formidable Opus-Earth eagle who'd been visiting the gamma/delta bird planet at the time of the debate and had volunteered to join the expedition rather than go home.

Warbler could tell Jigsy was annoyed by the Aquila's public expression of doubt and flew next to him.

'I'm a believer in Aquila instincts, Jigsy. That said, they've been wrong before. Not all of their questions and speculations are future facts. I think you should stand firm on this one.'

The Aquilae were highly revered. Although Jigsy was grateful to Warbler for his support, he felt it would be too divisive to challenge the Aquila's prescience.

'You make a good point, Qybil. There is a risk. However, I ask that we still try the expressway and I promise we'll only touch the tanks if we need them for a short burst of air,' suggested Jigsy. 'Worst case, we'll have to fly back and take the long route through the nesting stations.'

Qybil nodded and the flock agreed and Warbler gave Jigsy the flaps up.

Jigsy dived after another ten or so minutes of super-fast flight and took the birds down a narrow corridor. 'This is not the ancient expressway, it is the corridor leading to it,' he explained.

After a long spell of silent gliding, the walls darkened and the distant blurred lines of stars disappeared. Their surroundings were like a night sky suddenly obscured by clouds and even the air inside the corridor seemed to be part of the gloom.

'Those with the keenest eyes to the front, everyone else stay close,' ordered Jigsy. 'We're in the ancient expressway, folks. The corridors didn't always offer a view of the cosmos,' he smiled.

The flock huddled together. The smaller birds filled the gaps between the larger ones and they flew on like a jigsaw puzzle made up of variously sized pieces.

They settled into a rhythm, each bird comfortable with his or her place in the pattern, and every once in a while they opened their sacks at precisely the same moment and treated themselves to a tasty parcel of food-infused air.

'Reduce speed,' cried Fovea after about an hour. The birds immediately came out of their trance.

'Full stop!' she yelled. 'The corridor is sealed not far ahead.'

They drifted forwards, then hovered. 'There's a tiny cut in the end wall,' warned Fovea. 'It's sucking air out of the corridor.'

'That's a trapdoor into space,' said Machian. 'Don't go anywhere near it or you'll get dragged into oblivion.'

'We should repair the cut,' urged Warbler. 'The Skulls may never find it, but it does give access to the network nonetheless.'

'Wait here,' Jigsy instructed. He flew within metres of the tear, forcing his way back against the vacuum. 'The skin is ancient. I think we can work with it though,' he said.

As he turned, Jigsy noticed what looked like a diamind lying hidden below him in a corridor fold. There was a faint light inside the casing, only just visible in the murky interior of the tubeway.

He picked it up and brought it back for the others to inspect. 'What do you think? A Skull weapon, but perhaps not a recent one?'

Warbler examined it. 'Trapped light, a tear in the corridor, it must be a Skull diamind, but the faded state of the light tells me it's a relic from another age,' he said, calming the anxious birds.

When it was Jonathan's turn to hold the ancient diamind in his talons, he felt an immediate connection with the light. 'There's something alive inside the casing, and it's trying to escape. It's the light,' he cried.

Jonathan was drawn to its struggle and understood its pain. It was dying. His pulse slowed without him even asking it to and his mind conjured an Opening. He then lifted the diamind into his wings and took it with him into Twilight.

Jonathan cast a spell of freedom and a pinhole appeared in the casing. A narrow wisp of light instantly crawled out of its prison and Jonathan was struck by the most overwhelming sense of joy and relief.

He let the Opening close and the birds stared in amazement. The light hovered in front of them before moving one way, then another, as if looking at them.

It then wrapped itself around Jonathan's ankle and whispered a message to the osprey, 'Thank you, thank you. I have battled for so long to break free. My name is Alea and you, you are an osprey of great power, what is your name?'

'Jonathan, Jonathan Powers, from Centurian,' he answered. 'I am so glad my spell worked. I could not bear to have left you imprisoned.'

The wisp of light pulled Jonathan towards the cut and without thinking he began to sew the corridor skin together with a spell of healing and the tubeway wall was repaired in a matter of seconds.

The birds wondered at the osprey's magic and gazed in awe at the silver creature of light circling his ankle.

'Is it one of the sapphire lights?' asked Machian.

'It has to be,' smiled Jigsy.

Some knew of these legendary sentient beings—rings of light that had protected the birds from Skulls and the demons of the Arc of Darkness in the Gazongian war many thousands of years ago. None had seen one.

Alea heard them and spoke to the whispering flock, 'I am indeed one of the sapphire lights. Thank you for finding me and gifting me another life.'

The birds were overjoyed and asked if they might be allowed to touch her. Alea was delighted and the birds marvelled at the soft radiance of her ancient light as she curled across their feathers.

With the expressway blocked, the birds now had no choice but to fly back to the corridors and take the long route to the Tau 6 chasm. Qybil had been correct. The expressway had been torn, just not in the way they had imagined.

But as they readied themselves to leave, they noticed Jonathan staring at the corridor wall. 'What's troubling you?' asked Jigsy, flapping impatiently at the front of the troop.

'That,' gasped Jonathan; a silver oval was forming where the cut had been and two bird-claws were being stitched together inside the circle.

Jigsy was ecstatic. 'An emergency lapisphere,' he declared. 'A seriously old one. You remember I told you about these once, boys?' Squigbox, Squigsy and Squijy nodded frantically. 'Fixed gateways in the walls,' continued Jigsy. 'They provide passage between two adjacent sealed corridors that used to be one tube but were somehow separated.'

The excited jabiru addressed the troop, 'The bird claws don't show unless the lapisphere on the other side is intact as well. The shortcut is back on, everybody!'

'Wait,' objected Warbler. 'We can't simply dive in. The creators of these lapispheres specified who was allowed through and we're not on any ancient white list as far as I'm aware. The gateways may contain hidden spells or curses.'

'The diamind would have broken any spell, don't you think?' said Jigsy.

'But the lapisphere has now been remade,' cautioned Warbler.

'Wouldn't the creator still need to reconjure the curse?' argued Jigsy.

Everyone looked at Qybil. The Aquila smiled and Jigsy didn't wait for any further opinions. He pressed his feet into the lapisphere's claws and spoke the avian spell of corridor flight.

Moments later, he and the troop were darting through the gateway and exiting the lapisphere on the other side.

The air in the far corridor wasn't as clean, but it was good enough for them to fly on without tanks.

'Yuk,' spluttered Squijy, getting used to the stench.

'Oh, come on, son. It's no worse than your breath after breakfast when you haven't bathed yer beak yet,' teased Jigsy. Squijy grinned and blew a parcel of smelly air into his dad's face.

'This corridor hasn't been fanned by flight for hundreds, perhaps thousands of years,' coughed Warbler.

'In which case, we should give it a jolly good airing; let's see those tiny warbler wings make some jabiru-sized waves,' roared Jigsy.

Warbler laughed and the birds shrilled in triumph, 'Omicron interchange, here we come!' they chorused, launching themselves into the corridor.

32. The World of Birds

Sound Capture

The merry band of birds had been flying for several hours and according to Jigsy they were making good progress. He'd given regular updates, praising the troop for maintaining their speed despite the unpleasantness of the air and the corridor's near total darkness.

Other than Jigsy's check-ins, the only sounds in the ancient expressway had been Alea's voice answering questions about her life and the gasps of incredulous birds as her stories were relayed throughout the flock.

Squigbox, the oldest of the jabiru leader's three sons, glanced at his dad.

Jigsy smiled. 'I know what you're thinking.'

'Bet you don't,' chuckled Squigbox.

'Of course I do, you want to perform. The fact that there's been no singing for hours is driving you nuts,' answered Jigsy.

'Well, obviously, but that's not all that I'm thinking,' winked Squigbox.

Squigsy and Squijy were intrigued, as was their father.

'Go on then, don't leave us hanging,' demanded Squigsy.

'I want to convert the smell of this corridor into a sound,' grinned Squigbox.

'I'd rather have silence,' Squigsy protested.

107

Squigbox was desperate to give it a go. 'I tell you what, I'll capture the stench as a sound but only play it briefly inside a song you like and in an appropriate place so all it'll do is make the song better.'

Squigsy hesitated. 'Alright, go on then, but don't foul it up,' he sighed.

'Minim, my love!' cried Squigbox, turning towards a beautiful woodpecker a few rows back in the bird formation. 'Your husband needs you, we're going to mix the smell of this corridor into one of our songs.'

Minim was from Gazong, the Earth-like planet famed for its music and inhabited only by birds.

Gazong lay in the Beta sector of the birds' universe and birds flew between the planet and the corridor network via estuary tubeways that were similar in design to those that surrounded Opus and Centurian.

Gazong's landmasses thrived, they were lush and green, but its oceans were waterless. Hundreds of tiny moons floated in the empty seas and these moons had become home to musicians who hoped their songs would one day make the waters return.

Minim was an exceptional percussionist who often toured the Tymporian moon as it drifted across Gazong's widest ocean.

Her musical prowess and startling colours never failed to dazzle her audiences and Squigbox had fallen in love with her the first time he watched her play.

He'd darted up to the brilliant woodpecker straight after her final encore and told her she'd knocked him out with what he called the perfect punch; pounding loudness, delicate touches and long sections of well-rolled rhythm.

Minim had laughed and blushed, and made him promise to come to her next concert and Squigbox had been at the front of the queue for every other concert on the tour.

Minim flew beside her husband and they sang a Gazongian ballad called "The Journey", a tale of a bird's search for the love of his life; a striking golden Aquila who'd been captured by an envious foreign overlord. The bird's hunt took him across the archipelago moons and farther than he'd ever been from home.

'Hear that? We did it!' yelled Squigbox as they finished.

'Didn't hear anything different, thank goodness,' replied Squigsy.

'You weren't listening closely enough. The evil overlord's song part,' cried Squigbox. 'It was the smell-sound of this corridor. We nailed it, didn't we, Minim?'

'Certainly did,' cried the woodpecker, racing up and down her arpeggios in preparation for another performance.

While Squigsy, Squijy and Jigsy hadn't made the connection between the foul air and the evil overlord, Jonathan had. He'd been listening all along to their conversation, then the music and had spotted the sound capture even though he'd never heard the song before.

Jonathan tried to hide his tears as memories of Rockmore consumed him. The birds noticed. Alea did too and she wrapped herself more tightly around his ankle.

'Hey buddy, what's up?' said Squigbox, nudging Jonathan gently.

'You did nail it, but too well for my liking, I'm afraid,' choked Jonathan.

'How so?' asked Squigbox.

'It brought back memories, wonderful memories, of friends I miss,' he replied. 'What do you call what you just did?'

'Magic-music, sound capture to be precise,' answered Squigbox. 'Have you ever given magic-music a go?'

'Yes,' said Jonathan, forcing himself to smile through his tears.

'We can work on stuff together then,' enthused Squigbox. 'And once this whole adventure is over, we'll take you to the Gazongian archipelago. Minim and I will show you around.'

Squigbox and Minim told Jonathan about the music school they'd attended on Gazong. It was called the Awkward Academy and was named after a group of birds whose songs sounded terrible until they invented a magical hearing adjuster.

It was not the easiest thing to wear, hence the group's name, but its effects were beyond anything any bird had imagined possible and it opened up a whole new world of supersonic sounds and pulsating rhythms.

Squigbox had achieved the Academy's highest grade in the sound capture category, classification A***, which meant "Astounding", while Minim had received the same commendation for moon-drumming.

They'd also both graduated magna cum loude—with great volume, a phrase that was a bastardisation of a human accolade and just one of the many things that birds had copied through their fondness for humans. Magna cum loude also gave Squigbox and Minim the right to swap the word bird for bard whenever they chose.

'Tell me, Squigbox, what was your first big sound capture?' Jonathan asked.

'The one which every Awkward Academy student attempts at the end of their first year; an original recording of the atomhawk's echo, the heartbeat of Naumachian,' smiled Squigbox.

'When the great atomhawk gave his life to save Gazong from the Skulls and the Arc of Darkness all those thousands of years ago, he left an echo of his heart behind.

'It can be heard in many locations across Gazong so it is up to each student to choose where they capture it.

'I flew a complete circle of Gazong's largest continent, right where the land meets the waterless seas, and I recorded the echo all the way round.'

Jonathan listened in amazement as Squigbox sang samples of his sound capture. Jonathan wished Filia was with him. The empty seashore waves of Gazong sounded just like Elephant's Trunk exhaling the dust rings of the Tilmenian corona.

'I'm more of a moon-girl,' interjected Minim. 'Nothing can beat the atomhawk's echo as it ricochets off the deepest of our ocean moons.'

'Here we go,' cried Squigbox. 'Remember, Jonathan, she's a drummer, a Tymporian moon-bard,' he laughed, poking Minim with his wing as if it were a drumstick.

'And what's wrong with drummers? You're jealous, aren't you?' responded Minim. 'You're incapable of playing a single rhythm for more than five seconds, isn't that right, Mr Schizophonic? You're just one big box of sound-oddities.'

Jonathan smiled. 'How my friends Filia and Julius would love to meet you two. Filia and I have conjured some crazy sound constellations and Julius recently gave our magic-music an entirely new angle.'

'Tell us more about your friends, Jonathan, your home, how you came to be here with us in the corridors,' beamed Squigbox.

Jonathan stared down at the passing gloom. He had so far not talked about his life on Centurian, conscious of Agnostus' judgement that he should be treated as a bird.

He looked up at Squigbox and Minim. They were becoming the closest of friends. He wanted to tell them everything and he could no longer to hold back; he hoped Agnostus would forgive him and understand if he said too much.

'I lived a happy human life on Centurian until only weeks ago when I suddenly discovered that I could no longer use the magic of my world,' Jonathan wept.

'I did not understand the change, nor did my people. I was the object of suspicion and they tried to take me away but I escaped by becoming an osprey. I've no idea how that transformation happened.'

Jonathan's eyes welled with more tears. 'Now I am the bird in your song, a bird who longs to be with the love of his life and the love of my life is my friend, Filia.

'She means everything to me and I must journey far from home if I am to see her again.'

Jonathan paused, choking as he wept. 'And if I do one day set eyes on her, who can say whether I'll be able to touch her again with my own hands?

'No one understands the magic that has taken hold of me, not even the powerful robin.

'Maybe I will reach home and change back into human form. But will my people then lock me up? My strange departure has probably already sealed my fate.

'Perhaps, therefore, I will choose to live my life as an osprey, separated from my family and friends, watching them from the skies and speaking with them in secret.'

Jonathan turned away, then he glanced at Squigbox and Minim again. 'I see so much of myself and Filia when I listen to you. That is also why I weep.'

Squigbox and Minim bowed their heads.

'No, do not be sad,' said Jonathan. 'I am grateful that we have discovered each other, and each other's love of magic-music because that is something I thought I might never experience again.'

Jonathan cried and cried as he told Squigbox and Minim about the triumph of Elephant's Trunk and the torture of his last visit to Rockmore.

'Jonathan, one day, you, Filia, Julius, Minim and I will fly the Tilmenian run together,' said Squigbox firmly, resting his wing on the osprey's feathers as they flew.

'Thank you,' Jonathan wept, embracing Minim and Squigbox. 'Thank you for understanding me, and for helping me find my way home.'

33. Centurian

School Trip to the Spellenaria

Filia boarded the dronibus for school and messaged Julius, Albert and Lorna, telling them she was opening a four-way communication channel.

Filia had taught Julius the long-distance messaging magic Mizmiq had showed her. Albert and Lorna were already familiar with it and had told Filia and Julius how to link the individual communication frequencies together.

'I can see you in your window seat, Filia Wrens!' exclaimed Albert from somewhere in the skies above Bushley Park.

'We have you in our sights too, Julius Fog,' declared Lorna. 'Don't board that dronibus, Filia's on the next one. She'll be at your stop in three minutes. Eye in the sky, over and out.'

'Message received by legs on the ground. Thank you, eye in the sky,' smiled Julius.

People at the dronibus stop glared at Julius. They hadn't heard him; his mind had spoken his words. They simply saw a sixteen-year-old boy grinning from ear to ear and wondered what on earth he was thinking.

'Now that we're all in the chat, I've got some news!' announced Albert. 'I've been selected for a standby position at today's Spellenaria festival.'

'You're in one of bird-teams?' gasped Julius.

'Yep, the pigeons were that impressed with my speed and precision in the trials,' Albert replied.

'We're so proud of you,' messaged Julius.

'You're a superstar, Albert,' added Filia. 'And what's more, we'll be in the crowd to cheer you on. We're joining the school trip to the Spellenaria. You've got to be sixteen to go so this is our first time.'

The Spellenaria festival took place not far from the capital, Geocentrian, in Centurian's largest stadium, the velocodrome at Silverrock.

One of the highlights was what Centurians called the great avian game. It was also known as the Silverrock 600 because six of its rules contained the number 100.

One hundred teams of birds dropped stones onto a circular one-hundred-metre-wide board drawn out in the arena dust.

The board had one hundred segments of varying size, each with a different points score; the bullseye being the highest—a hundred points.

Teams were allowed one hundred drops and their stones had to be released at an altitude of a hundred metres or more. There was also a points-multiple for speed; the faster you flew, the higher your score.

The number-obsessed Centurians couldn't come up with a quick-fire rule for a tie that included their favourite number, one hundred. If there was a tie, the victor was decided by sudden death single drops.

Birds had argued long and hard about whether to cooperate with humans in the Spellenaria contest. It was horses who had in the end persuaded them to participate.

Centurians had traditionally run horse races at the Spellenaria. The horses were treated well but not many of them enjoyed racing. The birds did enjoy racing, almost without exception, and the disgruntled horses repeatedly begged them to find a way to replace them.

The birds refused until the horses asked them soon after Centurians thought they'd identified magic paths that translated their words into a language birds and other creatures could understand.

The birds decided to play along, but only in this one aspect of Centurian life out of sympathy for the horses.

Communication wasn't necessary for the birds to propose a format for a contest that suited them. They flew across the velocodrome when it was empty, dropping stones in the dust.

Centurians began suggesting rules and the birds complied, leaving people aghast at the effectiveness of their magic.

The birds never used verbal responses or obvious sign language so there were no interactions that looked like a conversation. Their secrets were safe and they revelled in the contest as much as the festival crowd. The horses were, of course, delighted. They immediately stopped following their trainers' instructions and the people of Centurian soon lost interest in horse racing.

Albert and Lorna shared other news—information they'd collected from the chatterati during their dawn updates. It was dominated by speculation around which team of birds would win the Silverrock 600.

Julius boarded Filia's dronibus, which was also buzzing with opinions on the Spellenaria birds. Filia and Julius looked at each other and laughed; the humans were all confidently predicting the peregrine falcons would win. The birds' analysis had been far more sophisticated.

The traffic was horrendous as everyone sped out of town to get to Silverrock. Fortunately, the levitator orderlies were out in force, deducting spell counts from anyone foolish enough to stray into the dronibus lanes and although Filia and Julius arrived after assembly and registration, they made it in time for the school trip.

The Tempo Chorium School of Magic and Music was in no lesser state of frenzied excitement. 'Go falcons!' whooped Fergus Hydren and Grace-Miracle Jones, bounding up to Filia and Julius.

Fergus and Grace were Filia and Julius' closest friends alongside Jonathan. Grace's parents had tried for decades for a child and were so surprised by her arrival that they celebrated the miracle of her birth with their choice of name.

They had also sewn the date she was born into her baby clothes—01 01 1000 AI.

Filia, Julius, Grace, Fergus and Jonathan had all been born in the year 1000 AI, one thousand years after the birth of Illumeter, the god-like figure who'd discovered magic and founded Numberalism.

Grace, however, had the most-sought after date of birth there was, the first day of the second millennium. It was as if Grace's parents had been fated to wait for their child.

'Is Jonathan still locked up in a government facility?' Fergus asked.

'Yep. It's bad,' replied Julius. 'They won't let him out of isolation until they've found the source of his Destructive Interference. Only then can they know whether it's contagious. We're not even allowed to talk to him.'

'Explains why my messages haven't got through,' said Fergus, shaking his head. 'Can't believe Larry Dyers might actually have been right about something.'

The government had instructed Filia, Julius, Presette and Lucius to tell people that Jonathan was in medical isolation and to say that potential contagion was the reason for the precaution.

They had explicitly forbidden them from talking about the government's own version of events—that he'd gone into hiding. The Numberalists didn't want people to think there might be blind spots in their all-seeing infrastructure.

Mizmiq had also insisted that they keep the truth to themselves. It wasn't merely a matter of bird secrets. Speaking to anyone, even family and friends, about the existence of powerful magic outside the grid would only increase the chances of Jonathan being taken away when he returned.

Filia was about to elaborate further when they were interrupted by an out-of-breath voice coming up behind them. 'Filia Wrens, Julius Fog, better late than never,' exclaimed Mr Archaneus, their ancient history and premagic world teacher.

'You've both been docked ten spell counts for missing school without credible explanation.' His voice lowered to a whisper, 'The Plasmatron wanted to double the penalty.'

This was the name everyone used for the head of their school, Mrs Deirdril. To pupils and teachers alike she was a terrifying matriarch, renowned for dealing out punishment freely and with apparent pleasure.

It was widely rumoured that Mrs Deirdril was the Numberalist government's leading candidate for the job of education minister at the next election. She oozed discipline and control and not least because she spied on everyone from her office at the top of the school's central tower; an imposing pillar with windows angled purposefully so she could monitor every inch of the school grounds.

Mr Archaneus pulled Filia and Julius aside, looking up at the control tower before continuing, 'I also successfully negotiated down the punishments relating to school energy-saving on the basis that this has been your first truancy.

'Filia, you will have to put the orchestra instruments away by hand for two days, saving the school a good number of storage spell counts.

'Julius, I'm afraid you've been hit with lugging the entire drum kit in and out of rock, jazz, magic-music theory and big band classes for a week. You'll have to break it down and set it up by hand as well.

'That, however, is the end of it; no other punishments and the case is closed.'

Mr Archaneus' expression changed to wide-eyed glee. 'And what's more, no chores today because we're off to the Spellenaria!'

'Thank you, sir. We're so grateful,' smiled Filia and Julius.

If they'd ended up in different interrogation rooms inside the Plasmatron's tower, they would have been caught lying. The Plasmatron was able to spot inconsistencies in even the most carefully crafted excuses and the penalty for dishonesty was the most feared school punishment of all—zlashings; powerful zaps administered to the palms of the hand.

Zlashings sent pain scurrying up the arms and back down the spine. They were also known as SCIDs—student crucifixions indoors—a phrase Mr Archaneus, a Temporium alum, claimed to have invented.

'Is there time to grab a late breakfast from Professor Harvester?' pleaded Julius.

'Go on then, my lad, and bring one back for me, will you?' smiled Mr Archaneus. Julius set off towards the café in the main courtyard.

'Two vast choccy croissants, please, Professor Harvester,' said Julius after battling his way to the front of a particularly voracious crowd of students.

'Birdside too, Fog?' shouted Professor Percy Harvester, taking orders from at least ten pupils at once.

'Definitely, sir,' answered Julius.

'The right choice, especially on Spellenaria day,' declared the professor who taught creature communication and environmental spellcraft and was delighted when the boys and girls served the birds as well as themselves.

'When you say vast, Fog, do you mean extra-large or even bigger than that—inflated?'

'Extra-large, please, Professor. Spell-enhanced food doesn't really do it for me. Same for the birdside, all natural please.'

Professor Harvester handed over two fabulous choccy croissants and a box of mini-croissantettes. 'For our dearly beloved bird-friends,' he grinned.

'Levitation in two minutes!' cried Mr Archaneus. Julius hurried to the maxi-dronibus and gave Mr Archaneus his croissant.

'Thank you, Fog, I shall enjoy this en route. Poor Jonathan, still very sick I hear. He's going to miss a truly heliogabalactic day.' Julius and Filia nodded in reply as they boarded the bus.

'What the heck is heliogabalactic, Julius?' asked Filia as they sat down.

Julius laughed. 'It's a replacement word for epic. Mr Archaneus told me about it last week. He said epic was far too small a word for a festival like the Spellenaria. It's a corker, don't you think?'

Filia smiled. 'You and he are peas in a pod with your word-smashes and verbal inventions.'

'That we are,' grinned Julius.

Mr Archaneus stood at the front of the dronibus and spoke the magic path of public speaking.

'I'll have your ears now, please, you lucky lot,' he boomed as the bus set off.

His voice carried perfectly throughout his audience of nearly three hundred ecstatic pupils, all of whom were either in their penultimate or final year at the Temporium.

'First up, the only boring part of this trip: the briefing. However, fortunately for you I have prepared an interesting version.

'There are four rules that everyone must follow. One, you cannot donate spell count to enter the wagering system. Yes, I know it's good for the grid, it saves energy, but you're not eighteen, most of you, and those who are know full well that wagering's against the school rules, so don't try it.

'Two. Only use the spell of meeting at the end. It's a costly high-energy spell so you only have one a day, and if you want to get home you'll need it. You won't find me or the maxi-dronibus otherwise. Remember, there'll be two million people at the velocodrome.

'Three, don't lose anyone you don't want to lose because you'll be tempted to cast multiple spells of meeting to locate your friends and find the maxi-dronibus when the festival's over, and what would that mean?'

'Zaps!' everyone yelled at the top of their voices.

'Very good, what a sensible bunch you are. Now, rule four; who's Rod?'

There was a strange mix of silence, murmuring and laughter.

'Go on, have a guess,' grinned Mr Archaneus.

'Actually, forget it, you'll never guess,' he said, a moment later, 'not even you final-year students—Rod wasn't here last year. Besides, I can't wait to introduce him to you. Rod, is, are you ready?'

'Yes!' they screamed.

'Rod, is, you: Raucous Obedient Decorum,' howled Mr Archaneus, throwing his arms in the air. 'Rod is your behaviour and state of mind on this school trip, and don't you forget it. Have fun but follow the rules,' he bellowed triumphantly.

All three hundred pupils stood up and cheered madly.

'And now, quiet please, quiet, thank you, and now my fellow Rodites, it is time to make your selections. Bring me your choice of winning bird-team on a piece of paper and if you can't find the species you're looking for, comb the team lists.

'For example, Team Urban is a hotchpotch of city-dwellers. If you're after a muscular pigeon or another beefed up streetwise avian, then that's the place to look.

'I'll think up some appropriate prize, probably an extra hour of premagic mythology; exactly what's at the top of your desired prize list,' chortled Mr Archaneus.

Filia and Julius had already chosen. She was going for Team Osprey and Julius for Team Urban, hoping to see Albert steal the show.

They strode down the aisle to the front of the dronibus and handed their pieces of paper to Mr Archaneus.

'Ah, good choice, Miss Wrens, wonderful creatures, ossifragus by classification, the bone-eater,' remarked Mr Archaneus. 'And one of the outsiders for you, Mr Fog, another good choice; I think they're long overdue success,' he winked.

'Thank you, sir,' grinned Filia and Julius before making their way back to their seats.

34. The World of Birds
The Spell of All Souls

'We rest here for an hour,' declared Jigsy. 'By my calculation, we're one-third of the way to the Omicron interchange.'

The birds settled down to sleep, nestling together in the curved base of the ancient tubeway, its once-smooth skin now wrinkled and hardened with age.
Warbler and Jigsy were the last two birds to close their eyes and they were moments away from sleep when Warbler heard a slow tapping sound. 'Did you hear that?' he whispered.

'What?' replied Jigsy.

'Tapping. It's an echo. I'm not sure which way it's coming from,' answered Warbler.

Jigsy studied the corridor and nodded.

'Let's move on,' said Warbler.

'Agreed,' sighed Jigsy.

'Wake up, we're not stopping here after all,' announced Jigsy to the exhausted birds. 'I got my calculations wrong. We're not as far as I thought.'

There was grumbling in the flock. 'Jigsy hardly ever admits he's wrong about distance estimates, something must be wrong,' muttered a worried falcon as the nervous troop flew on.

'Everybody hover,' ordered Jigsy after a few hours of silent flight. He and Warbler conferred briefly and when they were satisfied that the noise was no longer there, Jigsy told the birds to get some sleep. 'You can have ninety minutes,' he said.

Jigsy kept watch first, Warbler followed, then Fovea, Machian and others in ten-minute slots.

Eventually it was Jonathan's turn. The only source of light in the otherwise dark, rank stillness was Alea who was clinging tightly to the osprey's ankle.

Tap...tap...

Jonathan spun around. The noise stopped.

He flew a short way along the corridor in the direction of the Omicron interchange and made out the lines of a shadow on the wall.

Jonathan's heart rate immediately slowed as his mind told him to cast a spell of protection and seconds later he'd placed a faint but powerful shield of light across the corridor.

The shadow grew into a human shape and Jonathan was astonished to see a dishevelled old man walking towards him. Jonathan hovered anxiously behind his protective barrier but the man stepped straight through and looked the osprey in the eye whilst resting on a staff.

He gazed down at Alea, then back up at Jonathan and Alea shone more brightly than ever as the man started to smile. 'She's a dear old friend. Where did you find her, young osprey?' he asked.

Before Jonathan could reply, he found himself morphing back into his human form and felt a surface underfoot, the same invisible walkway that the strange haggard man was standing on.

'I'm sorry,' the old man exclaimed. 'I cast a spell of understanding and didn't expect it to return "human". It's gone too far and shown me your original form. Don't worry; I'll keep the platform where it is.'

Jonathan was overwhelmed. He stared at his human self. He was Jonathan Powers for the first time since diving through the lapisphere in his music room. He looked back at the birds, wondering what they might think. They were all asleep.

Alea left Jonathan's ankle and wrapped herself around the old man's wrist, and he leaned to one side, placing his ear next to her.

'Is that right, Alea,' he mused. 'Quite some boy then.'

He lifted his bushy eyebrows and Jonathan felt a new wave of examination moving through him from head to toe.

'I am grateful to you for freeing Alea, Jonathan Powers,' said the old man. 'She's a brave, strong robin but even she would have died in that prison.'

'Wh...what, a robin? When was that, Alea?' gasped Jonathan.

'A good many thousand years ago,' laughed Alea, her circle of light twisting playfully around the old man's arm.

'And that's about how long I've been stuck in this tube,' added the wizened bedraggled man. 'How on earth did you and your friends get in?'

'I managed to repair something called an emergency lapisphere,' Jonathan replied.

'Extraordinary,' grinned the old man. 'This corridor was sealed by a very powerful bird, a bird that didn't want anything flying in or out. You've a mighty fine box of tricks at your disposal, haven't you, young man?'

'I–I guess so, thank you,' answered Jonathan. 'But wait a minute, you said the corridor was sealed by a bird. Why would birds block their own corridors?' asked Jonathan, confused.

'Ah, sounds like the universe is more peaceful than it was. Birds have not always lined up on the same side,' mourned the old man. 'What is your destination?'

'The Omicron interchange, then the Tau 6 chasm, and from there, Eskatar,' said Jonathan.

The old man appeared concerned. 'A chasm you say, on the way to Eskatar. There is much for me to catch up on if we're able to get out, which, come to think of it, we should be able to do.

'If you've reconjured the lapisphere at one end, the likelihood is that the lapisphere at the other end is now working too; they were bound by the same spell.'

The old man chuckled. 'You've rescued me as well as Alea, Jonathan Powers. I will come with you to Eskatar, if that's alright; the air and healing of the Emerald Lands is exactly what I need.'

Jonathan glanced at the birds, then at the mysterious old man. 'I would like you to join us but we have to get there urgently. Why don't I ask my friends if we can carry you, some of the way at least?'

The old man laughed. 'I've a better idea. I should try and grow some wings. I will need help though, I've not taken bird form for who knows how long.'

He placed his fingers in the palms of Jonathan's hands. They were ice-cold and shaking. Jonathan wondered how he'd survived.

A glint of fire sparkled in the old man's eyes. 'Thank you, Jonathan. The spell of rekindling only passes warmth from one life to another if its source has great healing power. You have quite some flame inside you.

'Now, what bird shall I choose? Something small to start with, I know, a little robin, yes, some of my dearest friends were robins, like our magical Alea here.'

'Should I also take my robin form?' asked Alea.

'I think stay as you are for the time being,' smiled the old man. 'Atomhawk spells alone can gift sapphire form and I rather suspect there are none of those great creatures left. The magic of Naumachian would have freed us long ago.'

A tiny robin suddenly fluttered where the old man had been. It landed in Jonathan's palm and he felt more of his rekindling warmth flowing out of his hand and into the bird; the robin almost shone in delight.

Jonathan thought about asking his mind to return his body to osprey form. He hesitated. He wanted to be certain he could conjure the old man's spell and become himself whenever he wished.

'I don't believe you'll have any trouble becoming human again,' winked the old man, as if hearing what he was thinking. 'You are more than capable of the necessary magic.'

Jonathan cast a spell of changing. His transformation into osprey form was instantaneous and he peered down, smiling at Alea who was circling his ankle once more.

When the birds woke from their slumber, they were flabbergasted. How could a robin have lived in the corridor for so long?

'It is yet another miracle,' declared Jigsy, welcoming the robin, 'and there's plenty of time for stories on the way. Everyone ready for the second two-thirds?' he laughed, trying to make a joke out of his earlier miscalculation.

The birds chuckled politely and shot off after their leader who'd already accelerated into the blackness of the ancient expressway.

The robin started fielding questions but he and the birds became distracted by a rapid rise in the corridor's temperature.

The foul air was different too. It was thick with dust that settled in the birds' lungs and they rasped and coughed as they flew. 'I can't breathe properly, my throat's all clogged up,' Squijy sputtered to his father.

'Air-tanks everyone?' suggested Jigsy. There were no objections. 'Slow down a little as well. That'll reduce the amount of oxygen you consume.'

Machian and his squadron of logistics falcons had distributed the largest possible oxygen-tank to each member of the troop at the gamma/delta bird planet, taking account of everyone's size and striking a careful balance between air quantity and speed-sapping weight. All in all, each bird had approximately two hours of air.

Unfortunately for the birds, they soon faced another challenge that oxygen-tanks couldn't solve. The smoky dust began to irritate their eyes and stick to their feathers. Their wings felt like lead and they eventually came to a near standstill.

The old robin sent Jonathan, Alea and Jigsy a message. 'This cannot be. The heat and smouldering ash come from a creature, one I fought hundreds of years ago. I thought it had withered and died. It must have been sleeping in the shadows. I fear it has been woken by the scent of fresh prey.'

Before the robin had a chance to say anything else, a stream of fire spun towards them. Jigsy dived and the flock followed, and the fireball thankfully shot past.

But as soon as they looked up, they saw a burning shadow and the terrifying sight of a vulture in flames.

The creature was vast and its wings were barely able to fit between the corridor walls but that did not stop it from fighting its way towards them at speed.

The firestorm surrounding the vulture quickly engulfed the birds. A few died straightaway, dropping like blazing coals to the corridor floor while others were wounded or killed by the creature's claws as it lashed out inside the inferno.

'Warbler!' screamed Jonathan as he emerged from the flames. The warbler finch was no longer beside him.

Jonathan turned and to his horror saw Warbler vanishing with the creature into the corridor. He'd been caught by the vulture's grasping talons.

'Fly for your lives, everybody. We cannot stay to mourn our friends. The monster will make another pass,' shrieked Qybil.

The petrified birds fled and Jonathan sent a message to the old robin as they flew, 'What is that creature?' he wept.

'It is a demon of the Arc of Darkness. It cannot be defeated with our spells of destruction. I am too weak. Not even a spell of consumption could kill it.'

'What's a spell of consumption?' cried Jonathan, desperate to help Warbler.

'A spell of consumption offers victory even if the battle is a draw, but at the cost of one's own life.

'The spell calls time on the fight by consuming everyone in its circle when it senses neither side is winning.

'It is known as the spell of all souls. No life escapes, if neither side prevails.'

Jonathan was devastated. 'It has Warbler. He was one of my first friends as a bird. I cannot leave him to die.'

'I'm sorry, Jonathan, I am too fragile to cast a spell of consumption. It requires incredible strength.

'I would also be of no use during the fight inside the spell's circle. I would not be able to hold the demon in stalemate even for a moment,' sighed the old robin.

The roar of flames grew louder and with fire came scorching heat. 'Speed up, use the tanks, whatever you need,' yelled Jigsy.

'But if one side wins, then that side survives you say?' choked Jonathan.

'Yes,' replied the robin.

Jonathan decided he had to leave the flock and confront the demon. He might equal its power for a short time and save the birds, or he might conjure a miracle and defeat it.

Tears flowed from Jonathan's eyes. He knew that the most likely outcome was death, and that his journey was almost certainly at an end.

He thought of his parents, Filia, Julius, Fergus, Grace and his other friends and whispered goodbye to each of them in turn, speaking their names and telling them how much he loved them as he wept.

Jonathan looked down and begged Alea to stay with the robin but she refused and pressed herself against his skin.

Jonathan left the birds and prepared to face the demon's fire. As it drew closer, he saw Warbler lying either dead or unconscious in the beast's claws.

'Give me back my friend,' Jonathan cried, his pulse slowing as he conjured an Opening into Twilight.

The vulture laughed, its tongue both dark and red-hot from the ash-laden flames spewing out of its throat, but its expression changed to one of surprise when a circle of glass-light appeared around the osprey. Jonathan knew that he had successfully created a sphere of consumption.

The demon chose to enter the circle and half the sphere instantly blackened and shards of glass-light erupted where the line formed between the two sides.

The temperature rose as the vulture's flames burned inside the circle and Jonathan found himself unable to stop the darkness advancing across his side of the sphere.

The demon taunted him, 'You chose the wrong spell, osprey. You cannot match my power. It is time, yesss, I sense the fear in your soul, and you feel it too, don't you, osprey?' hissed the creature.

Jonathan cried in anguish. There were no spells he could conjure to slow the demon's progress but as he bowed his head he saw Alea slip away from his ankle without the vulture appearing to notice; the flames seemed to conceal the sapphire light, but not touch her.

Alea made her way towards Warbler and into his mouth. Warbler started to move. His eyes opened and he glared up at the hellfires inside the vulture's heart.

White light shot from Warbler's beak and pierced the demon. It screamed and Jonathan's side of the sphere gained ground, but the vulture quickly recovered and held the line of contention at the halfway mark.

Warbler struck the demon again and again and Jonathan poured all his strength into the spell of consumption.

The vulture raged and burned as it defended itself but the line stayed where it was and moments later the sphere imploded.

Glass-light, flame, smoke and fire consumed them all. Warbler and Alea's intervention had been enough to create the tension and pressure needed to trigger the spell. But there had been no victory, only death.

35. Opus-Earth

A New Life

Rose perched on the hospital windowsill, one eye on Florence, the other on the London night sky.

After telling Lord Agnostus that Filia, Julius, Albert and Lorna were somehow able to talk to one another the Chief Justice had asked her to visit Jonathan Prior again. Rose had reluctantly agreed, calculating that she would just about be able to catch up with the birds before they reached the Tau 6 chasm.

Agnostus had concluded, like Rose, that an unknown magical force must have existed in Jonathan Prior or surrounded him in some way. Albert and Lorna were proof of it. There was no other explanation for why Filia and Julius were only able to hear the two Battersea Park pigeons.

The Chief Justice was also convinced that if this mysterious magical power was still present in Jonathan Prior it might be the reason why his raft had returned to the Opus souls' embarkation point. It was imperative that Rose examine his body again; this time for signs of magic, not lingering threads of life.

Rose gripped the window ledge, frustrated and ready to give up. She'd spent hours searching for magical notes. There was nothing, only silence.

Rose sent a message to Gardencrates, the inquisitive starling who'd attended her Christmas lecture and who had asked Jaden and Enchoir a string of probing questions about human eternity.

Gardencrates had been so inspired by Rose, Jaden and Enchoir's revelations that he'd decided to become London's foremost expert on eternal consciousness edge cases.

Comas were clearly an area that could benefit from further study and Gardencrates was observing a patient on life support in another ward when he received Rose's message.

The starling opened the tiny parcel of air and read the robin's words with sadness: 'I must leave at sunrise if I am to join the osprey before he arrives at the chasm.'

Gardencrates flew to the window where Rose was watching Florence. 'Is there still no hope for her?' he asked.

Tears welled in Rose's eyes. 'I don't think so. I have drawn so much from Twilight but my spells of healing will not last and she is determined to die.'

'I will remain here, with her, until the end,' choked Gardencrates.

As Rose and Gardencrates wept for Florence, a doctor hurried into the room and the two birds listened intently to what he had to say.

'I've just been looking at the latest blood test results, Mrs Prior, and I have some wonderful news. You are pregnant,' exclaimed the doctor. 'We must have missed it in previous tests. I've no idea how. I'm so sorry for our mistake but I can tell you with absolute confidence that it is there, I mean he or she, or rather the beginnings of he or she. We are certain,' he beamed.

Rose and Gardencrates nearly fell off the windowsill and when Rose cast a spell of understanding she cried with joy and astonishment at its answer. The doctor was right. Florence was pregnant.

Rose really was utterly dumbfounded. Birds did not believe they possessed the magical power to create new life. Their greatest magic was the onward journey of human souls after death.

Either it was indeed possible to draw enough strength from Twilight to create new life or this was another example of their invisible power transcending known magical boundaries. Rose's first thought was that the latter was probably more likely.

Gardencrates was as blown away as Rose, but unlike her, he was all but certain that the pregnancy was Rose's doing. The most powerful bird he'd ever met had discovered a new dimension to Candela Lumen power and he had been the first bird to witness it.

Florence spent the next hour asking questions in total disbelief while Rose and Gardencrates listened as she and the doctor talked.

Florence, at one point, asked for food and water and Rose and Gardencrates could barely hide their glee at the sight of her looking after herself again.

'I must rest now,' Florence mumbled to the doctor when she could no longer find the strength for further questions, 'and do not to tell my husband of this, please. I need some time to think.'

Florence stared at Jonathan and wept. Nothing could console her in her guilt. She was also frightened, wondering how she would cope, and she thought about giving up again and fasting once more so she could be with Jonathan.

Florence touched her womb and cried for the life that was growing inside her. 'No, I must go on,' she sobbed. 'I will do all I can to care for this child.'

Florence prayed for the first time since holding Jonathan after his accident. 'Thank you, God, thank you for this miracle. I think I understand. You cannot save Jonathan but you wish to help me. You forgive me, and have offered me this child so I might cherish my life once more. Thank you, thank you for loving me,' she wept.

Rose and Gardencrates punched the air with their wings. 'Florence will live, Gardencrates, she will live,' proclaimed Rose. 'Look after her and I will return as soon as I can.'

Gardencrates nodded and rejoiced as Rose flew down to the hospital car park, darted under a bush and conjured a lapisphere into Opus-Earth's estuary corridors.

36.   The World of Birds

Rejoining the Flock

Rose used all her magical power to speed her flight and she did not rest until she reached the messaging cluster in the Epsilon Gamma superhighway where she'd picked up Mizmiq's news of Filia and Julius' friendship with Albert and Lorna.

Rose added a new message to the thousands of air parcels that floated near the tubeway wall right before the entrance to the gamma/delta corridor; a message to Elgarian, asking the lord of eagles to speak to Agnostus about what had happened on Opus so she could hurry on and catch up with Jonathan.

The little robin then plunged into the gamma/delta corridor and arrived at the bird planet a few hours later.

She made straight for the kernel's sumptuous turf and while she ate and drank, the birds told her about the Skull attack and how Jonathan had saved Squijy's life.

Scipio, the jacana stationmaster, spotted her and flew across. 'Rose, you should know that Jigsy was eager to shorten the journey by taking the ancient Omicron expressway.'

'But it is not possible to enter that corridor,' Rose responded.

'Perhaps they found a way in with the osprey's help,' Scipio smiled.

Rose sighed. 'Even if they did, I think the foul air may have forced them back. Nevertheless, my next stop will be the Omicron expressway. Thank you, Scipio.'

Rose made herself a sack of food and water and set off towards one of the bubble's exits.

She careered along the gamma corridors at many times the speed of Jigsy's troop and when she arrived at the expressway lapisphere, she hurtled through without stopping to wonder how it had appeared.

The spell of consumption had left a trail of echoes that crashed up and down the corridor and Rose made out the cries of dying birds inside the sound and her heart filled with dread as she flew further into the ancient tubeway.

Rose hovered when she came to the place where the spell had imploded. The walls were charred with smoke and ash and the bodies of those who'd died trying to escape the demon lay blackened and petrified in the corridor folds.

Rose knew what she was looking at: the destruction and remains of Arcan fire. She flew on, weeping and fearing the worst.

After several more hours of high-speed flight, she saw the troop. Her heart raced. They were exhausted and flying slowly, but a good number seemed to have survived.

Rose was surprised to see an old robin at the rear of the flock. She cast a spell of understanding and was overjoyed when it returned "grandmaster".

The old robin looked back, sensing her spell. 'Dear Rose!' he exclaimed in delight, leaving the birds to fly ahead.

Rose stared at him, trying to place his voice. Then it came to her. 'Nomadiq?'

'Yes, Rose, yes, missing for thousands of years, locked away in this corridor, but now free!'

The two robins dived and weaved around each other, celebrating with every turn.

'Are the young grandmasters doing a good job keeping an eye on things?' grinned the old robin.

'Ah yes, a very good job,' laughed Rose.

'I always thought they would,' mused the robin. 'Fine pedigree,' he winked.

As they caught up with the flock, Rose searched for Jonathan. 'I don't see the osprey. There was a young osprey who joined the troop, Nomadiq. Where is he?'

The old robin bowed his head. 'He is no more, Rose. He fought a demon of the Arc of Darkness. He cast a spell of consumption and battled so valiantly. The spell took them both.'

Tears flowed from Rose's eyes as she mourned Jonathan. The grandmaster also told her about the discovery and loss of Alea. Rose was beside herself. The sapphire light had been one of her dearest friends.

'We must carry on, Rose, and ask the priestesses to help us confront the growing might of our enemy. I have learnt much from these birds and I am worried about the Skulls' resurgence.' Rose nodded and the flock was heartened greatly by her arrival.

The air quality started to improve and the birds were able to fly faster. They were silent as they sped on. Their grief was terrible, and not least for Jonathan.

The osprey had been so much more than a friend; he had saved them and he'd been a saviour whose magic they had only begun to know.

Jigsy eventually asked the flock to sing the birdsong lament for Jonathan, Warbler, Alea and the other friends they'd lost.

The opening words of the requiem were always sung by a bird of paradise and a dazzling peacock-plumed exemplum of the species flew next to Jigsy.

The bird of paradise sang her solo, the sorrow of the deceased as they travelled to Nihilimb, the place birds believed they went when they died.

The flock then launched themselves into the requiem's first choral movement and the power of their voices in unison lifted their spirits, reminding them of the strength of their companionship. The passing of Jonathan, Warbler, Alea and their other dear friends would not be in vain.

Squigbox flew to the front after the lament and began singing "The Journey". Minim went with him and comforted her husband as they sang.

Every bird in the flock joined in, and Squigbox missed Jonathan more and more with each phrase and sound. Their passion for magic-music had brought them together so quickly and the jabiru's cheeks flooded with tears as he remembered how much alike he and Jonathan had been.

'Minim, we must never forget how fortunate we are,' he wept, looking back and following the echoes of their final notes into the gloom.

Squigbox started singing the song again but paused during a flurry of notes at the top of his range and turned to his father. 'Have you noticed it too? I think we should slow down.'

'What, son, what?' said Jigsy. 'We need to keep moving.'

'The air. It's thinning, I can't hit the high notes as easily as beeeeefoooooorrrrr,' sang Squigbox, illustrating his point.

'You all okay?' bellowed Jigsy to the troop, 'Squigbox is wondering if the air is thinning.'

'We think we're okay,' everyone shouted back.

Moments later, Fovea announced that they were approaching a wall across the corridor. 'It's the end of the expressway!' declared Jigsy. 'Look, a perfectly intact emergency exit awaits us.'

While the lapisphere appeared to be in good condition, there were perforations in the wall and the corridor was leaking air.

'There was a change in the air after all; well spotted, Squigbox,' grinned Jigsy.

The jabiru leader addressed his flock, 'Now, my friends, you will experience the greatest of the old marketplaces, the Omicron interchange. Not a bird planet, too small for that, but an original ancient corridor junction.'

The birds shot into the lapisphere circle one at a time. Jigsy waited with his sons until everyone else had dived through. 'I visited the Omicron interchange once when I was about half your age, Squijy.

'It was full of birds reconstructing the market stalls exactly as they used to be. I got lost in the crowd and had to be summoned over the airwaves, really embarrassed my mum and dad in the process. Ha!

'Here we go lads, our turn,' he signalled.

They swooped towards the lapisphere circle and emerged safely on the other side but what they found horrified them.

There were gaping holes in almost every part of the bubble's skin and tens of thousands of dead birds were floating inside the sphere. The old marketplace had been destroyed by Skull diaminds.

'These birds died recently, their wounds are fresh,' wept Jigsy.

'Does this mean the Skulls now have the firepower to break a bird planet?' asked Squijy. He'd said what was on everyone's minds.

'No, son, never,' howled Jigsy angrily.

'We must use our tanks and move on,' said Machian stoically. 'There is no time to gather the corpses or lament the dead with birdsong. We risk being seen.'

The flock wept for the massacred birds and mourned the destruction of an irreplaceable part of their past as they glided to the once magnificent eastern corridor opening.

'It has been sealed,' cried Fovea who was flying at the front. 'The birds must have shut it off to keep the Skulls out of the corridors.'

'I can cut into the tubeway wall nearby and weave the skin together again,' said Rose. The birds were speechless. They didn't know it was possible for any single bird to break into the corridor network and then repair the damage and they watched with gaping beaks as the robin cast spell after spell until the threads began to tear.

The embattled troop dived inside and a welcome breeze touched their weary faces. Rose spun new threads across the transcendent tubeway wall and when the corridor had finally closed behind them the birds wept with relief. They were safer than they had been for a long while.

Jigsy gave the shattered flock a minute to breathe in the refreshing corridor air before speaking to them again. 'There will be no respite, I'm afraid. We must fly straight to the Tau 6 chasm.'

The courageous birds knew the need for urgency was greater than ever and not one of them questioned their leader as they shot after him into the Omicron corridor.

37.   A Place Between Life and Death

Twilight

Jonathan drifted. He was not far from the ancient expressway and could see the old robin and the band of birds. 'Hey!' he cried out. 'I'm here!'

There was no response.

He kept calling their names, and when he saw Rose catching up with them he yelled with joy, but even the powerful robin was oblivious to his cries.

'They cannot hear you, osprey,' said a voice, softly. 'You are with us, the stars. You are in the place the living call Twilight.'

Jonathan looked about. He couldn't see anyone, only the glittering galaxies. 'Am I dead?' he wept.

'No. There is life, death and inbetween. Inbetween is where you are,' replied the voice. 'Almost all birds, humans and other creatures exist in their own particular realms of life and death, but occasionally one joins us here in Twilight.'

'Wh–why me?' asked Jonathan.

'Because you died in Twilight, inside your spell. Those who die in Twilight do not pass on to death until their time inbetween has come to an end.'

'Can I not conjure an Opening back to the living world, and return to my friends?' said Jonathan.

'No. You cannot go back. You are no longer alive,' replied the voice. 'It is true that living creatures enter Twilight briefly through their Openings but they are only here for the duration of their spells.'

'Then can I at least talk to my friends?' pleaded Jonathan desperately.

'That too is not possible. The living see us, the stars, and we also watch them, but no form of communication can pass between us. We share the same universe but we exist in very different places.'

'Then which star are you, please?' wept Jonathan, losing sight of Rose, the old robin and the flock.

'The living call me Pleione and I have chosen that name for myself. I sit in the constellation you birds, humans, Skulls and other creatures call the Pleiades.'

Jonathan sobbed as the birds disappeared into darkness. 'My name is Jonathan Powers. I am from Centurian, and that is where I belong.'

'I'm sorry, Jonathan, but that is no longer who you are, and Centurian is no longer where you belong. You will shortly become a star, either a new star, or you may join yourself to one of us. You are in Twilight and although you retain your memories, you have in fact begun a new existence and it is my role to welcome you.'

Jonathan was inconsolable. 'Do you know if my friend Warbler Finch came here? Or the sapphire light, Alea? They were inside the same spell of consumption.'

'Warbler Finch, yes. The sapphire light, no. I expect she passed on to death with the vulture. The Arc of Darkness often takes its own creatures straight to its realm even if they are destroyed in Twilight. We prefer it that way too.

'The Arc's demons also do all in their power to carry the conscious souls of others with them. Such will have been the sapphire light's fate, and I doubt it is something we could have stopped.'

'Then may I speak with Warbler?' cried Jonathan.

'Once you have chosen a star name,' answered Pleione. 'Warbler was quick to select a name when we told him he'd be able to speak with you after he'd chosen and he found a perfect match; Gamma Cassiopeiae.

'He said Gamma was home to his favourite bird planet and Cassiopeia, the constellation where his star sits, was the name of a young finch he'd once loved, but lost. And not only that, Cassiopeia, as you will know, is a "W" shape. I expect you'll want to be part of a "J"?'

Jonathan did not reply. He simply wept in silence.

'We will do all we can to find something that is right for you, Jonathan,' continued Pleione. 'It is common for beings to ask for a representation of their former selves when they enter Twilight. We understand that parting with who you were, while you still have memory, is not easy.'

Jonathan was completely crushed. He realised that he was not going back. The spell of consumption had indeed been the end of his journey.

Tears poured from his eyes, and he sensed Pleione weeping too. 'This is the worst part,' she whispered gently. 'I have welcomed so many who, understandably, do not want to stay.

'Please, look to your right, Jonathan, and you will see a place where we turn the tears of new arrivals into stars.'

Jonathan gazed across the universe and saw a myriad of shining lights. 'I know those stars,' he cried.

'Yes; some humans call them the Milky Way,' said Pleione, 'but their Twilight name is the galaxy of tears.

'Things will get better after you choose your star name, Jonathan. Most come to accept that they cannot go back or influence the lives of those they've left behind,' sighed Pleione.

Jonathan wept and wept, picturing his mother and father, Filia, Julius, Fergus, Grace, and his other friends. He would never hold them or speak to them again.

'I would,' he sobbed, 'like to ask for my own sign in the stars, if it is possible; an FJ with an exclamation mark, please. My friends and I created a magic-music constellation that had such a shape.'

'I can see the pattern in your thoughts,' said Pleione, 'and what you wish for will, I think, be possible.

'Please also choose a star name; your conscious mind will sit within one of the stars in your constellation. Your star name is what you, I and other entities in Twilight will use when we strike up a conversation, and I'm afraid the name must be different from the name you had in the living world. Remember, you have begun a new existence.'

'I can't even begin to think about a name right now,' choked Jonathan. 'Please will you give me some time to decide?'

'Yes, of course. You will be here a long while so it is important to be comfortable with your choice,' answered Pleione, leaving Jonathan to think and drift.

38.   Centurian

The Dictionary of Magic

Filia sat daydreaming on the maxi-dronibus, imagining the Spellenaria ospreys whisking her away after the festival so she could be with Jonathan.

'Hey,' said Grace. 'You too, Julius, listen up. You both missed an unbelievable triple Spellology lesson on the origins of magic. Mr Archaneus also gave us our copies of Calculus Agrippina's Dictionary of Magic and I've got yours in my bag; here you go.'

Filia and Julius clutched the fabled books, the first written list of spells and their magic paths. Students received a copy in the school year they turned sixteen as part of the Spellenaria celebrations and their names were inscribed on the inside front cover next to the signature of the serving Calculus.

'At the end of the lesson Mr Archaneus announced that he had organised a private viewing of the actual dictionary in a few weeks' time,' smiled Grace. 'And he's pulled some serious strings,' added Fergus. 'The chief librarian will be there, turning the pages with spells of reading.'

'No way,' gasped Julius, 'we get to look inside the holy of holies?'

'Yep,' nodded Fergus.

Filia opened her copy, staring in awe at the magical tome. 'Thank you, Grace. It's beautiful.'

'The seventeen and over paths are greyed out just in case we're tempted to get ahead of ourselves,' laughed Fergus.

'You'd never do that, would you, Fergus? Learn a few of your older brother's brewing spells?' winked Julius.

Mr Archaneus yelled 'RAMP!', interrupting their conversation. They held tight as the maxi-dronibus veered upwards suddenly, then shot forward and back down again.

'There'll be more of those, so watch out,' warned Mr Archaneus. 'We're in an area where the government has introduced new crossovers so levitators can pass above and below each other at right angles without braking. No more four-way stops or roundabout delays. Hooray!'

Filia released her grip on the seat in front and began flicking through her dictionary.

'The index has a spell-enhanced filter,' enthused Grace. 'You can view Agrippina's original list on its own or the later spell additions, or both. You can also see how count allowances for age groups have changed over time.'

'It says you can search by profession too,' exclaimed Julius. 'Arrest, arrest when faced with resistance, stopping a suspect from using magic—the descriptions are superb, even though the paths are greyed out. Maybe I'll ditch engineering and go for a career in law enforcement after all.'

'No, absolutely not,' cried Grace. 'You'd be even more of a liability than you're going to be anyway with your intertonics.'

'Interwhatsits?' blurted Julius.

'Intertonics, you've never drunk one?' grinned Fergus.

'No, you never offered me one,' roared Julius. 'Grace, put me out of my misery,' he demanded.

'Intertonics is Mr Archaneus' newly invented word for spells conjured by computer automation. It's his replacement word for multiples,' laughed Grace.

Julius searched excitedly for the filter that listed computerised spells.

'You won't find any intertonics in these books I'm afraid. Mr Archaneus said that the government thinks they'd make the book too unlike the original,' explained Grace.

'That sounds like an excuse for hiding the truly supersonic spells,' grinned Julius. 'Even though engineering didn't exist way back when, computerised spells should be added. It's a spell-enhanced dictionary, for goodness' sake!'

'Can't you ask Jonathan's mother for a list?' winked Grace, knowing the answer would be "no". What happened inside engineering stayed inside.

'Which reminds me, here's Jonathan's copy, Filia,' said Grace. 'You okay to give it to his parents on your way home? I hope they'll be allowed to send it to him at least.'

Filia held the book tight and her mind wandered again. 'Filia?' repeated Grace.

'Yes, of course, I'll give it to his parents,' she replied, staring blankly at the front cover as Mr Archaneus shouted 'RAMP!' and everyone looked out of the window.

Filia turned back to Grace. 'Did Mr Archaneus say anything about the development of concept spells? You remember he talked about a spell of hope the last time he mentioned the subject?'

'Yes, he's not sure concepts will ever be transformed into magic,' said Grace. 'He told us he's becoming more and more convinced that spell outcomes need to be specific for sound to exist in the frequency band of magic.'

'What if there was another magical band that catered for such spells?' Filia wondered.

'You mean an entirely different spectrum?' said Grace.

'Yes,' smiled Filia. 'Illumeter discovered magic once, so maybe we can find it twice? The possibility of the impossible?'

They were interrupted again by Mr Archaneus but this time it was to announce their arrival: 'The velocodrome!' he cried.

Everybody jumped out of their seats and the maxi-dronibus shook with excitement as Silverrock came into view.

'And there is the Velossos!' declared Mr Archaneus, pointing at a brightly coloured statue of a peregrine falcon standing over one of the entranceways to the velocodrome. It must have been several hundred metres tall.

'Look at it, students of the Temporium, the Velossos of Silverrock, the ultimate icon of avian athleticism,' proclaimed Mr Archaneus, enthralled by the imposing splendour of the famous falcon, the only bird ever to have made one hundred consecutive hundred point drops at a speed of more than a hundred miles per hour and the reason the contest's highest scoring bird was given the title "velossos".

They descended through the most chaotic traffic they'd ever seen and disembarked. Mr Archaneus then led everyone up a maze of steps and they eventually entered the stadium at the three hundred and ninety-third level.

It was a fairy-tale world. The magnificent statues of past winners towered over the velocodrome, their marble talons clinging to the arched passageways above the topmost rows of seats.

Filia, Julius, Grace and Fergus gazed across the stadium, struggling to take it all in. Two million people were pouring into the giant oval and the noise was deafening as the crowd cheered wildly in the build-up to the contest. They could not have imagined a greater spectacle.

39.   The World of Birds

The Lifeless Corridor

Jigsy and Rose had led the troop through the corridors and bird planets between Omicron and Tau. They had stopped just once and that was only to refill their tanks and sacks. They were now entering the Tau 6 corridor, the final part of their journey to the chasm.

Every bird they'd passed had been stricken with fear, their watchful eyes scouring the darkness of space for the next Skull attack and the only birds daring to venture through the air planet hatches had been the duckbills and the brave volunteers guarding them.

As Jigsy's troop shot along the Tau 6 corridor, Rose cast powerful spells of opening that let them fly through the thickly woven skin that stretched between the walls of the tubeway at regular intervals.

Skulls had tried many times to enter the Tau 6 corridor via the chasm. These protective layers had so far prevented them and Rose sealed each one carefully as soon as they darted through.

After several hours navigating the defensive barriers in the deserted corridor, Jigsy ordered Squigbox out in front. 'Tell us when the air thins, son. It will indicate that the chasm is near and we'll believe you this time,' he smiled. 'You're in charge now, my lad, briefly. We'll slow down on your signal. The Skulls must not see us.'

The jabiru's heart raced as he felt the weight of responsibility on his youthful shoulders. He was leading his father, brothers and some of the most experienced bird folk in the universe towards a place of extreme danger and it was his job to make sure they weren't spotted.

Minim smiled with pride as Squigbox whispered his highest notes to help him detect any thinning air and after a short period of nervous flight Rose and Nomadiq suddenly flew next to him. 'I felt something too,' said Squigbox, sending one more whisper into the air. 'Yes, we are close.'

Squigbox gave his father the nod and Jigsy pointed to his tank so the flock would be ready to use their oxygen if they had to.

After a few minutes of silent gliding, the birds caught a glimpse of the severed tubeway opening and there was no sign of Skull ships.

They flew, slowly, to within metres of where the corridor ended and its torn silver threads trailed off into the emptiness of space. 'I can't see the other side,' Fovea gasped, staring into the distance.

'Look down, not across,' said Rose. 'Be careful though. If you fly beyond the edge, you'll need a lot of oxygen to power your way back,' she warned.

'You know this place well,' said Jigsy.

'I do, my friend,' sighed Rose. 'I come as often as I can, to mourn the moment all was lost and to wonder what more we could have done.'

'You were here when it happened?' gulped Jigsy.

'Yes, I battled the Skull ships that tore the corridor threads and the demons that were sent to aid them.

'It broke my heart. Not even the priestesses could stop the enemy, and it was here, in this very spot that we were forced to wave farewell to the angels of Eskatar.'

Rose surveyed the chasm and became tearful and concerned. 'The Tau 7 side is farther than I expected,' she muttered. 'The Arc's poison is destroying the weave at an ever faster rate.'

The birds immediately went to work, knowing the Skull ships would come.

They cast spells of traction across the void that would bring the flailing threads of the Tau 7 corridor closer. The birds had to reduce their flying time in open space to no more than a few hours so they wouldn't run out of oxygen. A few of them would then risk crossing the chasm and try to reach the nearest thread without being seen.

Bridging spells could then be conjured from both sides, each spell only needing to stretch halfway. The smallest of air-tight tubeways would be enough to give the remaining birds a transcendent path across the void—a flight that would take only minutes, perhaps seconds.

Rose bowed her head in despair; the Tau 7 threads were not responding to her, or the other birds' spells of traction. 'It is useless,' she groaned. 'The strands have lost all their transcendent magic. The air in the Tau 7 corridor must be cold, lifeless. Arcan corrosion has devastated the weave.'

'I will go,' offered Nomadiq. 'And if the Tau 7 threads do not answer my spells as I fly I will glide on to the corridor opening.'

There was silence. The birds knew such a long flight was suicidal; the falcons had calculated the odds.

Jigsy opened his beak to object, but Nomadiq had set off before he or anyone else could challenge him. 'The grandmaster's strength is growing,' smiled Rose, marvelling at the fluttering robin.

The gamma/delta troop stared at the tiny bird, hoping he would somehow survive, and as Nomadiq flew further into the gloom the birds were shocked and overjoyed to see his shape changing. He was getting bigger, much bigger; even though he was already some distance away.

Rose beamed in delight. 'Grandmaster Nomadiq used to come and go in many forms,' she grinned. 'Last time I saw him, thousands of years ago, he was a hawk, and a mighty fine one too.'

40. Twilight

Stars Gazing

'Pleione, are you there?' cried Jonathan as he searched for her constellation in the horizons of starry space. 'Please, is there any way I can watch the birds again while I choose my star name?'

Pleione replied straightaway, 'We would normally wait until a new arrival has chosen a name before allowing them to gaze. However, I want to do all I can to help you and will be happy to let you look upon your friends for a short time.'

'Thank you, thank you,' answered Jonathan. 'How can I see them please?'

'We stars use each other's locations to observe the living world. My eyes, and those of others, are yours as it were. Tell me where your friends might be and I will find the nearest star.'

'I think we will find them at the Tau 6 chasm,' Jonathan replied and moments later he was looking at the birds hovering at the edge of the Tau 6 corridor.

'Rose!' Jonathan yelled, but the robin did not hear him, and no matter how much he shouted to his friends there was not even a hint of them noticing him.

Jonathan saw a great hawk gliding across the void. He didn't recognise the bird but cried out to it anyway. There was no response.

Jonathan wept and he eventually lost sight of the birds again. 'I'm sorry, Jonathan,' sighed Pleione in her gentle mournful voice.

'I would like to look somewhere else, please,' sobbed Jonathan.

'I am reluctant to allow that. I must ask you to choose a star name first,' said Pleione. 'Every being that joins the Twilight realm comes with new light; a light that is shared across the stars, contributing to the brightness and longevity of us all.

'You see, Jonathan, you bring far more than your conscious mind to our world.'

'Then take whatever I have and let me go,' begged Jonathan.

'Alas; light cannot be shared in limbo—our name for the place where you now reside,' answered Pleione.

Jonathan cried and cried and Pleione was silent for while, pitying him as she listened to his tears. 'There is another way,' she said finally, 'another way to be close to the living. Creatures touch Twilight when they dream and we are able to join the worlds they imagine. I will permit this once, in the hope that a little of what is to come will help you look forward, rather than back.'

'Th–thank you, Pleione. How do I join my friend's dream? She is human, and she's from my home planet, Centurian,' wept Jonathan.

'Then your passage into her mind will be through her host planet—you must speak to Centurian.'

Jonathan gasped. 'Planets also exist in Twilight?' he cried.

'Yes: planets, moons, and all the other entities of space,' replied Pleione.

Jonathan was speechless and it wasn't long before he heard another voice. 'Hello, Jonathan, welcome to Twilight, I am Centurian.'

He was totally dumbstruck; he was talking to his home planet. 'H–h–hello,' he fumbled.

'Who is it you are looking for?' said the voice of Centurian.

'F–Filia Wrens, please.'

'Can you be more precise?'

'Bushley Park, south Geocentrian, thank you.'

There was a short pause. 'I have found her and she appears to dream regularly so you have a good chance of joining her soon. The gateway into her mind is now open for you.'

Jonathan instantly heard something, it was breathing, and he somehow knew it was Filia even though he couldn't see her or hear her voice.

'The connection that you are experiencing will tell you when she enters a dreaming state because you will see the images her mind creates,' explained Pleione.

'If the connection is lost, which can happen, Centurian will let you know when she begins to dream.'

'Can I listen to her, to what she's saying, while I wait?' cried Jonathan.

'The gateway has no other power or purpose, I'm afraid,' answered Pleione. 'It cannot bring you closer to her in any other way.'

'Then will I be able to talk to her when I'm inside her dream?'

'No. You will be as she remembers you, not as you are now, nor as you might wish to portray yourself.

'You will, however, feel as though you are with her; you will see what she sees. You will also find it possible to influence the dream sequence and show her things or take her to places in her dream if she chooses to follow. I hope her dream brings you great happiness,' said Pleione softly.

Jonathan was lost for words. He wondered what Filia's dream would be and he couldn't even begin to comprehend what the experience of joining her dream might be like.

41. Centurian

Testing Conditions at Silverrock

Harriers, falcons, swans, swallows and many other species cruised above the one-hundred-segment velocodrome board, analysing wind patterns in microscopic detail.

Filia's fabulous ospreys were among them. So too was Albert and the other city dwellers of Team Urban.

The birds cast spells of noise cancellation to block out the roar of the crowd and help them identify the most volatile pockets of air. This was their last opportunity to evaluate what appeared to be unusually windy conditions before the contest began.

Tortriq, the Calculus' special adviser on magic, was talking animatedly to the Numberalist leader in the government box while Mizmiq and Sporadiq circled high above them, listening to their conversation. Tortriq had so far not managed to discover the true purpose of the engineers' explosives.

The Calculus was interrupted by an official who indicated it was time to announce the start of the great avian game and Augustus VIII stepped forward and greeted the two million hysterical Centurians standing on their marble seats inside the stadium.

'Welcome to the velocodrome, the arena of speed, precision and celebration!' he declared. 'Today, we honour extraordinary skill and great sacrifice.'

The Calculus pointed to a hundred men and women who were sitting nearby. They were the Centurians who'd used the least magical energy over the past year. Some had foregone their entire spell allowance for weeks at a time and they basked in the adoration of the spell-crazed crowd while Augustus recounted examples of their incredible abstinence.

When the Calculus had finished, the master of ceremonies cast the spell of commentary and each bird-team's wager tally materialised in mid-air above the giant oval.

Wagers were placed by donating part of your spell count at one of the thousands of gifting terminals situated in the stadium's shaded walkways.

The government paid out far fewer spells in prizes than it took in wagers. That, coupled with wagering's popularity, meant the system reduced overall spell count significantly and wagering had come to be lauded as an important part of the government's efforts to conserve the scarce natural resources that powered the planet's spell-casting infrastructure.

Those who picked the winning team did however share a large prize pool, adding hundreds, sometimes thousands of spells to their annual allowance.

Some donated these spells to the government. Those who didn't were expected to carry out many good deeds with their increased spell allowance and were obliged to give an account of their benevolence on the morning of the following year's festival. Exaggeration and references to the underachievement of past winners were commonplace and Mr Archaneus had told the Tempo Chorium students that this was one part of the festival they could afford to miss.

Albert sent Filia and Julius a message from the dugout. 'I'm in, I'm taking part, I'm no longer on standby. The first and second choice pigeons are both sick, a batch of dodgy fodder in the camp, can you believe it?'

'Go Albert!' replied Filia and Julius, delighted at his good fortune.

'I hope he's alright up there,' added Lorna; 'some of the birds are predicting a summer storm.'

Albert laughed. 'I keep telling her that testing conditions will make it a game of chance as well as one of skill, and that's going to suit an oversized amateur scavenger like me,' he chuckled.

Filia and Julius wished him well as the first bird left the dugout carrying its dropping stone in one of the specially designed Spellenaria pouches.

The master of ceremonies cast a spell of projection and the birds' scores were displayed across the sky. The crowd, however, was not happy; swirling clouds were obscuring not only the scores but other crucial in-game wagering information such as which bird was dropping and its past performance. The poor master of ceremonies tried all his usual tricks but was unable to fix the problem and the grumbling continued.

At the halfway point, there was an intermission. Albert had done far better than expected with an average score of ninety-two and he messaged Filia and Julius to tell them he'd been selected to fly again in the second half.

Filia hurried off to get a drink from one of the stalls in the velocodrome's vaulted passageways, excited for Albert and eager not to miss his next drop, but her heart sank when she joined the queue. Not far ahead of her was Lucius, Jonathan's father.

Filia apologised to the people in front of her and Lucius hugged her tightly when she reached him. 'They're keeping Presette locked up and under interrogation until they find Jonathan,' he wept. Filia gripped his shaking arms and cried with him for Presette.

The gong went for the beginning of the second half and they moved to one side of the passageway to let people past. Lucius clenched Filia's hand and stared at the Centurian sky through one of the narrow-sighted vaults. 'I'll see you soon, with Jonathan,' was all he could say as the tears poured from his eyes.

'Yes, soon,' Filia wept and they embraced once more before making their separate ways back to their seats.

As Filia stepped carefully around the other people in her row, there was an announcement, 'Due to poor weather, the second half is delayed.'

The crowd became agitated, then angry as news spread of what was going on in the dugout; the birds were refusing to fly.

'I'm going to demand my spells back,' snapped one man.

'What a mess,' remarked another.

'You should leave your spells where they are as charity for the grid unless you've really gone for it,' said someone else.

Filia sent a message to Albert and Lorna asking them what was happening.

'The wind is so strong the birds are worried they'll hit someone in the crowd,' Lorna explained. 'And what's more, the Aquilae, prescient eagles, are saying it'll get worse. Everyone's panicking. Hang on, there's another meeting. I'll send you an update shortly.'

Filia sat down next to Julius, Grace and Fergus and they watched in astonishment as all the birds suddenly left the dugout and careered off towards a gathering mass of storm clouds.

Filia and Julius messaged Albert and Lorna, but it was Mizmiq who answered. 'Get out of the stadium,' shouted the grandmaster. 'This is much more than freak weather. I may not be able to message you for some time; the same will be true for Albert and Lorna.'

Filia and Julius stood up immediately and went over to Mr Archaneus. 'It doesn't look like they're coming back, sir. Shouldn't we leave now to beat the rush?'

'I was thinking the same thing,' sighed Mr Archaneus. 'Listen to me, everybody, there's little chance of the contest resuming. Make your way to the maxi-dronibus,' he yelled.

Mizmiq and Sporadiq sent a message to Tortriq as they flew with the birds. 'Where is the Calculus?'

'He's leaving. I will not let him out of my sight,' replied the grandmaster.

'It is time to give up our search for an answer, Tortriq. The storms are a Skull attack and the Calculus must be destroyed,' insisted Mizmiq.

'As soon as he is alone, I will confront him and do what I can,' messaged Tortriq in reply.

42. Centurian

The Ancient Terror

Mizmiq, Sporadiq and the birds approached a wall of black clouds. Thunder and lightning clapped and flared inside them and Mizmiq spoke to the preregrine falcon at the front of the flock, 'Felix, beware, that is a battleship coming out of matterline.'

'We are ready,' cursed Felix, sniffing and spitting out the air.

As they soared up through the thunder, the cylindrical metallic hull of a Skull warship bulged into view. It was general Kazeg's ship, the Turpitude, repaired and restocked with a mighty arsenal of diamind artillery.

Kazeg held his arms aloft in triumph as the wind blasted his ten-foot frame and the Turpitude completed its transformation into physical form.

The birds accelerated and attacked the Skulls lining the ship's platforms, shattering their bones with shockwave spells of destruction.

Kazeg ordered his crew to stand their ground and many of the birds were killed or wounded by the lightning streaking from the Skulls' diamind-tipped rods.

Mizmiq and Sporadiq dived towards one of the bow platforms and diverted the Skulls' attention away from Felix who darted into the warship.

The falcon glided barely a foot above the metal-grated gangways of the Skull vessel and rounded its corners like a levitator pilot pursuing the racing lines on a speedway.

Felix eventually spotted his prize, the centritube, the breathing vent that ran from base to bridge of every Skull ship like a truss rod. It was the part of the ship that enabled Skulls to change from shell to wind-form and back again. It was also the device that gave the vessel its ability to cloud and become weather.

Kazeg had anticipated the danger and stood between Felix and the centritube.

Felix did not stop to think, and with electrifying speed he cast a succession of shockwave spells that catapulted Kazeg against the transparent wall of the tube. It bent as it was designed to do but it did not break or even fracture.

The pitiful frightened eyes of wind-form Skulls becoming skeletons stared out of the chute, wondering if they should stay as air to escape the unexpected invader rather than continue morphing into shell-form in preparation for taking their places on the battle platforms.

Felix sent a spell of destruction towards one of the narrow joins that circled the tube to keep it intact while it curved. He missed his target by no more than a few inches and the tube recoiled from the blast but remained undamaged.

Kazeg responded by hurling his diamind-tipped rod at the falcon. It spun like the sword-blade wheel of a chariot, flung from its axel at a crucial turn.

Felix swerved, only just managing to avoid the diamind and the rod's serrated edges but as he conjured another spell his concentration was shaken by a deafening explosion coming from the velocodrome.

The falcon sped away, terrified by what it could mean, while Kazeg took wind-form and entered the centritube—a shortcut to the bridge.

As Felix shot out of the battleship, there was another explosion. It was quickly followed by a further eruption, then another. The explosions were coming from the counting board at the centre of the arena.

'The dropping stones are diamonds. They coated them to hide the light,' cried Sporadiq in horror, realising that they'd discovered the purpose of the engineers' bomb-factory too late.

'The warship is a diversion,' yelled Mizmiq to the birds. 'They wanted us away from the stadium so that we wouldn't cast spells of containment around the stones. Leave the Skull ship. We must protect the crowd.'

Lorna fled the dugout as the diamonds continued to explode. Albert had made her stay behind and promise not to fly towards the storm.

She searched for her husband when the flock appeared again but there was no sign of him so she began to follow the exact path she thought he would have flown.

The gales grew stronger the higher she flew but she steadied herself and battled on, never once losing her sense of where she was and where she believed Albert might have been.

When Lorna saw the Skull ship she feared the worst, but her heart leapt when a whispering breathless message passed her in the breeze. 'Help me…my love…below the Skull ship…falling…' Albert had been struck by a Skull weapon.

Lorna dived, tears flowing across her cheeks, and there, spiralling down, was Albert. She drew alongside her dear husband but as she opened her beak to reassure him all would be well, a shockwave from one of the bombs in the arena separated them and they crashed to the ground outside the velocodrome.

Lorna sent Filia and Julius a message, 'We need help…southwest gate…in the dust…please…'

Filia heard her and grabbed Grace by the wrist. They had lost sight of Julius and Fergus in the panicking crowd and Filia had not been able to make contact with Julius using the birds' magic. Mizmiq had not responded either.

They rushed towards one of vaulted passageways. 'No,' shouted Grace. 'It is too dangerous. It will collapse.'

'We have to risk it, there's no other way past the crowd, someone's in trouble and I can help them,' wept Filia. 'I'll tell you more when we get there. Please trust me,' she begged.

Filia sent Mizmiq another message as they ran through the crumbling passageway, hoping he might be able to help Albert and Lorna but there was no reply.

Mizmiq and Sporadiq were circling the velocodrome and they were channelling all their magical energy into creating silver spheres and sending them into the crowd. One sphere could hold a few thousand people and when the containers were full, the grandmasters were conjuring spells of flight to lift them to safety.

The magical power required to raise the spheres over the velocodrome walls drained as much energy from their minds as the process of creating the spheres themselves. They were exhausted and were almost at a point where they could no longer move the containers away from the blasts.

'It is hopeless,' mourned Sporadiq. 'Hundreds of thousands are dead and more are dying and we can't even save a fraction of the rest.'

The Centurian birds did not possess the grandmasters' magical power. There was nothing the contestants or any of the other birds flying to the velocodrome could do.

The cruelty and scale of the carnage was beyond anything anyone could imagine. People were being crushed and killed in every section of the stadium as the seats and vaults collapsed around them.

In a desperate attempt to save lives, a few of the birds tried to carry diamind bombs away from the arena only to find that they exploded as soon as they touched them.

Mizmiq and Sporadiq summoned the strength to cast one final spell of flight but as they followed their silver sphere through the billowing clouds and over the velocodrome's outer wall they went white with fear. 'No, it cannot be,' Sporadiq muttered, his voice trembling in horror.

Mizmiq lowered his eyes in despair. 'It is. It is the ancient terror, our greatest dread. After thousands of years of silence, the Arc of Darkness returns.'

A blanket of shadow descended over the stadium and the ground where the board had been fell in on itself.

The grandmasters fled and as they shot away, they were tormented by the harrowing cries of not just the living but the dead. The souls of one million people were pouring into the cavity at the centre of the arena.

The birds' magic meant that the dead sensed the enemy, even though they did not know who the enemy was, nor what was at stake—their own eternity.

The dead were fleeing to the planet's lumenest core and Arcan devilry had created an open path that was far quicker than flying through Centurian soil.

'A million souls making for the core together will weaken the earth at the bottom of the cavity, and with more bombs, it will become an abyss,' warned Sporadiq.

Mizmiq glanced up. There was no sun and no light. Silverrock was shrouded in darkness.

'It is not merely bombs that I fear, Sporadiq. A Greylight is forming, the Arc's mantle of shadow. What we have witnessed is only the beginning.

'Poisonous winds will ravish the earth, just as they did Gazong. The Arc will try and break the planet. We must protect the lumenest. We have to go back,' cried Mizmiq.

Sporadiq bowed his head—they were unlikely to survive if they went back. But he also knew that Mizmiq was right. Centurian's eternal core would be exposed.

The grandmasters turned and dived. They, like the birds, would give their lives to defend human eternity. They would follow the terrified dead into darkness, even if it meant their own destruction.

43. Terminus

Astronomic Bomb

Duggerrid ordered thousands more Skulls to join him on the upper platform of Pleonec Tower. 'We must channel more lightning into the container or the bomb will not fill in time,' he howled.

The Skulls clambered up and pointed their diamind rods towards a great vortex of whirlwinds that had formed in the thundering skies above Terminus and the maelstrom answered by sending ribbons of crackling energy cascading down the walls of Pleonec Tower.

But Duggerrid had calculated that the Pleonec megalith alone would not draw enough lightning into the container, even with his army threatening the skies with their diamind-tipped rods.

He had therefore ordered four funnels to be built around the tower, each one designed to channel more destructive energy into the encasement chamber beneath the planet's surface.

One of the funnels was not yet complete and Duggerrid leapt onto his shuttle and shot across to the pillar, raging at the lack of progress.

His commanders responded by throwing weaker Skulls from the funnel and replacing them with new recruits from the diamind factories below.

Duggerrid had divided the Skulls into cohorts of a hundred, each led by a commander and his attention was drawn to a cohort strengthening the girders around the unfinished funnel. They were hopelessly far behind schedule.

The commander, Zaritin, had risen through the ranks of violence, serving for a period as helmsman on Kazeg's Turpitude. Zaritin was smashing Skulls off the scaffold at a higher rate than any other cohort commander.

The rank of commander came with a name, chosen by Duggerrid. Every other Skull's identity was a series of four symbols scratched across the forehead and these anonymous slaves were known as Quadits.

'You have one minute to finish that join,' snarled Zaritin to one of the Quadit Skulls. But to his surprise the Skull was able to complete the task in seconds. 'Almost a minute ahead of schedule, commander,' it smirked.

Zaritin glared at the impertinent Skull and struck it full in the face with his rod. The Quadit lunged back at the commander, piercing his eye sockets with its thumb and forefinger.

Zaritin shrieked with pain and slipped off the scaffold and his shell disintegrated as soon as it hit the unforgiving Terminus rock.

'Hey, you, get over here,' demanded Phlegatin, overall commander of the funnel. 'Weld the next ten joins at the same speed.'

The Skull made short shrift of the work and the joins were sealed in a matter of seconds again. 'Done, you doubting fool,' it spat.

Phlegatin was outraged and raised his diamind rod but the Quadit severed his head before he could strike. The funnel commander's broken body fell towards the ground while his empty skull soared skywards, blown and battered by the storm-force winds.

The Quadit then threatened other Skulls with the same fate if they did not work harder and the towering funnel was quickly back on schedule.

Duggerrid summoned the Quadit to his audience chamber and the fearsome Skull made its way into the dungeons.

The guards outside Duggerrid's chamber stood aside as soon as they saw the Quadit's shadow and the Skull strode in and knelt before its master's throne. 'You are an unusually powerful Skull,' grinned Duggerrid, pleased with the strength and merciless brutality at his disposal.

'I do not believe in failure or weakness, my lord. We will destroy the Gamma 12 planet and its core,' replied the Quadit.

Duggerrid smiled. 'I want you to do something for me before you travel to Gamma 12,' he said. 'A group of powerful birds has arrived at the broken Tau 6 corridor. They must not cross the chasm.

'We have always defended the void successfully and very few have passed into Eskatar since our victory—none for a long while. The priestesses too have not been able to enter the bird corridors and their power must not join our war, whether exercised directly or through others. Go now and destroy these birds. I will oversee the work on the funnel. The bomb is all but ready.'

'As you wish, my lord,' answered the Skull, bowing before his master.

'There is one further matter,' smiled Duggerrid. 'From now on, you shall be called Ornifrac, the bird-breaker,' he declared. 'I give you command of the Stowaway, one of our most formidable warships. You have shown your skill and determination. Do not now misplace my trust, commander. As you well know, I do not forgive failure,' warned Duggerrid.

Skull commander Ornifrac marched out of the dungeons and onto his ship and ordered his crew to embark.

Snaking cables whistled away from their moorings, whipping the harbour Skulls as they twisted free and the Stowaway's helmsman grinned proudly as he steered his mighty battleship about.

Not only was he piloting one of the greatest Skull warships, he and the rest of the crew knew exactly who their commander was—the fearless Quadit who had ridiculed and butchered his superiors. He was a commander any Skull would want to follow and obey.

Ornifrac looked back and he and his death marines cheered as raw lightning energy poured into the dungeons of Terminus. The container was almost full and the crews of the main battle-fleet were making their final preparations for the voyage to Centurian.

Duggerrid's ghostly voice rallied the Skulls as they gathered on the harbour front. 'Human eternal consciousness is about to die, and when it does, you will all be free to invade a human life. There will be no roll call, no waiting, no craving.' Roars of triumph erupted from the dockside below Pleonec Tower.

'And when your human lives are over, you will be rewarded again. You will join me, and our masters, as eternal elemental powers, the voices of judgement and justice.'

'Flesh, life, justice,' yelled the Skulls, hammering their rods against the stones of the harbour wall while Duggerrid stretched his arms towards the turmoil in the skies, celebrating the storms that had given the Skull race its weaponry and power.

Duggerrid ordered the bomb to be raised and the Skulls rushed to their ships as the weapon broke through the rock strata of Terminus.

The funnels crashed to the ground without so much as scratching the weapon or slowing its monumental birth, and Pleonec Tower buckled but it did not fall.

Skull vessels began surrounding the bomb and attaching hooks to the container but they could not control it. The bomb was being dragged upwards by its lightning wanting to rejoin the volcanic storms above.

'Should we turn back and help them, commander?' asked the Stowaway's helmsman. Ornifrac watched and smiled when he saw Duggerrid instructing the Skulls to scatter diaminds to one side of the bomb, drawing it to an alternative magnetism. 'No,' he replied. 'Lord Duggerrid has anticipated everything. He is as clever as he is powerful.'

The Skull fleet regained control of the container and towed the bomb away while Ornifrac's crew shook their fists, confident their lifetime of misery and craving would soon be over.

As the main fleet readied themselves for matterline travel, Ornifrac addressed the Skulls aboard his ship, 'We have been given a special task by Lord Duggerrid. We travel to the Tau 6 void. The enemy is attempting to cross the chasm.'

The Skulls cursed the birds and Ornifrac silenced them before continuing. 'They will not last long, I can assure you, for I am Ornifrac, the bird-breaker, and all who confront me die,' he howled, smiling and relishing the battle ahead while his crew rejoiced at the strength of their commander. Their victory would be swift.

44. Twilight

1054 AD

Pleione spoke to Jonathan, 'We are ready to place your FJ constellation amongst the stars. Once it is there, will you choose your star name?'

Jonathan wept. 'I will, but I would like the constellation to be clearly visible in the Centurian night sky above the planet's capital city all year round. Is that possible?'

Pleione did not at first answer and Jonathan wondered if he'd asked for too much.

'We have found a way,' replied Pleione moments later. 'Some of our Twilight friends have offered to adjust their brightness. Stars are always eager to help new arrivals leave limbo. I will now move your gaze close to Centurian so you can look up at the constellation in the way you wish it to be seen. Please tell me whether you are satisfied?'

Jonathan didn't sense any movement. He simply felt as though he'd blinked and his eyes had opened in a different place, a place he knew well.

In front him, straddling stars he recognised, was the perfect FJ with an exclamation mark. 'It is beautiful, Pleione, thank you,' he sobbed. 'May I look at it for a short time? I'm not sure which star should be my home.'

'Yes, but while you're deciding, I would like to ask you to help me with something.'

'Of course, if I can,' answered Jonathan, wondering what he might be able to do to help her.

'There is another being of human origin who arrived recently. He is here, like you, because he was wrapped in Twilight when he died.

'He insists on becoming a planet inhabited solely by birds and the creatures needed to sustain them.

'The trouble is, whilst there are such places, the so-called bird planets you are familiar with, they are not Twilight entities so they cannot be joined. They exist entirely within the living world. They were not born into the Twilight realm.

'Planets, stars, moons, all whose hearts lie in Twilight host many chains of life or none. Even the planet that the birds call Gazong is not inhabited by birds alone and the creatures that sustain them. Other beings lie hidden in the archipelago's empty seas.

'I think you are well-placed to persuade this person to move on from limbo, Jonathan. You have been both human and bird. You are also of similar age. Friendships formed in limbo often help inbetweeners make the leap.'

'Which part of Centurian is he from?' asked Jonathan.

'He is not. He's from the planet the birds call Opus,' said Pleione.

'I was told of Opus while I was in Savanna,' gasped Jonathan, 'but the birds were unwilling to tell me about its people and history; not only while I was beside the lake—on my journey too. They thought I would probably become human again and felt uncomfortable whenever I asked them anything specific. Please, will you tell me more?'

'I would be happy to,' replied Pleione. 'The humans of Opus call their planet Earth, the same name Centurians used for their planet before they discovered magic a thousand or so years ago.

'Earth actually has a more or less identical premagic history to Centurian and still measures time by the chronological system your founder Illumeter abolished when he began counting again from his birth year.'

'You mean they continued on from 1054 AD with the same premagic religions and society?' cried Jonathan, astounded.

'Yes, and they are yet to find the sound spectrum that enables human spells,' said Pleione. 'They've had another thousand years of evolution without magic. I think you'll be fascinated to hear more about what could have come next.'

Jonathan felt exhilarated at the prospect of meeting such a person, someone with both a shared and divergent history. He wondered how the people of Opus-Earth had evolved and what their inventions would have been.

Jonathan suddenly became aware of another being. He couldn't see anyone but was overwhelmed by a deep bond as soon as the person spoke.

'Hello, Jonathan. Pleione told me your name. I was called Jonathan on my home planet, Earth. She said we had lots in common, not just our names but our ages too; I was fifteen when I passed into this place. It is great to m–meet you.'

'It's amazing to meet you too, Jonathan. I'm sixteen, or rather was sixteen. How did your life end so early? I'm sorry to ask if it brings back terrible memories.'

'That's okay. I was killed in an accident. I got hit by a bus while I was stumbling across a road—my eyesight wasn't right,' he choked. Jonathan felt the grief and tragedy in the boy's voice.

'I hope you didn't suffer too much,' Jonathan sighed.

'No, it was over quickly. I had no chance,' he replied.

'You said you were stumbling so I'm guessing your buses travel along the ground?' asked Jonathan.

'Of course; why, do yours fly or something?'

'Yes, they do, would you believe? On my planet, humans use magic for pretty much everything.'

'Magic? You mean spells, that sort of magic?'

'Yes, exactly, and it's not only humans who cast spells, birds do too. I hear you're a fan of our feathered friends. What's your favourite species?'

'I'd have to say robins. I love songbirds. I love birds of prey too though. If I had to choose one of those magnificent creatures I'd pick ospreys. My parents took me on holidays to a place called Scotland and I'd stare at the ospreys all day. I hated camping out in the rain but it was worth every moment, watching those majestic birds swoop and pluck their prey from the lakes.'

Jonathan's heart jumped. 'I love robins and ospreys, but camping—you've got me there. I'm picturing premagic soldiers at war, not a family enjoying themselves on holiday! You'll have to explain.'

'Ha! It's common on Earth. I guess you people are able to magic invisible roofs over your heads if you need one?'

'As a matter of fact, yes,' laughed Jonathan.

'You've never touched the inside of a tent and got wet when the rain's pounding down?'

'No!'

'It's magic, but not in a good way,' he chuckled. 'Water trickles in, then the canvas turns into a sieve and rain streams towards you like iron filings drawn to a magnet.'

'Hilarious!' cried Jonathan. 'The way we live sounds completely different but I reckon our birds look the same, judging by your osprey description. Now, get this, the birds' spells are far more powerful than any human magic. They even helped me take bird-form; that of an osprey no less. I expect the birds on Earth have the same secret power, they're just doing a darn good job of hiding it, like the birds on my planet.'

'Th–that blows my mind. To think I could have one day become an osprey, or a robin, incredible,' the boy exclaimed. 'I knew there was so much more to birds. I think I was close to understanding what they were saying. I used to sit under a tree in my local park talking to the chattering tweeters.'

'They heard you all right, and there's more,' said Jonathan. 'Birds have created a network of corridors that transcend time and space. Their corridors allow them to travel between the stars and planets that you and I know, as well as ones we don't. Their corridors also lead to vast bird-only planets.'

'That's what I want to be!' cried Jonathan's Twilight friend. 'I've been trying to persuade Pleione to allow me to join a bird-only planet. Why didn't she mention these bird planets?'

Jonathan was interrupted by a familiar voice, it was Centurian. 'Jonathan, it is time.'

'To join my friend's dream?' asked Jonathan excitedly.

'No,' replied the silver planet. 'To choose your star name, please. The brightness of your constellation is something that you should be contributing to, I'm afraid.'

'I'm sorry, I have to go,' Jonathan sighed.

'Hey, no worries, I'm just so glad you're here,' answered his Twilight friend. 'It's funny, my only friends on Earth were birds and in you, I have a friend who was both bird and human. But quickly, before you take off, who were you hoping to dream with?'

'Someone I loved, very much,' wept Jonathan. 'Pleione said I could join one of her dreams while I was still in limbo. Have you experienced that yet?'

'No. Pleione did tell me about it and offered me the chance to do it. I've been trying to pluck up the courage to enter my mother and father's dreams,' he choked.

'They were in a bad way the last time I was allowed to gaze. I would like to help them but I don't know how. I fear I might make things worse if they see me in their dreams. It would be great to talk about it with you, an older boy as it were, get your advice on what you think I should do. I can't tell you how happy I am to have met you, Jonathan. Come straight back, please.'

'I will and we'll compare osprey notes too. Having been on the inside, so to speak, I can promise you those creatures are even more remarkable than they seem.'

The two Jonathans laughed and said goodbye, certain that theirs would be a long and happy friendship; one that neither life nor death could end.

45. Centurian

Letters from a Friend

Julius and Fergus lay suffocating in the ruins of the velocodrome, terrified that it was only a matter of time before they too would be killed by the collapsing seats.

A boulder spun out of the darkness and smashed into the rubble metres from their faces. 'We have to get out,' screamed Fergus.

Gasping for air, they crawled towards a narrow opening. 'Filiaaaa, Graaace,' they yelled desperately.

Filia and Grace did not hear them. They had escaped the devastation and were outside the velocodrome hurrying to the southwest gate where Filia hoped to find Albert and Lorna.

Filia tripped and fell as she ran but Grace hauled her up and as she wiped the dust from her eyes, she noticed the flickering of stars peering through the gloom.

Filia knew her constellations and these were stars she did not recognise. She looked at them more closely and as soon as she'd made out their shape she broke down in tears. 'FJ,' she sobbed. 'It is, it is! It's a sign,' she cried, hugging Grace.

'I can see an FJ, yes, but you think it means something?' asked Grace.

'It means Jonathan, it's a sign that he's alive, it's the exact constellation we made at Rockmore! It is a precise match, that's too much of a coincidence,' wept Filia.

Grace looked at her blankly, 'Jonathan's sending us a signal from space? Have you gone mad?'

Filia told Grace everything: the existence of secret corridors between Centurian and distant stars, Jonathan's transformation into an osprey, his journey to a place called Eskatar and much more besides.

She then sent Mizmiq a message as Grace tried to wrap her head around what she'd said. 'Can you hear me, Mizmiq? I'm at the southwest gate. Look up, do you see an FJ constellation with an exclamation mark? Have you seen it before? It's a new constellation, isn't it? It must be a sign from Jonathan; it's a copy of a magic-music shape we made at Rockmore!'

Mizmiq heard her message as he and Sporadiq sped down into what was becoming an ever deeper abyss; many of the diamind stones from the arena had been set to detonate only after they'd struck the earth at the bottom of the cavity.

Mizmiq looked at his fellow grandmaster. 'We're going back up. Filia says there's a sign from Jonathan in the sky, a constellation—astonishing if true; such a miracle could only be conjured with the hands of Eskatar, and even then, magic on that scale, the formation or movement of stars, it's beyond anything we could have foretold. We fight with fresh heart, my friend.'

Mizmiq and Sporadiq turned around and spotted the FJ gems as they neared the mouth of the cavity. The stars glistened above the Greylight veil like silver studs puncturing thick black leather. 'Look at them, Sporadiq,' Mizmiq roared with delight.

The grandmasters shot across what remained of the arena and flew up over the wreckage of the velocodrome's seats. 'Wait, over there,' said the vigilant owl suddenly. 'It's the boy, Julius.'

'So it is!' declared Mizmiq triumphantly.

They landed beside Julius and Fergus, looked them up and down, and having decided that they were lucky to be in one piece, proceeded to carry them over the stadium's outer walls.

'You're right, Filia! That is a new constellation,' messaged Mizmiq as they glided down to the southwest gate.

Filia was overjoyed. 'I knew it, Mizmiq, I knew it,' she yelled, marvelling at Jonathan's constellation in the heavens and remembering how he'd scribbled his initials into the golden dust rings outside Elephant's Trunk. A sign in the stars was so Jonathan. There could be no doubt—this was indeed him.

The grandmasters found Filia and Grace and laid Julius and Fergus on the ground next to them, and while the friends hugged and wept with relief at seeing each other again, Mizmiq spoke to Filia and Julius.

'Centurian is being attacked by the evil I told you about when we were with Jonathan; the creatures we call Skulls. The explosions, the massacre, the darkness. It is all their doing.

'I and my friend here, this wonderful owl with brilliant eyes, must leave you. Shelter outside the walls. You will be safe for a time. The enemy's deadly intent now lies elsewhere.'

'But when will you be back?' complained Filia.

'Soon,' answered Mizmiq, raising his wings.

The hawk and the owl shot off into the blackness before Filia could quiz them further.

'You had a conversation with those birds?' cried Fergus, stunned. Filia brought a flabbergasted Fergus up to speed, sharing everything she'd said to Grace about Jonathan's journey, and more.

'Do his parents know?' gulped Fergus.

'Yes,' wept Filia, hoping Lucius had been as lucky as them and survived.

'Can two-way bird communication be taught?' asked Grace.

'According to the hawk, it can only be gifted by a few birds,' Filia replied. 'Although I have to say I'm not sure how reliable he is on that point. It was Jonathan who gave us the ability to converse with birds before he left.'

'Agreed,' added Julius. 'There are clearly other ways of doing it.'

Mizmiq sent Filia and Julius a message. 'I heard that,' he laughed. 'I'm as reliable as I can be, which is very, and I would wager there isn't a single bird out there able to make head or tail of Jonathan's magical might.'

'You've been listening to our conversation? How rude!' objected Filia.

'Oh, I was merely testing my, er, wand, a device I use to monitor the airwaves. It, unlike me, is unreliable and regular checks are obligatory,' chuckled the grandmaster.

'Well, seeing as you're out there somewhere, snooping, you can tell me which birds do actually have the power to gift two-way communication?' demanded Filia.

'I will tell you about one, then I'll sign off and further questions will have to wait,' Mizmiq replied. 'The bird's name is Rose. She is accompanying Jonathan and you would never guess her magical power by her appearance. Her favoured form is that of a simple busy robin.

'I'm sure you will meet the little woodland wonder when Jonathan returns. In fact, I expect you've already met her, without realising it, of course. Now, time to go; Mizmiq the hawk, over and out.'

Filia and Julius told Fergus and Grace what Mizmiq had said. 'I'm never going to look at robins in the same way again,' smiled Grace.

'Me neither,' gasped Fergus, 'how many secret bird-friends do you have?'

'Not many,' laughed Filia. 'That said, the reason we're by the southwest gate is two pigeons. They…'

'Lorna!' cried Julius, interrupting her.

Lorna was moving slowly, flying then dropping to the ground as she tried to lift Albert through the dust.

Filia and Julius ran to help her. 'He's barely alive,' wept Lorna. 'My brave Albert, I should have done more to break his fall, and I should have discouraged his obsession with this stupid contest.'

As Filia and Julius consoled Lorna and tended to Albert's wounds, the Greylight skies began to darken. Filia sent Mizmiq a message, 'It's getting worse, the blackness, whatever it is; please help us.'

The hawk answered immediately, 'Do not be afraid. What you see is the Centurian night closing in—Jonathan's magic will shine more brightly than ever.'

The grandmaster was right. The FJ gems sparkled beyond the Greylight veil and Filia, Julius, Grace and Fergus set about finding a place to shelter.

They eventually lay down amongst the rubble with Albert and Lorna beside them, exhausted and gazing up at the constellation for one last look whenever their eyes threatened to close.

46.   The World of Birds

Ornifrac

The band of birds willed Nomadiq on. The grandmaster was not far from the Tau 7 side of the chasm. The flailing threads had not responded to his spells but he'd somehow managed to glide almost all the way to the corridor opening.

'You seem distracted, Fovea,' said Rose.

'Something's moving in the distance,' replied the eagle.

'Where?' asked Jigsy, 'I don't see anything.'

Everyone stared at Qybil. 'I see something and it doesn't give me a good feeling,' warned the Aquila.

'Skulls, a battleship,' shrieked Fovea.

Jigsy marshalled his frightened troops. 'We must intercept them. If they stop the grandmaster, we'll have no chance of casting a bridging spell.'

'I will go with a squadron of eagles and falcons,' said Fovea.

'You go too, Minim, please,' asked Jigsy. 'They will need your metal-pounding skills. You have your drilling sheath?'

Minim nodded and Squigbox wept and held her tight as she prepared to jump. 'Now,' cried Fovea.

Ornifrac ordered the Stowaway to plot a direct course towards the birds. The Skull ship accelerated and it was not long before the two sides clashed.

Fovea was first to engage the enemy, grabbing the helmsman's diamond rod with her talons and tossing it into space. The weapon disappeared in a swirling circle, like a pin into darkness.

The birds lashed out at the Skulls lining the battle platforms and the Stowaway slowed as furious exchanges commenced.

Minim drilled into one of the weather tubes, atmospheric sensors that spooled like tentacles across the outer shell of the ship. It burst and the birds cheered her victory.

Buoyed by her success, Minim targeted another tube. She hammered away with all her percussive might and was close to splitting its skin when she saw the Stowaway's ferocious commander lowering himself from an upper platform to attack her.

Minim fled under the hull and back up the far side of the ship, and Ornifrac, angry at having lost the woodpecker, redoubled his efforts to clear the Stowaway's path. 'Forward, faster,' he raged, spinning his diamond rod indiscriminately and slaughtering any birds who dared to come near.

Nomadiq had changed back into his robin form so the Skulls would have less chance of noticing him and when he reached the Tau 7 corridor he grasped one of the threads that hung from the opening. It was lifeless, just as Rose had predicted.

He held the strand in his tiny feet and fluttered his way up onto the lip of the corridor. The air was ice-cold and Nomadiq cast a spell of warming to breathe what life he could into the tubeway's frozen skin. The corridor had to be revived if a secure bridge was to form across the void.

The threads began to brighten and Ornifrac realised the danger. 'Turn about. Ram that creature,' he howled.

Nomadiq heard an echo of the Skull commander's voice in the darkness and saw his ship hurtling towards him but suddenly stopped casting his spell.

The birds reacted with dismay when they saw the Tau 7 threads losing their brightness and wondered what could possibly be wrong. 'Why is his spell not working, Rose?' they screamed. 'He's going to die!'

Rose was silent, shocked. She had no idea what was happening.

As the Stowaway closed in, Nomadiq changed his appearance again. He became the wizened old man Jonathan had found tapping his way along the Omicron expressway, except he was now wearing a cloak of shining silver threads.

Nomadiq raised his arm and pointed at Ornifrac's jawline. White light shot towards his target and at the same time, a slither of brightness lifted itself out of Ornifrac's mouth.

The grandmaster's stream of magic and the tiny strand of brightness curled and twisted until they'd tied themselves together in an unbreakable bond.

Ornifrac tore at the long line of light but his skeletal hands passed straight through it. He was unable to touch the grandmaster's magic.

The birds gawped in amazement as Nomadiq dragged him overboard and began pulling the monstrous Skull towards him while the Stowaway's crew steered about and fled.

'That, my friends, is a true display of grandmastery from a wizard in all his glory,' Rose smiled.

Nomadiq sent a message to Rose, 'There is a sapphire light in this Skull. I heard it when the Skull spoke.'

Rose was dumbfounded and looked at the birds. 'Grandmaster Nomadiq has detected the sound of a sapphire in the Skull's voice,' she gasped.

'How can anyone hear a living voice inside the words of a Skull?' asked Squigbox.

Jigsy grinned. 'I don't know, but our clever little brains can remember the voices of those we knew and loved long after they're gone. Think of it like music. The old robin recognised a familiar song,' he winked.

'I bet that grandmaster's got tens of thousands of songs stored in his head,' beamed Squigbox.

'More,' Rose chuckled.

'No way, how many, Rose?' cried Squigbox.

'How long is a piece of string, as our human friends would say?' answered Rose and everybody laughed.

Nomadiq bound Ornifrac in a silver weave and wrapped his mind in a spell of sleep before laying him down on the corridor floor. He then conjured a spell of understanding and messaged Rose, astounded.

'The sapphire is Alea, but that is not all. There are signs of human life in this Skull. It is not merely a Skull. Dare we hope for a trace of Jonathan in this creature?'

Rose's heart leapt. She did not know how to answer. Nobody knew what happened to those who lost their lives in spells of consumption.

Nomadiq gazed into the Skull's mouth and saw Alea spinning inside. 'How is this possible?' he whispered.

She did not reply and Nomadiq held out his hand, inviting her to circle his wrist, but Alea moved away and darted frantically from one side of the Skull's mouth to the other.

'You believe the Skull will die if I release you?' asked the grandmaster.

Alea calmed her movement and Nomadiq knew her answer was "yes".

'And nor will you speak, for using your own words might separate you from the Skull, putting something of Jonathan at risk?'

Alea shone brightly and Nomadiq's eyes welled with tears as he realised that what he'd said was true. 'I understand, we will ask the priestesses to help us,' he said softly.

The grandmaster sent Rose a message, 'There is much hope, my friend. Alea too believes there is something of Jonathan, alive, inside this Skull.'

Rose and the birds at the Tau 6 corridor were overcome with joy and they sent messages to Fovea, Minim and the others who'd survived the sortie, letting them know what the grandmaster had discovered as they drifted back towards them.

Rose addressed the whole flock as soon as they landed, 'The time has come for us to bridge the chasm,' she declared, and not a second later threads of brilliant silver shot from her beak and arched their way across the divide.

The same spectacular threads of glistening silver spilled from Nomadiq's fingers and a solid line was formed. 'We have the beginnings of a corridor,' announced Rose triumphantly.

The birds and the grandmaster wove more and more of their transcendent magical threads and eventually stopped once they'd created a thin tube of air.

The birds then flew off in single-file but as they approached the Eskatar side of the void, their narrow passageway began to wither and tear. 'It's the poison, hurry,' warned Rose.

They pressed their wings against the widening cuts in the corridor skin to keep as much air inside the tubeway as possible, switching to oxygen whenever the gaps were too big.

Some of the larger birds fainted after gulping down their last few bubbles of air and had to be carried by groups of smaller friends and everyone was forced to walk at least some of the way. They waddled like a group of drunken humans crossing an abandoned rope-bridge and when they finally collapsed onto the Tau 7 ledge, they didn't just shrill with relief, they laughed. Never had a band of birds looked so ridiculous.

Rose recognised Alea instantly and the robin cried and cried with happiness as she watched the sapphire light twisting in jubilation inside the Skull's mouth, 'I have found you after so many years of searching, dear Alea,' she wept, overwhelmed. 'There was barely a day when I did not think of you and sing to you.'

Alea curled ever faster, creating tiny bright letters and spelling them out one by one into a message, 'How I have longed for this moment also, Rose. We will share so many stories when we arrive in the Emerald lands.'

Grandmaster Nomadiq, still resplendent in his wizard's robes, took robin form once more and cast a spell of miniaturisation so the Skull and Alea would be stowed safely for flight.

The crazy gang were on their way again. *Whatever next?* they thought, flexing their wings and shooting off into the ice-cold air.

47. The World of Birds

Emerald Lands

Alea noticed the Skull turning and stretching awkwardly as Nomadiq carried them along the Tau 7 corridor. It was as if something was trying to find a way out of its shell.

'Jonathan?' she whispered, circling the Skull's mouth. There was no reply.

'Jonathan?' Alea repeated as the Skull grew ever more restless.

'Alea?' mumbled a voice.

'Yes!' cried the sapphire, recognising the voice as Jonathan's.

'Alea! You have joined me in Twilight?' exclaimed Jonathan.

'Twilight? No, Jonathan, that is not where we are,' she replied, confused. 'You and I are trapped inside a Skull's shell, but we are also travelling to Eskatar with our friends. They crossed the chasm. The old robin is carrying the Skull. We are hoping the priestesses will set us free.'

'The birds made it across the void?' Jonathan gasped.

'Yes,' answered Alea.

'But we are bound to a Skull, you say?'

'Yes,' Alea replied.

Jonathan was silent for a moment. 'Wait,' he said, 'I was a Skull of great strength, the memories are coming back. How did I become a Skull?'

'I do not know,' said Alea, 'but I can tell you how we came to be here. The old robin, grandmaster Nomadiq, heard my voice when the Skull spoke. The wonderful wizard fought the Skull at the chasm and put the creature to sleep.'

'Wizard? Grandmaster?'

'Yes, Jonathan, yes. The old robin, as you know, is able to take human form but it will not surprise you to learn that he is no ordinary human. A wizard is perhaps the best way to describe who he really is in your language.'

'And his wizard name is Nomadiq?'

'Yes,' answered Alea.

'Is Warbler with the birds too? Did he find a way back from Twilight?' asked Jonathan.

'No, I'm so sorry. But Jonathan, tell me please, where were you? You speak of Twilight as a place where you and Warbler existed after the spell of consumption.'

'We spoke with the stars, Alea. It was like another life, another dimension of being.'

'You had conversations with the stars?'

'Yes,' Jonathan replied.

'Then you've discovered a part of Twilight I do not know,' said Alea, utterly astonished. 'As far as I and others have always understood it, Twilight is a place of energy, of light, not a realm that hosts life. It is where we expose the living world to Candela Lumen power. We have never known there to be sentient beings in Twilight, let alone ones that are associated with the stars.'

'Well I can say with absolute certainty that animate beings do exist in Twilight, Alea, and those beings are the stars, incredible though that may sound, and I think I understand at least one reason why Warbler is not here,' sighed Jonathan, grieving for his dear friend. 'He chose a star name whereas I had not yet decided. I doubt I could have returned if I'd chosen my star.'

'What is your last memory of Twilight, Jonathan?' asked Alea, enthralled and baffled by what she was hearing.

'I was with Filia. You remember me talking about her with Squigbox and Minim when they told me of Gazong and their magic-music?'

'Yes, I do. Was she with you in Twilight?'

'No, I was able to enter her dream, although she did not know it. It's mind-blowing, isn't it, to think that the stars are not only sentient beings, but they can join our dreams?'

Alea was completely dumbstruck as Jonathan rejoiced in recounting Filia's dream. 'I was in my osprey form and Filia was a graceful golden eagle,' he said. 'I led her high above the Meadowlands, a stunning part of our planet.

'We dived to within feet of one of the glasslike lakes and I watched her as she marvelled at her colours in the water, the paler brown feathers along her wings and the bright white flecks which she knew to be the markings of a younger eagle.

'But then I found myself being taken away, and although I could still see her I could tell that she'd lost sight of me.

'At first she laughed and accused me of hiding, but as she soared upwards above the lake, looking for me, she became worried and angry. 'Not funny, Jonathan,' I remember her yelling as she searched.

'I begged the stars to let me stay in the dream and I caught one final glimpse of her feathers as I crossed a col between two peaks.

'And now I understand why the dream was ripped away from me. It wasn't the stars at all. I have been given a second life,' wept Jonathan, his voice choking with elation. 'My journey continues: Eskatar, then home, Eskatar, then home,' he sobbed. 'Alea, will you tell me all you can about the Emerald lands?'

'I would be delighted,' wept Alea, crying with joy. 'There is a song that describes them best, a song that was sung by those who hoped to one day travel to the Emerald lands when creatures first knew of them.'

Alea started to sing and Jonathan's mind raced with thoughts of home, his parents, friends, Filia and happiness:

Shapes of darkness do not linger
On the staircase valleys of Eskatar
No poison soils the welcoming earth
Or the aegis of the angels' star
And all who alight are lightened
Of burdens from a darker star
For spring follows summer on Emerald Eskatar.

'It's beautiful, thank you, Alea, but how does spring follow summer?' asked Jonathan.

'Eskatar begins and ends its years with the spring and autumn Equinox; there is never a time when darkness is greater than light,' answered Alea. 'Eskatar's flowers bloom in perpetuity; they are the visible fabric of its being and the planet's creatures possess a healing power that I believe will free us from this Skull.

'Eskatar is like no other place we know, Jonathan. We sometimes call it a star, sometimes a planet. No other world is comparable.'

'Please sing your song again, Alea, and if I fall asleep, please keep singing,' whispered Jonathan.

Alea sang and Jonathan drifted off to sleep and dreamt again. He was in his osprey form once more and he was also gliding above the Meadowlands mountains.

He looked for Filia, but instead of finding the golden eagle, he spotted a boy hurling skimming stones across a lake.

He landed beside him. 'Are you my Twilight friend? Are you Jonathan from Earth?' he asked.

The boy grinned and nodded furiously; he'd joined his dream but because he was in Twilight he was unable to speak using his Twilight consciousness.

Jonathan flew in circles around him and his Twilight friend held his hands aloft, amazed at how close he was to such a magnificent osprey, and not only that, an osprey whose name he knew.

Jonathan asked if he'd plucked up the courage to enter his parents' dreams and he raised his thumbs before starting to wave. He was saying goodbye.

Jonathan woke and instantly knew why his Twilight friend had waved. He'd sensed the dream coming to an end.

Jonathan also knew that his friend could not have been part of his dream without Pleione's help and that meant the stars in Twilight had found him, and could see him.

Jonathan lifted what he thought must be his hand as if to wave back. He tried to imagine the consternation he must have caused by leaving Twilight, and he wondered if his friend had finally chosen a star name, and if so, what it was, or whether Pleione had allowed him into his dream while he was still in limbo to encourage him to choose.

Jonathan became distracted by a change in the air. 'Alea, can you hear me?' he said.

'Yes, do you feel the breeze?' she replied.

'I do, what is it?'

'We are arriving, Jonathan. We are arriving at our most precious star,' cried Alea triumphantly.

48. Centurian

The Lost Jewels

Filia bolted upright and stared into the darkness of the rocky shelter outside the velocodrome. Her mind was still in the dream. 'Jonathan, Jonathan, where are you?' she cried, searching for the osprey.

She crawled out and gazed up at the night sky. To her horror, there was no FJ, but every other star and constellation was exactly as it had been when she'd fallen asleep.

Filia was inconsolable. 'Get up, Grace, Julius, Fergus. I can't see the FJ,' she cried.

The friends leapt up, as did Lorna, while Albert moved as best he could; his wounds were more painful than ever.

No one could see anything other than empty black circles where the FJ had shone.

The air began to stir and the wind swirled in menacing spirals as it raced across the fallen rubble. 'There's another dust storm coming,' warned Lorna as dirt and grit lodged in their throats.

They hurried back into their shelter but even there it quickly became harder and harder to breathe.

Filia sent Mizmiq a cry for help and the grandmaster heard her as he and Sporadiq flew down into the abyss. Mizmiq was beside himself when he listened to her words. 'The FJ has gone, Sporadiq, and our friends are suffocating. You carry on. I will take care of them.'

'Then should we not ask Tortriq to help me? I will have no hope of defending the core alone if the enemy gets that far,' said Sporadiq.

'Yes, you're right, he must join you, whether he's dealt with the Calculus or not,' Mizmiq replied.

Mizmiq messaged Tortriq as he shot upwards and out of the abyss and Tortriq set off from Numberalist government headquarters straightaway. He had not yet chosen his moment to confront the Calculus.

Mizmiq battled his way through the storm, scanning the Greylight shadows for the constellation, but he too could not see it.

'Why has the FJ gone?' messaged Filia as the grandmaster flew over the velocodrome's outer walls.

'I do not know, I do not know,' was all he could say.

Mizmiq found Filia, Julius, Grace, Fergus and Lorna choking and gasping for air. Albert, however, lay motionless inside the shelter. The wind had blown the dirt and dust deep into his wounds and the brave Opus pigeon was dying.

Mizmiq wrapped Albert in a spell of healing, but it was no good. 'I'm so sorry, Lorna, I can't keep him alive for much longer,' mourned the hawk.

'My love, forgive me,' Albert wept. 'I should not have taken part in that contest.' Lorna cried and cried, holding her dear husband. 'I would not have wanted you any other way. I love you more than you can know, Albert. You've brought so much adventure and laughter to our lives, and to everyone who has known you.'

'Th–thank you, my love, and please, lay me beside the oak, in our park, our home.'

Lorna nodded and stroked his tattered feathers but Albert's eyes began to close and his heart gave way.

Lorna poured her tears into the dust, and Filia and Julius wept with her and tried to console her. A much-loved husband had been lost, a dear friend, and the life and soul of every park he'd visited.

The storm was gathering strength and Mizmiq spoke to the friends as they cried for Albert. 'I'm going to take you somewhere safe, all of you,' he said.

Grace and Fergus' mouths dropped open in bewilderment; they could suddenly hear the hawk's words.

'Don't be alarmed,' smiled the grandmaster. 'You're not losing your minds. I've cast a spell to translate my words into your human language. In fact, I can do quite a number of human things,' he chuckled.

'My spell will also make Lorna's avian speech travel to your ears as human words within your audible range. You'll be able to understand what she's saying as clearly as Filia and Julius.'

Grace, Fergus and Lorna looked at each other and Grace and Fergus knelt beside the grieving pigeon. 'We are so sorry for your loss,' whispered Grace.

'Thank you,' wept Lorna, 'Thank you.'

'Now listen carefully, please,' said Mizmiq, closing his eyes for a moment to protect them from a violent gust. 'Lorna, you are to carry Filia and Grace, and I will carry Julius, Fergus and poor Albert's body. He shall have a proper birdsong lament where we are going.'

'How in heaven's name will I be able to carry them?' objected Lorna. But as soon as she'd asked her question, her feet began to grow and she watched in dismay as they became long enough to curl around Filia and Grace.

'Don't worry, it's temporary,' Mizmiq reassured her, smiling.

'A–and, where are we going?' said Lorna nervously, still staring at her feet in shock.

'To my home, a castle at the end of the corridors,' beamed the grandmaster.

Lorna looked at the hawk, aghast, and Mizmiq smiled at her and placed a wing on her shoulder, 'You have nothing to worry about and you will not get lost on the way. I will be conjuring spells to help speed your flight, spells that will allow you to fly fast, very fast indeed.

'But don't get ahead of yourself once you become used to it. You are not to exceed one hundred miles per hour in the tubes or the humans will squidge up, and remember, one hundred miles per hour is flying speed; the distance we'll be covering in the transcendent corridors will, as you know, be far, far greater,' he smiled.

'I will watch my speed, I promise, Mr Hawk,' gulped Lorna, weeping again for her dear Albert. How he would have loved to have seen the farthest corridors and a magical castle full of powerful hawks.

49. The World of Birds

Phantom Traces

Mizmiq conjured a lapisphere and a fresh breeze welcomed Lorna and the four friends as they plunged into Centurian's estuary corridors.

Filia, Julius, Grace and Fergus gazed beyond the transparent tubeway walls in stunned amazement. They were racing away from Centurian's sun and hurtling past its neighbouring planets.

'It–it's taking, only minutes, wait, seconds, for us to leave our solar system!' exclaimed Fergus.

'What sort of bird would you be, Filia, if you could become one of these incredible creatures?' yelled Grace, leaning back with her arms outstretched, exhilarated.

Filia smiled, remembering her dream, 'Auburn locks, hazel eyes; a golden-brown eagle,' she answered, pretending to glide over the Meadowlands lakes with Jonathan.

'We're going to speed up,' announced Mizmiq, 'and unfortunately that means you won't be able to talk. Your cheeks will contract in the air, other parts of you as well I expect, but you'll be quite safe.'

'Speed up?' cried Julius. 'That's impossible!'

Mizmiq laughed. 'Thankfully, it is possible; otherwise you'd be middle-aged by the time we reached our destination.'

They accelerated and Julius, Filia, Grace and Fergus' cheeks compressed so quickly they couldn't even scream. 'You see, you don't really need to talk after all, just enjoy the experience,' chuckled the grandmaster.

The Centurian solar system disappeared behind them and despite their incalculable speed, the only sounds that the friends could hear were the whooshes of swerving birds and the odd word of explanation from the grandmaster.

Mizmiq and Lorna eventually slowed down after many hours of shooting past the smudged dots and blurred lines of stars and Filia, Julius, Grace and Fergus gawped in wonder as they entered a vast open space full of tens of thousands of busy twittering birds. 'Where…what is this?' they cried.

'Welcome to one of our greatest gems, the beta/gamma bird planet,' declared Mizmiq, signalling for Lorna to pause so that everyone could admire the bubble which was surrounded by millions of glasslike panels, each the size of a Meadowlands field.

'Every so often, one of the Beta 9 star systems drifts towards the planet, sending kaleidoscopic patterns shining through the panels. It's an awe-inspiring spectacle and we call it the northern light show, a phrase we stole from a place where something similar can be seen,' Mizmiq winked, glancing at Lorna who smiled knowingly back at the grandmaster.

'The musical festivities that accompany the light show are, well, out of this world I would say,' added Mizmiq.

'It's certainly the biggest disco ball I've ever seen,' exclaimed Julius and everybody laughed.

'Can you get me a ticket to the next show?' begged Lorna.

'I will, and I'm delighted to have been the first bird to introduce you to this special place, even though our visit is fleeting.'

Mizmiq led Lorna up to one of the giant rectangular ceiling panels and asked her to hold Julius and Fergus. He kept Albert with him.

Lorna decided the best way to carry Julius and Fergus was to press them between Grace and Filia.

'Shove up, Julius, you oaf—I can't breathe!' cried Grace.

'I'm sorry, but I honestly can't move,' answered Julius hysterically. 'It's an all-male Centurian sandwich.'

'I won't be long,' laughed Mizmiq.

The grandmaster disappeared behind the panel and returned almost instantly. 'This way,' he smiled, taking Julius and Fergus back.

They passed through the glasslike skin and into another corridor. It was narrow and meandered sharply so Lorna and Mizmiq flew in single file.

'This is the Alpha passageway,' grinned the grandmaster. 'It is a shortcut across this segment of space.'

'Alpha?' gulped Lorna.

'Yes, don't worry about falling off the edge of the universe. At the end of this tiny tube is the entrance to my home.'

After another hour or so of flight, Mizmiq asked Lorna to wait and carry Julius and Fergus again while he darted off. A moment later she heard his voice in the darkness but couldn't see him. 'It's okay, come, and when you feel the ground underfoot, land,' he called quietly.

Lorna flew forward and came to rest, placing Filia, Grace, Julius and Fergus on a stone-paved floor while Mizmiq laid Albert's body next to them, cushioning it with a soft fabric of woven silver threads.

The hawk then turned to his guests and with a wave of his wing filled the room with sunlight and birdsong. 'Welcome to Castle Spinneret,' he declared.

Everyone gasped at the scenes of spring painted on the glorious domed ceiling above them. The most astonishing thing of all, however, was Mizmiq.

Where there had been a great hawk, there stood an old man in a silver-laced cloak with sparkling blue eyes, a long grey beard and the broadest of welcoming smiles. 'You see me in my original form, dear friends, and this is my observatory,' beamed the grandmaster.

Mizmiq pointed at the ceiling and the colourful skies suddenly became a cosmos of glistening stars. 'This observatory is not merely a planetarium, it is a looking glass,' he announced proudly. 'It allows distant horizons to be viewed close-up because places that I and my kin have visited and committed to memory may be enhanced and searched in detail. We call it a mirror-mind.

'Oh, and that comfy chair over there is where I sit in my most peaceful and most troubled moods,' he smiled.

Mizmiq's eyes, mouth, hands, every bit of him stretched with excitement as he paced across the floor and delighted in explaining how the observatory worked.

The friends stared at the sprightly old man in wonder. 'Who, I mean, what are you, if I may ask?' said Filia. 'You mentioned your kin—are there many of you?'

'We have a rather fancy title, I'm afraid; we're known as grandmasters,' smiled Mizmiq, 'and we are twenty or so in number. A few are missing but we hope they'll turn up again. Think of us as wizards if you like, although, like all wizards in the stories we know and love, there are many shades of wizard.

'You'll be here a while and will no doubt discover our quirks, and once you have, you can tell me where you think we stand in the panoply of weird and wonderful wizards,' he beamed.

'One thing I will say, though, is that we're a collaborative bunch. We each have an observatory in the castle and always share our memories. We help paint each others' ceilings as it were,' he laughed.

'Refining the mirror-minds is also why we like to travel, not just gaze, and why grandmasters are rarely found in the same place at the same time, and even if we do bump into each other, we tend to notice and record slightly different things, adding to the richness and precision of the mirror-mind's presentation.

'You see, grandmasters are a bit like probes. We take close-up pictures to enhance a telescopic view,' he smiled.

But Mizmiq's mood darkened as he strode up and down. 'This is where our FJ briefly appeared, between the constellations of Cepheus and Cygnus, and as we saw at Silverrock, it is no more.

'However, that is not what bothers me most. I expected to see a phantom trace, a faint representation of the FJ from the mirror-mind's recent history.

'I committed the FJ's shape to memory when I saw it, as did the owl, Sporadiq, a fellow grandmaster, but there is no record of our memory in the mirror-mind. It is as if it was never there.'

Filia fought back tears. The idea that Jonathan may not have placed his sign in the stars at all was impossible to accept or comprehend. She'd seen it as clearly as any other constellation.

Mizmiq put his hand on her shoulder. 'We will find him, Filia, we will find him,' he sighed.

Mizmiq began inspecting the ceiling again when a tall, extremely well-dressed, human-like figure entered the observatory. 'Grandmaster, the council awaits you,' he said.

'Yes, of course,' Mizmiq nodded. 'Everybody, this is Hennington. He's been my friend for many a stratospheric age and he will look after you. My assistant Skrieg will appear shortly too; he's very attentive and will probably follow you if you don't follow him. I will be back in an hour or so.'

Hennington sent Mizmiq a private message. 'Grandmaster, Skrieg was invaded by a Skull. He has been destroyed.'

'Impossible, an invasion here in Spinneret?' messaged Mizmiq.

'Yes,' Hennington replied. 'We found him passing secrets to Terminus. I'm very sorry,' he said, as Mizmiq hurried out.

Hennington cradled Albert in his hands and led Lorna, Filia, Julius, Grace and Fergus out of the observatory and into a garden courtyard full of flowers that seemed to smile at them quite naturally.

At the centre of the courtyard was a mosaic depicting a group of students at school. 'Don't be surprised by what you see,' grinned Hennington as Filia, Julius, Grace and Fergus looked down in amazement.

'That's us with Professor Harvester!' cried Julius.

154

'And there's Jonathan at his dronibus stop,' gasped Filia.

'These are grandmaster Mizmiq's gardens,' smiled Hennington. 'The mosaic changes with time, and with his thoughts. Everything is influenced by the images captured on his travels. What you see is the result of the same mirror-mind magic that improves the observatory's accuracy.'

'Hennington's voice is so exquisitely beautiful, don't you think, Filia?' whispered Grace, as intrigued by him as she was by the grandmaster's magic.

Filia smiled. 'Yes, it's mesmerising. He'd win all the Numberalist politeness awards,' she laughed.

Hennington ushered them along a cloister and into another courtyard where a marble sculpture of Albert stood at the centre of a fountain. He was flying and his windswept face was full of determination while his beak was curved in an elated smile.

'This splendid sculpture appeared shortly before you arrived,' said Hennington, laying Albert down beside the fountain on a soft bed of moss and magenta flowers. 'I now understand why. There will be a birdsong lament this evening.'

Lorna wept and kissed her husband's body and the sculpture's expression changed for moment into one of peaceful happiness before remoulding itself with lines of adrenaline and speed. 'I will stay a while,' choked Lorna. 'Go on, please.'

Filia, Julius, Grace and Fergus followed Hennington into another courtyard and ambled along a colonnade, stopping several times to run their fingers up and down the columns' fluted curves.

They then entered a rustic quadrangle that was neither inside nor out and Hennington led them to the far corner and up a spiral staircase. He pushed open a door and they found themselves standing in a circular gallery, looking down across the largest collection of parchments they'd ever seen.

'Welcome to the Spinneret library, one of the castle's greatest treasures,' proclaimed Hennington, pointing to a multitude of aisles and shelves with no visible end.

'This is the centre of the library and from here you can descend the stairwell and walk in whichever direction you choose, browsing the annals of everything that eyes have seen and minds have imagined.'

Hennington invited Filia, Julius, Grace and Fergus to explore and they immediately set off down the stairs.

'The domes above each section tell you which subject you're in,' explained Hennington. 'And don't worry if the paintings change as you pass—they're allowed to pick and choose what they show you, as long as they don't stray from their subject.'

Filia looked up and decided to climb a ladder to get a closer view of the dome above her.

'Be careful of the parchments on the top shelf,' said Hennington, watching her. 'Some are what we call living scrolls. Read only a bit at a time and if you feel like the scroll is trying to draw you into its story, put it down.

'We've had visitors who did not return for a while—some out of choice, others because they got into trouble and found it hard to escape the scroll.'

'I rather like the idea of being part of a fairytale in a fairytale castle,' quipped Julius as he raced down one of the aisles with Fergus.

Hennington frowned. 'I said be careful, Julius Fog,' he boomed, his voice somehow carrying throughout the library. 'It is not always obvious which scrolls have been inked with such magic, and you, particularly, should read in short bursts.'

50. The World of Birds

Shadow in the Sun

Jigsy's merry band of birds flew out of the Tau 7 corridor into clear sunlit skies. 'Eskatar,' they chorused in delight, gazing across a vast expanse of snowy mountains.

Jonathan and Alea heard and saw nothing of the world beyond their confinement inside grandmaster Nomadiq's spell of miniaturisation. They could only sense a change in the air.

The birds soared over Eskatar's towering peaks and laughed as they made faces at each other in the thick glacier ice.

'Where do we go, Rose, Nomadiq?' enquired Jigsy after a while. 'When it gets dark, the temperature will plummet,' warned Machian.

The two robins looked flustered. 'This is not the Eskatar I remember,' said Nomadiq.

'The planet has been covered by an ice age,' muttered Rose. 'The lack of warm corridor air has had a far greater impact than I imagined.'

The flock flew on. There was hardly a difference in the shape of each snow-laden summit and the ridges that joined them were continuous and unrelenting.

They searched for a way down, but there was no snowline, vegetation or watery green valley as far as the eye could see and they dived into a wide crevasse in a vain attempt to find a path beyond the ice, but it too offered no way through.

'We should fly higher so we can see further,' suggested Fovea, and the flock summoned the energy to glide upwards but they saw only snow as they climbed.

'We must rest,' cried Squijy, looking hopefully at his father.

'We fly back to the corridor,' announced Jigsy.

The troop agreed but Jigsy, Rose and Nomadiq darted off in different directions. 'Which one of them's right, Qybil?' asked Machian.

Qybil touched her brow with her wing as if trying to soothe a stabbing headache. 'I do not know,' she groaned.

The birds opened one lapisphere after another but there was no corridor behind any of them, only the same chilling breeze.

They flew higher again, resuming their desperate hunt for food, warmth and shelter. 'I see something above us,' cautioned Fovea. 'There's a thin shadow lying across the sun. Wait, it's moving.'

The birds hovered, hoping Fovea would elaborate quickly so they would know what to do. 'That is no shadow, it has wings,' she cried.

With incredible speed, a great bird of prey swept towards the weary band of travellers and circled them.

It eyed the birds without speaking or giving any clue as to its intentions and at every turn, it would look away across the mountains, then back at them. After ten or so circuits, they heard a deep, whispering voice. 'Were you followed?'

Rose spoke first, 'We weren't. A Skull ship tried to stop us from crossing the chasm but the Skulls fled when they lost their commander.'

The mighty bird jerked its head and looked directly at Nomadiq while continuing to circle the trembling flock.

'You hide something. It is evil.'

'I hold something very dear and strange which I can only partially explain,' replied the nervous robin.

The great bird completed another circuit of the shivering troop. 'Yes, strange indeed. Come, you will need these.'

The colossal bird came to a sudden standstill in mid-air and began giving out air tubes. 'There is one for each of you,' it said. 'They are exactly the right size. I created them while I was watching you.

'Go on, take them, I will not harm you, but this place will, it was once called Eskatar, a land of friendship, happiness and healing, but no more.'

The birds stared down at the frozen world below them. They were devastated, speechless.

Jigsy broke the silence. 'May we know who you are, please?' he choked, threading the tube-fastenings through his feathers.

'I am the guardian of Eskatar, but that was not always my role,' answered the bird.

'When I last traversed your world, in times that were as dark as these, I was Caerulean. I believe the two robins remember me, although shock or disbelief, or both, is making them hesitate before saying so. I'm fairly certain I remember them, or a version of them. I have not been out and about for a long while, but that is a story for later.'

While Rose and Nomadiq blushed, the other birds almost fell out of the sky.

'Dad, it's Caerulean!' cried Squijy.

Every bird knew of the mythical Caerulean. Many had first heard of the great atomhawk when they were younglings playing a game that the birds had copied from humans called top trumps.

Caerulean was one of the most sought after birds in the game. His points tally was second only to that of his father, Naumachian. He scored one hundred for attack and an outstanding ninety-nine for wingspan and defence.

'The real deal's much bigger than I imagined,' gulped Squijy to his brothers.

'There's no stack of wow words huge enough to describe him,' gawped Squigsy.

'We are invincible! Aaaaallllrrrrrrr,' shrilled Squigbox, letting rip an ear-splitting cry of victory.

'Calm down, please,' said Caerulean, raising his voice ever so slightly. 'I realise an atomhawk coming out of the sun to the east is quite some omen, but I haven't established for certain whether you were followed or not.'

'Silence, boys,' added Jigsy, introducing himself and his sons to the atomhawk.

'Thank you, Jigsy. I miss my father,' mused Caerulean. 'I hope to one day see him again. He once told me that the spell of hope is the only spell that requires no magic. It is always there. We have only to search our hearts to conjure it. I must learn to delve deeper and be more hopeful.'

The birds hung on Caerulean's every word and committed the sound of each of his syllables to memory so they'd be able to tell their friends and families what the great atomhawk had said.

'Now, saddle up, as the human horsemen used to say, we journey to the warmth of my sun,' he grinned, letting out an almost inaudible shrill. The birds laughed, quietly and set off after the atomhawk.

'Do not be afraid of the heat,' messaged Caerulean as he led them higher. 'I have surrounded you with a spell of protection.'

Spots of fire erupted as they approached the mysterious sun, scorching everything but them, and the birds examined their feathers after every flap but there was not even a hint of singeing.

The air too was still and the flabbergasted birds flew on through solar flares and rivers of molten rock with the ease of a windless summer's flight.

'This Caerulean is special beyond our wildest dreams,' gasped Squijy.

'Too right; defence should have been a hundred. A supernova explosion would bounce off him,' added Squigsy.

They maintained their speed as they neared the hydrogen corona. 'The hottest gases will raise the temperature only a touch,' messaged the remarkable atomhawk.

The birds braced themselves for the subtle difference between one thousand and two thousand degrees and barely broke a sweat as a narrow corridor opened in front of them. 'Not far now,' announced Caerulean and minutes later, they had arrived at a cave and felt the spell of protection fall away.

'This, my friends, is my home. You will be safe next to my hearth,' smiled Caerulean.

The birds landed and set about making themselves comfortable. They were exhausted and no words were sufficient to express their gratitude; they'd been flying nonstop since crossing the chasm.

They also sensed that the ancient atomhawk was glad of their company and that he was happy for them to nestle down in whatever part of his cave they wished.

Caerulean, meanwhile, gazed at his guests, worried that they would not find spaces to suit them. Eventually, when every bird was content and asleep, Caerulean relaxed and smiled, pleased not to be alone, but happy too with the silence and stillness he'd known for so long.

51. Castle Spinneret

A Contentious Council

An exceptionally tall, earnest grandmaster welcomed Mizmiq as he entered the council chamber.

'We know of your gallantry on Opus and Centurian and are grateful, my friend.'

'Thank you, Master William,' Mizmiq replied, acknowledging the greetings of the dozen or so grandmasters who rose from their marble seats as soon as they saw him.

Grandmaster William accompanied Mizmiq to his place in the chamber and shared some terrible news as they walked.

'We have just received word from Elgarian that the sickness of Gazong is deepening. Its landmasses are crumbling and falling into the empty seas. The lord of eagles himself cannot recall such a sudden and catastrophic change in the planet's state.'

Mizmiq went pale with fear as he listened. 'Elgarian's message arrived only moments ago,' continued William. 'He and hundreds of thousands of birds are flying to the archipelago. You know full well that the atomhawk's echo and Gazong's survival are as precious to many of the birds as even the Centurian and Opus lumenests.'

Mizmiq sat down, deep in thought, while William called the council to order.

The grandmasters quickly concluded that they should fly to Centurian without delay and help Sporadiq and Tortriq, calculating that the poison pouring out of the skies above Silverrock could erode the planet's structure in a matter of weeks, extending the abyss to the core.

Mizmiq spoke last. 'We must fly with all haste to Centurian, I agree. However, I am not convinced that we will be able to stop, or even slow, the Greylight's corrosion without Elgarian and the other birds who have flown to Gazong, and we cannot be certain of when they will return, or how many of them will come given the peril of their beloved planet.'

'You underestimate us,' objected grandmaster Ballistiq. 'Besides, we have no choice. We must do what we can and hope the birds will join us if we struggle to contain the Greylight. There is no other power that can help. The priestesses cannot leave Eskatar while the Tau 6 air spills into the void. The Emerald lands will die without their spells of warming.'

'There is, in fact, another power,' smiled Mizmiq.

The grandmasters glared at him.

'Who? Where?' demanded Ballistiq.

'You will no doubt have heard of the osprey who healed the dying petrel in the supreme court of Savanna?' said Mizmiq. 'It is much talked about in the corridors.

'I expect you will also be aware of the osprey's origins; he is a sixteen-year-old boy from Centurian. What you will not know, perhaps, is the nature of his magic?'

The grandmasters fixed their eyes on Mizmiq.

'I was with him when he cast the spell that gave him osprey form and I can tell you that turning himself into a bird was not the most astonishing thing that he did. He created an Opening into Twilight with spells that I was unable to hear.'

The grandmasters gasped.

'He is travelling with Rose to the Tau 6 chasm. My hope is that they will cross the void so the priestesses can help him, and us, understand the true extent of his power.'

'Mizmiq, the chasm is watched and it has widened as much in the last ten years as it did in the previous hundred. They will not reach the Tau 7 corridor,' warned Ballistiq.

'Then we should not hesitate to go there and help them,' responded Mizmiq sternly.

Muttering filled the chamber. The grandmasters and birds had tried and failed many times to cross the chasm when it had not been nearly as wide and the thought of ignoring a visible enemy on Centurian to make another attempt was impossible for some to accept.

Disquiet became open argument, then disarray. 'Silence, let the grandmaster finish,' yelled William, noticing Mizmiq getting up to speak.

'We should first go to Tau 6 so that Rose and the boy have every chance of crossing the void, and from there fly to Centurian, with or without them,' Mizmiq urged.

'That will add days to our journey,' exclaimed grandmaster Ballistiq. 'The Omega passageway, Tau 6, back here again, Alpha, then Gamma; that's our fastest route. With all due respect, Mizmiq, what you propose is madness. We'd be more than quadrupling our journey time to Centurian.'

'Sacrificing a few days for the possibility of bringing an extraordinary power into the war is what we must do,' insisted Mizmiq.

There was uproar. 'We will reconvene in ten minutes,' shouted William. 'Remember, do not panic, there is always a way,' he cried as the grandmasters hurried out of the council chamber.

Mizmiq and William sat alone. 'Thank you for your support,' said Mizmiq. 'I think we should use your qniform name more often, Donotpaniq.'

William laughed. 'I prefer the rough and tumble of a contentious council. The danger of interminable old age is that we become so terribly stubborn, immovable. It's good to put a cat amongst the pigeons from time to time, and you certainly did that today, my friend,' he grinned. 'Now, pass me one of those velvet cushions and tell me more of what you've seen. To hear news firsthand is a privilege—nothing against the observatory ceilings, of course. Where would we be without them?'

'Indeed,' smiled Mizmiq. 'And my ceiling is in fact where this whole thing started.'

Mizmiq told William about the moment he'd first noticed Centurian flickering in his observatory ceiling, and how he'd searched the silver planet for magical anomalies and found Jonathan.

William listened intently, treasuring every detail of the miracle that was Jonathan Powers and becoming more and more convinced that they should find a way to bring this incredible boy into the war.

52. Castle Spinneret
The Threads of a Lost Wizard

The endless aisles of the Spinneret library had kept Filia, Julius, Grace and Fergus captivated for hours. They'd walked for mile after mile, browsing parchments on astronomy, nature, history, magic, medicine and much more.

The friends had left the library for Albert's birdsong lament and had returned teary-eyed after sunset to pick out a few choice scrolls to take to their rooms.

Julius had selected one of the so-called living scrolls from a top shelf, "The creatures of Eskatar", and after reading the first chapter he'd put the parchment down next to his bed as Hennington had instructed.

He stared at the ornate wood-panelled ceiling in his room, running his eyes along the grooves as if they were pathways through a maze. 'I'll allow myself another read once I exit the other side,' he chuckled to himself. The scroll was quickly back in his hands.

When curiosity finally gave way to exhaustion, Julius placed the scroll under his plush burgundy pillow and was fast asleep in seconds.

Filia had also chosen a living scroll about Eskatar. Her's was full of maps and detailed descriptions of the Emerald lands and she too had come up with a way of stopping herself from becoming overly engrossed.

Painted eagles towered above the corner-posts of her bed. In between reads, she imagined these magnificently gilded birds careering off and completing a circuit of the castle, and each time she pictured them flying back into her bedroom she opened her scroll again.

Filia had also placed her parchment under her pillow before falling asleep and that night she and Julius found themselves in the same dream.

The two friends were in a cave that looked down onto a field alive with butterflies. They clambered out and ran happily through the brightly coloured waves of flowers that rolled away in front of them.

A swallowtail butterfly fluttered to and fro beside them as they sprinted. They noticed it darting off then coming back and realised it was trying to lead them somewhere.

They followed it up a steep hillside to the ruins of a circular temple and cried with joy when they got there. Jonathan was sitting on a fallen column and next to him stood an old man who they assumed to be Mizmiq. They couldn't see his face clearly, but his cloak was just like the grandmaster's.

They rushed to embrace Jonathan, but he didn't move. He was cold, frozen, expressionless.

'Jonathan, Jonathan,' they yelled.

His lips quivered. 'Air…air,' he coughed but the dream ended before he could say anything else.

As soon as they woke, they rushed out of their respective bedrooms and met halfway along the corridor. 'Did you see Jonathan too?' blurted Julius.

'Yes, at the temple,' exclaimed Filia.

They hurried back to their rooms, willed themselves to sleep and dreamt again, but this time they saw only fields of flowers and butterflies. There was no Jonathan.

Spinneret's dawn chorus began with a medley of breathtaking solos and quickly became a choral masterpiece as one bird after another added their voices to the music.

The yawning friends delighted in the performance as they wandered towards the dining hall and when they arrived, Hennington directed them to a table. The grandmasters were on the opposite side of the room, deep in conversation.

The four friends tucked into a feast of jam-filled toast-turrets and salmon-stuffed egg mosaics, Spinneret specials according to Hennington.

Mizmiq joined them. The grandmasters had been arguing throughout the night about whether they should fly directly to Centurian, or go to the Tau 6 chasm first. They'd given themselves until after breakfast to battle it out. There would then be a vote and everyone had agreed to support the majority.

'Both Julius and I saw Jonathan in a dream,' beamed Filia.

'Tell me more,' smiled Mizmiq.

Filia and Julius took turns to retell the night's events.

'You both adhered to the reading rules, short bursts?' enquired the grandmaster.

'Yes,' answered Filia and Julius.

'I read for about ten minutes at a time and put the scroll under my pillow when I was done,' said Julius.

'I did the same,' nodded Filia.

'I'm sure you followed correct procedure,' grinned Mizmiq, 'under the pillows, you say?'

'Yes, the scrolls never seemed to crease so I thought that would be okay,' Julius replied, worried he'd somehow damaged his parchment.

'My thinking precisely,' added Filia.

'Please, there's no need for concern, you're right, they do not crease,' laughed Mizmiq. 'However, they were doing something else. Living scrolls entice the mind into their stories if they're very close to you; they don't like the reading rules either,' winked the grandmaster.

'They mean no harm, but they're drawn to active minds because they like to be read—understandable if you're a scroll that thinks it's got something interesting to say.'

'Could we have seen a real representation of Jonathan in Eskatar?' asked Filia.

'I don't know,' sighed Mizmiq. 'Your visions have all the hallmarks of a fictional dream, I'm afraid. The butterflies, the fields, the temple. They're all things you will have read about in the scrolls, and Jonathan would probably have featured in any of your dreams, not only those of Eskatar. The ruinous state of the temple does bother me though, but again, we can put that down to your minds fearing the worst perhaps.'

'But Hennington told us the content of living scrolls can be changed so the parchments are always up to date. Jonathan could do that, couldn't he, from Eskatar?' suggested Filia.

'I'm not so sure,' Mizmiq smiled. 'If I tried to persuade the grandmasters of that, I think they'd be sceptical. Living scrolls can only be updated through the eyes of a grandmaster, as far as we know. The vellum is enriched with the same mirror-mind magic as the observatory ceilings.'

'What if the old man wasn't you? Maybe he was a different grandmaster. I just assumed it was you, although I couldn't see him clearly and his cloak wasn't exactly the same as yours,' said Filia.

'How was it different?' asked Mizmiq abruptly. 'A grandmaster's cloak is one of his most distinctive features.'

'The threads were moving,' answered Julius.

'Did they settle?'

'Yes, briefly, as curved N shapes, before moving again,' Filia replied.

'Draw the pattern, please, here, on this parchment,' said Mizmiq.

Filia and Julius did as he requested. 'Were there gaps between the lines?' asked Mizmiq, leaning over them.

'Yes,' nodded Filia.

'And were the N shapes arrayed vertically or horizontally?'

'Both,' replied Filia and Julius at the same time.

Lorna flew in as Mizmiq paced the floor. She'd decided to breakfast in the opulent Spinneret gardens rather than pick apart what she thought was bizarrely presented human food.

As she opened her beak to ask what was going on, Mizmiq addressed the room, 'My fellow grandmasters. I believe Jonathan Powers has crossed the chasm but Eskatar is on the brink of disaster.'

'How on earth did you come to that conclusion?' cried Ballistiq.

Mizmiq appeared on the verge of tears as he held up Filia and Julius' drawings, 'Grandmaster Nomadiq has spoken to us for the first time in millennia, through the living scrolls of Eskatar.'

The grandmasters gazed in wonder at the curving lines of the lost wizard's cloak. They wept, overjoyed, while Mizmiq explained his interpretation of the dream: the temple was the priestesses' home and its ruins were either its actual state or a cry for help from the grandmaster.

'This also means that a strand of Nomadiq's magic spans the void,' gasped William.

'Yes,' beamed Mizmiq. 'A living scroll can only receive new information through the mirror-mind threads woven by grandmasters into the corridor walls. Eskatar is no longer isolated. Perhaps it was Nomadiq's wizardry that helped Rose and Jonathan cross the void where all others have failed?'

'Well, what are we waiting for?' declared Ballistiq, placing his hand on Mizmiq's shoulder and looking him in the eye. 'We take the Omega passageway to the chasm. We fly to the aid of Eskatar, our old friend and the Centurian boy before hurtling back to the silver planet.'

The wizards roared their approval and William ordered them to be ready within the hour.

53. Castle Spinneret

Unexpected Journeys

Filia, Julius, Grace, Fergus and Lorna waited with Hennington in the dining hall while the grandmasters bustled about the castle, making their final preparations.

Mizmiq marched in. 'We're all set, bar one last thing. We would like you to come with us.'

'Yessss!' they cried, except Lorna who immediately stared at her feet. She was relieved to find they were not expanding.

'Calm down, calm down. I'm afraid *you* does not mean all of you, only Filia and Julius. Let me explain, and Grace, Fergus, don't be disappointed, there's plenty to explore here in Spinneret.

'We've been examining the Eskatar scrolls and can't find any of the imagery you described, Filia, Julius. The latest editions are still those that were published before the Tau 6 corridor was severed a thousand years ago.

'We do not doubt that what you observed was real. It is impossible for you to have drawn grandmaster Nomadiq's livery so accurately without seeing it. The most likely explanation is that Nomadiq's connection with the parchments has been broken.

'The corridors were poisoned when they were first attacked and the venom is as strong as ever. The grandmaster's threads may not have lasted long and we think the scrolls are not ready to include what they showed you. We believe they want to re-establish contact with the grandmaster first to check their facts. Living scrolls were one of Nomadiq's own incredible inventions and he designed them with free will so they could make their own judgements about the truth.

'In a nutshell, you saw what the scroll was being told before the connection was lost, and that knowledge may be critical if we are to find Jonathan, Nomadiq and

Rose. It is likely that they are in your cave. That is where your dream began and where the grandmaster's thoughts almost certainly originated. We know how to find the temple, the priestesses' home, but are unsure about the cave. We may need you to retrace your steps to help us locate it.'

Grace and Fergus were still not happy but before they could express their dissatisfaction, Mizmiq raised his hand to silence them, 'There is no reason to put you at risk, Grace, Fergus. Even if we find a way to cross the chasm, Eskatar's perilous state will present us with further challenges. You must remain here, and you will, I am sure, enjoy the magic of Spinneret. A new world of bird-lore and wizard-lore awaits all of you,' smiled the grandmaster. 'You too, Lorna,' he winked.

Filia and Julius leant down to stroke Lorna's feathers and she rolled her cheeks across their fingers. They then hugged Grace and Fergus tight. 'Next time we see you, it will be with Jonathan,' wept Filia as Mizmiq invited her and Julius to follow him.

The grandmaster led the two friends through a long colonnade and into a quiet courtyard surrounded by painted columns and a frieze depicting numerous bird species, some of which were familiar to Filia and Julius while some were not.

The birds changed whenever they looked at them, revealing yet more of the magical creatures, but the disappearing birds did not fade into the frieze, they glided down to a shallow pool at the centre of the courtyard and vanished in the water without a splash.

'The water has been blessed with the magic of transformation,' Mizmiq remarked as he walked past the pool. 'And you're going to dive in,' he smiled, stopping and turning to face them.

Filia and Julius were dumbstruck. 'I don't think we heard you correctly?' gulped Julius.

'You did,' chuckled Mizmiq. 'I'm not carrying you on the next leg of our journey. You are going to take bird form. I can travel faster without holding you and whilst I don't expect us to be separated, we don't know what we'll find when we arrive in the Emerald lands; you may need your own wings,' he grinned, as Filia and Julius glared at the water, terrified.

'The pool was gifted to the grandmasters by some very powerful birds. It is perfectly safe; you won't hit your human heads on the mosaic squares and you'll emerge fully feathered in the Omega corridor,' he beamed. 'And yes, you will be able to become yourselves again whenever you choose.' Filia and Julius were speechless.

Mizmiq asked them to think of a bird. 'Don't be pensive, first one that springs to mind,' he smiled.

Filia spoke first. 'Golden eagle,' she said, wanting to smile but too shocked and frightened to move her lips.

'Jabiru,' blurted Julius, 'I saw jabirus in our Eskatar dream,' he explained, swallowing hard.

'Interesting, very good. Now, when you dive in, I want you to think of yourselves as those birds, ready?'

They stood next to the shimmering pool and Mizmiq leapt in and disappeared. Filia and Julius hesitated, but then closed their eyes and plunged headfirst into the water, whooping and screaming.

*****

After Mizmiq, Filia and Julius had left the dining hall, Hennington asked Grace and Fergus to accompany him on a tour of the castle's meticulously kept gardens while Lorna shot off again, eager to meet more of the woodland locals.

Grace and Fergus were enthralled by the paradise of Spinneret's parks and meadows and for a long while refused to rest their legs at any of the glistening marble benches that adorned the pathways. When they did eventually tire, they chose to sit on the smooth white steps of a circular temple.

'This is a replica of the temple Filia and Julius saw in their dream,' explained Hennington.

'You're saying we're looking at an exact copy of the priestesses' home?' gasped Fergus.

Hennington nodded and smiled as he too admired the immaculately sculpted angelic figures that were the temple's columns.

'Butterflies, hundreds of them,' exclaimed Grace, pointing at a line of luxurious colours fluttering towards the temple.

'Those are Eskatarian butterflies,' smiled Hennington. 'They were visiting the castle when the Tau 6 corridor was broken and have not been able to return. They often congregate at the temple.'

'Look,' cried Fergus as a great eagle swooped past them and soared upwards before vanishing in the sunlight.

'And there's Lorna trying to keep up,' added Grace, laughing at the pigeon who was frantically flapping her wings some way behind the eagle.

'I wonder what Mr Archaneus would have said about a pigeon chasing a low-flying eagle,' chuckled Fergus. Hennington peered at him quizzically.

'Oh, Mr Archaneus is our premagic history teacher and divination is a favourite topic of his,' grinned Fergus.

Hennington raised an eyebrow. 'Here's an amusing fact about the premagic Centurian fascination with omens: some birds used to adjust their behaviour to avoid giving the wrong impression. They knew the seriousness of their actions.'

Grace and Fergus laughed and shook their heads in astonishment. They thought of Mr Archaneus, hoping he'd somehow survived the destruction of Silverrock. How he would have delighted in what Hennington had revealed.

Hennington excused himself and left Grace and Fergus to wander on their own for a while. 'Have you noticed his ears? Not small, are they? Rather pointed too,' whispered Fergus when he was certain that Hennington was out of sight.

'How rude,' responded Grace. 'I think his ears are exquisite; they resemble butterfly wings.'

'I didn't say they were ugly, just strange, a bit like his clothes. He's wildly overdressed, don't you think? I can't fathom why he'd want to hike around these parks and gardens wearing impeccably polished shoes and a bright blue blazer.'

Grace laughed. 'I love the way he dresses. He's so elegant, and you can't even hear his feet touch the ground.'

Fergus and Grace heard a light cough and jumped. It was Hennington; he was standing right behind them and his pursed lips were hiding a wry smile.

'Er, we were just talking, speculating, about you, Hennington. Would you mind telling us about your own history, please?' babbled Grace.

165

'Of course, I should have told you when we met, I apologise. As you can see, I look a little peculiar. I'm a butterelfly.'

'Sorry, Hennington, could you repeat that?' asked Grace, kicking herself for not listening more attentively.

'A but-ler-elf-ly. I am Eskatarian and have a long history of service to the priestesses no less.

'Like the butterflies, I am unable to return to my home while the Tau 6 corridor remains broken.

'My race can assume many forms, butterfly is one; I'm an Adonis blue,' he smiled proudly. 'I can also take bird form, as well as the almost human appearance you see now, although we've never quite cracked the human image,' he winked.

'I think you're lovely the way you are,' declared Grace, worried that Hennington had heard Fergus' mutterings about his ears.

'Why, thank you, Grace,' replied the butterelfly, bowing slightly, and blushing a little too.

Grace was about to launch into a series of questions when the gardens erupted. Eagles, hawks, kestrels, kites, crows, buzzards and numerous other bird species suddenly filled the cloudless Spinneret sky with anxious shrieking while a whole host of woodland birds shook the hedgerows as they took to the air.

Hennington appeared equally perturbed. 'The birds have sensed something,' he said. 'Come, let us hurry to Mizmiq's observatory.'

They rushed along the garden pathways and across the castle courtyards until they reached the grandmaster's rooms. Hennington went straight to the observatory and gazed up at the mirror-mind ceiling, horrified. Centurian was almost invisible, a dark circle.

To his, Fergus and Grace's relief, the silver planet shone again seconds later, but it then faded quickly once more.

The flickering persisted and Hennington became increasingly concerned as he watched. The extremes were far more pronounced than the light and dark that Mizmiq had observed and which had continued intermittently ever since he'd flown to Centurian to find Jonathan.

'What's happening, Hennington? Please tell us our home is safe,' cried Grace and Fergus.

Hennington strode up and down. He did not reply. All he could think was that such instability indicated a threat to the lumenest core, or the planet itself, and that the clarity of the mirror-mind's warning was perhaps a result of Sporadiq and Tortriq seeing the danger with their own eyes.

'I do not know what this means,' he answered finally. 'And I've only one suggestion: we must fly to Centurian and discover the truth for ourselves.'

Before Grace and Fergus could say another word, Hennington had disappeared. 'I'm here,' he called. 'In my bird form.'

Fergus and Grace stared at their feet and saw a hoopoe butterfly bird with a formidable Mohican crown.

'I'm going to cast a spell of miniaturisation,' he said. 'You will be carried within me; there is no other way to explain it. I will also send a message to Lorna before we set off so she knows we've left the castle.'

Hennington conjured his spell and Grace and Fergus found themselves cocooned, unable to see or hear the outside world. They then felt a sudden lunge and yelled in fright as the butlerelfly opened a lapisphere and accelerated into the Alpha passageway.

54. Centurian
The Owl and the Raven

Sporadiq and Tortriq hovered inside the abyss. They were halfway between Centurian's surface and the lumenest at the centre of the planet.

The diamind bombardment appeared to have stopped but the grandmasters wanted to be certain that there would be no more bombs before letting their spells of protection fall away. They would then focus their magical energy on filling the vast channel that had been gouged into the planet above them.

'Let us begin,' said Tortriq and Sporadiq nodded agreement.

The grandmasters criss-crossed the abyss, trailing thick silver threads, and they fixed them to the walls before every turn and poured healing magic into the weave, hoping to prevent the Greylight's poisons from undoing their work.

The first few miles were sealed quickly but the owl and the raven were then shaken by a massive tremor. Duggerrid had come out of matterline and ordered his container of raw lightning and diaminds to be released into the abyss.

The grandmasters looked upwards, petrified, and cast spells of understanding.

'That is no earthquake. There is a roar of hatred and anger inside its sound,' cried Sporadiq, struggling to interpret his spell's response.

The walls started to crumble and the grandmasters immediately conjured spells of protection but found themselves being swept down as the planet began to peel apart.

'We must stop and fight,' yelled Sporadiq.

'Not yet,' answered Tortriq. 'Whatever it is, it is too strong. Our only hope is for the planet to slow its descent first.'

As they fell, they saw dots of light shining through tiny cracks in the innermost layers of the planet. 'The eternal core,' exclaimed Sporadiq, his eyes fixed on the outline of the pearl-like oval which became clearer with every mile.

'It is time to stand our ground,' cried Tortriq suddenly, and the grandmasters took human form and wove threads across the falling rubble to stop whatever it was that was crashing towards them.

'Light the strands, now,' screamed Tortriq as the noise of violence intensified above them.

They set the web alight but the raging fireball ripped their hastily woven threads, like a stone smashing through a spider's web.

Sporadiq and Tortriq were carried beneath the bomb and as they neared the lumenest, they saw what looked like grey wisps of smoke passing inside the oval.

Sporadiq gasped. 'The souls of the dead,' he cried. It was a sight he'd never witnessed.

The container struck the lumenest and exploded, crushing the grandmasters and sending shock waves throughout Centurian and the oval instantly lost all but a slender line of its brightness even though its meshed threads did not tear.

Duggerrid gazed down from the bridge of the Marrowbone, howling with delight at his victory. The Spellenaria diaminds, the force of more than a million dead, the

Greylight and the great bomb had all played their part in giving the Skull lord a direct path to the core. Human eternity was about to die.

55. The World of Birds

Grand Mastery

Filia opened her eyes and wept in wonder. Her body was covered in soft brown feathers; she was the youthful golden eagle from her Meadowlands dream with Jonathan.

She looked up. Above her was a tall jabiru, dangling its red legs and swinging its black beak from side to side.

'Julius?' she cried.

'Filia!' he yelled.

They beat their wings and twisted awkwardly. 'You're doing ever so well, try not to overthink it,' laughed Mizmiq who was flying a little way ahead.

They flapped harder and caught up with the grandmasters but other than Mizmiq they couldn't tell who was who; they'd all changed into bird form.

'We're quite a mix of shapes, sizes and colours, aren't we?' remarked a hummingbird whose voice they recognised as William's. 'How do you feel?' he asked.

'Like it was meant to be,' beamed Filia, already getting used to the incredible sensation of flight.

'Strange, but sort of okay, a bit like myself,' answered Julius, and everyone shrilled with laughter.

The grandmasters ushered Filia and Julius into the middle of the flock and settled into a steady rhythm behind Master Velcrow, a granite-black crow who was introduced to them as the grandmasters' pacesetter.

'Whenever we go about our business in a group, he takes the lead; he's a superb judge of speed, time and distance,' William explained. 'And for some, it's the only way to keep up,' he winked, nodding towards Grandmaster Limpiq, a bird Filia and Julius did not know. 'He's a switch, and it's not merely his wings that are lopsided, the poor chap's legs got the gene too,' chuckled William.

'Oh, and you're so bloomin' perfect, aren't you, grandmaster splendid,' scoffed Limpiq.

'There is far more to Master Velcrow's role than simply keeping us together,' added Ballistiq, a magnificent red-crested rooster. 'He helps us reach our destination in the best possible condition.'

'And the rooster doesn't only mean physical condition,' smiled Mizmiq. 'Relaxing the mind so it can endure the labours of magic is equally important. Now, brace yourselves, I'm going to add you to the glue.'

'The what?' gawped Filia and Julius.

'The glue, our spell of attachment, the magic by which we stick to the paceman and fly without thinking: first-class travel as it should be,' grinned Mizmiq, as their speed increased. 'We are masters of the air travelling with the masters of the universe,' shouted Julius, enjoying the liberating feeling of being a passenger without a care in the world.

The grandmasters flew on for hours, stopping only once during their journey—at the tau/upsilon bird planet. They were eager to hear the local news and were told that a flock of gamma/delta birds had recently passed through the sigma/tau nesting station on their way to the chasm. No one had dared to fly to Tau 6 to find out what had happened to them.

The grandmasters replenished their sacks with food and water and Master Velcrow led them swiftly on.

After several more hours of high-speed flight, they arrived at the first Tau 6 barrier. William cast a spell of opening and they flew through. The grandmasters then crossed each section quickly but slowed down as soon as the air began to thin and master Velcrow finally brought them to a full stop a short distance from the chasm.

The grandmasters approached the Tau 6 ledge with caution and were horrified to see how far the gap had grown.

When it was clear that there were no Skull ships patrolling the void, William took charge and told the grandmasters how he wanted to proceed: 'We will cast spells of thread-creation, sizing, sorting, weaving and binding simultaneously,' he said.

'You all know where your expertise lies so divide yourselves up accordingly, but I don't want more than three of you working on the same task at once.

'Bring me the threads untangled and each one must be the same length. If you need to make adjustments, ensure that the discarded strands are reused. Let's make every inch count so we don't lose any time.

'I will signal when I'm satisfied our threads are securely fastened to the lacerated edges of Tau 6 and we'll then move outwards at a steady pace.

'Ballistiq, at the first sign of Skull attack, engage the enemy. I will leave it up to you to decide who you take with you.

'Filia, Julius, hover directly behind me and try not look past,' instructed William. 'The silver light of a corridor weave is especially intense. The threads derive strength from their brightness as much as from their thickness. You've only just got your bird-eyes—make sure you don't lose them,' he smiled.

Filia and Julius stared at the hummingbird's back. He was suddenly many times his previous size and the light around him shone with near-blinding brightness.

The grandmasters began moving backwards and forwards across William's silhouette, coming and going as he bid. The dazzling hummingbird was composer, conductor and master builder all in one—the most extraordinary and brilliant magician the two friends could ever have imagined.

The wizards sang quietly as they wove, and from time to time Filia and Julius would glance through the turquoise waves of William's wings and catch a glimpse of the corridor taking shape ahead of them.

The minutes ticked by and became hours without even an inkling of a Skull ship, and as the grandmasters eventually drew closer to the Eskatar corridor, Filia and Julius noticed the temperature drop and kept close to the hummingbird to stay warm.

'Do we fly on now?' asked Filia, shivering, the moment they touched the Tau 7 ledge.

'Only you, Julius and Mizmiq will continue on to Eskatar for now. Unfortunately, the rest of us have barely begun our work,' sighed William. 'We need to cross the chasm tens, if not hundreds of times for our corridor to have any chance of remaining airtight so it can send warmth to the Emerald lands.

'There is good news, however, for the veracity of your dream. We found a few of Grandmaster Nomadiq's threads. He was indeed here not long ago.'

Filia and Julius rejoiced and raised their wings in readiness for flight, but they did not take off. 'Wait!' they yelled while the grandmasters fell about laughing; their wings had all but frozen over.

'I do apologise,' cried Mizmiq, casting a spell of warming. 'Some magical adjustments happen almost without thought. I'll be sure to monitor your temperature from now on,' he laughed.

Filia and Julius proceeded to fold their wings across their warming bellies. 'Amazing!' whooped Filia. 'The heat's travelling down to my toes.'

'You mean those great big weapons of yours, not your toes,' howled Julius.

'Can you feel it too?' cried Filia.

'Absolutely. My long trouserless legs are roasting!' Julius replied in delight.

'Ready?' grinned Mizmiq.

'Yes!' they shrilled, and the eagle, jabiru and hawk shot into the Tau 7 corridor, leaving the wizards to make their next pass across the void.

56.   The World of Birds

The Butterfly Effect

The birds opened their bleary eyes to find Caerulean preparing a meal. He was separating berries of different types into piles of equal height.

'You have been asleep for a long time,' smiled the atomhawk. 'There is no day and night inside my sun, or any other sun for that matter; nothing to trigger a dawn chorus.'

Jigsy's troops were starving and they gobbled up Caerulean's feast of dried fruits. 'These are fabulous,' chirped Squijy, tucking into a second mound of bilberries.

'I'm glad they suffice. They're conjured, I'm afraid. I dug through the snow and searched for some real food while you slept, but that proved fruitless,' he sighed, half smiling.

Caerulean shuffled off to a corner of his cave and left them to it. He lowered his head onto a rocky shelf jutting out from the wall. It seemed to have been designed for that very purpose.

Rose and Nomadiq followed and when he'd made himself comfortable they bowed before looking up at the aging atomhawk's silver-grey eyes.

'I know what you have come to ask,' said Caerulean, his words full of regret and sorrow. 'Alas, I fear the priestesses are dead. I failed them, and that failure breaks my heart all the more because it was they who saved me.

'As you will remember, I lay dying after the Gazong war nearly ten thousand years ago. The priestesses brought me to Eskatar and the world believed that I was lost.

'But the priestesses never stopped casting spells of healing and after endless years of darkness, my eyes opened. That was only decades past.

'I was dismayed to learn of the Tau 7 void and all those who'd died trying to cross the chasm during the thousand years since the corridor was severed.

'I wanted to act but the priestesses persuaded me to remain hidden in Eskatar lest the Arc destroy me while I was still weak. Reluctantly, I agreed, and they told no one of my return.

'At the same time, the void's freezing winds finally overpowered them. They could no longer sustain the seasons of spring and summer across the Emerald lands with their spells of warming.

'I made it my mission to help them and created this sun. I battled the ice from the sky while the priestesses sent their healing power into the earth from within the walls of their temple.

'But I fear we have lost our fight. The priestesses lie buried beneath the mountain glaciers. They refused to seek outside help, saying the planet would die if any one of them abandoned it, and that Eskatar's only hope was for them to care for the earth while I gave my strength to the sun.

'I will not rest until Eskatar is saved or I die. In every waking moment, I pour my energy into this sun, hoping to one day defeat the ice.

'But I am close to despair. I no longer feel the priestesses' warmth when I reach into the soil, and although the heat of the corona rises, it is not enough and I am terrified that I have failed the planet of Eskatar and the angels who saved me.'

The robins wept, and Caerulean turned away, fighting his own tears.

It was Nomadiq who spoke next, 'Caerulean, I hold two creatures who I wish to free. Do not be quick to judge; give me a chance to explain.'

Nomadiq took human form and placed the mighty Skull Ornifrac on the smooth stone floor.

'I was right; you have brought evil to Eskatar. The Skull must be undone,' declared Caerulean angrily.

But the great atomhawk's mood softened the moment he saw Alea. 'Sapphire,' he gasped. 'What is this?'

Alea curled in ever-quickening circles, astonished and elated as she realised who was staring at her.

'Do not harm the Skull, dear Caerulean, he is not what he seems,' she pleaded. 'I am also tied to him; it would be the end for both of us.'

'I will free you, then we will see about the Skull,' answered Caerulean.

The atomhawk grabbed Ornifrac and before anyone could utter a word, he shot out of the cave towards the raging fires of his sun.

Alea sent a message to Rose and Nomadiq. 'Jonathan is inside the Skull's shell, he spoke to me for a short time, but I fear it is too late; I can no longer reach him. I will help Caerulean understand.'

The atomhawk made short shrift of the distance between his sun and the ice-covered world that was once Eskatar, landing on one of the many snow-capped peaks.

'My dear sapphire, it is Alea, isn't it? Either I release you now and the Skull dies, or if you insist, I will leave you both here. The Skull's carcass will rot on the mountain and you will, in time, be free. If that is what you wish, I shall bring you warmth until the Skull is gone.'

'Yes, Caerulean, I am Alea,' she replied, her voice tearful and frightened. 'I am one of the sapphire lights who fought alongside you and your father in the Gazong war.

'I choose to remain here and I will do all in my power to pass whatever warmth you give me into this Skull because there is a living creature inside it, impossible though that may sound; a human, a boy who is my friend and who is able to take bird form.'

Caerulean let out a frustrated cry of such magnitude that the mountains trembled. 'Please, talk with Rose and grandmaster Nomadiq before condemning the Skull,' begged Alea. 'Rose, in particular, knows much about the boy.'

Caerulean touched Alea gently with his wing and she felt his warmth. 'Very well, let us hope there is another way,' he sighed.

Caerulean gripped Ornifrac carefully with his talons and soared upwards into the sun.

The birds rejoiced when he reappeared carrying the Skull and Rose, Nomadiq and Caerulean began casting every healing spell they knew, but they could not summon Jonathan's voice.

'The Skull has taken him,' mourned Caerulean. 'Your spell of sleeping prolonged his life, grandmaster, but it has not prevented his death. I am sorry. And you, my dear Alea, have done all you can.'

The birds were quiet, then muttering filled the cave as they wondered what else could be done to bring Jonathan back.

'Silence,' cried Caerulean suddenly. 'There are other creatures. You were followed—careless birds.'

The atomhawk hurtled out of his lair, taking the Skull and Alea with him.

'Get after him, quick!' ordered Jigsy.

The birds shot into the narrow tunnel outside the cave, petrified they would burn to a crisp if they didn't catch up, but Caerulean had stopped abruptly at the end of the corridor. 'The ice is melting,' he gasped. 'Ever so slightly, but it is melting, there is no doubt.'

'Look at that grin,' yelled Squijy. The birds were all thinking the same thing; what a joy it was to see happiness on such a sullen face.

Caerulean led the flock through the magically tepid heat of his sun. 'Three birds have exited the Tau 7 corridor. Do you know them?' he asked, transferring images into their minds.

'I know one of them,' exclaimed Nomadiq, careering off and leaving the others behind.

Rose cast a spell of understanding and darted straight after him. 'I know all three,' she shrilled.

Mizmiq spotted the two robins as they emerged from the sun's glaring rays. The rest of the flock were not yet visible.

Nomadiq raced past him. 'Follow me, young Master Mizmiq! Let us find some turf and retake our human forms,' howled the grandmaster.

Mizmiq wept as he chased him. He knew Nomadiq's voice as if it was yesterday.

'Who is that?' Filia and Julius shouted to Mizmiq.

'That, dear Filia and Julius, is the wizard you two discovered, my long-lost mentor and teacher, grandmaster Nomadiq. Come on, keep up!'

172

'What about the other robin? There's another robin coming towards us. Is he a grandmaster too?' they yelled, setting off in pursuit.

'No,' Mizmiq laughed. 'He is a she and her name is Rose. She's the woodland wonder I told you about in the dust outside the velocodrome, the bird with the power to gift creature communication to humans and much else besides.'

Rose caught up with them and flew alongside Filia and Julius. 'Hello, Filia Wrens and Julius Fog,' she smiled, inspecting the golden-brown eagle and bright white jabiru. 'What fine additions you are to the world of birds,' she beamed.

Filia and Julius grinned as widely as their beaks would stretch and all five birds landed on a tiny patch of wet grass below the melting snowline. 'I think you've earned a brief respite from flight,' declared Mizmiq, casting a spell of changing over Filia and Julius who were delighted to find themselves standing on their human feet once more.

The grandmasters also took human form and embraced. They were ecstatic. 'You were lost for so long; how…how is this possible?' choked Mizmiq.

'I have to admit, I thought I was a goner too,' Nomadiq joked, recounting his imprisonment in the Omicron expressway and how he'd come across the band of birds.

But Nomadiq's mood then darkened. 'Some have not survived the journey to Eskatar, Mizmiq. I'm sorry, the osprey is no longer with us. Rose has told me how important he was. But all is perhaps not lost. One of the ancient sapphires, Alea, who the osprey himself found and rescued at the entrance to the expressway is tied to a Skull who recently spoke as the boy. The Skull is here, and safe, but the boy's voice is silent.'

Filia and Julius were inconsolable. 'Jonathan can't be lost. We've seen him in the same dream as you.'

As Mizmiq explained Filia and Julius' dream and their friendship with Jonathan, the grandmasters, Rose, Filia and Julius noticed Caerulean's shadow coming out of the sun and saw the Skull lying motionless in the atomhawk's grasp.

Mizmiq was dumbfounded by the sight of a great atomhawk descending towards them and bowed in awe and respect. Filia and Julius quickly did the same.

Mizmiq sent Nomadiq and Rose a private message, 'That is Caerulean, if I'm not mistaken? Naumachian's son is alive?'

'I am indeed,' boomed a voice inside Mizmiq's head. 'Welcome to Eskatar, grandmaster. Mizmiq, isn't it?'

'Y–yes, Caerulean,' said Mizmiq, overwhelmed.

'Were you not attacked as you crossed the void?' asked the atomhawk.

'It was unguarded. We believe the Skulls have deployed their ships elsewhere,' Mizmiq replied.

'Did the three of you come alone?' said Caerulean.

'Here, yes, but not to the void. Fourteen grandmasters are weaving a corridor across the chasm. They will do what they can while their luck lasts,' answered Mizmiq.

'Ah, then that is the reason for this sudden spell of warm weather,' smiled the atomhawk.

Caerulean thanked Mizmiq and laid the Skull gently on the ground. 'Do not touch it, Filia Wrens and Julius Fog, nor you, Grandmaster Mizmiq,' he ordered. 'It is evil. It is not your friend.'

Mizmiq placed a finger on Alea's circle of light, being careful not to brush his hand against the Skull's mouth. He wept as he recognised her. 'Mizmiq, yes, it is me,' she whispered. 'And there is hope. There is no doubt that Jonathan is inside this Skull.'

Filia and Julius were overcome with grief, wondering how something of Jonathan could have found its way into such an abomination of human form and they cried and cried, imagining his pain, as everyone congregated around Alea and the Skull, weeping and at a loss as to what to do.

Squigbox and Minim were the first to fly over to Filia and Julius and the tears flowed more than ever when they talked about how Jonathan had longed to be with them in Rockmore's magic-music halls.

As the minutes passed and everyone began telling each other their stories of how they'd come to be where they were, Caerulean noticed a butterfly flying towards them. It ignored everyone and made straight for the Skull, hovering above its open jaw.

'A swallowtail,' smiled the atomhawk. 'They're adventurous mountain Eskatarians.'

The butterfly was joined by ten, twenty others and as they fluttered to and fro across the Skull colours started to appear on its bones while Alea's brilliant white light streaked with green, blue and rich yellow lines.

Fovea then spied a shadow that sparkled in the sunlight as it swooped over a ridge and flew down into the valley. 'Hundreds, thousands more butterflies,' she exclaimed.

The butterflies swarmed around the Skull, dropping spice-like grains of colour from their wings, and colour became flesh as many of them remained inside the Skull's changing body and new layers of skin formed over them. 'How will they get out?' cried Filia and Julius.

'They won't,' mourned Caerulean. 'These butterflies are not only creatures of beauty, they are beings who bring colour from everything that grows in Eskatar to those in need of healing.

'They are reviving your friend using the bounty of the Emerald lands. Their spells are those of reformation, spells that are cast with the sacrifice of life. This is the closest that magic comes to creation. They must have fled to the mountain caves when the ice came. We are fortunate they are still alive.'

'Look!' wept Filia. 'The face, it's Jonathan.'

Filia, Julius, Rose, the grandmasters and all the birds who had accompanied Jonathan on his journey to Eskatar cried with joy.

'Stand back, please, be patient,' cautioned Caerulean. 'I think we'll be a little while yet.'

Jonathan's features eventually neared their fully formed state, and when his mouth began to close, Caerulean whispered a tearful message to Alea.

'Goodbye, dear sapphire, we will remember you always when we look upon his face.'

The great atomhawk's eyes welled with tears and Rose, Nomadiq, Mizmiq and all the birds wept with him, as did Filia and Julius, realising that Alea, like the butterflies, had sacrificed her life to be certain of Jonathan's return.

57. The World of Birds

Revelations

Jonathan couldn't see anything; his eyelids were shut tight. Nor could he hear even though he was awake.

He felt his eyes being pulled from side to side and tried to stop them moving but was shocked to discover he had no control over them.

He concentrated his mind on his vision and saw coloured spots, then blurred lines. He followed them and watched them curl into complex shapes and patterns. It was as if his eyes were being sewn together, pixel by pixel.

Jonathan heard his heart thump. He waited nervously. It thumped again and started beating with an irregular rhythm before settling and pounding with the slow thud of a human heart inside a Twilight Opening.

Jonathan then found himself able to influence the movement of his eyes. He could also feel his hands and feet, and he relaxed and smiled. 'I'm alive,' he mumbled. 'I am the chandelier, being put back together inside an Opening. Alea, are you there?'

But it wasn't Alea who replied, it was another voice, the one he'd longed to hear more than any other. It was Filia.

'Jonathan?' she wept. 'Jonathan, this is Filia!'

'And Julius!' cried his dear friend.

Jonathan's pulse raced as the Opening fell away, and Caerulean smiled and nodded to Filia who fell to the ground, kissing his head, hands and mouth.

Jonathan opened his eyes and wrapped his arms around her, weeping with joy while the grandmasters and birds cheered in triumph.

'I have dreamt of this moment in every minute of my strange journey,' Jonathan sobbed.

'I will never let go of you again,' wept Filia, running her fingers through his hair and caressing every part of his face with her lips.

Julius hugged his dearest friend. 'Unbelievable,' he bawled. 'I've got zero one-liners to describe this.'

Jonathan held him tight and cried and cried. 'I'm sure it won't be long before you come up with one,' he choked. They laughed as they wept.

Jonathan noticed an old man he did not recognise standing above him.

'Jonathan, you remember the chandelier, which means I suspect you also recall meeting a clumsy hawk?' asked Mizmiq, beaming with delight.

'You're Mizmiq the hawk?' Jonathan gasped, thinking not only of his music room at home but also of his conversation with Alea about wizards and grandmasters.

'Yes, I am indeed the awkward hawk,' Mizmiq laughed.

Jonathan stood up and put his arms around the grandmaster while Nomadiq joined their embrace.

Caerulean spoke next, 'And I, Jonathan Powers, am also a hawk—a very different kind of hawk however; an atomhawk,' he smiled. 'Welcome to the Emerald lands.'

Jonathan knelt, astonished, remembering how he'd first heard of these mythical creatures in Savanna. 'Thank you, I—I am honoured,' he replied, trying to find the right words.

Squigbox and Minim then darted over to Jonathan while Rose and the other birds hurried after them, and Jonathan stretched out his arms, attempting to offer all of them a perch.

Jigsy's troop proceeded to land on his shoulders, head, hands, arms and anywhere else that it was acrobatically possible to place themselves.

Everyone laughed and Caerulean spoke to his jubilant guests as they began to recount their tales of adventure. 'I'm going to complete a circuit of the Emerald star and I don't know when I'll be back, but it will be no later than sunrise,' he said.

The birds glanced up at the evening sky and Caerulean smiled. 'Yes, even my sun sleeps from time to time,' he chuckled.

They spent the night under a clear starry sky and stories of heroics were frequently interrupted by songs of celebration. There were also moments of terrible sadness.

Filia and Julius told Jonathan about the Spellenaria massacre. Jonathan was devastated and while he was relieved to hear that Grace and Fergus were safe, he struggled to come to terms with the fact that Mr Archaneus and most of his classmates were unlikely to have survived.

Jonathan wept and wept for his father. He knew he would have been inside the velocodrome even before Filia had told him of their chance meeting. He hoped desperately that some miracle might have saved him.

Jonathan cried too for his mother, afraid that she would be punished harshly by the government for his disappearance.

The night was also one of revelations. The greatest of all for the birds and grandmasters was the existence of a state of consciousness in Twilight.

Mizmiq, Rose and Nomadiq were as transfixed as Jigsy and the gamma/delta birds as they listened to Jonathan talk about Pleione, Warbler and another human called Jonathan.

Filia and Julius were equally dumbstruck to discover the existence of a second human planet, and not only that, one with both a shared and divergent history.

Rose knew instantly from Jonathan's description that the boy he'd spoken to was Jonathan Prior, even though Jonathan did not know his surname.

The evidence was overwhelming—his age, the nature of his accident, the timing, the boy's name, albeit a common first name—they all pointed to Jonathan Prior. There was also Jonathan's statement that only those who died in Twilight existed there as conscious beings. Rose could well believe that Jonathan Prior had conjured an Opening the moment before he was tragically killed. The boy from Opus, like Jonathan, was a magical anomaly she did not understand. His spell would have been the same sort of magical explosion that had gripped Jonathan when the chandelier had crashed towards his music room floor—an instinctive reaction to imminent disaster.

Rose could hardly contain herself as she listened; Twilight consciousness was yet another example of the extraordinary, mysterious magic that existed in the two Jonathans.

Rose did not tell Jonathan that he'd had a conversation with the boy whose soul had joined him. Agnostus had been adamant that Jonathan should be treated as a bird when it came to matters of eternity. Rose had agreed and even though these were the most exceptional of circumstances, his human past was not something she was prepared to disclose. There was no reason to.

'A new Spinneret scroll needs to be written,' declared Mizmiq when Jonathan had finished.

'I would say a whole new shelf of them,' exclaimed Grandmaster Nomadiq.

'Incredible,' beamed Rose. 'But perhaps not so surprising in hindsight. After all, we spend our time watching the stars, so why wouldn't they be watching us?' she smiled, staring up at the glittering galaxies.

Rose glanced at Mizmiq, Nomadiq and the birds, and then at Jonathan, Filia and Julius. 'I think it is time to share a revelation with our human friends,' announced the little robin.

'Jonathan, Filia, Julius, please pay careful attention to what I am going to say. The birds and grandmasters are at war with a terrible enemy and you should know what is at stake. You exist in our world and it is therefore only right that we tell you.'

Rose turned to Jonathan. 'It is especially important that you know precisely what we stand to lose, and how to protect it, Jonathan Powers. I believe you may have the magical might to influence the outcome of our war.'

Rose looked at the three friends. 'What we are fighting for is human eternity. The planet Jonathan just told you about and Centurian are linked by much more than their mere existence in the same universe.'

The three friends were speechless as Rose described how human souls journeyed to the lumenest cores of Centurian and Opus-Earth at death, and how they then travelled on to Savanna before joining a new consciousness on the other planet.

Jonathan knew much of what she said from talking with Agnostus, but Rose also went into far more detail. She wanted him to be ready to fight for every precious thread of the birds' eternal magic and Jonathan was astounded by what he heard.

Filia and Julius wept, as Jonathan had done in Savanna when he'd been told the answer to the greatest question of all: what happens to humans when they die?

Filia and Julius wanted to know if human souls from Opus-Earth had joined them, and if so, who they had been.

Rose refused to tell them, just as Agnostus had refused to answer the same question when Jonathan had asked him. She did not need to delve into individual eternal pasts to explain the nature and severity of their war.

After countless questions and further revelations, Rose bound Filia, Julius and Jonathan to a spell of secrecy.

No matter what the temptation or pressure, they would never be able to reveal what they knew to other humans unless she released them from the spell; the truth would be stopped the moment it tried to leave their minds and become words.

The birds, grandmasters, Jonathan, Filia and Julius talked long into the night and the more they spoke the more their conversation changed from one of celebration and sadness to one of worry and fear.

Jonathan felt an immense weight of responsibility as he thought of home. The challenges confronting him were suddenly so much greater than avoiding being locked up in a Numberalist laboratory or curing his Destructive Interference.

The birds were expecting him to go to war alongside them. He would be returning to Centurian to fight not only for his own survival, but for his planet and the eternal lives of humankind. Going home was supposed to have been the end of his journey. This felt far more like the beginning of a new life.

58. The World of Birds

The Hands of Angels

Caerulean's sun blazed once more in the Eskatarian sky and the warming Tau 7 breezes continued to whistle across the Emerald lands.

'Those wizards are master weavers,' observed Nomadiq proudly. 'Of course, Caerulean's fireball is pretty potent too,' he chuckled.

'If I remember rightly, those wizards were taught by someone with rather deft hands,' said Mizmiq, grinning affectionately at his old mentor.

'How very kind of you, young Master Mizmiq, although I shall have to stop calling you that,' Nomadiq laughed.

Caerulean appeared in the distance, his long shadow rolling over the dew-laden valleys, and as he approached everyone saw that he had the broadest of smiles. 'I have some wonderful news,' he announced, landing beside them. 'The priestesses are alive. Come with me, please.'

Everyone rejoiced and Filia, Julius, Jonathan and the grandmasters quickly retook their bird forms and the merry band shot off after the great atomhawk.

The three friends twisted in the wind together while Squigbox and Minim raced around them and sang "The Journey", the Gazongian ballad they'd performed in the Omicron expressway.

'Again, again!' Jonathan yelled, having taught Filia and Julius the words as well as some of the whirling manoeuvres that accompanied the chorus.

The flock eventually arrived at a circular temple overlooking a steep hillside. 'This is the priestesses' home,' declared Caerulean.

Filia and Julius cast their eyes across the mountains and down into the fields of flowers below, wondering which was theirs. Eskatar was even more stunning than it had been in their dream.

'Jonathan, please, you should go in first, on your own,' smiled Caerulean.

Jonathan changed back into human form and walked towards the temple. Circling each of its twenty columns was a flutter of butterflies that seemed to dart and dive with growing excitement as he made his way towards them and up the steps.

As he entered the temple, its columns became graceful maidens with pearl-silver eyes and one of them spoke to him as he passed inside. 'Welcome to the Tholos of Eskatar, Jonathan Powers,' she said gently.

'Th–thank you,' answered Jonathan, bowing then glancing up and wondering whose voice it was that had spoken to him.

'We understand why you are here; you wish to control your Candela Lumen power,' continued the voice. 'We also know that the birds are hoping you will help them defeat the Skulls and their shadow. We will give you what we can of our magic. Alas, we must remain here in the Emerald lands and tend to our planet while you fight.'

One of the marble figures appeared to step out of herself and walk towards him. She smiled and touched his palms with her fingers and Jonathan saw a spiral of silver vanishing inside them.

'My name is Ythia Gamma. Whenever you recall my image, you will create Twilight Openings that are blessed by the hands of angels.'

Jonathan stared into the Ythia's eyes, mesmerised. 'You are, angels?' he mumbled.

'That was the name given to us when we first set foot in the land of Eskatar,' replied the Ythia.

'We came to the Emerald star in an age when it was not possible for us to return to the living world. That is why we were named angels by those who knew us, and knew of us.'

'You mean this was a place of afterlife?' gulped Jonathan.

'Yes, Eskatar was once a paradise after death, in a time when there was no eternal consciousness for humans,' explained the Ythia. 'Our planet is now a part of the living world and it has been joined to your world for thousands of years. The temple is our home and we are now called priestesses, although we are the same beings that we always were. We have the same minds and a single thread of memory for the entirety of our lives on Eskatar.'

'Th–then, who were you, if I may ask, before you came here?'

'We were humans,' smiled Ythia Gamma. 'Fortunate humans whose souls were marked out for paradise after death.'

Jonathan was silent as he tried to comprehend what the Ythia had said. They were like him. They were humans who'd journeyed to a place of consciousness beyond the living world and had somehow found a way back, only it wasn't merely them who had passed between dimensions of existence, their planet had crossed the same invisible lines as well.

'Was Eskatar also a part of the living world before it was a paradise after death?' he asked.

'No, Eskatar was created outside the living world as a haven for the souls of the dead. This is why we cherish it so, not only because it is our home,' answered the Ythia.

As Jonathan gazed at her in wonder, she spoke to him again, 'I believe you wish to know how to cast human spells without conjuring Openings?'

'Yes, yes, I do, thank you,' Jonathan replied.

Ythia Gamma asked him to reach into Twilight, but when he cast his spell she could not hear many of his magical notes. There were long periods of silence that she knew must be filled with sound.

The Ythia was astonished, just as Mizmiq and Rose had been when they had first listened to Jonathan's Twilight spells.

Jonathan looked at the Ythia hopefully but sensed she'd found something she hadn't anticipated.

'I'm afraid that only you can control your Openings, Jonathan. There are parts of your magic that I cannot hear. My hands have given your Candela Lumen power new depth and brightness, but that is all we are able to offer you.'

Jonathan fought back tears. He still hoped to continue his life with Filia if he and the birds overcame their enemy and he wept as he realised that the original purpose of his journey to Eskatar had amounted to nothing. And although he had expected answers to the nature of his magic, he did not feel it was right to blame Rose and Mizmiq for his disappointment—they would be as surprised as anyone that the priestesses were unable to hear his spells. The truth behind his magic was something he would have to discover alone.

The Ythia wrapped her pearl-white fingers around his hands, sending a calming warmth throughout his body. 'Something is at work in you, Jonathan, a power we do not understand. You yourself must bring it to light if you are to control it,' she said.

'But as you step into the unknown, do so with hope, not with sorrow, dear Jonathan. Your magical power is more than capable of seeking out the answers. You will find things that none can foresee. You already have. You are the only being we know to have experienced human, bird, Skull and Twilight consciousness.

'Indeed, until Caerulean told us of your journey, we, too, did not know of the sentient state of stars in Twilight.

'We've long believed there are formulations of life and death that we are unaware of, and we often wonder if our conscious minds will ever experience a final resting place.

'We also believe that the universe is constantly striving to turn its many worlds into better dwelling places for those who inhabit them. Something out there is rooting for you, Jonathan. It is trying to achieve something good, through you.

'If you win the battle for Centurian, continue your journey and search for your mysterious ally, the source of your magic.

'But if there is one thing, more than any other, that you should remember as you leave our temple, it is this: do not settle for what you think is possible when you conjure your magic, ask for what you really hope to see. No one knows where your magic ends, Jonathan. Your imagination is perhaps the only limit to your power.'

'Thank you, thank you for helping me understand,' Jonathan choked.

Ythia Gamma gently brushed away his tears and Jonathan smiled. He then made his way towards the outer circle of the temple, but before he left Ythia Gamma spoke to him again, 'Jonathan, look after Caerulean. He is not what he was and he is very dear to us.'

'I'm sure he will stay here with you?' answered Jonathan, surprised.

'I am not so certain,' sighed Ythia Gamma.

'Then I promise to do all I can, I mean, everything I imagine I can,' he fumbled.

The priestesses smiled, closed their eyes and the temple's columns were glistening pillars of marble once more.

Filia and Julius were waiting for Jonathan on the temple steps. He embraced them and wept, 'Not even the priestesses can hear my magic. I must find the answers myself, and I will, I tell you, I will. They believe I can too,' he cried.

Filia and Julius held him tightly for a long while and when he was ready, Jonathan wiped his eyes and strode over to the flock.

Mizmiq and Rose bowed their heads in bafflement and sadness when he told them what the priestesses had said. But bitter disappointment wasn't the only thing they heard in his voice. There was a newfound determination. Jonathan clearly knew that no one could help him, and he had accepted it. He, alone, would now decide where he went and what he did, and he would succeed in uncovering the truth, the purpose of his magic, the hidden meaning to his life.

'I will come with you,' announced Caerulean when Jonathan had finished. 'In fact, I will carry all of you to Centurian. I can fly long distances through open space, a much quicker passage than the air corridors,' he grinned.

The birds' beaks dropped in disbelief. 'I honestly don't know how to pass on the magic; otherwise I would, of course,' exclaimed the atomhawk, holding his mighty wings aloft in apology.

Jonathan smiled. 'Based on what I learnt inside the temple, I'd have a chance of catching you,' he winked, reverting to his osprey form.

The birds didn't know how to react. They were flabbergasted by the impertinence of a young osprey challenging an atomhawk in a contest of speed and endurance.

'That's my boy,' laughed Caerulean. 'Look at him, everyone, he's full of the Eskatarian spirit—never say never.'

The birds immediately relaxed and Caerulean touched Jonathan's osprey feathers with the tip of his wing, 'I am also able to protect you, and everyone else, from asteroid storms and other cosmic splinters with a home-grown spell of deflection. I suppose you think you can do that too, eh?'

Jonathan raised his wings in surrender, enjoying the laughter of his friends. He then looked up at Caerulean. The great hawk loomed over him like a big brother, not merely a sensational addition to the band of birds, and it was Caerulean who now roused the troops.

'It is time,' he declared. 'Go, all of you, receive the blessings of the priestesses inside the temple while Jonathan and I wait here. We fly to war, and to victory. The Arc of Darkness will never again defile our world.'

59. Centurian

Queuing for an Eternity

Sporadiq and Tortriq opened their eyes and glanced about. Their last memory was being crushed between the bomb and the lumenest.

'We're inside the eternal core, for Spinneret's sake,' whispered Sporadiq. 'How long have we been lying here?'

'Incredible, I've no idea,' answered Tortriq.

The lumenest's single chamber was crammed with hundreds of thousands of dead souls. All were full-size shadows of their former selves but they were also weightless and each one, on its own, appeared to occupy hardly any physical space at all.

The dead souls ignored the grandmasters; their devastated faces staring this way and that, wondering where they were.

'To be here, we must be dead?' said Sporadiq.

'I don't know,' replied Tortriq. 'I feel alive but dead is our logical state.'

The grandmasters got up to inspect the lumenest wall and moved through the shadows of grieving men, women and children with ease.

'The core is intact,' gasped Sporadiq.

'The weave is badly damaged though,' cautioned Tortriq. 'And the few remaining silver threads are rapidly losing their brightness.'

Sporadiq cast a spell of finding, asking it to locate faces he'd recognise. 'Magic's working!' he exclaimed.

'What spell did you cast?' asked Tortriq.

'Finding. There's someone I know nearby,' Sporadiq replied.

Tortriq followed him into the crowd. It was Jonathan's father, Lucius. Sporadiq had seen him going in and out of the Powers' Tildesline Avenue house after he and Mizmiq had flown to Centurian to investigate how Filia and Julius were able to understand Albert and Lorna.

Sporadiq was tempted to begin a conversation but he didn't know where Jonathan was, or whether he was safe. There was nothing of comfort to say.

Near Lucius was another face Sporadiq knew from watching Filia and Julius in the velocodrome shortly before the massacre; Mr Archaneus. He was speaking to a large group of students and trying to count them. 'Be patient, stand still, twenty-five, twenty-six, twenty-seven…'

'Sir, we've lost track of how many times you've tried to count us,' cried one of his pupils. 'And not to be disrespectful, but you always end up with a different number. Can we please join the queue? It's what everyone else is doing,' begged another.

Mr Archaneus was distraught. 'Very well, but stick together. I don't know where we are or where this queue will lead us.'

Sporadiq spoke to Tortriq, 'I think exiting the core is the only way we're going to find out whether we're dead or alive.'

'Agreed,' nodded Tortriq, and the grandmasters joined the queue behind the Temporium students as Mr Archaneus began another count.

'…two hundred and fifty-three, two hundred and fifty-four, done!' he announced after quite some time and as the students neared the front of the queue. 'That's the second count that's ended in the same number. Looks like thirty-two are missing. I hope they're okay,' he sighed.

'They're okay alright,' boomed a voice ahead of him. It was the gatekeeper. 'Don't worry, no one has a clue where they are when they come here. I'll give it to you straight up. This is where the people of Centurian come when they die. You lot are dead and your friends are alive.'

The students' grief was unbearable and Mr Archaneus did all he could to console them while he wept at the realisation of his own death and the scale of their tragedy.

'But!' bellowed the gatekeeper. 'As you grapple with the fact that you're well and truly dead, I've got another nugget of information that'll blow your minds even more; life begins all over again—there's a new world beyond this gate.'

Mr Archaneus and the Temporium students glared at the narrow opening, wondering what could possibly lie beyond it.

'Only a few more, thank goodness,' smiled the gatekeeper, ushering a reluctant soul through the exit.

'What's he talking about, Mr Archaneus?' asked one of the students, panicking. 'Is he not going to let everyone through?'

Mr Archaneus was equally perplexed and worried. How could the promise of new life be taken away moments after it was announced?

The gatekeeper stopped one of the souls as it reached the exit and grinned, 'It's your turn to be gatekeeper, buddy. After ten thousand souls go through, there's a new gatekeeper, and that's now you—those are the rules.

'Our job is to maintain order and ensure that dead souls pass one at a time. There's no need to count; the total will tick inside what's left of your brain. And don't try to get rid of it, you won't be able to.'

The new gatekeeper turned and stared at the chaos inside the core, horrified by the prospect of having to control such a crowd.

'A full chamber's a good thing, you won't have to wait too long,' chuckled the old gatekeeper. 'Oh, and be certain to check that the next gatekeeper knows about the afterlife; it helps calm the crowd.' And with that, he jumped and the frightened gatekeeper took up his post.

'We're all still going through,' shouted Mr Archaneus, enlightened and relieved. 'There's no single gatekeeper; it was the end of his shift,' he yelled, astounded. 'The dead organise themselves and take it in turns. The gatekeepers are ones of us. That's not something that we, or anyone else, ever contemplated. I bet our premagic cousins were delighted not to be challenged by a grumpy boatman or a multi-headed hound,' he declared, trying to lift everyone's spirits while the first of his pupils prepared to jump.

Sporadiq and Tortriq watched as the Tempo Chorium students and Mr Archaneus leapt through, but when it was their turn to go the new gatekeeper stopped them. 'Hey! You two, the counter can't, er, count you. It's throwing up all sorts of messages. It says you've got working organs. Get out of the line,' he demanded.

The grandmasters moved away quickly. 'We're alive!' cried Sporadiq. 'Yes, yes, not so loud, my friend,' grinned Tortriq. 'Come on, let's find a quiet corner and stay out of trouble.'

60. Centurian

Race to the Core

Duggerrid towered above the other Skulls on the bridge of his battleship as it circled Silverrock inside the Greylight veil.

He smashed one of the metal-grated gangways with his diamind-tipped rod and cursed his ill fortune. The lightning container's explosion had shaken the planet with such force that rockfalls at the base of the abyss had prevented him from reaching the lumenest and he was worried that further bombing would only serve to fill the opening more.

But Duggerrid was also convinced that the ricocheting tremors and poisons carried by the Greylight's winds would eventually cause Centurian to fracture and offer him a new path to the lumenest.

'The crews grow impatient, my lord,' warned General Kazeg. 'Shouldn't we at least attempt to make our way through the rubble?'

'No, make them wait,' yelled Duggerrid angrily. 'The planet will break, I tell you.'

As soon as he'd given Kazeg his answer, the Skull lord roared in triumph at the images on the screen in front of him. Centurian had begun to crack.

'Retreat. No further than the upper atmosphere,' Duggerrid ordered and they sped away as quickly as they could.

Giant land masses wheeled upwards, killing countless Centurians and sending their wailing souls to the planet's lumenest core.

'Stay where you are, in a solid state. I will not have us lose sight of our prize,' barked Duggerrid as Skull ships were cast aside by the onslaught of broken Centurian.

When Duggerrid was satisfied that the danger had cascaded into space, he instructed his fleet to navigate through the wreckage to the centre of the planet where much of Centurian's structure still clung to the eternal core, and as soon as they had arrived, they began focusing their diamind bombs on a single point and forging a new passageway towards the lumenest.

Duggerrid saw birds gathering in large numbers behind him and ordered the bulk of his fleet to form a protective shield so the remaining ships could blast their way to the core unhindered.

Duggerrid also knew it would not be long before the most powerful birds joined them. The Arc of Darkness had poured its Greylight poisons into the oceans and lands of Gazong, diverting Elgarian and hundreds of thousands of others away. Nevertheless, the desolation of Centurian was certain to bring many, if not all of them, hurrying back.

Delighted with his defensive shield, Duggerrid commanded the Marrowbone's helmsman to steer his ship towards the core. 'This time, it will be the birds fighting to break through our shield. Let us see how they fare,' he smirked.

But as his battleship came about, it slowed. 'My lord, we're losing power,' shouted one of the crew.

'Impossible,' Duggerrid raged, but to his horror, he saw the shape of a great atomhawk tearing at the Marrowbone's metallic shell as he marched out onto one of the platforms.

'You, and your filth, are going to die,' howled Caerulean who had shot ahead of the grandmasters and birds after they'd exited his spell of transition. He'd then used all his stealth and speed to dive unnoticed through one of the few remaining gaps in the defensive shield right before it closed.

'Forward,' demanded Duggerrid as Caerulean raised his head above the platform and sent a spell of destruction hurtling into the Skull lord's eye sockets.

Duggerrid stood his ground, consuming then expelling its force through his mouth; the only defence for a Skull against such an attack.

Caerulean responded by lifting his wings and closing them in a thunderclap, creating a shockwave that ripped through the ship as it crossed its gangways.

The mighty atomhawk did not stop. Wave upon wave of devastating power pummelled the Marrowbone and its master, and Duggerrid just about held on as more and more energy shot into the dark circles of his eyes and out through his gaping jaw.

Kazeg saw Duggerrid's plight and the cracks in his buckling frame and steered the Turpitude in a wide circle before ordering his helmsman to extend the ship's beak and ram the hawk in the back.

Caerulean did not see the danger. His focus was Duggerrid and conjuring the necessary power to obliterate the Skull lord.

Jonathan, Filia, Julius, Rose, the grandmasters and Jigsy's band of birds screamed messages of warning to Caerulean as they approached the first bank of ships, but the atomhawk was too far ahead to hear them and Kazeg skewered him clean through.

The great hawk shrieked in pain and tried to fly free but the Turpitude ploughed on, keeping its shaft where it was while Duggerrid fell to the deck, crippled but released from the atomhawk's spell. 'Turn!' yelled Kazeg, narrowly avoiding a collision with the Marrowbone.

The grandmasters and Rose told Filia and Julius to stay behind while they and Jonathan joined the other birds and engaged the Skull ships along the shield.

The Skull crews had been stricken with fear by the sight of the monstrous hawk, a bird they had consigned to myth, and they were still terrified that it might break free.

The birds, grandmasters and Jonathan took full advantage of their fear and quickly broke through the shield and sped after the Turpitude which was now heading straight for the core. The Skulls tasked with opening a passage to the lumenest had achieved their goal—there was a clear line of sight.

Kazeg ordered the ships in front to move aside so he could strike the core at speed.

'Attack the Turpitude's bridge,' cried Rose, and she and the gamma/delta birds tore at the helmsman while Nomadiq, Mizmiq, Jonathan and others cast spells of destruction and crushed as many of the Skulls around him as they could.

'Even if you kill us all, the ship will not change course,' mocked Kazeg, hauling himself up.

Jonathan dived between the core and the Turpitude and cast a spell of shielding, opening his wings and picturing Ythia Gamma as he conjured a barrier that he hoped would stop Kazeg's ship.

Caerulean was bleeding terribly. He was powerless and unable to help him and the battleship's beak struck the osprey full in the chest.

But the ship exploded off Jonathan in a mass of splintered metal and the birds rejoiced at the miracle when they saw the osprey emerging without a wound.

The Turpitude plunged but as it fell, its beak slashed the side of the core, cutting the gateway from the lumenest and the souls of the dead poured into space and disappeared as wisps of smoke.

Sporadiq and Tortriq took their owl and raven forms and shot out of the gateway. The grandmasters had been concentrating their magical energy on trying to keep the lumenest threads alight from inside the core.

Jonathan shone in front of them, his back turned. He was channelling all his strength into his spell to prevent the Turpitude's stern from damaging the lumenest, and when the danger had past and the ship had spiralled away, he let out a tortured cry for Caerulean who had fallen with the battleship into darkness.

Jonathan then looked up and saw Duggerrid in a new ship hurtling towards the core. Hundreds of other ships were following him. He'd commanded the fleet to abandon the shield and make for the lumenest.

Rose, Mizmiq, Nomadiq and the birds engaged as many ships as they could while Jonathan prepared to attack the Skull lord, as did Sporadiq and Tortriq, but the osprey suddenly froze; 'Mother,' he whispered.

Jonathan had recognised his mother's voice on Duggerrid's ship. Sporadiq and Tortriq hesitated, taking Jonathan's lead, but not understanding, and Duggerrid rammed the lumenest next to the gateway. His beak cut all the way through the core's meshed threads and the oval lost its last slither of light.

Duggerrid revelled in his victory. 'The abomination is no more,' he cried in triumph. 'Return to Terminus. We must repair the damaged ships and preserve the rest of the fleet. Only then will we be able to take wind-form and embark on our final human invasion.'

The Skull ships navigated away, fending off the dejected birds and grandmasters who knew the battle was already lost. The cycle of life had been broken. Eternity was dead.

61. Centurian
An Exchange of Lives

Elgarian, lord of eagles, mourned the remains of Centurian's lumenest. He and hundreds of thousands of birds flying back from Gazong had shot out of Centurian's estuary corridors only minutes after the Skulls had fled.

William and the grandmasters who'd been weaving a new corridor across the Tau 6 chasm flew alongside the great eagle. They too had arrived not long after the enemy's escape.

Hennington, who had been in the thick of the fight from the very beginning, circled the desecrated lumenest with the grandmasters. Fergus and Grace were still safely stowed inside his spell of carriage.

Rose, Elgarian, Mizmiq, Nomadiq and the other grandmasters cast spells of healing but any threads that showed signs of silvering immediately darkened.

Jonathan too could not find the magic to heal the weave and he cried and cried as he gripped the lifeless strands with his talons, mortified by his failure to act. He had allowed the birds' most precious creation and humankind's irreplaceable gift to die.

Jonathan stared hopefully at Rose who was trying to revive the threads around the gateway one at a time, but even that was useless. They unravelled wherever she perched and the terrified faces of dead souls continued to fall into nothingness.

Jonathan gazed up at the Centurian ships orbiting the wreckage of his planet. They were carrying millions of refugees who were utterly at a loss as to why or how their world had been decimated.

Jonathan knew his father was not among them. Sporadiq had confirmed what he'd feared all along and had told him how he'd seen his father's soul inside the lumenest.

Filia and Julius flew over to Jonathan and landed next to him, but he pushed them away.

'Jonathan, you mustn't give up,' wept Filia.

'It is too late,' he yelled angrily.

'This is not how it is supposed to end,' sobbed Filia.

'It has ended,' Jonathan screamed. 'Face the truth, Filia. I marched out of the priestesses' temple as the birds' new hope, but I proved to be a disaster. Not only did I fail to protect the core, I allowed it be destroyed.'

'You are not a failure, Jonathan,' she cried.

'Everyone got me wrong, Filia, from the moment I was told I had Destructive Interference. That was a disease, not some strange magic. I am a false promise.'

'That is not true and you know it. You've conjured miracles time and time again,' answered Filia. 'You must not give up.'

'This is different,' wept Jonathan. 'I cannot create eternity. My role was to defend it, to defeat its enemies. There is only one thing left for me to do and that is to find Caerulean's body and bring it back to Eskatar.'

The osprey sped away, inconsolable, and dived into darkness until he caught sight of the Turpitude floating near a distant moon. It was mangled and abandoned.

Jonathan tempered his speed and went to the dead atomhawk's side, placing his feathers on Caerulean's face. Each one of his wings just about covered the giant hawk's wrinkled, bloodied cheeks.

'I'm sorry,' he cried to his lifeless friend. 'I failed you. You were a big brother to me, Caerulean. Tell me there is hope. Please, speak to me and tell me what I should do.'

As he pressed his silver-white feathers against the atomhawk's skin, to his amazement and joy, Caerulean spoke, 'Jonathan, my strength is gone. What little you see, this gift of speech, comes from your embrace,' he moaned, his voice as broken as his body.

'Dear Caerulean, I heard my mother on the Skull lord's ship. She has been turned into a Skull. I moved away, allowing Duggerrid to kill the core. I've failed everyone.'

'You did what any boy would, Jonathan. Take my butchered remains to the Skull lord and offer me in exchange for your mother. Let us rescue what we can. There is…' Caerulean slumped.

Jonathan loosened his wings then wrapped them firmly around the atomhawk's face. Caerulean opened his eyes again and smiled, relieved to have been given a second chance to finish his words.

'There is another hope. Find my father, Naumachian. He has the power to create a new core.

'He gave his all to Gazong in long lost age, as you know. No one can say whether the echo of his heart in the waterless oceans is a sign that he might yet live.

'And if you find him, please, send me a message, for I will be grateful, my brave little brother, even if your words do nothing but fall into the empty voids of space.'

'I will not rest until his fate is known. This I promise you,' sobbed Jonathan.

They cried together, grieving and hoping for the lives of a lost mother and father, and when Jonathan saw that Caerulean's tears had run dry and his eyes had closed, he gently opened them again with his wings, desperate for one more moment with his friend, but Caerulean could not be summoned.

Jonathan cast a spell of concealment over the atomhawk and flew in a direct line to Terminus in Delta 13.

He used the spell of transition that Caerulean had conjured to carry him, Rose, Mizmiq, Nomadiq, Filia, Julius and the gamma/delta birds from Eskatar to Centurian. Only Jonathan had been able to learn it.

But as soon as he spied the raging skies of Terminus, he slowed down and looked for a place to hide Caerulean's body, eventually laying the great atomhawk at the base of a deep crater on a peaceful, solitary moon.

After shrouding his mighty shape with a spell of invisibility Jonathan set off again, cloaking his brightness well before he approached the Skull planet.

He soared over Pleonec Tower, wondering how best to enter the Skull city and finally decided to slip through an opening in the rockwall beneath the upper platform.

The osprey was nothing more than an eddying shadow as it searched the flickering half-lit dungeons for the Skull lord, and it wasn't long before he found him. Duggerrid was sitting alone in his audience chamber, nursing the injuries inflicted by the atomhawk.

Jonathan took human form, knelt and bowed, and placed his hands on the steps leading up to the Skull lord's throne, and for an instant, Duggerrid was speechless, stunned by the sight of a simple boy miraculously appearing in front of him. Then he seethed with anger.

'You, you dare come into my halls and taunt me with your youth and human form,' he roared.

Duggerrid seized his diamind-tipped rod and was about to strike him but was stopped by the pain of his broken bones as they cracked along his arm.

'I have not come to challenge you,' wept Jonathan as Duggerrid shrieked in agony. 'Nor am I here to deny you the human life you will soon enjoy, the experience you call completeness. I am here to plead for my mother, and to beg you to pity me.

'I am human, yes, but for me, completeness is to see my mother again and to take her back. I heard her voice on your ship moments before you dealt the final blow to the lumenest. I bring you a gift—'

Duggerrid drowned Jonathan's pleas with fury. 'Who are you, boy? Answer me truthfully, for I will know if you lie.'

'I am the osprey who confronted you at the Centurian core but did not fight you. Our battle is over, you have won and I am here defenceless, at your mercy, a beggar.'

Jonathan raised his voice before Duggerrid could drown him out again. 'I bring you a gift to show that I understand the magnitude of what I'm asking, the atomhawk who wounded you so terribly.'

Jonathan opened his hands, revealing an image of Caerulean cradled in the nearby moon. 'May this gift—certainty that the atomhawk will never fight again— and your understanding of my sorrow be enough for you to grant my request.'

Duggerrid's pride swelled. Caerulean was indeed a great prize and he gestured to one of his guards. 'How many of the crew on that ship survived?'

'No more than twenty, my lord,' replied the guard.

'Bring them to me,' Duggerrid grinned.

The Skulls were sent for and the guard ushered them into the chamber. Jonathan couldn't contain his grief. There was one who he knew to be his mother.

He fell to the ground, weeping uncontrollably. Despite the Skull's disfigured fleshless face, he was certain it was her.

Jonathan was desperate to hold her and motioned towards her but she didn't acknowledge him. The torment of not being recognised was unbearable and Jonathan longed to become a Skull again and join her; she would surely know him then.

'Stop!' ordered Duggerrid as Jonathan moved closer to the Skull.

'Hear now my decision. You say this Skull carries a value to you that is equal to the immeasurable worth of completeness, a Skull's experiences inside a human soul.

'So be it. I offer you this Skull who you believe to be your mother, but only after I have obtained the same completeness that I give you.

'I will leave instruction that once my human life begins, you may take her and do what you will.

'Go now and bring me the atomhawk as the first exchange in our agreement,' demanded Duggerrid.

Jonathan was devastated. How could he possibly hand over Caerulean and leave without his mother? But Duggerrid grew impatient as Jonathan wrapped his mind in spells of calming to stop himself from exploding with anger and reaching out to grab her. 'What is your answer?' he yelled.

Jonathan hesitated, staring at his mother, then nodded.

'Good,' smiled Duggerrid. 'One of my ships will take you to him. Now go, lest the sight of this Skull leads you to act in a way that you regret,' he warned, straining to lift his diamind rod.

But Duggerrid, this time, raised the tip just enough to jab Jonathan lightly in the chest and drops of blood dripped onto the chamber floor.

Jonathan, however, hardly felt the cut in his anguish, and as he was led out, he cast a spell that he hoped would whisper a message to his mother in the Skull tongue. 'Goodbye, mother, I love you, and I will return.'

She glanced up and Jonathan saw the faintest of smiles. Tears of agony and joy flooded his eyes but he did not dare say anything more for fear of revealing his Skull past, and although he did not know it, he'd come perilously close to being found out; Duggerrid had been watching and for an instant the Skull lord had thought he'd heard a voice he knew. But in the same moment he'd been stung yet again by the pain of his wounds and had been forced to look away.

62. Centurian

Silver Planet

Jonathan was bound and dragged through the violent dungeons he'd once inhabited, but as soon as he stepped onto the harbour front, he retook osprey form, freed himself and fled.

The swiftest Skull ships could not catch him as he soared upwards into the thunderous skies above Terminus. Nor could they find a trace of his shadow in the darkness beyond the storms.

Jonathan lifted Caerulean's body from its hiding place and began his journey back to the desolation of Centurian in Gamma 12, using the atomhawk's spell of transition.

Jonathan raged at the sickening cruelty of the Skull lord who even in victory had chosen to make him suffer by keeping his mother from him, and his fury grew with every passing star so that by the time he reached the ruins of his home, he was consumed with hatred for Duggerrid.

The birds had conjured a platform which drifted in and out of the debris near the lumenest. Filia, Julius, Grace and Fergus stood watching the grandmasters, Rose, Elgarian and others as they continued to search in vain for threads that might respond to their magic.

Jonathan ignored them all and shot through the gateway and into the empty cavity. He set Caerulean down and sped in circles around the blackened lumenest, eventually slowing his flight and landing on the flailing gateway strands.

Jonathan closed his eyes. He cried for his mother and cursed himself for having let a creature of such evil destroy the core.

The Skull lord's voice stabbed his mind with its malice and as he listened, he felt not only outrage but a renewed sense of purpose and power.

Jonathan changed into human form and conjured an Opening, placing the image of Ythia Gamma at the centre of his thoughts. But rather than ask his spell to will anything into being, he simply wept for his mother and father and for his home, allowing the sounds of Twilight to overwhelm him.

He found notes he'd never previously heard and told his mind to repeat them, and as they echoed, something touched his feet.

Jonathan peered down and saw a thin line of silver jutting out into space and it widened until it spanned the gateway; he had recreated the first step of the corridor walkway to Savanna, the eternal bridge, the path taken by the souls of the dead to judgement.

The corridor's steps had fallen away when Kazeg had cut the gate from the lumenest. Jonathan's spell wasn't bringing them back, it was conjuring the beginnings of a new walkway.

Jonathan moved one foot forward and another step formed. He then glanced round and saw the gateway strands glistening with silver.

Jonathan looked across to Filia, Julius, Grace, Fergus, the birds and grandmasters; they were rejoicing on the platform. He wept, elated, and waved at them as he started walking towards Savanna.

He told his mind to repeat the same Twilight notes with every step and each time they sounded a new part of the eternal bridge appeared below his feet.

Rose carried Caerulean's body out of the lumenest and laid it on the platform before joining Elgarian and the grandmasters who'd flown over to Jonathan and were unfurling thread after thread to build out the walls of a new corridor around his steps.

Hennington, Jigsy and the gamma/delta birds helped where they could, straightening and binding the strands according to Rose and William's instructions.

Hundreds, then thousands of birds suddenly fluttered around them and small torches of light shone from their eyes so there were no mistakes as they tied the threads with their beaks.

The birds sang as they laboured and Jonathan's confidence grew with every step. He spotted Alesand shrilling in jubilation and little Naricorn. The young petrel dived between his legs and then back past his shoulders in playful flight, celebrating every stride of the miracle-boy who had saved his mother.

Elgarian glided next to Jonathan. 'Here we are again, my lad. You've found yourself in another unfamiliar corridor, although I'm happy to say you seem to know what you're doing this time.'

Jonathan roared with laughter, remembering his first precarious flight.

'Now look behind you, there is more to your magic than eternity,' smiled Elgarian.

Jonathan turned. Centurian was reforming. Scattered pieces of his planet were being pulled towards a brightening lumenest.

Jonathan gasped in awe at the sight. 'Your eyes do not deceive you,' grinned Elgarian. 'The silver planet is being remade.'

'The lord of eagles is right,' added Mizmiq who had taken human form and was now walking beside Jonathan. 'Those are the largest chandelier shards I've ever seen. Just imagine the sound of your harp once we're done,' he laughed.

Jonathan put his arm around the wonderful wizard who had discovered him. 'We will celebrate together in the music room when our work is finished,' he beamed.

Jonathan's strides quickened and the eternal corridor stretched across the stars, its magical weave transcending all the rules of time and space, and as soon as he glimpsed the Savanna Lake he howled with joy and ran, being careful not to miss a single step.

The agnostriches had managed to save a small part of the old corridor and one of them had clambered up into the exit and was encouraging frightened souls to jump down onto the sand. Many of the dead had seen what had happened behind them and were terrified that this new opening would be their end.

Jonathan greeted the agnostrich like a long lost friend before leaping out of the corridor and joining the chaos on the shoreline.

Jonathan saw Lord Agnostus in the middle of the crowd and shook his fists in triumph. The Chief Justice cheered and lifted his long neck and Jonathan could tell he was mouthing the words "thank you". He instantly replied with the same message.

Jonathan was about to make his way towards Agnostus to ask what else he might be able to do when he felt a bird land on his head.

'Boo!' It was Rose and she laughed as she prodded his thick walnut mop with her tiny robin feet.

She then leaned over, still clinging to his hair so he could see her face. 'Ouch,' he winced.

'Follow me to the Opus eternal bridge,' she grinned. 'It is important that the same magic sustains both corridors, which means you're only halfway done with your walk. I presume you're up for another lap of honour?'

Jonathan laughed and sprinted after the robin who had shot off in front of him.

The Opus corridor exit lay a mile or so away and Jonathan smiled as he ran, recalling the moment Agnostus had told him of the existence of another planet hosting human life. He'd been perched awkwardly on a window ledge in the courthouse, watching Opus souls spill onto the very grains of sand he was now running across.

'Thank goodness you're here,' cried one of the agnostriches as he arrived at the Opus exit. The shoreline was packed with anxious souls. None were being allowed onto rafts.

'It's not just the shoreline that's full, the corridor is overflowing too,' explained the agnostrich. 'We had to ask one of the poor human souls to hurry all the way back to the Opus lumenest with a message for the gatekeeper to stop anyone leaving the core. Lord Agnostus has instructed us not to let a single soul onto the lake until you've completed your walk.'

The agnostrich then drew breath and bowed. 'We've heard incredible things, Jonathan Powers, osprey. On behalf of all ratites, I'd like to express my gratitude.'

'Thank you, my friend,' Jonathan replied, beaming. 'I, too, am grateful, for your sacrifice.'

Jonathan leapt up and found Rose waiting for him. The threads inside the Opus corridor had darkened and were showing signs of loosening but Jonathan's steps returned the weave to its former strength and silver brightness.

Birds gathered again to help and Jonathan sang with them as he marched. Even the Opus souls seemed to cheer, sensing that something extraordinary was happening despite not having a clue as to what it might be.

'Will the Opus core be damaged as well?' Jonathan asked Rose.

'We won't know until we get there, but I imagine it'll be in a similar state to the corridor—intact but in need of new life,' she answered.

Jonathan hurried along the walkway, and when he saw the Opus lumenest shimmering with new silver light, far ahead of him, he smiled and paused to survey his work.

He noticed something moving inside the corridor walls and as he stared into the weave he saw the faces of dead souls sliding between the strands. He gawped in wonder and looked at Rose for explanation. This was a detail she hadn't mentioned in Eskatar.

'They are Centurian Savanna faces; Centurian souls who have passed beyond the moon. They are on the final part of their journey to an Opus consciousness,' beamed Rose, eyes twinkling at the sight.

'When souls rise up out of their rafts and glide across the moon, they lose the long shadows of their bodies. Only their faces remain, circled by a single silver thread.

'They descend and slip within the walls of the eternal corridor, never entering the hollow where we now stand, the path of the dead to Savanna.

'The faces then make their way to the meshing around the lumenest gate and from there they travel deep inside the weave, looking for the one strand that's an exact match of the silver around their faces. The two threads swap, keeping the core whole and each Savanna face then fades.

'This exchange of pairs guarantees that the right mind will be joined as the new thread leaves the lumenest to find its ordained consciousness.'

Jonathan gazed at the Centurian Savanna faces, searching hopelessly for his father, Mr Archaneus and his Tempo Chorium friends, and weeping for the tragic loss of life that had befallen his world. He then turned away, wiping his tears, and set off once more to complete his journey.

Jonathan cried with relief when he finally placed his foot on the Opus gateway and was overcome with joy when he saw the lumenest gleaming with the same silver brightness as the corridor.

'You did it, Jonathan, you did it!' Rose shrilled.

Jonathan held out his hand and the robin danced across his palm and fingers. '*We* did it, Rose, *we* did it,' he exclaimed, correcting her.

Rose twisted again in celebration before coming to a standstill and looking Jonathan in the eye. 'Now, quick as you can, make a run for it, or fly, so you don't get trampled on by thousands of Opus souls hurtling towards Savanna,' she winked. 'I'll see you back at the silver planet.'

'Where are you off to then?' grinned Jonathan.

'I'm going to visit a few friends on Opus before doing my damnedest to catch up with you. I don't know how to thank you, Jonathan Powers.'

'It is I who am grateful, Rose, to you and to Mizmiq especially, for finding me before it was too late, and for helping me understand myself and guiding me through your beautiful, magical world.'

'You have a generous heart, Jonathan Powers, and that is something all birds cherish as much as any magic,' smiled Rose. 'It was Agnostus who first said that to you, as you'll remember, after you healed Alesand's wounds.'

Jonathan nodded and the little robin waved farewell and opened a lapisphere into Opus' estuary corridors. The other birds did the same, not wanting to lose sight of Rose or eager to enjoy a well-earned feast at the kernel of a nearby bird planet.

Jonathan stared at the Opus lumenest, his foot still firmly planted on the gateway threshold.

He thought about where he'd been, who he'd met and what he'd done. He simply couldn't believe it. But it was all true. A sixteen-year-old boy from Centurian had rescued eternity for humankind.

Jonathan willed his Opening to end, but it didn't fall away. He thought nothing of it and cast the spell that gave him osprey form, but there was no change, and nor could he conjure a lapisphere into the bird corridors.

Jonathan repeated his spells and began to panic when they failed again and again so he cast a spell of understanding on himself and to his dismay it returned the words, "Centurian in Twilight".

'How?' he cried. 'I don't understand, I don't understand,' he yelled.

"A spell of sacrifice" was the magic's only reply.

Jonathan wept and wept. He suddenly understood and realised how he'd accomplished his miracle.

He'd remade his home at the cost of his own life. He had become the planet Centurian in Twilight.

And not only that, he'd remade his planet in exactly the way it had been; with an eternal lumenest at its heart.

Jonathan sent messages to Filia, Julius, Fergus and Grace, to Rose, Mizmiq and Nomadiq, but he couldn't tell if his words were even passing beyond his lips.

He frantically tried to create a new Opening, a lifeline to the living world, but as soon as he felt a connection, it shut.

'Pleione, are you there?' he sobbed. 'Can you hear me? Am I in Twilight? Have I, after all, chosen a home—the planet Centurian?'

Pleione answered immediately, as if she'd been waiting for a message ever since he'd left the Twilight world. 'We were so worried. We've been watching you. We are overjoyed that you are safe. And yes, not only have you returned, you have chosen.'

Jonathan cried and cried. He attempted to locate something of his life again. But as he failed repeatedly to break through, he noticed he was also losing his human form.

He'd always been aware of at least a semblance of his physical shape when he was drifting in limbo but he could now no longer make out even an outline of his human self. He was an entity of light and energy, nothing more.

Jonathan felt his mind moving, and he did not need to ask his destination. He was accelerating towards Centurian, whose conscious soul he had now become.

Jonathan gazed down as he raced away and saw his human body in the distance. It was precisely where he'd left it; at the gateway to the Opus lumenest, and he caught one last glimpse of its shadow as it collapsed and disappeared.

Jonathan wept and wept, knowing he had witnessed the end of his existence in the human world. He had taken his place in Twilight. He was, and always would be, the silver planet.

63. Centurian

Homecoming

Filia, Julius, Fergus, Grace, Mizmiq and Hennington floated high above Centurian inside a magical sphere conjured by the grandmaster, and as they marvelled at the planet's silver sheen they could not find one spot of flickering darkness.

Lorna was there too. She'd joined thousands of other birds who'd hurried from Castle Spinneret to the silver planet as soon as the full scale of the disaster was known.

Elgarian, Nomadiq, William and the other grandmasters had said their goodbyes, promising to return quickly and celebrate with the four friends, and with Jonathan.

Elgarian had taken a large contingent of birds back to Gazong, hoping that the planet's sickness had not worsened while their attention had been focused on Centurian. Jigsy and the gamma/delta birds had voted unanimously to fly with him.

The grandmasters, meanwhile, had left for Castle Spinneret the moment Centurian's silver sheen had begun to sparkle. They were impatient to compare what they'd observed firsthand with the luminescence of the planet in their magical ceilings. Their only stop on the way would be Eskatar where they would mourn Caerulean's passing with the priestesses before leaving his body in their care.

'I must apologise for the grandmasters' abrupt departure,' said Mizmiq. 'The mirror-mind's accuracy is as important to a wizard as the clarity of his own eyeballs.'

'Well, I hope their ceilings can see what I can; a perfect planet,' smiled Julius. 'When do we set course for home, Captain Mizmiq?'

'Once I've miniaturised you with a spell of transportation,' grinned the grandmaster.

Mizmiq assumed his hawk form and Julius suddenly vanished, and everybody fell about laughing.

'Hennington, please port Grace and Fergus. I'll stow Filia in my Fog cabin,' quipped the grandmaster. 'And Lorna, you're from fine speeding stock; you'll have no difficulty keeping up. We take the estuary corridors to Bushley Park.'

'What about Jonathan?' asked Filia.

'He's still busy on the other side,' answered Mizmiq. 'Remember, from now on, not a word of it, and besides, any attempt to indicate the truth will be magically stopped as you know.'

Rose had given the grandmaster permission to extend her bond of secrecy to Grace and Fergus. They too would never be able to share the revelation of eternal consciousness with other humans.

'So when and where will we see Jonathan?' demanded Filia, hands on her hips, requiring something more specific before allowing the hawk to subject her to the same spell of confinement.

'Very soon, at his house,' Mizmiq replied. 'The only question is whether we'll have broken into his music room before he gets there,' he chuckled.

The grandmaster opened a lapisphere and the hawk, pigeon and hoopoe butterfly bird dived into Centurian's estuary corridors with their cargo of excited humans.

The tubeway traffic was terrible. Chattering and storytelling had reached epic proportions, but no one minded the chaos amidst the joy of homecoming.

'Hey, not so aggressive in the corners!' shouted a miniature, pale Julius, as Mizmiq lurched from side to side.

'You're not going to be sick, are you, Julius?' gasped Filia, curling up into a ball to get as far away from him as possible.

Julius closed his eyes and gulped.

'No, don't you dare, Julius Fog,' shrieked Filia.

They felt a sudden deceleration and yelled 'thank you!' to their trusty pilot.

Mizmiq, Hennington and Lorna burst out of a lapisphere and landed in a dishevelled but exuberant Bushley Park.

Mizmiq and Hennington hid the tiny humans under a leaf and looked this way and that before casting spells of maximisation when they were certain no one could see them.

'The park's a mess,' exclaimed Fergus, stretching his arms and flexing his neck.

'The woodland birds will fix that, don't you worry,' said Lorna proudly.

Filia opened her mouth and immediately shut it. Mizmiq laughed. 'You may speak freely, all of you,' he declared. 'I'll keep the magic of translation working, and don't worry about the grid; even your government hasn't got it up and running yet.'

'In which case, I'm using rushing yards to get to Jonathan's,' cried Filia, shooting off towards Tildesline Avenue.

The four friends arrived to find the hawk and pigeon grooming themselves on the wall. 'Where's Hennington?' asked Grace.

An Adonis blue appeared out of nowhere and fluttered in front of her. 'I wanted to show you the real me, what do you think?' he whispered.

'Gorgeous, simply gorgeous,' she beamed, opening her hand and inviting the butterfly to settle on her palm.

Hennington landed and fanned specs of blue onto her skin. 'For you, to keep, all the way from Eskatar,' he smiled.

'Oh, Hennington, they're beautiful, how…how can I make sure I don't lose them?' she flustered.

'Don't worry; they won't leave you, no matter what you grip. I'm glad you like them,' he replied.

Grace nervously tipped her hand to one side, gazing in wonder as her palm continued to sparkle blue in the Centurian sunlight.

'Shouldn't Jonathan be here by now?' said Julius.

'He won't be long,' answered Mizmiq confidently.

Filia went up to the door and unlocked it. 'Ha! The spell of entry he shared with me still works,' she exclaimed.

Filia, Julius, Grace and Fergus ran into the music room while Mizmiq and Lorna bundled in via a top window, closely followed by Hennington who nimbly slipped through moments before it shut.

Mizmiq and Hennington changed into their human forms as soon as they touched the hard wood floor and after a few minutes pacing the room Filia asked where Jonathan was again.

Mizmiq replied at first with the same reassurances but eventually started to show signs of concern and cast a spell of finding. His face immediately went white. 'Jonathan is not, is not in the living world,' he shuddered.

Mizmiq repeated the spell, asking for more information. 'Nor is he dead; his soul is not travelling to a new consciousness.'

He searched again. 'There are, wait, words, a message from Jonathan; "Centurian in Twilight" is all it says.'

'What's happened to him, when will he get here?' cried Filia.

Mizmiq held his head in his hands before looking up at Filia, his eyes welling with tears. 'He has forfeited his life to rebuild his planet. He is Centurian in Twilight,' choked the grandmaster. 'He's not coming home.'

Filia couldn't bear it. She was not going to let Jonathan go, ever. Grief turned to anger and she rounded on Mizmiq, 'You knew, didn't you? You knew it would end like this, if he succeeded?'

'Filia, I did not know. This is as unexpected for me as it is for you. I'm heartbroken, Filia, please,' answered the grandmaster, numb with shock.

Filia lashed out again. 'I don't believe you. Find a way to bring him back,' she demanded.

Mizmiq placed his shaking hand on her arm and wept. 'I don't think there is a way to bring him back,' he replied, letting her go and wiping his tears.

Filia, Julius, Grace and Fergus cried and cried, devastated and unable to accept what the grandmaster was saying. 'Isn't there a chance he'll find a way to return, like last time?' sobbed Julius.

'I don't think so,' wept Mizmiq. 'He said he was able to leave because he hadn't become a star or planet whereas this time, in his own words, he has become Centurian.'

Filia, Julius, Grace and Fergus cried their way through memories: Bushley Park, the Temporium, Rockmore and all their recent adventures, and they kept staring at Mizmiq in disbelief, as did Hennington and Lorna, but the grandmaster was as grief-stricken and dumbfounded as them. Jonathan's words, and now his silence, pointed to only one possibility. Their dear dear friend was gone.

64. Centurian

The Sound of a New Planet

Filia, Julius, Fergus and Grace's families had been fortunate. They had all escaped the destruction in one of the thousands of Centurian ships that had shot into space as soon as the government had realised that there was a threat to the planet.

They were now coming home and were desperate to see their sons and daughters. It was time to say goodbye to Mizmiq, Hennington and Lorna.

The four friends waved to the hawk, hoopoe butterfly bird and pigeon as they took to the air and climbed towards the evening silver.

Anger had been put aside and despite their misery they'd come to accept that what had happened to Jonathan was not something that the grandmaster, Rose, or any other power could have changed.

Filia, Julius, Fergus and Grace walked to the top of Tildesline Avenue and held each other and wept for a long time before going their separate ways.

When they arrived home, their families were overcome with joy. They had not set eyes on them since before school on the morning of the Spellenaria massacre and their celebrations continued long into the glittering night.

Filia found it impossible to sleep when she eventually went to bed. She stood at her window in tears, hoping for a miracle; the FJ constellation, Jonathan flying towards her, or running down the street, but there was nothing.

She wondered if Mizmiq might have been wrong, and whether Jonathan had in fact begun a new life on Opus. She hoped that the people of Centurian and Opus would one day discover each other so she could go there and find out.

Filia lay down on her bed and turned onto her front as she always did, head to one side with her arms outstretched under her pillow, and she suddenly felt something in her hands.

Her heart raced and she switched on the bedside light; it was a scroll. Filia immediately sat up and opened the parchment and saw the faint lines of words at the top and began reading as fast as she could:

'Filia, I started sending you a message but I was afraid it might not reach you so I asked my words to take physical form and find you on their own.

'This parchment can only write its message while your hands are touching its pages, and while your eyes are bringing its words to life. It needs to know that it is in the living world, and that it is with you. I hope its magic is working and that you are reading this. Everything inside is for you, to help you understand.

'With all my love, Jonathan.'

Filia gripped the scroll in her quivering hands and gazed across the page,

'I have become Centurian in Twilight. I cannot return, Filia. I did not choose this end, but it is done; I have a name and a place in Twilight.

'I hope my explanation of where I am can somehow help you come to terms with my death. I'm sorry, I cannot think of another word to describe how I feel, or what has happened.

'I will struggle and wonder where our love could have taken us for as long as you live, Filia, and for countless years after you have passed on to a new life.

'I hope from time to time to look upon your eyes, your smile, your tears, and to dream with you. Do not think of those things though. I cannot come back. You must live your life without concern for what I might think.'

Filia wept and wept. There was no longer any shred of doubt; the love of her life was lost and she cried out her tears as she read,

'I have a request, Filia. I made two promises which I wish to keep and I would ask that you try to fulfil them for me, with the help of Mizmiq and Rose of course.

'One was to my mother, to free her from Skull captivity. I know something of her lives inside that evil shell. The other was to Caerulean, to find his father, Naumachian.'

Filia sobbed and whispered her answer, 'I will do all I can,' she wept, closing her eyes and kissing his words before gazing again at the parchment and waiting for more of his message to form,

'Lastly, dearest Filia, I have a gift for you; my sound, the sound of Centurian, the sound of our silver planet. Place your hands on the front and back of the scroll.'

Filia did as his words instructed. She could hear every sound and every piece of music they'd experienced together by willing her mind to move through the music: the dust rings around Elephant's Trunk, the FJ constellation at Rockmore, everything.

There were also notes and melodies that she did not recognise, but every song and sound had nevertheless been joined together in a perfect medley, and as she listened and held the scroll, she noticed more words crawling around her fingers. It was as if they were an outline of his hands trying to press themselves against hers.

'Goodbye, Filia, the boy who loved you is no more, hear the sound of what he has become, the sound of Centurian.'

Filia cried and cried as the words eventually crept back into the parchment, and when the last letter had faded and gone, she clutched the scroll as tightly as she could to her chest, knowing that this was the end. What he'd written had been a message of goodbye far more than it had been one of explanation. Her life would be a life without him.

65.   Opus-Earth

Jonathan Prior

Florence knelt beside Jonathan. She had made a full recovery and kept her pregnancy a secret from Stephen.

The time had come to switch off Jonathan's life support. After prolonging the moment for days, Florence had told the doctors that she was ready to consent and Stephen had agreed.

'I'm so sorry, my beautiful boy,' she wept. 'Forgive me, I love you, Jonathan, forgive me,' she sobbed, choking on her words. 'I love you so, so much.'

Stephen stood behind her. They had not spoken since he'd stormed out of the hospital, angry at her accusations that he'd been partly responsible for Jonathan's tragedy.

Stephen touched Jonathan's head and kissed his cheek. He broke down in tears. 'I–I'm sorry, Jonathan. I was a bad f–father,' he stuttered.

Florence looked at Stephen exactingly and he continued his apologies. 'I–I did not support your interest in the w–wonderful creatures that we have c–come to love, the birds. I love you, Jonathan.'

Stephen wept and wept, groping for Florence's hand and she allowed his fingers to brush against her wrist before pushing them away. 'I'm s–so sorry, Florence, I love you,' blurted Stephen. 'I see it now, y-you were afraid of my vile temper. Please, forgive me.'

Florence held his fingers then gently let them go and Stephen felt the most immense sense of relief.

Florence hugged Jonathan, knowing that this would be the last time she would hold him. She couldn't speak. She simply ran her hand through his thick curling hair and sobbed, recalling how as a little boy he'd say, 'Stroke my hair backwards and my back forwards, please, mummy', before falling asleep.

But as Florence turned to give her consent to the doctors, she saw Jonathan's lips moving. Her heart jumped. It was as if he was trying to say something.

'He's alive, my boy is alive,' she screamed while the doctors went into a state of panic as their artillery of monitoring machinery lit up with a mix of red, amber and green numbers and wildly fluctuating waves.

Stephen grabbed Florence's hand and glared hopefully at Jonathan whose eyes, incredibly, began to open.

Jonathan suddenly found he could see and hear and when he looked up and saw his jubilant mother and father, he smiled. 'Mum, Dad?' he whispered.

'Yes, Jonathan, yes,' Florence cried.

'Wh–where am I?' he said, listening to the doctors' frantic conversations.

'You're in hospital, you were almost killed by a bus outside school,' bawled Florence.

Jonathan gazed at his adoring parents and wept tears of joy as the reality of life hit him. 'The bus, yes, there was a bird too, a robin, warning me,' he smiled. 'I thought I'd lost you, Mum, Dad. I've been in a weird, wonderful, terrible, nightmare, no, a dream, I'm not sure.'

Stephen and Florence embraced each other and Jonathan, overcome with tears. Florence then stared at the doctors. 'Is he okay? Please say he's alright?'

The doctors were not ready to give an answer; they were busying themselves around a complex mass of tubes, dashboards and dials.

'Mum, I feel fine,' murmured Jonathan softly. 'You, on the other hand, your eyebags are worse than ever. Only tears of celebration and happiness from now on, okay?'

'Oh, Jonathan, thank you, thank you,' cried Florence. She wiped her eyes and looked at the doctors again. They too were battling tears as they analysed the biological miracle playing out in front of them and about a minute later one of them finally spoke, 'It is true, Mrs Prior, Jonathan is alive and by all accounts, very well,' the doctor declared, smiling at Jonathan in wonder.

*****

Over the next few days Jonathan passed every test with flying colours and was soon begging his parents to take him home. The only reason he was being forced to stay in hospital was the curiosity of medical professionals.

Coma specialists from all over Britain and further afield had examined him and none could make head or tail of his change of state.

He felt very inhuman, being described by all other humans as an anomaly, and the constant interrogation had begun to infuriate him; every inspection was a list of the same questions.

Florence and Stephen had remained at his bedside throughout and had told him how the birds had saved Earth from either an unidentifiable enemy or an inexplicable natural force. No one could agree which it was; the so-called Sky War was a mystery.

Jonathan had lost none of his passion for birds and was delighted to have returned to a world where his parents had more to say about these amazing creatures than even he.

'I have good news!' announced a doctor striding into the room. 'We are ready to discharge you, Mr Miracle.'

Florence, Stephen and Jonathan thanked the staff and hurried home, and as soon as they walked through the door Jonathan went straight to the television, eager for more pictures of the earth-shattering events that he'd missed.

The lead news story, however, was nothing to do with the Sky War for once. It featured interviews with a group of scientists who were claiming to have discovered a planet with all the right characteristics to sustain human life.

'Not an outlandish possibility at all,' remarked Stephen, joining Jonathan on the sofa for the next burst of headlines. 'After the extraordinary events of the Sky War, who knows what's out there. Wh–what do you think, Jonathan?'

'Yeah, I think you're right, Dad. Normally, I'd be the alien laughed out of school for suggesting it but I reckon we'd be in the majority on this one,' he smiled.

'Too right, the bird-nerds have it: nerd Jr with his even more nerdy father,' grinned Stephen.

Jonathan raised his arm, offering his dad a high-five. Stephen didn't have a clue what to do and began to shake Jonathan's hand. Florence walked in and shook her head at the two awkward clowns and everyone fell about laughing.

After another instalment of the same news Florence asked them to come into the kitchen and sit down. 'Jonathan, Stephen,' she began, looking directly at them to make sure they were paying attention. 'I've been feeling sick in the past week or so. The doctors have been watching me closely, and—here's your tea, dear–and digestive biscuit too? There you go—and, I'm pregnant!'

Stephen spat out his Earl Grey tea. 'How–how? Oh my love, you are certain?' he cried, wrestling with shock, joy and disbelief all at the same time.

'I don't know how, my love, but I am absolutely sure of it,' beamed Florence. 'There's a heartbeat, a little on the slow side, but it's there, plus I'm only fifty-four, so it's possible, and I don't care if it's a miracle anyway; let it be a miracle like brilliant Jonathan here or the existence of a distant planet inhabited by humanoids. It is true and that's all there is to it. We're going to have a second child, and Jonathan, you are going to have a little brother or sister.'

'Well, these digestive biscuits must be pretty powerful,' exclaimed Stephen as his mind continued to whirl uncontrollably. 'And you, my dear, are made of something special too,' he smiled, plonking his tea down on the kitchen table and hugging Florence tightly before getting up to perform a very shaky dance.

Florence stared at her husband, once a dour self-centred emotional catastrophe, now a terrible comedian with a heart. 'Best you sit down, I think, dear,' she laughed.

Jonathan was over the moon, 'That is aaaaallllllrrrrrrr!' he shrilled.

'Goodness gracious me! What is that howling gargle of a noise, Jonathan?' cried Stephen.

'I've no idea,' laughed Jonathan. 'Let's just say it's the trumpet of a very happy boy who is going to have a brother or sister,' he whooped in delight.

'Then keep trumpeting, and practising your trumpet too!' Stephen guffawed. 'Now, let us break open the sherry,' he announced, lifting his arm and talking to the ceiling. 'Well, I guess for me, oops, sorry dear.'

'That's okay, my love, I'll have a sip and here's to the blessing of new lives,' declared Florence.

Jonathan grinned with the broadest of smiles as he watched his parents, a couple of old fogeys, trying to behave like young adults; and why not.

*****

Jonathan woke early the following day. He was going back to school and was nervous.

Despite encouragement from his parents that pupils and teachers would celebrate his return, Jonathan was worried that he would hate it.

His parents' perspective made sense, but memories of cruelty seemed to have been hardcoded into his brain.

Jonathan stood in front of the bathroom mirror, groggy-eyed, trying to banish the remnants of a bizarre nightmare in which he'd been run over by a bus, reborn as a bird of prey then struck by lightning in the Sky War.

His heart pounded as he contemplated going back to the same traumatic spot where he'd almost been killed. He would be there in less than an hour.

'Jonathan,' called Florence. 'Eggs and bacon ready on the table.'

Jonathan dressed slowly. 'It'll be fine, it'll be fine,' he muttered, gritting his teeth.

Florence drove him to school and found a parking spot close to the gate but on the opposite side of the road; there were no free spaces next to the entrance.

Jonathan held her for a long while before saying goodbye and checked for traffic several times before crossing the road. There was a bus coming down the hill but it was at a safe distance and wasn't travelling fast at all.

He stepped into the road and the bus suddenly screeched to a halt even though it was thirty or so yards away and no one else was crossing.

A group of birds had decided to park themselves in the middle of the street and Jonathan ran up the pavement to get a closer view.

A pigeon, a robin and an assortment of other birds were struggling to lift a discarded bun. It was covered in fresh black tarmac and was stuck to the road.

The robin looked Jonathan in the eye and the same confidence he'd felt in Mrs Flowers' creative writing class came flooding back.

'I think that bun will taste pretty terrible, I'll bring you something better tomorrow,' smiled Jonathan, making sure no one saw him talking to them.

The robin gave him a wink and the birds flew off, carrying their breakfast with ease.

Jonathan froze, and grinned. The sticky-bun scene had been a scam; they'd stopped the bus for him, so it had no chance of getting close. And they wanted him to know it.

Jonathan bounced through the gates of Grovecourt School. A huge colourful banner was slung across the sports hall with the words, "Welcome back, Jonathan".

He was overwhelmed, the centre of attention. There was no need to craft the right moment for an introduction.

Patrick was the first boy to run up, 'Want to come to my house at the weekend? Joe and I are going to a party. We can ride together?' he smiled.

'Yeah, that would be ace,' answered Jonathan, delighted.

The bell went and the buzzing crowd made their way to assembly. Jonathan didn't recognise the headmaster, who greeted him warmly.

'Jonathan, my name is Mr Avius. I took over the role of headmaster while you were gone. Welcome back to Grovecourt.'

'Thank you, sir, it's great to be here and to meet you,' he replied.

Jonathan's eyes wandered to the rear of the stage. 'What's that, please, sir?'

'That, Jonathan, is our tapestry. Every school made one in the aftermath of the Sky War to celebrate the wonders of our feathered friends,' he declared proudly. 'And while you will know of the Sky War, you may not have been told that ornithology has become the third-most studied subject after Maths and English. It would probably be the most popular if pupils had their way,' he chortled. 'I've been an ornithologist all my life, in my spare time really. I'll be teaching some of your lessons, and look forward to getting to know you.'

Jonathan was ecstatic, remembering how his parents had described his interest in birds as a harmful diversion from "mainstream subjects". He stared into space, bowled over by the perfect world into which he'd been recast. 'What is it, Jonathan?' asked Mr Avius.

'Oh, it's okay, I'm just very happy,' he answered.

At the beginning of the school assembly, Mr Avius invited Jonathan onto the stage. Jasper and Carter Manley were holding an envelope.

Jonathan caught Mrs Flowers' eye as he strolled up. 'Don't worry, it's not a giant crossword!' she mouthed, rooting for him as she always had. 'Thank you!' he whispered back.

Jonathan opened the envelope. 'To Jonathan, from everyone at Grovecourt School: a course of flying lessons. You always loved birds, we have missed you and we would love to see you fly.'

'Th–thank you,' he choked, smiling at Jasper and Carter.

'Sorry, Jonathan, for how we laughed at you,' said Carter.

'I think you were ahead of your time, mate,' added Jasper.

Jonathan had his best day at school ever. Ornithology surpassed even his expectations. Mr Avius seemed to have an encyclopaedic knowledge of every bird species imaginable, from little robins to great birds of prey.

Jonathan ran home as soon as his last lesson had finished and leapt through the front door. 'Mum, Dad, my turn for an announcement,' he beamed, kicking off his shoes as quickly as he could without falling over.

'I've decided what I want to be. I'm going to be a pilot. I think my interest in birds was a way of telling me that I'm destined to fly. Look what they gave me!' he exclaimed, proudly sharing the contents of the envelope.

Stephen and Florence glanced at each other, then back at Jonathan. 'I think that's a fabulous choice, Jonathan, you will make a first-rate flyer,' roared Stephen, while Florence twirled in delight at Stephen's approval.

The next morning, Jonathan got ready for school in record time and rushed out of his house, impatient to see his friends.

There was a sudden frenzy in the garden and a group of birds shot into the air. They appeared to follow Jonathan up the road.

Florence gazed lovingly after him through their music room window and laughed. 'The boy who chased the birds is now being pursued,' she declared, looking away only when they were out of sight.

Florence then sat down and dusted off the book she'd given Jonathan for his seventh birthday; Mythical Strongbirds. She smiled at the magnificent hawk-like creature on the front cover, opened the book and started to read.

The End